Abundant Grace

Abundant Grace

The Seventh Collection of Fiction by
D.C. Area Women

Edited by Richard Peabody

ISBN-10: 0-931181-44-5
ISBN-13: 978-0-931181-44-3
First Edition
Published in the USA

Some of these stories have previously appeared: Shirley Graves Cochrane's "The Smell of Apples" first appeared in *Gargoyle* #30/31, Dini Karasik's "Ghosting on the Rio Grande" first appeared in *Literal Magazine*; Barbara F. Lefcowitz's "The Pink Suit" first appeared in the February/March 2014 issue of *Portland Monthly Magazine*, and Amanda Miska's "Sam and Dee" first appeared in *Cartagena Journal* 2014.

Book design by Nita Congress.
Cover by Lisa Montag Brotman, © 2015, *Belladonna*.
Printed by Main Street Rag Publishing, Charlotte, NC.

Paycock Press
3819 North 13th Street
Arlington, VA 22201

www.gargoylemagazine.com

for Deanna D'errico, Carolinda Hales, Wilkie Leith, and Mary Lynn Skutley

"Only the Writer knows the exact combination of excess, self-denial, flagellation, whiskey, and medicinal massage that will enable Writing."

— Louise Wareham Leonard

*T*remendous thanks to everybody who steered new names and faces my way or helped us contact old friends: Jonathan Agronsky, Hildie S. Block, Michelle Brafman, Molly Burnham, Frederick Foote, Diana Friedman, James Grady, Shelby Settles Harper, Liz Huergo, Mary Ann Larkin, Mary Overton, Quentin Paquette, Michelle Parkerson, Patrick Pepper, Leslie Pietrzyk, Susan Pietrzyk, Sarah Pleydell, Marjorie Schwartzer, Debra Lattanzi Shutika, Rose Solari, Seema Srivastava, Virgie Townsend, Julie Wakeman-Linn, and Paula Whyman.

Contents

Introduction

*T*his is my last go round.

I'm grateful to have had the love and support of the DC Lit scene during the twelve-year-long "Grace and Gravity" project. How lucky to be surrounded by so many talented women writers, let alone coexist in a time and space where I could shepherd their work into print.

After seven volumes, I'm moving on to other projects. Time for somebody else to step up. While I managed to find almost three thousand pages of short fiction by close to three hundred local women, I was never able to print every local name. As a microcosm of writers in any city, any country, this has been only a sampling.

But I'm especially pleased to include works in this volume by three established writers who recently passed away—Shirley Cochrane was one of the first champions of my fiction, Faith Reyher Jackson came my way via Jonathan Agronsky, and Barbara F. Lefcowitz (who was a fixture at the Bethesda Writer's Center for decades) was made available by her daughter Marjorie Schwartzer.

Each of the seven volumes have had subliminal themes, subject matter that has risen out of the collective id of the writers and never by theme or command. *Abundant Grace* seems to be about picking your battles, paying attention, phantasmagoria, spirit animals, and death/change.

Caroline Bock's flash fiction could be the foundation for this collection, maybe the entire series. "We drink more wine, weep, scream, howl, beat our fists against one another, laugh gulping for air, a certain power in us to write about anything." Combine that with the not-so-subliminal message that men seem to miss everything when it comes to women, especially women writing.

Here we offer a roller coaster ride of lost fathers, missing husbands, cheaters, forked dicks, pedophiles (real and imagined), men named George who live in Georgetown, dogs, fish, crows, a marriage breakup at the Air and Space Museum, unexpected pregnancies, bomb shelters, the indignities of aging, voodoo altars, incest, fire and water imagery, miscarriage, gelato, ghosts, thalidomide kids, dog heads in bowls of soup, and how little we actually know about others no matter how close we think we are.

The title of Frances Carden's story, "Nature's Graveyard," is also in play throughout the collection. "Today everything seems like an omen," she writes.

And there is death in abundance. Bobbi Carducci kills off Oprah. A quarry in Alison Fairbrother's flash fiction is used only to make tombstones. Reflecting the times, there are funerals a plenty. Madelyn Rosenberg's Harold Crane paints eyes for the dead. Pam Risdon's Sara, in "Sarah's Way," smuggles a corpse into her bed. And Atossa Shafaie's character Ferri Khanoum works as a professional mourner.

There are plenty of wicked yucks, too. Jess Stork Glicoes shares a *Get Smart*-ish vision of resume fodder and the workplace, Amanda Miska updates the Samson and Delilah legend, Melody Schreiber posits the "Robin Hood of food," Abbey Mei Otis imagines sex robots falling out of the heavens, Dahlia Shaewitz's fifty-year-old Adrienne hooks up in a Key West sex shop, and Jourdan Woo imagines a Tim Burton-ish zombie makeover shop dubbed "Curl Up and Dye."

Both Barbara Lefcowitz and J. Howard's stories use JFK, Jackie, and Camelot as touchstones. And Jackie O. gets a passing mention in others.

In "Black Ice," Caron L. Martinez portrays a family whose "mood turns on the whim of just one person, and that person, inexplicably, is one of the children."

Melissa Scholes Young's "Oxygen in Use" is a heartbreaking mother-daughter end-of-life story with a feisty mom and a daughter conflicted over whether or not to ease her pain.

Debra Lattanzi Shutika's "Mirrors" puts Kate in a bossy plastic surgeon's nightmarish office.

Morowa Yejide's story, "Heathens," lends the perfect final touch to this volume and perhaps to the entire series. Mia Taylor is the Everywoman attempting to navigate the social and workaday worlds of the nation's capital amid stress and diminishing returns. She tries to keep up appearances with family and neighbors as the train wreck of her life becomes increasingly clear.

"Regrets come either way—whether you do a thing or you don't," Fiona J. Mackintosh says in her story, "Penitentiary."

Washington, D.C., is a transient city. Nobody ever seems to be from here, or to stay here for very long. I regret missing out on writers who moved on before we could connect. I regret not having the time or money to include all of the other writers who remain.

Those we missed include—Sally Amoruso, Susan April, Nicole Arthur, Meredith Banks, M. S. Bartley, Barbara Benham, M. L. Bishop, Margaret Blair, Judith Bowles, Connie Brisco, Julie Ann Britt, Beth Brophy, Courtney Angela Brkic, Eleanor Brown, Molly Burnham, Zofia Burr, Mary Carpenter, Cecilia Cassidy, Michele Chubirka, Halley Cohen, Susan Storer Clark, Jennifer Close, Lisa Couturier, Ellen Crosby, Carla Danzinger, Tracy Daugherty, Ashley Doherty, Pat Dowell, Meghan Drueding, Juli Duncan, Danielle Ellison, Nora Engel, Lora Engdahl, Danielle Evans, Siobahn Fallon, Laura Fargas, Stephanie Faul, Merrill Feitell, Gillian Foster, Marie France, Candida Fraze, Tana French, Isabel Fucigna, Caimeen Garrett, Jody Gerbig, Kathryn Gerhard, Susan Jane Gilman, Heidi Glenn, Mimi Godfrey, Marita Golden, Stephanie Grant, Jean Grenning, Mary Halnon, Ellen Hause, Marcy Heidish, Judy Hruz, Monica Ivey, Tania James, Alexis Johnson, Nubia Kai, Lynn Kanter, Sharon Keir, Caroline Keith, Rita Kempley, Anne Lacy, Jane Leavy, Susan Leckie, Nancy Lemann, Kimberly Libby, Jan Linley, Reb Livingston, Beverly Lowry, Lindsay Maines, Alice McDermott, Heather McDonald, Ann L. McLaughlin, Kathleen McCleary, Kathleen Meade, Beth Milleman, Emily Miller, Christine Montgomery, Kyoko Mori, Phyllis Reynolds Naylor, Katherine Neville, Joanne Omang, Shannon O'Neill, Michelle Parkerson, Sara Pekkanen, Dorothy Phaire, Jennifer M. Pierson, Zena Polin, Lauren Rabb, Liz Roca, Doris Rochlin, Teresa Rogovsky, Holly Sanders, Julie Shields, Tamara

Showalter, Susan Shreve, Helen Simonson, Jennifer Skala, Rachel Louise
Snyder, Pragna Soni, Gwen Sparks, Seema Srivastava, Silvana Straw,
Lydia Strohl, Meghan Thoma, Alison Thomas, Willett Thomas, Vanessa
Thurman, Kyra Todd, Rene L. Todd, Julia Tonkovich, Karen Trimbath,
Jane Vandenburgh, Jackie Walker, Rangely Wallace, Joyce Warren, Helen
Winternitz, Rosalind Wiseman, Sara Wolf, Becky Wolsk, Andrea Wyatt,
Martha Young, Zane, and Alex Zapruder.

A writer asked me the other day if I'd consider boxing the seven volumes
together as a set. I like the idea. I'd also love to see some intrepid critic tackle
the entire box. In a tangential vein maybe I should gather a collection of
works by women who used to live in the area? Guess we'll see.

Enjoy the ride.

—Richard Peabody
September 2016

Gigi Amateau

Good Bean

GIGI AMATEAU is the author of seven books for teens and young readers including *Claiming Georgia Tate* and *Come August, Come Freedom*, which earned a Library of Virginia People's Choice Fiction Award. In 2012, she received a Theresa Pollak Prize for Excellence in the Arts. A graduate of Virginia Commonwealth University, she has devoted nearly thirty years of work in the nonprofit sector toward improving access to resources for older adults, people with disabilities, and family caregivers. She lives in Richmond, Virginia.

An electrical storm so righteous, so potent that it summons a mother to the windowsill to pull her curious children and their brave dog away from the sting of its path, strikes a dead branch from a white oak—a branch unnoticeable and unremarkable, except perhaps to certain woodpeckers and other tree climbers with an acquired taste for saline. To anyone who might witness a leg of the fallen limb's half-mile pilgrimage from the backyard of the once-happy family to the river, this dead chunk of oak is now mere debris from the storm, now flotsam forging toward the place.

A northern flicker watches the violent muddy creek swallow up the branch and thinks *what a shame to lose such a reliable trough*—so abundant, so diverse in its daily offerings of beetle larvae and wasp eggs. Just a hop downstream, the crow cheers as the branch victoriously resurfaces, launching itself into the river. The bird lingers, considers hitching a ride, just for a ways, just for the thrill of surging the river.

From the hill, the oak itself oversees the journey of the dead, defoliated part of itself.

For a year or more, the tree has stayed alert, waiting for the woman to empty out the grief from her loss, filling the branch with the brine from her tears. When, finally, the emptiness and fullness converged, the tree conjured up this explosion, conducting quick fire with a passing storm, drawing lightning near enough to dispatch with the limb. A death self-inflicted by the oak with care and purpose.

And tenderness.

Tenderness for the woman inside the cottage, her four children, and even the wild puppy. The oak loved this family and had from the beginning. Loved them because they breathed upon its bark and it felt good. Loved whenever the family gathered beneath the shade of the oak's canopy to enjoy a meal outdoors. Loved how they tried to teach the puppy to fetch, and especially the way they all laughed out loud when the unbroken thing refused to bring the ball back, teasing as if she might. The oak treasured the family's laughter most of all.

Had they noticed—and at times, the littlest ones did but had no language to explain what they saw—the people would have seen curious swirls of steam rolling from the oak's bark. *Laughing*, the oak thought. *Laughing with them.*

This was not an oak that could be climbed anymore. Its lowest limbs towered above the cedar roof of the cottage. Not that anyone in the family had ever wondered what all the oak could see from way up, the tippy-top-up of its green self, but if they had asked, the tree would have told them. *Everything. I can see everything from here: the creek, the flat water, the dam, the rapids, and, even, the newly built row of white mansions, side by side nearly blocking my view of the falls.* The oak would have likely added, *I liked it better before.*

But how well can you see? As well as the eagle? The heron? Even better than the owl? The people might have wanted to know.

Glorious steam rolled from its dark wide fissures just thinking about how to reply.

How to answer that I am the one who shifts the wind in order to draw the heron's eye toward its dinner? Would that convey the vision alive in a white oak such as myself? How to explain that the very words "see" and "vision" only measure the smallest fraction of what an oak tree can know or tell?

The oak stopped imagining here, for it knew that disclosing such honesty—*I can see everything*—would invite other questions.

What did you see?

No, the woman and her children couldn't comprehend what the oak had done and dispatched—scarified—for them. Or why.

Yes, the oak liked it better before.

Before the dead limb, before the phone call.

At first, the family was only the woman and a man and an old dog—blind, half deaf, crippled in the hips, but a good bean. This is a phrase the tree heard from the man, and it made the oak love him. "You're a good bean," the man would often say to the first dog, who would not leave his side, even in wet heat, which was no good for her aching joints and cancerous lungs. Either those precise words—"good bean"—or the precise warmth in the man's voice made the dog lick his hand.

"You're a good bean," the man said to his wife, too, whenever she would bring him something cold to drink on Sunday mornings in August. Back then, before the children, before the wild puppy, the man worked outside most days. When it got too hot, too cold, or too wet, he would think about staying in but never could. Before the children, she worked beside him, minute for minute, hour for hour, and this also made her good. When the wife took care to remove that suffocating scourge of the south—English ivy—from the tree's bark, the oak understood what the man meant. *Good bean.* She watered the living things beneath the oak—the azaleas and hosta, the phlox and bleeding heart—judiciously decided which volunteers could stay—the dogwood and the honeysuckle but not the cedar—and coddled nothing. The woman, aware that she lived nearer to the river than many, used no insecticides, no herbicides at all, only water and sunshine and her hands. *You are a good bean,* the oak wished to tell her.

Soon a baby, then two more at once, and now, recently—only a few weeks before the tree started deadening the branch—another child. The wife, long since now also a mother, worked differently in the yard, but no less. For years since now, she had brought babies and toddlers and the first boy out with her. She picked up leaves and sticks, dug holes for new plants, and tried planting more flowers, which sometimes even survived the curious hands of a three-year-old or the deliberate jaws of the puppy. Mostly, she laughed at the children and followed them around, keeping spiders out of their mouths as best she could, teaching the names of whatever grew or perched or fed just beyond the tip of her extended finger. *Eastern towhee, day lily, Carolina wren. Echinacea, dragonfly, Baptisia, robin.*

It never did surprise the oak to see the children trying to bejewel the old or new dog with white Shasta daisy tiaras or golden dandelion necklaces. Such play made everyone laugh, as when the twins tried to force feed the new dog red clover singing, *clover for supper, Puppy, clover for supper* over and over until the puppy figured out how licking a big baby's face brings on enough giggling to make small hands retract.

The oak recalled these bygone games with the young widow. The entire garden served as the oak's radial bed. Each time she touched a root hair in her digging and weeding, the oak stored up the images and memories she released. With each shed tear that reached its fine feeder roots, the tree absorbed her grief.

Tell me, what did you see? What did you see after the dancing and playing and pretending? After all that?

She asked without knowing she had asked anything at all, yet the oak received everything that poured out from her as she worked the earth. The tree wondered if the woman herself even knew they were in conversation.

How could this man who loved the river drown in the river? The oak knew. *Did you see it happen?* The real question.

The oak feared that the woman would one day ask out loud and reckoned that for the woman this ordeal did not start with a sight but a sound. The oak would begin there too. A phone call—a wrong call to the right number—telling her she was no longer a wife, now just a mother. The oak saw her run out of the house with one hand to her mouth and the other welded to the phone. She had leaned against the south side of the white oak to breathe. Had the oak not held her up, she might have fallen into madness, eroded away from sadness. She went there because its trunk—so old, so wide—could hide the whole of her trembling, fragile self from the sight of her children. She wept from a well so deep that her tears watered the tree and everything growing in the bed. The oak knew the salt would soon take a toll.

A volunteer to distill her tears? The tree asked. Every limb, every leaf, every woody stem of the cottage yard offered it up but the oak could not draft another, so selected from itself a branch on high that would go unnoticed for a long, long time. Until her grief could subside enough for her to go on living. Then, the branch would fall and face its mission.

For days and weeks and months after the phone call, she heaved behind the tree, filling the earth with tears of a love and loss so enduring that her entire garden flourished with brilliant greens, bold yellows, and radiant whites. The plantations in the woman's flower beds—all anchored by the oak—stood tall and springy to the touch, even as neighboring gardens wilted, turned crisp and brown from the late July dry spell. As the oak sent and stored the salt to the martyr limb, her grief-well nourished all life on the cottage grounds.

Even in winter, the oak attended her. When the ground froze over and all its leaves dropped away, the hundred-fifty-year-old oak kept awake—galvanizing nearby coniferous trees and shrubs to nurture her by returning breath for breath. Even in winter, she came to the garden—her grief a riverbed of lava to keep her from freezing. She sat in the garden with her tears and a notebook, her hands tearing across the pages, as they had torn through weeds in the spring. The oak knew her so well that the prayer she wrote in her book spread out and rose up throughout the roots and trunk and branches and bark:

I will wait by the river, for bufflehead in winter, and for you to come back home.

Her sorrow knew her husband would never return, yet she must have known how something of him lingered still, so she asked the tree, again, *What did you see? Tell me.*

The oak recalled the day of the drowning, how life and death had unfolded within full view. Even the old tree admitted that the man's death had come as a surprise. The mother, the wife-no-more, had taken children to the river for lunch with their father. They met on the south bank, at the halfway point. She carried the baby in a cloth secured across her chest and toted lunch in a pack strapped around her shoulders. The twins, both contained in blaze orange life vests, walked ahead of her. The firstborn lagged behind—cajoling the wild puppy to keep up. The oak had observed worry in the woman's demeanor. Little things: skinned knees and sunburn, hydration and nourishment; things she had planned and prepared for that morning. All of this the tree saw.

On that day, the oak heard the man greet his family, "Tell me, what did you see today? What birds did you see or hear?" He was still wet from rolling—his favorite practice of capsizing and righting himself over and over in the kayak. The lingering water formed small pearls on his skin. His bottom lip—cold and blue already—foretold what awaited him downstream after lunch.

"I saw a mall-ahd!" said the oldest twin, oldest by five and a half minutes.

"A her-won," followed the younger.

The older boy had long outgrown his lisp. "A pileated woodpecker, Dad, a female. Three goldfinches, two cardinals, and a mocker."

The man smiled at his children, but it was his wife he held his arms open for. "What about the baby, Mom?" her husband asked. "What birds has the baby seen today?"

"The baby saw the kingfisher, again. Right when we got here, over by Rattlesnake Creek. That baby, she loves the kingfisher."

His family wanted to know what he had seen, too, this morning on his paddle down to meet them. He didn't tell about the faded-blue sneaker trapped in an eddy. He left out the beer cans and plastic bags and Styrofoam cooler tops. "I saw a log!"

"A log?" The oldest boy sounded disappointed. "How big?"

"About half the size of the big oak around back."

"Dad, that's not a log. You saw a floating tree."

"Yep, three rogue crows surfing the river on a floating tree, dude."

She passed out sandwiches, juice, and cookies to her children first. When she got to her husband—the good-bean-father—their eyes locked, for the one hundred thousandth or, perhaps, ten millionth time. "I can't look at you or I'll want to kiss you," she said.

"Please do kiss me," he said, and those would be the last words he spoke to his wife.

She did lean over; she did kiss him. The newborn slept and didn't stir when the top of her head brushed her father's chin as he stretched across the chattering twins to meet his wife's lips. With his hand on her hip, he steadied her. He wanted to ease her efforts to balance the baby, their lunches, and the extra weight she still carried.

She shook the sandwich at him, urging him, "Here, take your lunch." The tree, not so far off, had watched the family at the river, like always.

What else did you see?

The oak wished she would stop asking that question in her tears, on her pages, but her grief would not relent.

In the half century since the white oak's crown had crested the roof line of the cottage and surrounding homes, since the river first came into the oak's circle of concern, the tree had seen men, women, and children lose their lives by the river's turn. Drowning most commonly took them, to be sure. Some few jumped to their deaths from the train bridge. Now and then, the body of an old black man or the remains of a pink girl-just-turned-woman might simply appear—bloated, swollen, mostly intact cadavers—floating down through the cityscape with the cans and stumps and old shoes. A rare but memorable lot left this world in a way no one should—not a tree, not a bird, not a human being. The oak wished it had not absorbed those horrific and torturous scenes.

Tell me, what did you see?

She asked this of the oak every day now. She asked about the depth of her late husband's love, if he really could have been so good, as good as she believed. She found it hard to remember now. Only after hours of gardening, could she recall, again, the concentrated truth of their love. She returned to this truth every day and, when she did, when she came back to this realization that everything she felt from him was true, she would set down her trowel, walk behind the tree and cry, cry in hiding from her children. Except for the baby.

The baby came out of doors. The oak relished that its aerial roots grew at an angle that the mother deemed perfect for holding the baby in her chair, for keeping the baby safe. The oak shaded the little one with its crown and let nothing drop onto her face—not an acorn, not a stick, nor a small chip of bark.

Tell me.

And the oak surrendered its memory to her.

I saw everything.

The kayak. The floating tree carrying three thrill-seeking crows, lodged between two boulders. They watched, too. The sharp rock that jutted out just enough to jettison the kayak up, and send the man down, down into a massive strainer made of logs and junk, a barge of river trash that let the water pass but held the man under. How he had tried to roll, how his sycamore-white legs swayed in the current, kicked out, then disappeared. Tangled up in his river. The rescue team could only rescue his body. Something of him lingered.

The oak wants to end this recollection there. *I have told you everything*, the tree tries to say to this widow but cannot because there is something else, something the oak sees even now at the drowning place. The eaglets know it and avoid landing there. The heron fish up stream of the spot. The mallard drake and his lady take a different passage downstream.

Something else.

The man—his spirit or his heart or the thing that made him him—is still there between the sharp rock that stopped him and the built-up debris that trapped him. He has no garden, no oak, no new baby to distill his grief. He waits for some word from her.

In spring, the woman fills a new hole with a handful of potting soil, stands up, and massages her lower back. Today, she doesn't cry. She goes to the oak and rests her head, closes her eyes. Holding the baby firm in its roots, still watching the waiting drowned father from afar, the oak breathes onto the widow. *He waits. What may I tell him for you now?*

Reclined against the tree, the true part of her knows how the oak has stored and absorbed, secured and anchored the breaking and mending of her heart.

The baby wakes; the crying child needs her mother. "You're a good bean," the wife tells the tree. "I love you."

Yes, the oak thinks, dispatching her message to the salty, dead branch.

It's time to go.

Janna Bialek

At Seven I Had a Dad

JANNA BIALEK was associate editor of *Audubon Naturalist News* for many years, and has written essays for numerous anthologies. Her work has been published in the *Washington Post*, *Baltimore Sun* magazine, and a monthly column for the *Urbanite*. Her most recent story, "Love and Rockets," appeared in the *Washington Post Magazine*.

My father was the grandson of Tsar Nicholas II, the abandoned child of Princess Anastasia. He lived in the world of fables that I made for him, and although he never told me this, I knew.

Or goodbye. He never told me goodbye either. I was seven when he left, but I knew in the bottom of my heart that I was his favorite, so he still could have said goodbye. I don't blame him though. I blame my mother. She could have made him listen. Maybe it was because I was a princess, and she was not.

Even though we both had this royalty in common, and even though we were just alike and I knew I was special and important to him, I didn't spend my life waiting for him to return. I pretty much forgot about him, or if not forgot exactly more like stopped wanting. In the family I was left with, wanting what you couldn't have wasn't a very acceptable thing. It was dramatic. I knew I was dramatic, that was my nature, but also that it wasn't a good thing to be, like a nose-picker or a tattle-tale. And also my grandmother told me that if I talked about my father, it would kill my mother. I remember this specifically, how I sat in the baby's room while she was ironing and asked her a question about my father and although I don't remember what it was, she sat down the iron and looked at me, and even though I couldn't stand my mother because she was weak and useless and not my father, I still didn't want to kill her. I'd lost one parent already.

Another thing I couldn't have besides a father was a sister who was not a bully and a brother who was not annoying. It would have made things easier if I had better siblings, especially since I was in charge of them because my mother worked and there was no money for after-school programs. Every day I had to tell them what to do so they wouldn't get in trouble and also peel potatoes for dinner. I got to be good at the potatoes but I was never good at keeping them out of trouble.

When I was in third grade, a TV arrived, a small plastic one just came out of nowhere and onto our front steps. My mother said to no one at all, especially not to me, "He thinks it'll be OK because he leaves us this?" So I guess that meant that the TV came from my father who didn't say goodbye. Which would mean that my father knew where we lived, which would mean that he could come see us, which would mean that he didn't. But I didn't think about this too much.

Since I was the oldest, I got to keep the TV in my room, but I never used it or even really touched it, ever. I didn't imagine my dad bringing it, or wonder if his fingerprints were on it, or think about how he must have picked it out for us. Even though this would have been a perfectly normal thing to wonder about. But I didn't, because it would have been dramatic. I just let it sit in my room. It probably did make my brother and sister really angry that I got it and they didn't, and that was good. But I'm only guessing.

Did I mention that there's a picture of us, sitting on my dad's lap, just my sister and me? My brother, I think, wasn't born yet, but my sister is supposedly reading my dad a book and I'm sitting farther out on his knees, and even though he's paying attention to the book my sister is supposedly reading to him, here's the thing: his finger is resting right there on my leg. It's like a signal, like he was saying, "Yeah, I have to listen to your little sister, but I will always be connected to you, I will always love you best." I don't remember when this picture was taken, but I like it not only because of that and because I was wearing my favorite purple twirly dress, but also because it looks like my dad belongs there, in this chair, that he was really once my dad. I know he was sending me a message that he loved me forever with his finger on my knee because I am looking straight into the camera, and you just know. My mother must have taken the picture, but

I don't like to think about this. She probably would have told me to wipe that smirk off my face. I didn't know what a smirk was until much later, but it sounded like a pretty bad thing, so I smirked a lot.

I don't know how I knew I was descended from royalty; I think I found out sometime around the time the book came out about my great-grandfather, Nicholas, and Alexandra. It was a really good thing that I had this lineage, because it's very hard to be special when you have a bratty brother and an evil sister and your mother is overworked and doesn't love you very much and you don't have that many friends. Knowing this didn't make me very popular at home; maybe my father's heritage was a sore spot. More than anything, I was not supposed to be special, the rules were very clear about this.

When I was old enough, my father died. He didn't die because I was old enough, he died because he was in a plane crash, but when I found out about this I was in college and I guess that's better than finding out when I was little, because I could cry about it when no one was around, like my mother. It was confusing, trying to cry about someone you spent your life not thinking about. And exhausting. I cried until I realized I didn't know what I was crying for, and then I stopped.

There was nothing I could do about him being dead except, I guess, if I wanted to, I could find out things, now that we knew where he went after he left me. Finding out things sounded dramatic, like something I would do, but not finding them out seemed more dramatic for some reason. Like I was supposed to be curious. So on purpose I went to the big library to look through old newspapers and find out things. It's really gruesome when a jet crashes into a neighborhood, and also when you fall out of the sky at three thousand feet. So I looked for other things instead, like how he got his own special stories in the newspaper even though over a hundred other people died, and how he built houses for happy families all over the desert. One story said he was a "family man," so he must have been real happy with the woman in the convertible that was in the driveway waiting for him when he left my mom, and loved the two kids they had together to replace us. They didn't find out that my father was the Princess Anastasia's long-lost son when he died, so I guess that will always be my secret, and that's OK because it would be a lot of trouble if anyone knew anyway.

I think my dad would have taken me with him when he left in the convertible with the woman who had a lot of money. Maybe he was mad that my mother didn't let me go too, and that's why he didn't say goodbye. There isn't any way to know the answer to this except to ask the woman, if she's even still alive, but I don't want to do this, for obvious reasons, and also because of their children, who I guess are related to me, and I have too many sibling issues anyway. But I think he would have taken me because he knew I would have acted exactly like a perfect little lady, like the princess that we both knew I was.

Once, really, my dad did exist. I used to think that the photo versions of my dad were the real dad, that this was enough to make him real enough for me. I liked thinking this because it was happy and contained the reality of him and me together. Except all the photos of the rest of my life that didn't have him in them. You can't really see something that's missing, which is what I used to believe about my dad. He was missing, which is sort of different from running away. Better.

When he fell out of the sky in the plane crash, other people must have had their lives torn apart by his death. His two other children probably missed him a lot. His wife who replaced my mother must have missed him a lot. There must have been buildings and houses that needed to be built by his company; the circle of his life would have been pretty wide. I feel sorry for these people who must have missed him a lot (except for the woman in the convertible, who deserves terrible terrible things to happen to her). They did not know who my father used to be when he was my father. Nobody, ever, I think, knew about us, except for the woman in the convertible, and she probably wasn't talking. So my father and I had something in common: we both didn't exist to other people.

I think about this: what if there was a knock on the door and a woman who looked just like me (which means, just like him) was on the other side, and she said "Janna?" and I knew it was his daughter. I always thought I would just close the door, not giving her the satisfaction of having traveled all the way from California to meet her half sister and ask me questions. I think I would love to slam the door in her face for the father in the business suit that she got to have because I didn't. I could find her on the Internet, track her down, stalk her, or do terrible things to her on Facebook. If I found out she was evil, troubled somehow, traumatized by an alcoholic mother and an uncaring father, I could turn around and go home and be happy. But I don't think this would be the case. I think she probably turned out fine, because that's pretty much what happens when you have rich parents and a mom and a dad and a house in Malibu. That's who you get to be.

Once, when I turned into a mother, my mother started talking about my father as if he weren't a mystery that would have killed her. We went to a coffee shop and she just started talking, telling me about the woman in the convertible as if she were my friend and not my mother. I asked her why she had never talked about him before. She said: "I guess I always figured that if you wanted to know, you would have asked."

This is why I don't trust my mother. In one sentence, she rewrote my entire history. How dare she. I was given a gag order, right? That's true, right? My grandmother said to seven-year-old me, as we were sitting in the baby's room, as she was ironing and I was reading a story, "Don't talk about your father. Don't ever talk to your mother about it, do you hear? It'll kill her if you do." This is true, right?

I was seven.

Now, after thirty years, answers were lying on the table just like the knives and forks and spoons we used to stir our coffee. All I had to do was ask.

As I tried to swallow pancakes and hold back tears, I knew there were too many years behind us. Where would I start? Where would I even start?

I had lost more than my father. I had lost my story. The one that would have placed me in the middle of the lives of the two people who were supposed to love me most, the story lucky children take for granted. When you know your parents exist, you have a throughline to the future.

No. I would not ask. I had altered my life the way clouds alter sunshine. I was very happy with the father I had, the father who was the grandson of the Tsar Nicholas II and who gave me butterscotch candies and the TV and the finger resting on my leg. It was enough.

Caroline Bock

The Critique Group

CAROLINE BOCK is the author of two critically acclaimed young adult novels: *Lie* and *Before My Eyes* from St. Martin's Press. Her short stories and poetry have been published or are forthcoming with *Akashic Press, Fiction Southeast, Gargoyle Magazine, 100 Word Story, F(r)iction, Ploughshares, Vestal Review,* and *Zero Dark-Thirty.* Her poetry has been nominated for a 2016 Pushcart Prize and she is the 2016 winner of the *Writer Magazine* short story competition judged by Colum McCann. She lives in Maryland and is currently at work on a novel for adults.

We talk about giving birth and menopause, about celebrities we would jump in bed with if we had the opportunity, about being married forever from one of us, and not having a date in eighteen months, shit, maybe more—and about your grandmother: How is she? Her home in Chevy Chase is being sold. Ninety years old, and my parents have decided that she can not live alone anymore—the unreliable furnace and those long flights of stairs leading to all those unopened rooms. We gather closer to her, the youngest among us, and urge her to write more, about her grandmother, about what matters and what terrifies. What we think to ourselves: How did we find one another? How lucky we are—four women poised between twenty-nine and fifty. What we say aloud: We should meet more often. We drink more wine, weep, scream, howl, beat our fists against one another, laugh gulping for air, a certain power in us to write about anything. And he always arrives late, slick with sweat, riding his bicycle on even the coldest of nights, changing the pheromones in the wide-open room. When he says: Did I miss anything? We say: We haven't even started.

Frances Carden

Nature's Graveyard

FRANCES CARDEN reviews for *Readers Lane* and has had pieces published in *Through the Hourglass*, *Magical*, and *Answers I'll Accept*, to name a few. She has an MA in writing from Johns Hopkins University and works as a technical writer for a large consulting firm by day. At night, she works on various writing projects, including a novel.

She goes down to the shore with the portent of the crow behind her back and the blustery skies arching over her stooped frame. A plastic sack is clutched in her right hand, looking the same as the one she carried the day before, a year before, time immemorial. Her gray hair is curled tight to her head in the style of her youth, her shoulders sagging under the weight of the sky, her faded pink sweater swinging back and forth over narrow hips, her withered feet clad in thick, no-skid boots making her look like some kind of feeble monster, all thunderous walk and no bite.

She is here to beach comb, an activity that at 6:50 a.m. sharp every day is religiously respected. As the tide ebbs out, she ebbs inward, scouring through the remains of the ocean for the perfect treasure: a broken bit of shell, a beer bottle in pieces, buffeted and scrapped by the pounding surf into a sea offering of piercing beauty, a sea urchin covered in green spikes, edging itself with a fragile illusion of protection that shatters to let hungry beaks into the soft underbelly: an animal of useless defenses.

Today everything seems like an omen. The unbidden thought skitters around her mind like a frantic crab, claws grabbing and snapping at blurred conceptions that lap around the edges of sentience, and she does not acknowledge where it comes from and why it comes today.

She stands with the bag in her bony fist and begins the careful process of searching while keeping her footing, crunching over rocks covered in dry barnacles that look like mummified mouths, trying to avoid the snails in their rounded houses, clinging in untidy bunches along the slippery edges of large and small boulders, waiting for the ocean to rush back in and drown them in the dark.

And suddenly, she remembers back to the time when she was a little girl, sure footed as a mountain goat, precocious and desirous of all the mysteries of the deep. She feels the memory rush over her skin in the cold caress of the ocean that day which swelled about her puffy ankles as she launched into the surf, calloused feet skidding carelessly over the glossy rocks and pieces of glass, child hands diving beneath lapping waves in a kinder world where the sun reflected off the surf, making the rocks glisten gem green; the shells were washed into her hands by a beneficent ocean like a mother hen feeding her young. She took the broken shells and strung them into a necklace which she wore until one day, ten years later when the string broke and the shells fell apart, weathered by the passage of a hard decade, scattering through her clasping hands and shattering on the hard-tiled floor of the greasy truck stop café she had been working at. Each shardlike surface hard, the sun gem shine gone, pinioned against a dirty floor and crunched into particles to disperse on the feet of each trucker, each semi taking a small piece onward, unseen and gritty on floorboards in other lives.

She stares down between her feet at the battered remains of a mussel shell, purple and white, peeling on one corner with a sizable chunk missing from the bottom, and for a minute she thinks it is a piece of her long-forgotten necklace, and she reaches out to take it, but the shrieking of a gull delighted with the discovery of a stranded sea urchin tears her from the dream and suddenly she is aware of the thunderheads rolling in and the ocean stretched out in front of her, the hard, unbreakable gray of a dirty mirror, like the one she found that day in her teens when she first dealt with the ramifications of loss, cleaning her aunt's house, smelling the cancer that had seeped into the walls and dusty wooden boards, wafting from the folds of the curtains and eddying around her ankles, a phantom serpent that emerged from her aunt's skin to glide into everything she touched.

The gray of sky and land are intermixed in front of her and the ocean is strewn with feasting gulls and sea urchins, shells crunching underfoot and severed crab claws lying on top of slippery rocks. Like a flash flood, her former feelings are washed away, the years of love and adoration for the ocean replaced by a sudden and inexplicable repulsion. The light from the memory is extinguished and the ocean is an angry parent, ready to punish. The wages of sin, it whispers. Broken things wash in to shore and pool around her boots.

And suddenly the emotion is gone, as soon as it came, leaving her thoughts to whirlpool, concentrically drawing into themselves, a vortex under the waves.

Her ankle is beginning to throb with the pain of walking over the jagged rocks. She can feel the edges seeking the soft flesh, trying to push through her shoes. And she blinks dazed in her surroundings, shocked that this once-familiar place is suddenly so foreign and cold. All the years, through childhood, through her first year in high school, her first boyfriend, her first disappointment, her first lost child, her first divorce, her first taste of adult freedom, and her first desire to be a child again—through all this the ocean supported her with a daily calm, a little pile of treasures washing in every morning just for her. The endless repetitive lapping of the waves over the rocks, the concentration in moving from one to another like Indiana Jones, skirting the pitfalls, the clumps of soggy seaweed, the jagged edges, the occasional claw-happy crab, to finally attain the prize laid out just for her. A prize she would cart home, and, sitting in the pool of sunlight falling across the battered oak kitchen table, carefully and reverently place inside a giant glass vase, always clear. Each day she would do this, until one day, a week later, two weeks maybe, the vase was full; then with a flourish she would tie a ribbon, always a different yet vibrant color, around the fragile glass neck, then place it on display. She had begun this at five, a tradition passed on from her mother and her grandmother before her. She supposed she had made thousands of shell-filled vases by now. Giving some away to relatives, keeping her favorites, selling them in her shop, storing them in the basement. She was dedicated to them. Her life itself seemed whirled around them and even in the bleakest moments they were there, and she never missed a day. Not even the day she got married. Not even the day she caught him with another. Not even the day she left him. Not even the day the divorce was final. And now suddenly, these treasures feel brittle, feeble. Strangely macabre. Chalky and slimy in her hand, as though they were covered in invisible poison.

She walks away, shaking her head to dislodge clumps of half-formed and insidious thoughts, blaming a night of shocking sleep, dreams populated by monsters and lovers, friends and enemies that came and went with the tides of the year, all ominously intermixed and wanting something that she did not want to give, something that went nameless in the dream but pulls at her mind now.

A tower strand of high boulders, still wet from the receding tide stands ahead of her, and she slowly and surely stoops over to begin the climb to the other side of the beach where there is a brackish pool filled with torn-apart shells, layers and layers, protected by a family of crows that send up a cacophony of warning. This is the best spot, the crows' feasting area. This is where she once found her favorite shell, a rare and exotic thing she was never able to identify, blood red and conical, some offering she pictured coming from the very deepest part of the ocean, some dark place where ships rested hundreds of miles below the surface and giant sea beasts that had never seen the light of day skulked through abandoned hulls. This shell never went in a glass vase. This shell was on her mantle, sitting on a specially made wooden platform. This was her talking piece, her special sea treasure. The permanent mystery that she enjoyed for its very enigma. Even her friend in ocean research couldn't figure out what it was—or had once been.

But she knew or always felt she had. This was the ocean's gift for her constant dedication.

Today, bag in hand, she is climbing back to this spot that she has been returning to for sixty years, waiting for another sea miracle that, as of yet, has not come. As she climbs, one hand steadying herself, footing carefully chosen to step between the clumps of seaweed and the clinging snails, memories flood back on the pounding surf and her mind is half torn between concentration and a strange wondering that has overtaken her, the restlessness of a formerly quiet mind.

She is ten, fifteen maybe—the childhood years, they merge. She remembers her green bathing suit and a tangle of rusty hair blowing in front of her eyes. Her mother has just taught her where the real treasures are—the collectibles. Pulling back a piece of seaweed, as shown, she looks for shells but instead finds two crabs. They are both about the size of her childish hand and each is a pale, translucent green. Tiny little legs pump with fear and the crabs try to hide, both running apart, holding their pinchers close in to their little chests, fear making them prostrate. She feels a surge of sudden and overpowering love for these creatures. So afraid, so admitting to their helplessness, using their weapon hands to hide and not fight. She reaches out and carefully strokes the back shell of one and it stands immobilized, attempting to squeeze into the back of the seaweed. She lowers the plant fronds, hiding the treasure of life, and does not ever look under the plants again. Whatever treasures rest there should not be intruded upon.

Her heart constricts again with love for those long-ago crabs just as her concentration shifts and her footing slips. She clasps the rock in front of her, back in the here and now, feeling the first mist of rain as the palm of her hand scraps into the rock, peeling back skin and exposing vibrant red to the gray of the scenery, painting a small portion of herself onto this landscape. Her ankle is at a painful angle and she is aware of the familiar sensation of a sprain, having done herself injury on this beach since she was a child. Now it takes longer to recover. Now it isn't just the wound to display at school, proving a tomboy sense of adventure.

She recalls what her doctor said last Thursday and thrusts it out of her mind with enough violence to get her moving again and help her clear the top of the rock pile, where she stands for a minute and scans the beach, looking for hints of sea offerings, but a blurred monotonous image comes back, where rocks blend together and sea meets horizon and becomes one. She is reminded of a picture one of her old boyfriends took once. It was a beautiful day, and she was posing with her best friend in the sunshine, their backs to a glittering sea, but something had been wrong with the camera—something about the lens she thinks, or maybe the film itself, and the picture had come back a solid and fathomless brown, looking like a spot of quicksand, with tiny grains that when pieced together formed two ghostly, smiling faces hidden in the depths.

She shifts her attention to the ocean, watching the waves grow as the winds pick up and tiny prickles of cold rain sting her skin, making her feel suddenly and pleasantly in the moment, a part of the scenery again. She remembers herself at some far-distant age, some moment of childhood that stands out in a cluster of unconnected and inexplicable memories. Some unnamed location on the map of time finds her walking, shin deep, in the bone-chilling waters, a smile etched deeply across her face at the discovery of a lone starfish, very much alive and throbbing a vibrant purple, a find that is so beautiful, so incredible, that it lasts forever, the moment highlighted in colors more vibrant than real life, the starfish eternal in this one memory of cold water and first experiences. She left it as she had found it and her mother had been angry. A collectible lost. But to her, like the crabs, it was another living treasure. She was never as good at combing as her mother, as fierce with her collecting. Generations seemed to dilute priorities and expectations waxed and waned but were never fulfilled.

The rain begins to dash against her skin harder, a swift slap from nature that brings a smile to her face. She is at one with the landscape again, feeling it, and for a moment the throb in her ankle that has grown and left her putting most of her weight on her other foot is diminished as she abandons herself to the much-loved wildness of the sea at its fiercest. She stands for a moment on the tallest rock, facing into the wind, and it feels as though a portion of herself, missing, is returned. She stands for an hour. A minute. A second. Time doesn't seem to have much weight or meaning these days. But the sea, she is still herself and today she is angry, wonderfully so. She will take it out on the land, she will throw watery fists at the sky and knock birds out of the air and scare the crabs into the depths of their seaweed mausoleum where tiny green stalked eyes will watch the big picture unfold, shrouded in fake protection, a house built upon the sand.

She feels herself merging with this growing storm. She looks across the ocean and she feels it returning, this emotion that has haunted her of late. This feeling of seeing everything differently, a compunction to reexamine which had grown and then waned with her collection of years, suddenly buffeting her like the promised storm. She looks down as the ocean shakes with thunder and the land trembles in response, looks down and sees the broken shells, animal husks, and destroyed homes littered about her feet. She bends, a process that is accompanied by the ominous creak of bones, a sound mercifully hidden by the rising wind. These, her treasures. She runs her fingers over them, like a farmer sifting soil. What are they really? She feels the knowledge now, a submerged thought. This is a collection of the dead. Little skeletons for decoration. Sea skulls to show to your friends. See what I did. See what I found? I looted the dead. And they will all dutifully ooohhh and ahhh and collect the little carcasses to place in clear vases with brightly colored string adorned at the top, a showy grave marker. And these vases would rest on piano tops and fireplaces, on top of tables with intricate dollies underneath Walmart lamps with ubiquitous white shades. And these dead would just become a part of the surroundings; sterile pieces of unambitious suburbia. Their true meaning, that they had once been living, that they had once breathed and hungered and survived, would be forgotten in the mélange of decoration. They become, ultimately, worthless. Five dollars for two pounds at her souvenir shop with the weathered awning and cheap Bar Harbor T-shirts. The shop she will have to give up now. That too, a dead thing.

She sighs under the weight of the thoughts and looks at her wrinkled hand which is now carefully holding a spiny urchin, its soft underbelly cracked open by a gull, the viscera washed away on the ocean tide; she clenches her fist, feeling the dead animal's inadequate spines bite into her skin and bring the blood rushing to the surface. The sea does give up her dead. And we collect them and put them in vases. Death becomes decoupage and the tide just keeps ebbing and flowing.

An image impales her mind. She sees a cave somewhere far beneath the sea, a shadowy den for a predator. In the middle of this cave is a little vase filled with the eyes of dead sailors, limbs sheared off by calamitous storms and misfortune, lovingly collected and stuffed into a pleasant decorative array filled with screaming mouths, wide, decaying eyes, and hands reaching for a sun that will never be felt again. Was it all relative? Were sunken ships and breathless captains slumped over the ship's wheel beautiful to the creatures of the deep that slide through the waters into the bulky gracelessness of humanity's attempt at intervention? Was the ocean decorated just as our living rooms are, with the beautiful dead?

She hurls the urchin as far into the sea as she can. It plops into the water about two feet away from her. Her beach comb holds no pleasure today, and images of bloated bodies floating in the deep are submerged just below her eyes, eddying across her consciousness, a ripple that predicts an impending squall.

She gets up, turns, and makes her way slowly back up the beach. Somewhere along the line she has let go of the plastic bag and the wind has carried it away. She did this once, deliberately, as a little girl. She remembers that it was very windy that day. Not the wind of a storm. This was a day so bright that it hurt, like being submerged in someone's Technicolor daydream, a coma victim reaching out toward imagination's painted sun, unreal and beautiful. She was young enough then to see the individuality in days before the collection of time merged things into categories. She was young enough to let go. She held the bag to the wind in her chubby child fingers and let go, to see where things would be carried. The wind lifted and tumbled, over and over, that white grocery store bag, up into the pure blue of a serene sky with the sun shifting off the white like an errant cloud, and as the wind tore at her hair she couldn't stop watching that beautiful thing, almost alive in its boisterousness, set free and leaving her.

The wind is pushing her now and she welcomes the smell of the angry ocean, the sea salt alive. She used to be afraid of the ocean when it was like this. As a child, she did not understand such violence and it frightened her. But, after the divorce, it was a comfort. This rebellious side of nature, this side that stormed and stamped and shook the Earth and rattled the sleeping things of the deep with its incipient rage. It released something in her that couldn't be let go. It tore something from her, and in this tearing there was a raw element of healing. She still found the ocean somewhat terrifying in these moments, but they touched her too and the smell of churning waters, a certain musky scent of decay given off by exposed tidal flats, the sea sucking back into ever-larger waves, called to her today and she stopped walking away. Even after the divorce, she watched the storm from the shelter of a house, afraid to fully be a part, but today, she loved the assaulting scents in the ocean just as much as she hated them, because the death of all things was in that pulling back, that exposure as the ocean got ready to kill and cough up the dead, filling happy child hands the next day while she sat back sated, the purge complete.

She feels torn, a new loathing mixed with a new desire to turn around and just watch, just see how beautiful and awful this thing-to-be was, to immerse herself in the scenes of life and death hitting headlong in a fist-shaking denial by nature herself. She hesitates and for a moment, almost turns back, almost looks over her shoulder, drawn as she is by something in the ocean, something that has called the women of her family for generations. She hesitates as the wind rises and blows out the careful curls, the salt-soaked air leaving a wild frizz, the hair of a harridan, a beach gorgon in oversized boots, stoop shouldered.

She turns her head slowly and looks at the waves, sucking back and revealing the underbelly of the soft ocean before hurling themselves at the shore and she sees another day, waves rising and falling harshly, a storm far off the coast, or was it a hurricane, making the ocean wild on a gentle summer day, a day she saw him leaving for the beach when he was supposed to be at work, a day she followed and found him with her sister. A day when the call of the ocean wasn't for her, but for two new lovers. The memory, unfolding before her as vivid as the day she first saw it, no longer has a pull and she lets it go, lets the wind tear it away. Instead, she looks at the waves, their crests forming into sharp razor points. She sees the soft clouds cloak themselves with the iron of rain and feels the first, hard-driving fists from the heaven smashing her upturned face. She closes her eyes and lets nature wash away the tears. Tears not for the man or long-ago memories of the beach. Tears that have been there, intermittently, since the visit Thursday, since she was told. Tears that the stinging rain cleanses.

The salt is soothing, the ache in her joints receding in the cold deluge, the thundering and roaring all around her stealing the loneliness, but despite all this, ultimately the smell is too much. Not the smell of the salt. The smell of the things she knows are washing up. The decayed quagmire muds of the tidal flats and the pool where the crows beat each little sea urchin or clam into an edible mush of fractured shell and soft innards. She always knew about this murky side of the ocean, but her sense of smell is increasing lately and it is too much, too much to bear. Again, the image of the ocean depths and a collection of tidy dead in a bottle in some monster's cave, seaweed floating on top of the water like a drowned woman's hair, Ophelia floating by, the weight of her skirts making her a decoration of the deep. All these beautiful, treasured dead. Collect them.

No, she cannot stay. She turns away from the ocean but she does not run or rush. She has a dignity about this parting, although the image, the realization, will not leave her. Today, for the first time since that introduction to the sea at an age cloudy with distance and the newness of having just come into the world, she collects nothing, brings nothing home. Even the day she found the man with her sister, even that day she brought something home, picking the perfect shell as her husband and her sister curled into each other on the jagged stumps of dead beach things, making new life on top of an ocean graveyard. Today, only, she has not collected.

She walks to her house, thirty minutes in the chill of drenching rain and harsh winds, three times blowing her over, each time accompanied by the scraping and bleeding of getting up. But she does it quietly, herself a creature of the sea, wrinkled salt-pickled skin a testament to a life devoted, a Captain Nemo of the land who skirts near the beloved but never takes the plunge. Waters that eddied into nighttime dreams and seeped into a life. She doesn't begrudge the ocean this battering but instead dreads coming into her house, the memory of her aunt, a woman who seemed so old at the time but really wasn't, and cleaning out that attic with dusty mirrors and a window into cancer and disease.

The storm is lifting, a pattering of rain, as she opens the door to her house and she sees them everywhere, all her bottles with all those ribbons. Reds, greens, blues, yellows, pinks. Lines and lines of them, each with white shells, brown shells, rippled shells, broken shells, speckled shells, conical shells, large shells, small shells, purple black peeling mussel shells. Rows everywhere. She sits at her oak table, the gray light falling slatelike over the normally colorful kitchen and diluting everything, sight ebbing as her sense of smell becomes immaculate, precise. She sees the vase, her last, that she has been working on, the teal blue ribbon the color of oceans in a storm, sitting beside it placidly, this one not half full but finished anyway, she knows. She reaches over to begin knotting the ribbon in that special, final-touch way, her sweater dripping onto that pristine floor that she mops daily, her boots dragging mud and the scum of ebb tide across the tiles, pools of salty water forming beneath her in the chair. She works at that ribbon, putting the cork in the bottle first, working the ribbon around in that precise way she has done since she was a little child and had to stand on the chair while working over her treasures. All the time, with the house fading the ocean smell into dilution, she smells the cancer in the walls, on the curtains, over the mirror in the hallway, and mostly, emanating from her skin.

Bobbi Carducci

The Day Oprah Died

BOBBI CARDUCCI is a freelance writer and blogger and caregiver advocate. She is the author of *Confessions of an Imperfect Caregiver*, a memoir of her seven years as a caregiver for her mentally and physically ill father-in-law. Her work has appeared in multiple newspapers and magazines. She is the Vice President of Pennwriters, a nationally recognized writers group with over four hundred members. www.bobbicarducci.com; www.theimperfectcaregiver.com.

John Henry stopped believing in God the day Oprah died.

It happened on a Sunday and, just as he had on every Sunday morning for forty years, John Henry rose early and ate a breakfast of one soft-boiled egg, a piece of rye toast (well done—no butter) and two slices of well-crisped bacon. He washed it down with a single cup of Lipton tea (one half-teaspoon of sugar and a splash of fat-free creamer) served in a bone china cup so thin and brittle he came to believe the bone must've come from an osteoporosis-riddled old crone. It reminded him of his late mother.

He left his dirty dishes on the table, taking perverse pleasure in the knowledge that the runny remains of uncooked egg would congeal and harden in the egg cup as he dressed for church. White shirt, brown gabardine pants, the tie he had bought on sale the day the Walmart opened, his brown oxfords and, of course, his suit coat. Single breasted—the middle button missing. If he remembered his belt he'd wear it, if not, he didn't care a whit if it stayed home and had a true day of rest. God didn't seem to mind either.

John Henry always walked to church. It wasn't far and he used the time to collect his thoughts. If it rained, so be it. That's how life is sometimes. He would arrive early and stand across the street next to the rusting Civil War cannon, incongruously aimed directly at the church, and watch the pious arrive. At least they pretended they were pious despite evidence to the contrary throughout the week. He didn't give a shit. God said Sunday is a day of forgiveness and that was good enough for him.

Until the day Oprah died.

On that day he didn't stop when he reached the church. He went right past that old cannon rubbed smooth by the asses of teenaged boys straddling it obscenely every summer and kept on going until he reached the train station on the other side of town. It took him more than three hours to get there, due in part to his slow gait, but mainly because he took a detour to piss on the mayor's lawn. It relieved him greatly to do so.

Once at the station, he took his time reviewing the schedule posted on the wall. The idea of train travel intrigued him. He imagined boarding the 2:10 to Chicago, grasping a ticket in his left hand. The dining car would be filled with women reeking of J'adore perfume, all talking at once. He would select one for later use (as if any would go with him willingly) and back away before she sensed his intentions. He pictured a woman in his room late at night, her body all pink and white, her lips red from cherry Kool-Aid he'd mixed himself. He never got to what came next. John Henry was a man of limited imagination.

Until the day Oprah died.

Boarding the train to Chicago, he decided to attend her funeral. He knew he'd have to be creative if he was to get anywhere near her. Even in death you could only see her if you had the right connections. Too bad Maya Angelou was already dead, but Tom Cruise would be there, maybe even one or two of the folks who got a free car that time; only the ones who didn't bitch because they had to pay the taxes on it would be allowed in. He'd probably see Maria Shriver and a bunch of other politically connected millionaires, but they didn't give a shit about people like him. Never had, never would. No, they wouldn't see him or notice what he was up to until it was too late.

Oprah's the only one who ever paid him any attention. She spoke to him through the TV. Kept him from going ass-over-teacup crazy. She knew just about everything in the world worth knowing and it was uncanny how she always found a way to get a message to him whenever he needed a good talking to.

Her passing had left a hole in the world too big to be filled by anyone, although her best friend Gayle might want to give it a try. Trouble was Gayle didn't have a past to live down. No childhood incest to cry about, no recurring weight problem to keep folks tuning in to see if her pants still fit. Gayle would soon realize there wasn't no use in being the best friend of a ghost and soon after the funeral she'd just up and disappear.

John Henry wouldn't be in town long enough to find out if anyone went to look for her, he certainly wouldn't have time. He had bigger plans for the rest of his life and it was time to get started.

On the day Oprah died.

Shirley Graves Cochrane

The Smell of Apples

SHIRLEY GRAVES COCHRANE (1925–2015) was a poet, fiction writer, nonfiction writer, editor, and teacher. With a master's from John Hopkins University, she taught at American University, Georgetown University, Catholic University, and the Writer's Center. She was a freelance editor for Duke University Press, Yale University Press, and the *Shakespeare Quarterly* and the author of *Burnsite*, *Family & Other Strangers*, *Everything That's All*, *The Jones Family*, and *Letters to the Quick/Letters to the Dead*.

It was Stephen's favorite time of day—the children out back for one final hour of play, odors of food rising through the floorboards of his study. "Stephen is in his ivory nutshell," Elspeth would tell callers. Even in their present chaos, this hour was still his—a last remnant of Elspeth's wifehood guarded it. He almost regretted that Max was coming, although waiting for his visit partly accounted for his present euphoria.

He reread the opening for his article: "Maxwell Stallings, minor poet, major scholar, distinguished Rawlings Professor of Literature on the prestigious campus of Lester College…" All wrong. Major poet, minor scholar would do as well. Max was neither major nor minor, simply unknown outside the world of scholars and students. "Major influence"? Better. "The priest bone in him"—coming now. The whole thing in one easy flow.

Once started, anything might come. A poem even. It was the time of day when poems could best be caught. Sometimes a cluster of them. Word gifts. Better than the carefully trapped ones. ("Stephen Hastings, moving further from his mentor, Maxwell Stallings, is speaking increasingly now in his own strong voice…"—the young Johns Hopkins man, in *his* recent article.)

Below, the front door slammed, the house shivered.

Stephen looked out the window, saw Elspeth pause at the gate, frisk her saddlebag purse, go toward the park.

An errand to the mom and pop market? Nothing for alarm, surely. Yet a nervousness played over his scalp.

At the exact moment Elspeth entered the park, Max came into view at the other end. His manner suggested scissors, cranes, Beerbohm's Wordsworth. Stephen felt a rising excitement. Like a secret witness to a murder, he watched them move toward each other.

MAX STOPPED AT THE CEMENT circle of the park, needing to savor the fall, identify its smell. Apples. Leaves, of course—musked, trampled underfoot. Somehow transmuted into apples. In his youth, spring held a sadness for him, autumn an exhilaration. Now it was autumn that left him sad. Were you saddened by the season your age matched? Tonight the melancholy rode just above his head, not quite coming down upon him.

A woman walked toward him. There was something wrong with her— Max wondered if she might be disfigured, like the girl in his T. S. Eliot seminar whose scars were not immediately apparent but at close range revealed themselves shockingly. The woman moved toward him swiftly now. Max sucked in his breath. Her face was unscarred, yet it had an ugliness, made out of—yes!—former beauty.

He moved toward the familiar voice. "Elspeth?" He recognized her as a caricature of her mother. Even her greeting—a circling motion, the Queen Mother wave—was her mother's. He paused; she offered her hand. He was not expected to kiss her, then. Relief. Regret.

"Max, you dear," she said, speaking through the mother-mask, "I see you have brought wine. I was just dashing out to get some." She eyed his rucksack bulging with books and bottles. He handed her the wine bag, expected her to exclaim over the selection—red, white, rosé, choice for any menu—but she merely held it like an additional burden.

What had happened to her? Walking beside her, Max faced the question. She walked with head down; watched her own feet kick leaves, as though feet, leaves, pavement, equally, were no part of herself. Her greeting now seemed like memorized lines: spoken, over.

"Six children now, is it?" He knew their number—never the sort of thing he forgot. Merely something to break the silence.

"Yes," she answered slowly, as though counting them.

"Four born to us. To establish Stephen's masculinity. Two adopted to establish his liberalism."

"And you love them equally?" The question was what came to him. He avoided analyzing her ugly tone toward Stephen.

"Oh come now, Max. How can you love them equally? How can you even love them consistently? They are my enemies. I try not to kill them. That's the best I can do. I survive each day. They survive each day. That is all."

Had all the old Elspeth been sham? he wondered; *this* the reality?

Stephen and Elspeth were his surrogate children, born the same year, a continent apart. He had sent them identical silver cups. Their parents, equally dear friends to him, were strangers to each other. It had never occurred to him that the young people would even meet, let alone marry. And then suddenly there they both were, at Lester College, in his Freshman English class. *Of course*, he had thought, watching them choose adjoining seats, still unintroduced. *Of course*—watching them leave together.

Last month Stephen had written: "Elspeth has had a breakdown. The trauma of the modern woman. Yet she mends. And you will be a tonic for her." An inadequate warning. The present encounter seemed to Max like some particularly gross masquerade: a woman playing the part of Elspeth with not one suggestion of her special grace.

They reached the house. Larger, more imposing than the one he had last visited. "Ah, interesting!" he said, fiercely missing the old one.

"We outgrew the other one," she said, as though guessing his preference. "But how I loved it! The old contained life. I knew who I was then."

The streetlights, just come on, revealed her despair.

Max reached toward her, but she turned swiftly to the task of finding key, unlatching door. He followed her into the house.

FROM THE LANDING STEPHEN STUDIED Max. The usual bag of presents. Passing out books to the children, even the visiting neighborhood ones. Like the elongated figure of Saint Nicholas, he moved among the children, bowing, presenting. A beautiful way he had of touching their heads. "A fatherhood never directly experienced but exercised instead upon surrogate children—now, surrogate grandchildren." The unfinished article ran on inside Stephen's head.

Max noticed him, uttered one of his "ah's." Stephen descended. "Four years!" Max exclaimed.

Stephen studied Max for signs of shock. Nothing showed but impeccable good manners. Had Elspeth appeared in the costume of a dancing bear, Max would have registered only bland politeness ("Ah! Interesting!"), looking, perhaps, to see how the thing was made.

"So many children!" Max marveled.

"Four are neighbors," Stephen explained, realizing no one was getting them home. He began separating the neighborhood children, getting them into sweaters and jackets. A howl went up from Christopher and he ran sobbing to the kitchen, struggled back, pulling Elspeth, who ordered: "Leave them alone, Stephen—they are meant to be picked up by their parents. Don't mess everything up." She spoke as though he, an inept older brother, had deliberately created this chaos. Her face had that strange ugliness to it.

Christopher, provoked by a neighborhood child, set up another howl; Elspeth slapped him in the face.

Stephen saw Max move as though a spring had been released inside him. The au pair girl moved toward Christopher as Elspeth rushed back to the kitchen. Stephen wished that he loved the boy more. "Christo is at a perilous age," he told Max, then dropped all pretense. "We have problems."

"Ah yes." Max looked toward the fire. He plainly needed sherrying.

"Your usual sack?" Stephen asked. "Or what about some hot buttered rum?"

Max considered. "The sack, I think. Yes, yes, the sack."

Pouring the wine, Stephen wondered what his life would have been had he remained a bachelor like Max: holding steadily in his head the names of students, classes, references, traditions, stray lines of poems, dates, places, ceremonies, occasions—like Bishop Berkeley's Mind of God, keeping it all in place.

Max, in his turn, was mentally trying on the life of Stephen, wondering how he might have lived surrounded by children. Could he have produced them, nourished them? His mind hovered over the possibility, as though there were still time.

Parents came for children; finally only those of the household remained. All of them but Christopher settled in one corner of the room selecting crayons, taking scissors from egg carton holders. Max was strangely moved at the sight. One little girl came over to show him a picture.

"A heart," he guessed.

"A fish."

"Ah!" Max tried to see it that way. *But it is red*, he started to say. Christopher sat across from him, sucking his two middle fingers. He had a dirty blanket hung about his neck like a muffler. "My bucky," he explained to Max, through fingers.

Max had a sudden dreadful premonition that something terrible would happen to the boy. A suicide? Better not speculate. When Christopher grew older, perhaps he could come out for a visit. Though perhaps the first obligation was to his godchild, Maxwell Stallings Hastings—Maxie—the slender, serious, somehow burdened eldest child who called him "Sir." He read a book at the end of the work table and arbitrated disputes among his siblings. There were Laura, the young girl who had drawn the fish/heart; another girl who looked like a younger version of her...*Teachy*, some nickname like that; then a dark-haired, jet-eyed boy—*Manya*. Mexican? One of the adopted ones. But wasn't there another adopted one?

As though to answer this question, Stephen now entered carrying a small girl in yellow pajamas. She spread a hand toward Max. "This," she said, quite distinctly.

"Yes," Stephen said. "This is Max. Can you say *Max*?"

"This," she repeated.

Her cheeks were bright as apples, a fine high color; her eyes deep blue, darkly lashed and browed.

"A beauty!" Max said. Something in him approached —almost—hunger. To have such a being as this, sprung from his loins; or even, as in this case, adopted.

"Jennifer came all the way from Austria to join our family, didn't you, Jen?" Stephen jumped her gently up and down. The other children gathered around her. Even young Christopher came to tickle her toes. She pointed to each child in turn and said "This."

"Her one word," Stephen explained.

"A useful one." Max extended his arms. She leaned out, but when Max was ready to take her, moved back to her father.

"A flirt," Stephen said, kissing her cheek.

Suddenly Elspeth appeared. *Medea*, thought Max.

"Stephen!" Elspeth said, "they must all go upstairs. Mam'selle has them a picnic supper which they will have before the fire."

"Let me go up with them," Max said to Stephen. "I can read to them while they eat."

"Splendid!" Stephen agreed.

"Dinner will be served very soon," Elspeth said in the same admonishing tone.

DECIDING ON NO REPLY, MAX mounted the stairs, holding young Christopher by the hand, his blanket dragging and tripping them both. Ahead of him went Mam'selle with the child Jennifer. "This," she said, splaying a hand toward him. Max felt it was a benediction.

Stephen followed Elspeth into the living room and pokered the fire. In earlier, simpler times, he would have seized this moment to tell her that the planned dinner was too elaborate; that it was not the day to have had child visitors, especially ones whose parents did not arrive on time, "You're right, you're right," she would have agreed, looking at her hands. Were they not better off, Stephen wondered, even with this moderate oppression? Now he had stopped all criticisms, yet nothing improved. "Slaves rebel," Elspeth had recently told him, "only after the first shackle is removed."

"You haven't had your drink yet, have you?" he asked.

"Scotch on the rocks," she ordered.

Returning with her drink, he asked carefully: "Dinner under control? Anything I should do?"

"It's on hold. Later you can make the gravy."

Her mood seemed moderated, almost pleasant. He began to relax, enjoy his own drink. Too strong—this would have to be his last.

"A question," she began. "One that has been circling through my brain seeking an answer. This is it: Can Max be a pedophiliac?"

"Do you know what that term means?" He chose the tone he would use to a child testing a new obscenity.

"It means," Elspeth said carefully, "a refined molester of children. At least that is my definition."

"What in the name of God makes you think that Max—noble Max— would molest children?"

"It's the way he puts his hands on them. It is sexual. He handles them sexually."

She spoke with the certainty of her derangement, accepting stray feelings as sure facts. If you challenged her, she fixed you with her cunning look as though you were a part of the conspiracy. No wonder the sane feared the insane, Stephen thought; they tried to shape you to their paranoia.

"He touches them as a father would," he told her. "You have forgotten the nature of tenderness." But once knew it, he reminded himself. She had liked to comfort crying children. Sometimes, it seemed to him (although he could never be sure of this), she would wake them just to know the pleasure of comforting them back to sleep.

"Nevertheless, Stephen," she was saying, "I want you to be watchful."

Anger suddenly suffused him, and he strode toward her. "If you so much as hint at this subject again, or if you insult Max by even one look, I will have you sent to an institution."

She gazed at him for a long time. "Poor Stephen," she said at last, "you think it is still the days when a man can lock his wife away."

ENTERING THE DINING ROOM, MAX walked toward the picture of Elspeth as a young girl.

"I was a beauty, wasn't I, Max?"

"Incomparable," Max agreed.

"Would you say Ophelia?"

"More Miranda." Max felt a terrible sadness. Briefly he and Elspeth were alone, Stephen performing some final rite in the kitchen.

"Max, do you remember how grateful I used to be? For a book of poems.

A flower How thrilled I was if a cat looked in the window? *Out* of the window, for that matter." She laughed—almost the old Elspeth.

"Yes, yes, there was that about you."

"A child's joy. Fires. Do you remember how I loved fires? I used to have a *crush* on fires"

"Yes, I remember how they mesmerized you."

"I still love them. Only now it's more like pyromania. I want the fire to leap from the grate, consume the drapes, the walls, the house—everything. *Us*, Max—I want the fire to consume me. Oh Max, what is to become of us? Of me?"

"You are exhausted," he said carefully. "You must try to conserve your strength. This meal, now. I can see that you have spent too much energy preparing it."

"Nothing, nothing—in the old days I could have done it and fed a baby, finished a dress, done a washing, made an index... Now I am like an invalid. Or a high-grade moron. One thing at a time and that done poorly."

Max felt a clamp of helplessness encircling his chest.

Stephen entered with a platter. Relieved, Max sat down. He did not dare look at Elspeth. She was indeed mad.

Stephen began asking questions. An *interview*? Had Hotchkiss pressed Stephen into writing that retrospective study he'd been threatening? Damn Hotchkiss. He found himself saying: "My gifts are played out. I am reduced to writing children's poems." He had intended light irony, but Stephen leaned forward as intently as though he had revealed a terminal illness: "God, they've loaded you with slave work, Max."

"Always have. Give up everything but your main seminar."

"Why should you teach freshmen?""

"But I prefer freshmen." He could enter English 101 the first day, pick (by "a tingling of fiber") the faces that would be in his final honors seminar. World War II veterans, angry blacks with combs riding their bushes, hirsute Jesuses and Che Guevaras—he had culled winners from them all. The tingling of fiber seldom failed him.

Odd—Elspeth had produced the tingling of fiber, but not Stephen.

Across the table Elspeth asked questions which Stephen chose not to hear, talking over her words as one talks over an old tape, eradicating it. Eradicating her?

"Yes," Max said to Stephen, "I prefer teaching freshmen to any graduate seminar."

"WHAT HAS HAPPENED TO ME?" Elspeth realized this was the second time she had asked the question.

Stephen glanced at her warningly, then back to Max, who looked steadily at his plate, his ears growing pink, completing the rabbit image he often suggested.

"Poor Max," Elspeth sighed. Aloud? As in dreams, she was never sure when she spoke, since no one seemed to hear her anymore.

"What has happened to me?"

Perhaps there was no answer to that question. One day—or so it seemed at the time—she awoke to find her old life gone. Suddenly she was no longer beautiful, no longer even a woman. She moved from Stephen's bed—the act of love become for her "making the beast with two backs." She'd wanted to scream when a child touched her, that feather-bed capacity for mother love gone totally. Yet she now saw, this change had been preceded by a year of hell—her mother's death, Stephen's love affair…that wretched dark-haired weeping girl, dredged up by Stephen from the bowels of the Library of Congress. The necessary abortion (Elspeth herself finding the best clinic). Then (how odd Stephen's desires were!), almost immediately, the adoption of Manya, whose dark looks and unexplained weeping fits could almost make him the child of that wretched mistress.

And—final blow—Christo's terrible retching illness, still undiagnosed, that left him a pale wraith hung about her neck. Then the importation of Mam'selle, arriving almost the same time as Jennifer and oddly resembling her. (Another worrisome coincidence.)

Then therapy, first suggested, ironically, by Stephen, who now believed that he knew more than *they* did—"they" being the entire medical profession. Locked in a cork-lined room, made to scream out obscenities with people obviously crazier than she. The first day she'd been hideously cursed by a bent sparrow of a man—impotent, she felt sure. In four sessions she had been flayed of her skin, the dimensions of her hatred for Stephen revealed.

Had it not been better to collapse with a migraine, nurse constant low-back pain, disguise frigidity, keep the crouched pose of constant mothering, look forward to early death? In such a traditional life a miracle sometimes occurred: sudden wealth, purifying widowhood, a second, sounder marriage.

Now what she wanted was escape—leave Christo and his mystery ailment, Jennifer and her loaded diaper, Maxie and his cruelties hidden behind a façade of manners. Escape also the mixed-breed dog, the two tortoise-shell cats, one male and therefore valuable, the pair of gerbils she suspected Maxie of torturing, the parakeet that endlessly repeated, "It's a lovely," never completing its sentence.

"Max, why did you never marry?" Her question surprised her—she had not meant to ask it.

Stephen and Max both looked at her, quickly glanced away. Did they think she talked to the walls, the cat beneath the table?

"The dinner is dreadful," she said. "Not even edible."

Yet they ate, even with a certain gusto. She raised her voice: "I think I must have omitted something from the sauce." They raised their voices, Stephen thumping the table with an index finger, a gesture filched from Max.

Again, they did not hear her—or chose not to. Stephen had probably warned Max: "Don't be alarmed if she talks to herself. It's best to ignore her."

Max turned toward her, and she felt a flicker of gratitude. "Elspeth, did you ever revise the Donne article you sent me some time back?" he asked.

"Oh Max, dear, that was the other Elspeth who wrote that article. That sweet-faced girl who baked bread and sat at the feet of men, listening to their talk like Desdemona, that smothered darling. The Elspeth you see before you has lost her looks. How? I really don't know, except that perhaps they depended on expression, preferably beatific. Now, Stephen tells me, my face constantly registers obscenities. That is really rather witty of him, don't you think? And perhaps even accurate."

She became aware of the chaos of her own laughter.

"And her brain, Max," she continued, "I'm talking now of the brain of the new Elspeth. Ah Max, if you could but see into her mind, you would be horrified. Like looking into a volcano. Few can stand the sight. Dr. Berens must rest for an hour before seeing his next patient after my session with him."

Stephen looked steadily into his wineglass, reddening to match its color. Max gazed at his long fingers, like blanched minnows. And then Stephen spoke to Max, changing the subject.

"Well," Max responded, "as my mother always said…"

"Ah Max!" Elspeth cried, "I remember your mother!"

Max looked at his nails; then, rather too loudly, finished his sentence, turning pointedly to Stephen.

Elspeth continued, "She was tiny, beautifully dressed, like a doll." An apple-head doll, the withered fruit masquerading as human skin, aged. Lace framing the desecration. Her jeweled hand held her wineglass, waved it toward her son. *I want to vomit up the memory of her.* Words like these came to her now. Where had they been lurking all her girlhood?

"Elspeth," Stephen said, "perhaps it would be well to go up and get some rest now."

She had said it aloud, then. How much? She wanted to spring across the table, put the carving knife to Stephen's throat. Perhaps nick him—he could stand to lose a little blood. "All right," she said instead, "I will go. So that you can talk about me."

FOR A FULL MINUTE STEPHEN sat silently with Max while Elspeth mounted the stairs. At the top she shouted back down: "You pair of motherfuckers!"

"I am at the end of my rope," Stephen said.

Max uttered his saddest "Ah!"

"She is midway through her therapy," Stephen explained. "I say midway. That is optimistic. What they do these days is take mildly depressed patients, force them into insanity, then cure them. Also, the whole family must go. Dr. Berens handed me over to a woman shrink. Young Christo starts next week with a child psychiatrist. Actually, I'm glad of that. But my shrink says Maxie should go too, since he'll soon be entering puberty. Oh, by next year, they'll have young Jennifer toddling off to group therapy, a paper bag with change of clothing tucked under her arm."

"I suppose we are all a bit insane," Max observed.

"God, Max, the expense! The drain of assets…you could not believe…" Stephen stopped, realized he'd committed what his father considered the cardinal social sin: "poor mouthing."

Briskly Max reached into his breast pocket, extracted checkbook and pen. He wrote out a check, talking steadily: so grieved to see Elspeth… welfare of children…the one thing I can…my ridiculous income…despite inflation…and no one but myself…

Stephen was primed to reject the check when Max passed it to him. But when he looked at the amount—five thousand—he felt he had been given a ticket to freedom. He could pay all bills, even afford the needed dishwasher.

"Max, I…"

"I wish to hear nothing. It is my pleasure. What, after all, can I better invest in than a family?"

And now his brusqueness gave way to visible sadness, and Stephen found himself remembering Max's one real confidence to him: a young woman he'd met in Paris right after the war. They had not consummated the affair—Stephen was not certain exactly why—but there had been "much body intimacy," as Max described it. A year later, as Max was planning a second trip to see her, he received word of her death. Max had showed him a framed photograph—Stephen remembered only her enormous eyes. "I don't know how to thank you," Stephen said. "Of course it will be a loan."

"Gift!" Max almost shouted, a sort of anger flaming out. He rose, saying: "I must use the plumbing."

Stephen waited until Max had left, then reached for the check and folded it carefully into his wallet. It was now possible to do whatever must be done. Elspeth's endless therapy. A divorce, which they often spoke of now. Or perhaps a better turn. A trip abroad? Or some success—a book of poems published. But at least get them through this hell-time. What he felt was self-congratulation; deliberately he moved himself toward gratitude, saying aloud: *Bless Max*—a benediction.

On the bathroom door a shirt board sign was tacked with a lipsticked message:

Some fucking fool tried to flush a diaper down the toilet. Please use upstairs bath.

Wincing, Max climbed the stairs to find the bathroom unbelievably messy, toilet unflushed, spitty toothbrushes lying on the lavatory. Carefully he flushed toilet, replaced toothbrushes, then took care of his own needs. Leaving the bathroom, he was drawn to the windowseat at the end of the hall. The window was partly open, the chill welcome. He breathed in the appled air. From the small adjacent room, he could hear a sound:

"Eh? eh?" No distinguishable words. Still, a clear question. He got up, went to the door, slightly ajar, and pushed it open. Young Jennifer stood in her crib, its side only waist-high. One pajamaed foot seemed caught between mattress and springs. He went quickly to extricate her. Privately he would warn Stephen—Elspeth might take offense.

He continued to hold her, feeling her body warmth. Fever? She bent away from him, staring into his face, circling a hand about her ear. One hand lightly touched his neck.

"This," he said. He straightened her mattress, raised the side, but still did not put her back. He held his face to hers, feeling the near burning of her cheek. Her breathing was that of young animals. His free hand traveled the small body. She was held in the immobility of wonder. His lips found the soft spot in her neck, below the ear. She winced. An ear ache? "My dear, my dear," he murmured. Had he aggravated the ear? Perhaps she'd suddenly realized a stranger held her.

Down the hall, Max heard a door open, a flurry; then Elspeth stood in the doorway, clicked on the light.

"Her foot was caught," Max explained. "Also, she had lowered the side. She was in a precarious position."

"She couldn't possibly lower the side. It takes pressure on levers on both sides to bring it down."

"Perhaps the au pair girl…"

"Are you accusing Mam'selle of neglect?"

"Of course not! A simple oversight."

The child began to howl, stretching her arms to her mother. Elspeth took her from him.

"Max, I know perfectly well what you came in here for. Don't you think I know what you're up to? My poor sweet baby. Corrupted!"

"Preposterous!" Max whispered. He felt a desperate need to flee—the room, the house, the city even. He turned, headed blindly for the stairs, almost stumbled, but continued his downward plummet. Some air, I must have air! he thought. He said nothing to Stephen, standing at the foot of the stairs.

FOR QUITE A WHILE AFTER Max left—leaving overcoat, rucksack—Stephen expected him back. Perhaps he had seen a friend passing. Or Elspeth had sent him on some errand whose importance he exaggerated. Idly Stephen walked over to the rucksack, extracted a book. Max's latest. The dedication read:

> *To my dear friends*
> *and surrogate family*
> *Elspeth and Stephen*
> *I present this*
> *my final child*

Stephen flicked through the scant pages.

> *Winter: it apples the cheeks of children*
> *Witch fingers beat rhythms on iced air.*

A complete poem. Another, entitled "Matriarch," read:

> *I shall*
> *open*
> *one final door*
> *and see her*
> *standing*
> *there.*

"…Maxwell Stallings, practicing poet for over forty years, was originally firmly grounded in the forms, his poems graceful marriages of traditional and experimental. But he has moved steadily away from the forms, and indeed from form itself, toward fragmentation and obscurity. Glancing over the slender poems in his latest book, a reader may well wonder if his next book may not be composed entirely of blank pages…"

"Has he gone?" Elspeth, calling from upstairs, interrupted Stephen's internal composition.

"Yes—ten minutes ago."

"Good!"

Stephen walked to the window and opened a shutter. Leaves swirled in the park. Two separate groups of street urchins converged at its center, as though stalking a common enemy. A dog walker, a uniformed man, two bent women, other walkers came, disappeared, Max not one of them. Stephen had a vision of Max scissoring wildly down some side street, hopelessly lost. Two ideas occurred to him. He could get the dog and go look for him or call the police. Slowly he abandoned both plans. He waited what seemed a responsible time, then closed the blinds, leaving on porch and hall lights, and headed upstairs. Above him he could hear Elspeth's voice: *There, there, there*, even though the child had long since stopped crying.

PJ Devlin

Signals

AFTER A civilian career with Fairfax County Fire and Rescue Department, PJ DEVLIN pursued an MFA in fiction from George Mason University in Fairfax, Virginia, where she studied with Susan Shreve, Alan Cheuse, and Courtney Brkic. Her novels are *Wissahickon Souls* (2014) and *Becoming Jonika* (2015); her short story collection is *Wishes, Sins and the Wissahickon Creek* (2016).

It's 11:40 a.m. Percy and a baby-faced brunette in a striped sweater and skinny jeans laugh as they trip up the steps to his third-floor apartment. Mrs. Sanchez, dark and silent, stands on the landing holding a basket of white hand towels she embroiders with blue flowers.

"*Hola!*" Percy says when they push past her.

As soon as they burst into his apartment, Percy locks the door, drops his backpack, then wraps his arms around the brunette's waist and twirls her completely around. The girl spins onto the worn brown sofa that smells of coffee. She grabs Percy's backpack and drops a thin book into it.

"A gift," she says.

Percy smiles, then looks around, feeling watched. On the kitchen wall, a Kit-Cat clock rolls its eyes back and forth.

"I'll be back," he says and goes into the bathroom.

In the mirror, he bares his teeth like a dog, swigs mouthwash, and spits. With a deep breath, he returns to the living room. The girl walks around the room picking up odds and ends. She stares at the photograph of Percy and Peggy at the top of a Ferris wheel.

"She must be nice," the girl says. "Is she really that fat?"

Percy doesn't want to think about Peggy. He wants to have fun, to laugh, to do whatever the hell he wants.

"You ready to work on calculus?" he asks.

The girl takes his hand and leads him to the sofa. She lies back and pulls him on top.

"Let's work on integration," she says.

Percy leans on his elbows and looks in her eyes. Her breath smells of cigarettes and Juicy Fruit gum. She takes off her sweater and its blue-white-blue stripes remind Percy of a signal flag he memorized in the Navy—*On fire, keep clear.* Her hands run under his shirt, across his back, and over his ass. She slides them below his navel and tugs at his zipper. He feels pain on his chest near his heart, where her breath is hot and moist and he likes the pain.

"Integration," he whispers, "the analysis of functions with…in con…tin…u…ous do…mains."

He feels on fire and knows he should keep clear, but his head explodes and he lets everything go—guilt, responsibility, trust.

❧

WHILE THE GIRL IS IN the bathroom, Percy uses his Pearl Jam T-shirt to dry the sofa cushions and decides to flip them over. He looks at the clock, then goes to the bedroom and tosses his damp shirt and red boxers in the hamper. From a pile on the floor, he grabs a white T-shirt and goes commando in his faded jeans.

In the kitchen, the girl licks peanut butter off a knife. Her head goes back and forth, following the Kit-Cat clock's eyes. Calculus class is in thirty minutes. Percy checks the living room, then ushers the girl out the door. Mrs. Sanchez passes them on the stairs. Percy's glad she doesn't speak English.

❧

IT'S 7:15 P.M. PERCY OPENS the apartment door to red boxers flapping like the signal flag—*Discharging explosives.* Inside, Peggy stands like a fighter. She throws the boxers in his face, then rips through a hole in his Pearl Jam T-shirt and drops it on the floor. He crosses the threshold laughing.

"What's wrong with you?" he asks.

Percy brushes against her, hangs his keys on the hook by the door, drops his backpack, and lays his laptop on the coffee table. His blond hair is tousled and his beard is gritty.

Peggy's red hair frames a face covered with amber freckles the color of her eyes. Her lips draw tight across the overbite he used to think was cute. Soft skin cushions her arms and legs—her body's no longer the physically fit one she flaunted before he married her. She clenches her jaw and spits out her words.

"I watched you put on these boxers this morning. Now I find them in the hamper—wet and nasty. Your toothbrush's wet too. When did you come back to the apartment, Percy? Why'd you change your clothes?"

He looks shocked and sad, tilts his head and blinks. A festering smell rises from his armpits and he concentrates on keeping his expression hurt and innocent.

"The bio professor canceled class, so I came home, jogged, took a shower, grabbed a PB&J, and drove back to school. What's the big deal?"

He smiles, puts his hands on her shoulders, and gazes into her eyes. The fragrance of White Linen floats from her clothes. When he bends to kiss her, she backs away. His mouth tastes of cigarettes and the girl.

"Look, Peggy, between studying and working out, baby, I got nothing left for anyone but you. You better now? Hungry? I'm starving. What's to eat?"

Percy goes to the refrigerator, grabs a tub of macaroni and cheese and slides it into the microwave. On the brown velveteen sofa from her parents' house, Peggy tucks herself in a corner. He hears her quiet sobs. Their bed, a mattress on the floor, came from her parents, too. The sheets are crumpled like they left them this morning when she ran to catch the bus to her job in D.C., and he drove her car to campus. She's still in her work clothes. Her wrinkled white blouse hangs over a black skirt straining against her waist. Peggy looks more like her mother every day and Percy wonders what he got himself into.

"I'll be back. Gotta take a leak."

Percy leans into the mirror. Stupid to ditch his nasty clothes. Peggy's powers of observation leap quantums beyond those of the most highly trained spy in the universe. His blue eyes peer out above dark circles. He brushes his teeth and tongue to remove the yeasty taste, pitches his shirt, and runs a towel over his chest. When he raises his arms, he smells sex. Deodorant coats a fresh sheen across his armpits and he feels better. At the microwave's chirp, he walks shirtless to the kitchen. He doesn't notice the purple mark near his heart.

Percy fills two bowls with macaroni swimming in Velveeta and carries them to the living room. He offers the smaller bowl to Peggy, but she shakes her head no. He retreats to the beanbag chair to eat both bowls and he's still hungry.

"Did you go shopping?" His smile is charming and boyish, designed for absolution.

"No, Percy, but apparently you did. Was it worth it? Did you get your money's worth?"

Her face flushes with patches of white and red and he thinks of the flag signal—*You are running into danger.* White noise buzzes in his head.

Percy crosses to the sofa, sits next to Peggy, and rubs his cheek on her arm, adopting the tactics discussed late into the night with his buddies on the super carrier, *USS Harry S. Truman.* Peggy's head twitches like a compass needle trying to find north.

"You must think I'm stupid. God, you never even take out the trash but today you come home to rearrange cushions and change your clothes?"

Percy sees hurt coursing off her body like heat. If he reaches out, he'll touch it.

"Look, a girl from my calculus class flunked the midterm and asked me to go over derivatives with her. I thought we'd concentrate better if we had a quiet place to study, so we came here. I spilled a soda on myself and the sofa so I changed before we went back to campus. I didn't tell you because I knew you'd go psycho. There's never anything good to eat around here. When do you get paid?"

"Goddamn it, Percy. You take my car. Would it kill you to pick up groceries once in a while? I bust my ass to pay the rent while you bring some girl here to help with calculus. Maybe you should help me once in a while." Peggy glares at him from amber eyes that flash yellow like a panther's. The dignity in her rage frightens him.

"In a year I'll get my engineering degree, then I'll make good money. I don't have rich parents like you to put me through college. While you went to football games and got drunk at parties, I protected this country. Now it's my turn. You knew what you were getting into when you married me."

"I had no idea what I was getting into. You begged me to get married. You cried and said all you thought about when you were deployed was coming home to marry me. You didn't give a damn about my plan to work a year then go to law school. Why was it so important to get married right away?"

His blue eyes burn with fatigue. Everything's so hard. He rubs his right biceps where a tattooed lion roars above a striking snake and takes a deep breath.

"I thought I'd lose you," he whispers.

The macaroni and cheese form a lump in his stomach and he wants to vomit. His hands tremble. Percy crosses the room to Peggy, takes her arms, and drapes her hands on his shoulders. She pushes him away.

Her chin juts out and her lip quivers. "After work, I rush home to be with you. But you're never here. You stay late on campus to go out with your friends. When you do come home, you've bought yourself pizza or tacos but you never bring anything for me."

He raises his eyebrows and his eyes open wide. "You never told me you wanted tacos."

"Oh my God," she says and punches him in the chest.

Percy slinks away to slump in the beanbag chair. He's still hungry and doesn't want to deal with this shit.

"It's no fun anymore, Peggy. You're always tired and you're always pissed. You have to know where I'm going, who I'm with, when I'll be home. You want to control everything I do. I had more freedom when I was in the Navy."

"What do you think it means to be married, Percy?"

He is sick of this conversation, sick of her expectations, her demands, her petty calculations of who does what, who pays for what.

"I don't think it should mean I have to get your permission before I go out or do anything. I love you but the more you nag, the less I want to be here. I don't want a mother." The anger in his voice shocks him.

"A mother is exactly what you want. You want me to pay the bills, clean the apartment, wash your clothes, buy your food, and make your dinner while you come and go as you please. What about what I want? You care more about a skanky teenage girl than you do about me." Tears run down her cheeks, but she looks angry, not sorrowful.

The soft vinyl of the beanbag is warm from his flesh and reeks of beer. He runs his fingers through his hair, then rubs them on his jeans and thinks it's time to go to the laundromat and wash everything, every piece of clothing, every towel, every sheet. Start clean and fresh. He opens his mouth to tell her this, but he's infuriated when she opens his backpack and pulls out the book that pathetic loser gave him—*Jonathan Livingston Seagull*. Peggy reads the inscription out loud: *Keep working on love. Begin by knowing you have already arrived. Thanks for being a great teacher.* ♥ *Sandy*.

Peggy rips out the page, crumples it, and throws it at him, then hurls the book like a Frisbee. It jams into the lion on his arm. "It's time you tell the truth," she says.

Percy's back and ass ache from sitting on the beanbag chair. This is a critical moment. He should ponder the problem and consider independent variables that influence the outcome. It's the random variable that worries him.

"We're going through a tough time, Pegs. You're busy, I'm busy. We're running in different directions. We hardly ever have sex. Maybe I'm trying to make up for everything I missed by joining the Navy. This sophomore girl, Sandy, has been flirting with me all semester. Anyway, I brought her here to study, only to study. I never cheated, Peggy, I swear. But when she pulled me close, honestly, I was tempted. I felt her lips but when I thought about you, I pushed her away. She was so pissed. She called me a loser and hurled her soda at me. It got all over my clothes and all over the sofa. I wanted to punch her. But I just changed my clothes, wiped up the spills, turned over the cushions, and drove her back to campus. Whatever you think, I'm glad it happened. It was a test and I passed. I choose you, Peggy. For better, for worse, in good times and bad, I choose you."

Percy takes Peggy in his arms. Her tears trickle down his chest. He smooths her hair and touches her face. He loves her soft skin. Peggy's the only thing in his life that matters. His resentment turns to sympathy and understanding. Desire. Near his heart, her finger traces a circle, over and over. It excites him.

Percy steers her to the bedroom and caresses her until she stops trembling. He feels powerful and heroic, with his arm a pillow for Peggy's head and the taste of her tears a salty completion. He sleeps in deep oblivion, floating in an ocean of childhood dreams.

∾

IT'S 9:10 A.M. THE SUN angles through the window, piercing his eyes like daggers. He burrows under the blanket and breathes the essence of Peggy's body.

"Peg?" he calls.

Percy kicks off the sheets but stays in bed, reliving last night. It's true what they say about make-up sex. His stomach growls. He hopes Peggy woke up early, got dressed quietly so as not to wake him, and any minute, will walk into the apartment with cups of sweet coffee, cinnamon bagels oozing cream cheese, and the newspaper. He feels himself rise at the thought of her setting down their breakfast, then jumping into bed with him. He has class at 11:00 but would blow it off for another time with Peggy. Damn, she must have gone to work.

He rolls out of bed, goes to the bathroom, and decides to take a shower, wash his hair, and start on the clean sweep their relationship needs. He squeezes a glob of Peggy's lavender-rose shampoo on his hair and sticks out his tongue to taste the soapy water as it cascades down his face. He cleans himself with her oatmeal soap, the tiny grains rough against his skin. With water tapping on his head, he sits in the tub and scrubs his calloused feet. Peggy always says he should get a pedicure and maybe he will—with bright nail polish to make her laugh. He takes her pink razor and trims under his arms. Percy dries himself with the only towel on the rack, a white hand towel embroidered with blue flowers. After he combs back his hair, he notices his hairline receding. Above the dark circles, his blue eyes gleam clear.

Percy feels better than he has in months. Today he'll tell Sandy they had a lot of fun, but his wife suspects and he won't risk it. He wonders how he could have been so stupid, bringing her here for sex. He's just damned lucky Peggy believes him. *Don't bother me anymore*, he'll tell the girl. *You mean nothing to me.*

He finds white briefs in the back of his drawer and pulls on the khakis he wears when he has to get dressed up. The only clean shirt in the closet is a green polo he hates, but he slides it over his head. He wants something to eat.

On the kitchen wall, the Kit-Cat clock's eyes go back and forth and it creeps him out. The refrigerator's empty. He'll be ten minutes late if he leaves now.

He'll come home right after class. They'll go shopping tonight, maybe grab some burgers, then stock up at the store. They'll buy good food—vegetables and fruit, apples and strawberries, stuff to make salad, and a Chablis. This weekend they'll cook together and Sunday, he'll take Peggy to the art museum.

The living room looks strangely sterile. On the sofa, the cushions lay askew, but he can't put his finger on what's different. Percy studies the apartment he entered as Peggy's husband—the walls he painted yellow, the worn sofa, the beanbag chair from his childhood bedroom, the photo of them at the top of the Ferris wheel, where he asked her to marry him and she said yes, where they looked down at the foamy surf smashing on the beach and touched infinity where the sky met the sea in a line so narrow it disappeared.

On the hook by the door, the car keys are gone. Percy sits on the sofa and reaches for his laptop. Across the smooth white surface, the girl's red and yellow thong twists through Peggy's wedding ring.

Percy sinks at the signal—*Man overboard.*

Jenny Drummey

Fireflies

JENNY DRUMMEY's debut novel *Unrequited* was published by Rebel ePublishers. She received an MA in creative writing from Temple University. She loves the smell of books and lives with a basement full of birds in Fairfax, Virginia.

*I*n the middle of the night, in the Tucker Motors men's room, in a slender crack between the cinderblocks, sat a note written on the back of a fortune. Charlie had just used a pair of tweezers to slide it in there. It jutted out only far enough to be seen.

He imagined that in the total darkness, the paper might emit the faintest glow. With equal intensity, he hoped that it would and would not be found.

⌘

"I FEEL AWFUL," CHARLIE SAID. He was sitting at the dinner table with his mom the next day. A half-eaten plate of fried chicken sat before her. She had cancer, but she didn't want to know it yet.

She didn't say a thing.

Charlie's dad wasn't there, which was normal. He mostly worked at his gas station, off of Ohio I-280. He may have gone to meet a vendor for a cheap steak dinner, or eat fried fish in the back office (which always smelled of fried fish).

Finally, his mom asked.

"How come?" She licked her fingers and put down a cleaned chicken bone.

"I think I ate too much expired candy at the store today."

That afternoon, his dad had filled a huge black plastic garbage bag with really expired snacks that hadn't sold.

"I'm not ordering this shit anymore," he said as he chucked whole boxes of Carlton's Extra Smooth Taffy into the bag. "I should never have listened to that bastard from up the street." Matt Tucker imitated the salesman's whiny voice. "'You'll make a mint, Matt! You won't be able to keep them in stock.' Pure bullshit."

He threw three tins of Peruvian Love Buttons on top of the pile.

When he was done, his dad told Charlie to take the stuffed garbage bag of snacks to the dumpster out back, and then get the hell home. The plastic stretched thin in Charlie's fingers as he dragged the heavy bag out the door.

Outside, Charlie went through that bag and ate everything he never got otherwise. These premium snacks had been stocked near the register and his father surely would have seen if they were gone. Now, finally Charlie feasted on Simple Times Fruit Gel, Juarez Bros. Hot-Os, and the mildly flavored Fuji SnoBar.

"Well," his mother said from across the dinner table, "it's your own fault then. What did you learn?" She felt a pain in her lower back, but she ignored it, like she ignored most unpleasant things.

Charlie shrugged. "Not to eat expired candy?"

"No," his mom said, wiping her mouth on her sleeve, "Not too eat too much expired candy."

She lit a smoke.

Her plate was full of bones.

〽

MATT TUCKER COULD COUNT ON a steady stream of revenue from Tucker Motors. Some months it was a trickle, some a creek, some a creek after a good rain.

Matt depended on the gas station's success for everything, not just for the money to put fried chicken and fried fish on the table, but for his own sense of worth. Sometimes his heart hurt when he worked behind the register, or he counted receipts in his office, or he helped seniors pump gas.

When he thought he might be having a heart attack, his first thought was not of his family but always: Who is going to take care of the goddamn gas station now?

Then the feeling passed, usually because he belched.

Matt Tucker would not have had so many of these secret pains and fears if he was not obese, or small-minded, or lonely, or mean.

But he was all of these things, as his heart reminded him every once in a while.

∾

IF A MILLION YEARS PASSED between the time Charlie was born and the time he died, and if his parents too lived that long, they would never, ever, ever understand him.

His dad was always hostile. His mom seemed oblivious. Sometimes when he walked into a room she looked shocked to see him.

Charlie learned to do a lot of things that kids his age had not yet figured out, like build a reasonable fire, or do laundry and not destroy the clothes. He also knew how to get in and out of the house at all hours of the night and never get caught. He dropped noiselessly from the window two or three nights a week and crept through the wet grass, passed the hulking garbage cans, and hustled up to Tucker Motors.

He took his own copy of the men's room bathroom key from his pocket, let himself in, and locked the door behind him.

Charlie was full of the biggest secret of all, and he knew it was only a matter of time before it came shooting out of him like a bottle rocket down a long narrow hallway. It would not be ignored. He would get into the most amount of trouble he could ever get in for letting it out.

He was constantly aware of the possibility of a spark.

He passed hours in the bathroom, breathing the rancid air, watching his warped reflection in the hand dryer spout.

He wished to become invisible.

He wished to stand in the corner by the plunger and scummy trash can and watch each man perform his own secret, familiar rituals.

A man unguarded, comfortable, ashamed of nothing.

This is how Charlie wished he could be all of the time.

One night, a midnight knock on the rest room door, unexpected, soft, a test. Charlie put his hand on the knob, and was filled with a thrilling tenderness. He did not turn the knob.

He needed nothing else but the possibility of connection, just then.

An hour after midnight he crawled across the threshold of his bedroom's windowsill, and landed, once again undiscovered, in hostile territory.

But soon he came to regret not opening the door. Infinite scenarios played out in his head: violent, mundane, sometimes both. Men's socks, pants, and wallets. Callouses in unfamiliar places. Breathing.

He hoped the note might entice someone to show. He wanted everything to finally begin.

෴

ONCE, CHARLIE'S MOM BRENDA AND his dad Matt had been young and hopeful and not so fat. They had been kind to him then, or at least he hoped so. From what he could tell from photos of family gatherings and what his Uncle Davey told him, all was easy until he was four years old.

Then his dad bought the gas station.

For the first few years, he had a mechanic who would, occasionally, fix things. More often than not, he was slow because he was stoned. He misplaced his tools and lunches, and once, his fingers. Two tips sliced off by the running engine brought an early retirement. Matt never replaced him, but he kept the name, Tucker Motors, because it sounded better than Tucker Gas.

The station became everything his dad focused on, and meant absolutely nothing to his mom. Because his parents had opposing feelings about their source of income, it meant that Matt did all of the work at the station, and Brenda stayed home stubbornly cross stitching.

It was like she was a jellyfish and he was a plumber. They had no use for each other.

Matt told Brenda one evening:

"All you ever do is sew those stupid pillows. Enough with the pillows. Why don't you come and help me just once? I try to hire counter help, but the only people who apply are hobos."

"Nope. Not my thing," she said. She was firm about it.

Brenda saw the gas station as a filthy waste of time. Sometimes when she drove past it, she closed her eyes so she didn't have to see her name in huge red letters.

She had no idea why her husband spent so much time in that horrible dirty office in the back, or behind the register beneath a teetering cantilever of cigarette cartons and sleeves of dip.

But mostly, she resented the fact that he put their name on it, that people would connect her to that greasy, stale, cramped convenience store with ads everywhere and nothing of value to sell.

∽

YEARS BEFORE, BRENDA TOLD MATT to come on out, to stop his hiding, she was ready. Matt was sitting on a log in the thick scrub that bordered the front yard. She could see the glow from his florescent cap.

Matt did not answer.

Brenda sat on the porch swing for a while and then she said, "You know what? You could have a forked dick for all I care. If that box don't have a ring in it, than I don't want to see you anymore."

Her brother Davey came around the front of the house from the backyard. He was carrying a fishing pole and tackle box.

"What's this I hear about a forked dick?" he asked, coming up the stairs.

"Never you mind," Brenda said.

∽

SHE WAS TIRED OF WAITING for Matt to ask her to marry him. They had been going out for two years. She had wasted enough time.

"Now it is time to get serious," her mother had said to her just that morning.

Her mother had not yet given up. She refused to wear a housecoat. As soon as she got up in the morning, she put on her shoes. Her husband was a slow riser, it took him hours to expand into full consciousness.

Her mother was always ready for the next opportunity.

She had been very patient with Brenda and supported her for as long as she could in her decision to stick with Matt, though, if Brenda wanted to really know the truth, she *could* have done better. A few years ago, when she was not yet thirty, she could have had her pick of three men.

"When I was your age, I had already turned your father down twice." But then, Brenda's mother broke both her legs in a skiing accident and it took the injury to slow her down long enough to let her future husband take care of her.

"I learned to walk," she often said when a chore went undone, "but I didn't learn to walk away."

꒰ ꒱

HUNCHED IN THE SCRUB, MATT felt he was balancing on the tip of a pyramid that had somehow been built beneath him without his knowledge. He was equally likely to tumble down any of the sides, not looking forward to the painful descent.

He appeased her with a ring that was just big enough, which was lucky because he was on the cusp of ugly. It would take only a few more years.

꒰ ꒱

MATT AND BRENDA GOT MARRIED on a cold day in February 1968 by a wheezing asthmatic priest. When they were done, it was one o'clock in the afternoon, way too early to go to the bars. Davey had tied cans and streamers to Matt's back bumper, but the whole mess fell off in two blocks, and the couple could see their neighbor Mr. Orton run out in the street and shake his fist in their direction, then shrink to nothing as they drove away.

They went to some wilderness area and stayed in a rustic cabin for their three-day honeymoon, and then they came back and pupated in Brenda's parents' basement for four years.

When they lay together in their bed in the dark, damp basement they did not speak, but instead listened to every footfall above them. They could hear the smoosh of Davey's dirty gray sneakers, the exclamation point of Brenda's mother's high heels on the kitchen floor, the shush of her father's house slippers. Brenda's father was a small lumpy man who whistled under his breath and avoided conflict. He didn't want any trouble. If he spilled coffee and there wasn't a towel around to sop it up, he would use his sleeve.

Brenda and Matt were trying to build a life together blindly, adding to it with Charlie's birth, cutting stuff out of it when they moved out on their own. All along Matt grew more atrocious.

One morning he looked in the mirror and recognized himself as an unwanted man.

Brenda looked anywhere but at Matt when she talked to him. She did not want to be reminded of the gravity of her mistakes every time he told her to pass the butter. She still helped him tie his ties, but she did so from behind. She imagined the knot in the fabric constructing itself from her fingers, and she pulled it taut quickly.

He thanked her sometimes.

Eventually, he learned to tie his own tie, and then they barely touched anymore.

When Matt first saw the station that would become Tucker Motors, he was smitten: a sudden eagerness leaped up inside him that made his scalp tingle.

Here was something he could give his name to that would turn out exactly as he wanted.

Matt could instantly see a busy parking lot and garage, a line of cars with busted timing belts, serpentine belts, fan belts. Matt would be standing at the front of this line with all of these belts draped over his meaty forearms, distributing them to competent mechanics in front of grateful customers who waited in a glass-enclosed room with a coffee machine, a television, a pile of current magazines, and a standing ashtray in the corner filled with sand.

When the number of butts in the ashtray reached five, Davey would come and clean it out and then rake interesting patterns in the sand with a fork.

Mothers would have the sense not to bring their babies to such a place, but young boys, from five and up, would be very welcome. When Matt took a break from looking over his mechanic's shoulders, he would come into the customer waiting area and teach the kids how to use a wrench, a real one, but a small one. He would show them how to turn the bolts, smiling at the mothers who smiled back. He would gladly give these normal boys their only useful lesson that day, and probably most of them would remember it, and probably most of them would be far ahead in life because of it.

When they grew up, they would seek him out to personally thank him for giving them a great start in life.

These were just some of the things that Matt saw as the image of Tucker Motors sprang fully formed in his brain.

But after receiving the meager bank loan and shoving the business up off the ground, he had come to realize that the only similarity between this vision and reality was his name on the large sign and the ashtray filled with sand.

❧

BRENDA DID NOT WANT TO see a doctor because calling to make the appointment was like starting a small, efficient engine that would generate power to run a ruthless machine.

❧

BRENDA'S BROTHER DAVEY LOOKED FOR anonymous comfort wherever he could find it. In parking lots, janitor's closets, and police cars, between the rows of scuppernong grapes in a vineyard one weekend in October with an heiress who never asked his name, and once in a koi pond, with a petite gardener and a persistent carp.

In each of these engagements he could have been anyone, though he was really a man of misunderstood ambition. He tied flies with finesse; he caught and released. He broke things that needed to be broken. He freed people.

Davey believed that food, whatever the quality, was meant to be savored and digested, not wasted. So too with the physical acts that indicated desire. He did not judge and ignored the judgments of others. He was emotionally self-sufficient, his only goal to bring pleasure. Some days he was clean, after an hour in the bathtub. Some days, dirty, after an hour in the lake, where he befriended frogs, fishermen, and the occasional miscreant.

But always, he was ready to give.

It was at a salad bar, when its attendant bent over to refill the pepperoncini, that Davey in early adolescence recognized the secret language between people. A slightly overweight woman in her early twenties bent below the sneeze guard across from him, placing each pepper deliberately in a pile, while Davey could not help but look down her shirt into the cavern where her breasts swung and wobbled.

She did not look at him. She continued to perfect the pepperoncini pyramid for quite some time. Davey's clear plastic salad container held one half of a hardboiled egg for the duration of the performance, which inspired in him above all else a sense of gratitude and respect.

Likewise, a tender encounter with a parking lot attendant at the age of fifteen—the smell of gasoline, a damp chamois hanging from a uniform pocket—would engender in Davey furtive longing in public settings not often associated with affection.

Each of these encounters helped build the armature of Davey's understanding: People did not need jobs to sustain happiness or purpose. His life's work could be dedicated to the pursuit of constant, sincere, and heated affirmation from people he would never meet again.

ↄ

CHARLIE HAD ALWAYS BEEN POPULAR, but he was smart enough to know that it was a tenuous position. It was like trying to stay upright on a spinning barrel.

When he was in elementary school, he wasn't sure what he did to keep friends, but for some reason people were drawn to him. Perhaps it was that Charlie had stuff kids couldn't get anywhere else, like free soda in a plastic cup with a lid and a straw, or snacks with "not marked for individual resale" printed on the package.

Friends stuck to him for a while, then they yanked themselves free and were gone.

But now that he had entered middle school, the dynamics of keeping friends changed. Being popular was good and bad. He could use this power to woo friends of both sexes, but under scrutiny every interaction was amplified with the very real prospect of discovery and humiliation.

He had to find that one kid, equally afraid of revealing his true nature, and lure him in slowly. He had to build trust.

Maybe they would go fishing on a gray lake early one morning, and Charlie would set the hook with ease, quickly piercing the worm. Or maybe they would bend in close, pretending to focus on the boat's small engine until their foreheads touched. Then, when he was certain they were simpatico, Charlie would spill his guts.

Here was a precipice which Charlie had only dared cross in his mind, but he hung from its edge perpetually. He could not anticipate how much harder and easier everything would be once he let go.

Instead, Charlie used misdirection and sleight of hand, and publicly wooed the prettiest girl with the biggest mouth: Deirdre Reed.

❦

ONE AFTERNOON AT THE GAS station, Charlie loaded her pockets with candy. She drank a thirty-two-ounce soda in about fifteen minutes while they counted the flies on the four pest strips in the corners. They appeared to be having a good time. Her laughter flew throughout the store. The counterman had stepped outside for a smoke when she announced, stuffing yet another piece of gum in her mouth:

"I gotta go. Where's the bathroom?" Charlie had not anticipated this.

The women's had been broken since the day before, after a bulimic teenager gleefully stuffed the bowl with a hot dog and bun, opting to forego the regurgitation for once.

He could not let Deirdre use his bathroom.

He could not let her be the one who found his note.

"It's broken. Sorry." His answer sudden, surprised him.

"What do you mean? You have to give people a place to go." She whined and crossed her legs. "Come on, Charlie." She pushed through the door and headed around the building.

Charlie followed her.

"Hey, I don't have a key anyway. Just go here." He pointed to weeds waist high to the girl.

"I'll watch out for you, no one will ever know."

She recoiled just enough.

She wondered if this was a trick to allow him to see her pastel underwear. Perhaps this would guarantee that she continued to get the attention and snacks she deserved. Charlie was a good catch. He was blond and did not smell like a dog.

Next to the lone parking space, she squatted in the tall weeds. She could have done a better job of covering herself, but he had been extremely generous.

It took a very long time.

Charlie looked at nothing. He hummed to himself so he wouldn't have to hear it.

When she was done, she stepped carefully over the soaked ground, and they both ignored the puddle that had spread into the parking spot. He walked her around to the front of the store, where her bike leaned against the pumps.

"You won't tell anyone, will you?" she asked.

She was breathing heavily, suddenly.

"Of course not," he said, though it was hard to hide his disappointment. His intention had been that both of them would chronicle this meeting to anyone who would listen. He had wanted her to show off everything he had given her, and whisper embellished truths to her squealing friends.

When she lay her head on his shoulder, Charlie stood perfectly still. She acted like she was absolutely happy.

He felt like a stuffed animal.

Finally, she left.

Inside the store, as Charlie fitted the plastic lid on his soda, he hoped that at least the counterman would tell his father about Deirdre hanging around.

Then, his father hopped in, cursing like a professional, removing his shoe, pulling off a drenched sock.

"What kind of a motherfucker does this behind a place of business?" Charlie did not answer, and his father did not notice.

With Deirdre gone, he could finally go to the bathroom.

He stood at the urinal and counted up five blocks and two over. He found the crack. He looked, then looked again.

The fortune was gone.

✂

WHEN HE GOT HOME, CHARLIE poured himself a huge glass of milk and sat down in the kitchen. He wondered who had found the message and what they would do.

Across the room, his mother talked on the phone. She had a pillow and a heating pad behind her back, and she was smoking and cross stitching in a frenzy, though her voice was calm. Her words did not reveal much, just a bunch of uh huhs and yes ma'ams and OKs. It made him nervous.

When she hung up, Charlie didn't ask, and she didn't offer. She sighed, put out her cigarette, and slowly got up. Then suddenly she ripped the heating pad's electrical cord from the wall and threw it in the trash.

"Well, at least now I know why this goddamn thing doesn't work," she said. She paced, and Charlie watched her. She stopped and looked at him, but did not open her mouth.

Everything would be different.

✑

THAT NIGHT, CHARLIE AND HIS parents went to visit Brenda's mother and brother Davey. In the paneled living room, Matt watched a game on the television while Davey flipped through a magazine about woodworking and giggled occasionally.

Brenda and her mother sat in the kitchen, having a slow conversation about nothing.

Brenda had told no one.

Charlie got bored. He went out to his uncle's incredibly messy car and hid in the backseat under a sticky blanket. It was easy for him to blend in next to a cardboard box full of old magazines, bottles of motor oil, half-empty cans of Davey's favorite snack, Pickle Nuts, and heaps of rags and old clothes. Charlie waited for twenty minutes, until he heard his uncle approach the car saying that he was going to town to cause just a little bit of trouble.

Davey rarely worked, but he was a sweet leech. He was easygoing, and he had a nice smile. When he asked people about their thoughts and opinions, he sincerely wanted to know. Because of this, and an inherent loneliness in everybody, he met people easily. The women were usually on the way down, and the men missed their sons.

From beneath the blanket Charlie did not make a sound, even though his body wanted to belch and cough and sneeze and sigh. The blanket became more uncomfortable the longer Charlie spent beneath it, breathing his own stale breath. When Uncle Davey took corners, it was hard to keep from rolling around.

Davey sang along with the radio and whistled and talked under his breath. He hummed and farted in ways that only solitary people do. Charlie wished he could see his uncle, but he had to be satisfied with the soundtrack alone. Finally, the car stopped, and Davey got out. He was gone for a long time.

It went from light gray outside to deep black. Charlie fell asleep. The car windows fogged.

Back at Brenda's mother's house, Charlie's parents were ready to go. They couldn't find their son anywhere. Eventually, Matt suggested they just leave.

"He'll turn up eventually. We've got all of his goddamn stuff back at the house, right?"

Brenda stayed and Matt went home.

Brenda's mom soon forgot her daughter was in the room. She looked at the TV, but as usual her mind was elsewhere. Tonight she was spitting in the Arctic Circle, and watching it freeze into abstract and surreal shapes somewhere between her mouth and the ground. Brenda's mom was on some blood pressure medication that made her hallucinate wonderfully. All she had to do to go on vacation was close her eyes.

Brenda sat on her mother's lumpy sofa with scratchy, stained upholstery and watched her mom watch TV. She worried only enough about Charlie as she thought was necessary. She knew he'd show up, then one of them would have to punish him, and it wouldn't make a damn bit of difference. Then she thought about what was growing in her and what her son had left to learn.

Now, she would have to be tender and more involved with him even though it was not in her nature.

Brenda was only half mad that Charlie had disappeared. For the rest of her life, she would always be half everything, the other half wondering when she would go (*Now? Next week?*) and what it would feel like. This terrified and fascinated her. As hard as she tried, she could not conceive of unbeing. She could not imagine never smoking again, never eating when she was starving. Would she be starving for all eternity?

She imagined cells dividing, dying, growing, giving up, rekindling, warping, puckering, shivering, dissolving. Some floated off where they didn't belong, then gathered in clumps.

She imagined one cell that refused to be transformed. Its membrane was impenetrable, no matter the angle of assault. But as it separated itself from her disease, it became insignificant. This was worse than succumbing: to exist and still to be nothing.

This was not her.

She had to be something.

What was she?

☙

IN DAVEY'S CAR, AFTER A few hours, Charlie was suddenly awakened by the sound of a door latch next to his head. He heard some quiet moaning, and some tiny wet sounds, like bubbles breaking on the surface of a pond. Then he felt someone lying down on top of him.

It was a lady. Then, on top of that lady, was Uncle Davey.

The swampy liquor smell instantly filled the car, and Charlie was terrified. He felt the lady struggle to get comfortable on top of him. He had never lain so still in his life.

Because the car was full of stuff, it was dark, and they were wasted, neither of them realized that Charlie lay beneath them.

Charlie heard his uncle and the lady grunting and whispering, faintly then frantically, right in his ear. Their elbows poked him. His head was pummeled by the back of her skull, and her pointed shoe heel dug painfully into his calf.

Even though it seemed like forever, they were done almost immediately.

The smell of liquor, perfume, sweat, cigarettes, and leather, plus the fact that a grown lady with a generous backside was crushing him, made Charlie feel sick.

Then, as sudden as an unexpected slap, he sneezed.

The lady screamed and she and Davey immediately leaped off of him.

Davey pulled the blanket down and a wave of cool air overtook him. Even though the air was full of foulness, it was ten times better than being stuck under that blanket.

At the sight of Charlie's sweaty, pale face, the lady pushed her way out of the car and ran shrieking into the darkness, and Davey laughed so hard he fell out onto the pavement. He gasped and yelled after her: "He's my nephew, it's OK!" but then continued to spew laughter. He waved his hand in the direction of her departure.

"Ah, fuck it," he said, and he held his head.

He didn't really care that much, but she had bought him three drinks, and she had looked pretty good in the dark. He'd also had two shots that he remembered, which the bartender slid to him and winked.

He would have to sleep it off for a while before he could drive.

Davey got in the piled-up backseat and shoved Charlie aside. "Move 'er over," he said. "You're going to have to sleep with me a little bit longer." He was soon out and his breath was appalling, catching and dragging through the snores.

Even though it was his uncle, and even though it was midnight in the middle of town, and the headlights from cars coming and going in the parking lot cut across them, and even though Charlie was completely exhausted and filthy, at least now he knew what it felt like to sleep next to a real live man.

↝

WHAT WAS SHE?

Brenda was a smoker.

She was a reluctant wife and, by extension, a distant mother.

She was the daughter of a distant mother. She was the daughter of a smoker.

Her mother would outlive her.

She had not outlived her father.

He was not a smoker, but it hadn't mattered.

He would have liked to have been closer to his daughter, but didn't want to cause any trouble.

Brenda was a woman who did not trust anyone who said that they had been truly blessed, as though a good life could only be granted by some ethereal, occasionally attentive, being.

Brenda found a pencil in between the cushions of her mother's couch. It was very late at night. This would have been the time that she would have written down all of the things she should tell the people who loved her.

Had she been so blessed.

❧

CHARLIE WOKE UP. UNCLE DAVEY was driving. He had the radio down low, but he was still wasted, so he was singing along, shamelessly, loudly. It had been a pretty good night for Davey, and he had one more thing to attend to. He pulled into the parking lot, across from Tucker Motors.

"Shh," he said to Charlie, even though Charlie hadn't made a sound. "We're going to go and hide out for a while. I got a lead on some funny business going on at your dad's gas station, and I want in." He giggled and dug around in the seat for a bottle.

"What funny business?" Charlie asked, pretending to be drowsy, though he was alert. This gap between what he felt and what he pretended to feel was so natural, he slipped into it even when it wasn't necessary.

"Shh," he said again, and opened the door slowly. No cars. They raced across the road and towards the tire pile behind the station, where last year Charlie had seen a copperhead curled around the very shovel that his father would use to kill the snake not two hours later.

Then, Charlie suddenly knew.

It must have been Davey who found the note, who was now waiting to ambush whoever approached the bathroom, who would perhaps jump on the man and beat him mercilessly, or stuff a tire around his middle and push him out into the road with a bag over his head.

Maybe Davey would blackmail him with a grainy photo from his disposable camera.

Charlie's mind writhed around the possibilities.

Never had he thought that his sweet wasted uncle was an enemy to boys and men like him. But of course, it had to be. Charlie had not yet found any allies. He was always behind enemy lines.

In Japan, there is a river that once a year becomes a beautiful spectacle, the sight of millions of synchronized flashes that illuminate the water, the signal of the fireflies calling to mate. Charlie did not yet know that his note was like one of these brief flashes, and had been discovered and discarded by a man traveling with his family to New Jersey who considered tucking it into his wallet as a souvenir, then realized that it would almost certainly be discovered by his snooping wife. This kind of trouble, he didn't need.

In fact, the Tucker Motors parking lot had played host to late-night encounters for years. Charlie could never have known that a few hours after he left the gas station bathroom at night, a secret with its own pulsing ember was coaxed into life with the tiniest of motions.

In the not-yet-gray light, Uncle Davey just sat on two tires, smoking. He wasn't even facing the bathroom door.

His gaze settled on the abandoned lot that stretched out into a ridge of silver trees with tresses of dried moss hanging over their shoulders.

Silence.

It was the ambling shadows Davey watched, the trees through the bright moon. They both heard a night creature's purposeful step. A million bugs singing.

"Charlie, dude, forget everything your parents have ever taught you. They're all upside-down. When you get hungry for something, the best thing you can do is eat." Davey put his hand on his nephew's back.

Then suddenly:

"Go on, go somewhere else for about fifteen minutes."

"Go where?" Charlie whispered.

"Go wherever you want to." A pause, then more serious, perhaps a hint of menace,

"Go."

ఴ

BRENDA CHEWED THE PENCIL. IF she could just figure out what to tell him, her son. If she could just figure out what was important enough to tell him, then she could finally fall asleep and not feel anxious, jangly, noxious, alive.

She could finally rest if that thing could be found. She had to tell him, her son. She had to tell him something that was important enough.

What was it?

What has she?

What was he?

He would have a hard time of it with only Matt, that was one thing. Maybe if she just told him that: "You will have a hard time with your father."

She tried to picture her husband's horrible face, but it was no longer clear to her. She hadn't looked at it in such a long time that she was no longer sure of its likeness.

Or maybe she was just tired.

Or maybe she was failing.

If she could just find that one important thing.

Brenda realized that just because something was important to her, it did not mean it was important to Charlie.

Perhaps that was important enough.

She wrote.

✌

CHARLIE STUMBLED THROUGH THE WOODS, bright with the moon. He knew the trees, the outlines in the jagged abstract landscape. Grateful for his own loud crunching footsteps, he did not want to hear anything other than the sound of his own movement.

In his mind, he visualized simple acts that had a distinct ending. He ate a tuna fish sandwich. He played Pong. He brushed his teeth and then cut in line.

He thought about how an embrace could transfigure momentarily into a trap.

It sickened and terrified him that he had unwittingly lured some stranger to his own humiliation.

Instead of Uncle Davey's charming smile and wretched breath transforming into something horrible and hate filled, Charlie tried to imagine all of the good things that might happen in his own life, but these were repeatedly pushed aside by the many ways he would disappoint and humiliate himself. How he would reach for a napkin at just the wrong time, and clash hands with an aggressive, resentful stranger. How he would glance at the wrong man, whose face would tangle into a sneer. How he would always see the world though the sick, bruised, and pinkish light of unwanted, shameful exposure.

It was as though Charlie always had to pretend he was comfortable while his shirt was clearly soaked with sweat.

He stepped into a deep hole and water rose suddenly to his ankle, shocking and cold, a cymbal crash in the dark.

His hidden life was leaving him. Uncle Davey knew, and others would too.

He had to stop.

He had to go.

It would be easier and harder. It would be impossible at home. He anticipated his father's reaction, a daily mundane violence that would be normal for a while until it wasn't.

He did not know if his mother would react at all.

He wanted to be a target that she hit, just once.

&

"LEARN WHEN TO WALK AWAY."

&

HIS UNCLE HAD BEEN VERY quiet. Perhaps he was still waiting to sabotage the nocturnal visitor. Charlie's allegiance to this unknown man was easier to assume than he thought.

Charlie thought of all the boys and girls who he would soon forget and who he hoped would soon forget him. He envisioned the interlocking jumble of their skeletons, so many weapons in those bones that he could use just now.

There were weapons everywhere in the trees too. He chose two rocks, and the top of a can of dip that had broken at a jagged angle.

He only needed to hurt Uncle Davey enough to let the man escape.

But what happened after that, Charlie didn't know.

He circled out through the trees and onto the empty road, back towards Tucker Motors. His wet sock started to warm. He crept close and peeked from behind a rotten trunk, a caravan of nocturnal beetles passed up and down its height. He strained to hear a voice hued with pleas, tones which caused a sharp pain to rise in his mouth, as though he had eaten something impossibly tart.

He tried to hear his uncle's voice, grinding with pleasure. He tried to hear what his uncle sounded like when he thought he had won.

The rise of thrilling tenderness surprised him.

For, where he had left Uncle Davey, he could now see two tiny lights not six inches apart, two brief flashes, cigarettes glowing and fading in the dark.

Alison Fairbrother

Hard Freight

ALISON FAIRBROTHER teaches creative writing at Stony Brook University. Her work has appeared in the *Southampton Review*, *Creative Nonfiction*, *Guernica*, *Salon*, the *Washington Spectator*, the *Washington Monthly*, and more. A five-year D.C. resident, she recently relocated to Brooklyn. She misses bike paths, Ethiopian food, and snow panic.

The bloody history of the Bethel quarry began in 1896, when the quarry owner's only son was killed in a railroad crossing accident. The owner vowed that from then on, the granite from his quarry would never build another bridge or home. It would only be used to make tombstones. During his final years he carved twenty-seven stones for his son, one for each of his birthdays. He wrote twenty-seven epitaphs. He couldn't afford plots in the cemetery for twenty-seven gravestones (and there was only one body) so he left them stacked like blocks.

Bevies of worms bundled in the crevices. A family of birds nested on the stone. They returned each spring to gather grass and sticks and mud over the words, "A Good Son Lies Here."

When the quarry owner died in 1903, granite-rich and penny-poor, the quarry lineage had run out. A new owner laid claim to the rock. The quarry was again a repository, a store of stone.

Bethel granite became hard freight. It traveled the tracks to St. Louis and Kansas City and then westward to San Francisco. It went south to Atlanta and to Washington, D.C., where it rests today in the planar grandeur of the National Museum of Natural History.

Workers flocked to Bethel to make their fortunes. They shaded their eyes and looked up at steam-powered derricks casting long shadows over stone. Bad weather stopped the work and therefore pay. Money was earned only when the material was in motion.

On barges and barrow-loads, Bethel granite roamed, its hammered face exposed to the sun. When one of the boats sank in the Potomac River, a day laborer was lost, a husband with a wife back in Bethel, the father of a son.

Some granite still lies at the bottom of the river.

The rest built Union Station, which opened on October 27, 1907. The head contractor boasted, "It is the first of the series of great granite buildings which is to make Washington a White City that will indeed be the wonder of the world."

And then one day the Bethel quarry sat empty, and it began to fill with rainwater. The first rainwater dropped fifty feet to find the bottom. The second rainfall fell forty-eight feet, five and a half inches. An unseasonable fall flood contributed more than a foot. In a single soggy year, the quarry grew by seven feet.

A sounder ascertains the depth of liquid by certain echoes. By October 27, 2013, the sound was needle thin. The quarry was full.

My father leapt in that day when the water was cold and black.

No one was extracting granite from Bethel anymore, so we bought marble instead.

Later, we found a note. "I'm going home on the morning train," it said.

Lydia Morris Fettig

For George

LYDIA MORRIS FETTIG spent her early life in coastal Connecticut and upstate New York before migrating west to complete her undergraduate work in social science at Reed College and Portland State University. After returning to the East Coast in 1998 to earn an MFA in creative writing, she met her husband, gave birth to three children, rescued several animals, and completed a short stint as a parole and probation agent for the state of Maryland. She teaches creative and academic writing at American University. Her work has been published by Rude Girl Press and in *Gargoyle Magazine*.

George, this story is for you. Consider it a gift. It's simple, really. This story is for you because when I told you that I was a writer you got worried. I could tell you were worried because you said something about hoping, and yet not hoping, that you would appear in one of my stories someday. That, to you, is what I write—stories. Story after story. But if you want to know the truth, really what I write are not stories but quasi-lists of all of my various violations. This may strike you as odd, perhaps funny. You may simply not know what I mean. But to me, George, there is nothing else. There is me and there are my perceived violations.

I feel the need—as the writer you deemed me to be, as the writer I did not deny myself to be—to begin this story traditionally. It's important to me that you see how a story is told, how it is written. Maybe then you will understand how every story is in fact the record of a violation.

Please understand that to tell this traditionally I can no longer refer to me as "me," or to you as "you." You must become merely "George" and "he," and I must become "she." Like this:

To start at the beginning, the problem with George was really his simplicity. But nothing can really be that simple. Maybe the real problem with

George was that she wanted him to be simple. Or maybe the problem with George had nothing to do with George. Maybe she wanted a simple situation (involving George), despite the fact that such a thing is never possible. Situations—like people, like George—are not simple.

And to begin at the real beginning, the whole thing was really about fish. Yes, fish. Or maybe women. Women and men. Relationships. One-night stands. And since everything is always about death—well, life and death—those two elements should be added too. Men, women, and fish all live and die. Honestly, it's rather repetitive.

It's hard to tell when, if ever, anything truly begins. Or when, once it has begun, it ends.

About those fish: We have all seen fish. Like people, they come in all shapes, sizes, and colors. And yet always we seem to be attracted to the bigger and more colorful fish. We watch them in their tanks (rarely do we see them in their natural habitats) and we wonder about them. We wonder about why they don't acknowledge us looking at them (even, and especially, when we tap obnoxiously on their glass houses).

Basically, we know very little about fish. We conclude often that they are merely a standard introductory pet. Goldfish are the easily disposable pets that we flush down our toilets when they die. But there are other fish: there are the giant fish who live and own the oceans and there are the beautiful, smaller tropical fish. The fact is that for some people the goldfish is too common. These types of people might have huge tanks of not only exotic fish (for this type of person finds only the tropical variety worthy of ownership), but tanks full of egregious flora and other such nonsense. But regardless of the kind—tropical, oceanic, the simple goldfish—we watch them intently, try to figure them out, and yet they remain a mystery. About the most we can do to rectify this is to name the ones we come to care for. We name our pets because it both simplifies and establishes interaction. Names confer identity. Names set the precedent, the foreground, for relationships.

Fuck the formality. Fuck tradition. Fuck the this-is-what-my-story-will-be-about introduction. Let's just talk about how we met, George. Though, of course, you and I are not talking. I am talking now to my audience, my reader—and you may or may not be included. George, do you read? I saw copies of *Penthouse* in your bathroom. Isn't there some stupid line that guys like you say about porn—that you buy it for the articles?

I saw your *Penthouse* right after I used your toothbrush. Your toothbrush was yellow. In fact, I saw the *Penthouse* while I was peeing. Urine is yellow. I was peeing in your bathroom, right after I brushed my teeth, and I saw—not in but next to a magazine rack piled high—many copies of *Penthouse*. And I sat there, peeing yellow pee, and I wondered about that. George, how is it at all sexually satisfying to be sitting on the toilet of all places and flipping through *Penthouse*?

I'm going to assume that you read more than just *Penthouse*. I am going to also assume that you remember how we met. But for my other readers, I should tell the whole story.

We met online. I lived far away from here, and we met one day in cyberspace. I was planning to relocate to D.C., and I thought that meeting you over the computer was a sign, a sign of a promising move-to-be, as you emailed me that you lived in Georgetown. Georgetown, you wrote, was part of D.C. Maybe it was not a sign. Maybe it was an evil omen.

You sent me photos of yourself. I will never deny that you are a good-looking guy, George. A devastatingly good-looking guy. And then you began to call me, even though at that time I lived thousands of miles away. You called because I had given you my number, because I wanted to know what a good-looking guy like you sounded like. Too bad about that Boston accent.

And then, and so, I moved here. We went out a few times. If I ever had doubts (and I didn't), I was pleased to see that you were good-looking in person. Photos are one thing, in person is another. Do you remember me, George? Yeah, the girl you met over the computer, then in person. I am relatively tall. Or at least I wear shoes that make me look tall. (Is that like lying if you wear shoes that make you look tall when really your height is only average?) I have dark hair, pale skin, and blue eyes. (No lies here, George. The hair is its natural hue, the eyes are crystal blue, and I wish I weren't so pale.)

Do you remember that I am thin? I try pretty hard to be thin. But I have gained weight since we last saw each other. I tell you this only because I feel you should know. I'd hate to surprise you one day. You know, run into you unexpectedly somewhere mundane, like at Safeway or in line at the bank. What would you say? Would you have the guts to ask me if I have gained weight? Save your guts, George, I am telling you now it is true. I think it might be as much as ten pounds.

And what did we do first? Oh, you came over to visit me. I hadn't found a place to live yet after my recent move. I was house sitting for some out-of-the-country friends of my family. Yes, I have a family. You never asked me about my family. It's pretty big. I have two siblings, parents, step-parents, aunts, uncles, four still-alive grandparents. It's big and everyone is divorced and remarried. No one shares the same last name.

So you came over to my house, which was not my house but someone else's house, and then we went out. You took me to a bar in Arlington, Virginia. You told me it was a hot spot.

Really, George, who says "hot spot" anymore?

The bar was sort of inside, sort of outside. The building itself was like a warehouse. Outside, under a large parking lot–sized metal awning we sat at one of many picnic tables. You told me that this place (wherever we were) was one of many hot spots that you frequented with your many, many friends. You went as far as to say that it was odd that you were able to see me that night because usually you were so busy.

That was when I first suspected that you had a rather large ego.

We had drinks. Well, beer. You told me all about how you didn't want to date anyone. Why should you have to, you asked me. You said a lot of mumbo jumbo about your job being very important. Something about how you couldn't afford to have a relationship that distracted you from your number one priority. You made it very clear that your number one priority was your job. Did you feel threatened? Did you think I wanted to date you? That I wanted you—to what? Quit your job, marry me, and live happily ever after, even though you wouldn't be happy because you would no longer be associated with your number one priority if we did all that? What were you thinking, George?

I didn't want to date you, George. I just wanted to sleep with you.

After that stupid conversation, we left that dumb bar. You took me to your apartment. You called it a house. You live in Georgetown. Think about that, George: You live in Georgetown and your name is George. This can't be helping that ego problem of yours.

Your house was a mess. In your bedroom, I couldn't help but notice that the sheets had imprints like two people had slept there the night before. There were two half-empty (or was it half-full?) wineglasses resting on a very tall speaker. It occurred to me then that for someone who didn't want to be dating you were definitely having sex. Not that I cared, George. Because, like I said, I never wanted to date you, I only wanted to have sex with you. It occurred to me then that maybe you wouldn't have sex with me if you were having sex with someone else—though of course not dating anyone else. My other concern at that time had to do with wondering whether I still wanted to have sex with you if you were having sex with someone else. I'd hate to think, George, that you sleep around.

Have you been tested for AIDS, George?

The thing you have to understand is that sometimes when we writers write stories we have to add things that aren't really true. Sometimes, all of what we write isn't true. Other times, parts are true and parts are, well, lies. I like to tell people (forget that it's a big fib) that when you took me back to my house-sitting house that you kissed me good night. You did walk me in, back into that house that wasn't mine. We each smoked a cigarette out on the patio that wasn't mine. It was awkward then. I was wondering if you would kiss me. I was hoping you would. Did you, George? When I walked you to my door that wasn't really my door, did you kiss me good night?

I feel I should tell you that as a writer I do lie. I lie all the time. I make stuff up for effect, for drama, for the sheer stupid fun of it. But it's not so much fun sometimes. I've lived most of my life, George, as a suspected and often accused liar. Even before I became a writer (as if one becomes a writer!), people always thought I was lying. I could feel it. Maybe because I was lying, maybe not. What business is it of yours? But my point is that all this suspicion—well, it has made me paranoid.

I imagine, in my day-to-day life, that everyone I know thinks I am lying about something, maybe everything. Do I really have a job? Am I really a student? Am I really a writer? Is that boyfriend I've been talking about for the last three months merely a fabricated figment of my imagination? I dream sometimes—I feel I can tell you this—of all my imaginary friends and coworkers, and fellow students, my boyfriend...I imagine them all meeting. They would all meet just so I could prove to each and every one of them that they all really do exist.

George, do you exist?

[Have you ever stopped to think about simplicity, George? Or do you think that everything is complex? I am continually debating this issue—are things really as complicated as I think (as I make them out to be) or is everything, is everyone, extraordinarily simple? I mean, what was it I liked about you? What, for several weeks, made me call you all those many times when you said that you would call me and then never did? Was it simply that I am desperate? Am I weak? Was it not about me? For instance, you are a very good-looking guy. You have a steady job. You have a home. Maybe I liked that about you—your good looks, your job, your apartment. Yet none of these things really attributes much to you or to the true nature of our relationship. Instead, while these reasons appear simple, they may be too complex—maybe even made up. I think, George, that sometimes I lie not only to everyone else, but to myself.]

It's too bad you never read, George, because the English philosopher John Locke wrote something interesting about basic truth—he was trying to define matter and finally he concluded that he just couldn't do it, that he simply didn't know. You are that way, George—completely abstruse and indeterminate. If anything, all I can do is create analogies. Example: If George were a fish, he'd be a satiated piranha.

But I don't want to lose you, so I'll get back to the story. Remember what we did on our second date, George? I went and visited you at your precious workplace.

It's good to meet the competition.

You were on the phone when I arrived. You were looking better than ever (you look like a J.Crew model, the kind of clean-cut, handsome, and rugged man my sister and I—yes, George, I have a sister—used to swoon over when we were both in high school). But you really rubbed me the wrong way despite your consuming good looks. It was so obvious that whoever you were talking to on the phone was a woman. And, George, you just sat there holding one finger up to me in some sort of perversion of good manners, while you went into flirt overdrive over the phone. Right in front of me! You said trash like, "Oh we should definitely get together soon..." and "Thank you so much for saying so..."

If you must know, George, it was pretty sickening. It really was.

If you must know, George, I think your real number one priority is you.

And so soon after we said our hellos, and then after you said goodbye to your phone-sex maiden, I left. It could have been a graceful departure, but you said to me then: "Hey, I'll give you a call before the end of the week." And, of course, this pissed me off, because who the hell says "before the end of the week"? I mean, it was like you were graciously scheduling me in. I got mad. Really, I hadn't been mad until then. I looked at you with the kind of hatred that God might have had in the Old Testament, and I said: "Yeah, we'll see if that happens."

And it didn't happen. I called you.

I called you because, while still house sitting, I had a guest from my faraway previous home visiting me, and I wanted to take her out. At least that was what I told you. I might have been lying. Yes, I told you that I didn't know where to take my friend. To put this in George-talk, to put it in a language that you might understand: I didn't know of any hot spots other than that bar in Arlington. At least not yet.

It's a good thing I wasn't lying because you invited yourself along with my friend and me for that evening. You gave me the address of a bar in Georgetown, told us to meet you there at nine. We were there at eight thirty. You didn't show until nine thirty. You brought four male friends with you. I wondered if one of them was supposed to be for my friend. Maybe you had some big testosterone plan involving you, me, my friend, one of your friends, and sex.

George, even the best plans go awry.

I feel that perhaps I should start over. I am not sure whether, so far, I have made myself entirely clear, and there are so many details I've neglected. In addition, I am having trouble figuring out when things truly began between us. To be honest, George, I am not even sure if they have ended.

George, do you remember what I told you after you asked me if I was a writer? I said, "I suppose I am a writer—whoever or whatever that is." It occurs to me now, George, that I am not a writer. I am a liar. Perhaps, just to show you the many ways one can tell the same lie, I will write this all over from a different point of view:

She met him over the Internet. He ran a construction company with two of his friends. He lived in Georgetown, but he had a Boston accent (they moved from the computer to the phone quickly). He was everything she hated and yet couldn't resist. He was what her friends called a player. He seemed to know just what to say and when. He had gone to college in Utah (later she found out that he'd never actually graduated) and was an active brother in a fraternity (and no doubt a date rapist wanted in twelve states). He was probably a Republican too. He had a lot of catchphrases, stupid little things he'd say over and over—mantras, if you will. It would take months before "absolutely" and "I'm a skier not a Mormon" finally echoed for the last time through her head late at night.

They met in person for the first time while she was house sitting. He came over, picked her up, and took her out for drinks. He had two beers. She had one. He said her name a lot when talking to her. She knew this was a sales strategy, and she wondered what he was trying to sell. It was hard not to picture him at one of his job sites wheeling and dealing, saying the name of his potential buyer over and over as he described in detail why aluminum siding would be better than wood, why that bay window wasn't really needed, how a screened porch would keep out bugs, until he'd made the sale. This was standard operating procedure, she was sure. *Well, Bob, I can see how you'd be concerned about those water marks, but when I look at your gutters I see a few simple and, keep in mind, affordable solutions…*

And three weeks later she was drunk and in his bed. Though first she was in his truck. And before even that, she had been with him in a bar with a girlfriend of hers and four male friends of his.

He had a big red truck. It was brand new, and he bragged about it endlessly, but always in a subtle and off-the-cuff manner. He would only refer to the truck in passing, never would he say outright that it was an amazing machine—which was clearly what he thought. Instead, there were numerous, yet pseudo-casual, references to the excellent mileage, alloy wheels, and turbo-charged engine. He had taken her into the truck to listen to CDs on the stereo that he had told her all about (as if the topic had come up naturally) when they were in the bar earlier.

Long after "Stayin' Alive"—during the fifth track of the *Saturday Night Fever* sound track, to be exact—he made his move. When you are drunk, in a small confined space, and all you can hear is the Bee Gees, little good can happen next. It was out of the truck, in their underwear at this point, and into his bed that he took her.

[George: How deep is your love? Am I more than a woman? If I can't have you...]

There were problems with George. One wouldn't want to say that there were problems with her because, after all, she shouldn't be portrayed as a victim. She knew what she was doing. Victims are violated. Victims don't know what they are doing. It's a game, and she, like him, was a player. She knew the rules, she just didn't know if she was winning or losing.

We meet these people, in bars, over the computer, at our workplace, at school, and we have expectations. An expectation can be as simple as: I expect that we fuck and never talk again. Her expectations were along the lines of: let's fuck, not think much of it, and talk again, maybe even fuck again. It's unclear really what George's expectations were, or if he ever stopped to draw any up. She told him, the morning after, that she didn't expect that just because they had had sex that they were now dating. God forbid.

She had this convoluted idea that if she let him know where she stood— (which was only really a corroboration of where she thought he wanted her to stand and her own vague notions about George (that he might be an asshole)—that he would call her within the week.

He never called. She eventually called him.

None of this really makes a story. See, George, a story has definition—a plot, a climax. (I hope you noticed that we are back in first person now). The thing is, George, guys like you are a dime a dozen, and confused women like me practically grow on trees. Excuse the clichés. My point is that people meet all the time, get drunk, and fuck like rabbits. Oops, there's another cliché. But we did fuck like a couple of rabbits.

The story is all the parts in between, George. The story is what happened between the bar, the truck, and the morning after. Come to think of it, even what happened after the morning after is material for a story.

So, to start at the beginning (and pay attention, George, because my crazy, lying writer self is at it again and from now on, or at least for a while, you will no longer be referred to as "you," but once again as "George"):

I met George five months ago. First, we communicated online through email. We sent each other photos, and soon we were talking over the phone. Eventually we made plans to meet. He was everything he said he'd be, everything he had been in the photos—tall and thin with short brown hair and hazel eyes. He did the typical outdated manly stuff like holding doors open for me, walking around to the passenger side of his truck to let me in, and he paid for everything.

To truthfully start at the beginning, one must acknowledge that, sadly, all George and I had were a series of moments. [George: please excuse this tangent, but I think it might be important.] I first learned about moments last year when I took a class on death and dying. It was a required course for my college major. One of my classmates was devastated by the death of her dog—a death that had taken place a full year before. She still regularly put food in his bowl.

One guy claimed to have been in a rap video. Two weeks after the video was shot, the rap star had been killed in a drive-by shooting. He simply didn't understand how such a thing could have happened. His words stick with me now: *how could that have happened*? [Can you hear it too, George? How do you think such a thing could have happened?]

Another girl had lost a friend in a car accident. She'd been in the passenger seat when the semi drove right into them. She said a helicopter came to take him away to a nearby hospital. He had died during the flight. She was there when it happened—holding his hand thousands of feet above ground. Later, in class, she talked for what seemed like hours about the moment before the semi hit them. She talked incessantly about the moment right before he died. She talked about how she had to pee before they got into his car but didn't stop to do so because they were in a rush. She had an elaborate theory based on a series of events that didn't happen.

Her theory went like this: if she had stopped to pee, they would never have been around when the semi ran the light and then ran into them. She talked a lot about moments. The moment she decided not to pee, the moment right before the semi totaled their car, the moment her friend was moved from the wrecked car into the helicopter. She seemed to think that if one moment had been just a little different, every moment that followed would have been different too.

I originally thought that George and I had essentially only shared one moment—our one-night stand. But I saw him again afterwards. [Remember that, George?] We went to a bar called Cactus Cantina. Sitting on high stools, across from each other at a very small table, with Mexican sombreros and tapestries suspended dangerously above us, I asked George if he knew who or what lived in glass houses. He looked at me blankly. "Never mind, it's just a silly cliché," I said and ordered another drink. I had two margaritas, one lime and one strawberry, both frozen, no salt. He had three Coronas.

Did I mention his name? He lives in Georgetown and his name is George. I hate to be repetitive, but this connection between his name and the part of town he lives is crucial in that his ego defies normal proportions.

Oh, George, this is all getting so confusing! Are you still with me? I'll tell you where I am now. I am in your apartment. Or I am imagining that I am. You have a huge fish tank in your basement. Two of them in fact. When I slept over at your place, after we left our friends at the bar, after I gave my friend money for a cab back to the house-sitting house I lived in back then, after we made out in your truck…after all that, I never slept. I sneaked out of your bedroom at four in the morning crying, trying to figure out how I could leave right at that moment and yet still see you again in the near future.

Do you know what Sylvia Plath said about neuroses? I doubt this was covered in any issue of *Penthouse*, so I'll just tell you, George. Sylvia wrote that to be neurotic one must want two mutually exclusive things. Well, I did not want to be with you at that moment, and yet I did not want to be away from you either.

So maybe it's neurotic, George, but I feel I must explain: I did not want to be in your bed next to you with your arms around me even though I must admit that a part of me liked it. See, I wanted mutually exclusive things in that there were two essential problems. The first problem was that I was convinced the only reason your arms were wrapped around me was because, in your sleep, you were thinking I was someone else. The girl that you drank the wine with, molded your sheets with—did you think I was her? The second problem was that I wanted to be in my own bed. Problem number two was particularly horrible as I did not have my own bed at that time. All I had was a temporary bed that I had slept in in the house that I was taking care of for the friends of my family for whom I was house sitting. Remember that, George? Remember that I was house sitting?

So I sneaked out of your bedroom and looked at the fish in the basement. This was my moment, George. I was alone and I had time to reflect upon how the moment I was having could have been very different if any given moment previous to it had been tweaked just a little. Like maybe I should have never gotten into your truck. After all, you had a CD player in your living room, and I've heard the Bee Gees before, surely that's enough. And what if the moments in the bar had been different? What if I, what if you, had not drunk so much? What if I had caught a cab with my friend instead of going home with you?

But that is not how it happened. Instead, I found myself crying and looking at your fish. You really should take better care of your fish. The tanks are obscenely dirty, and looking into them only made me cry harder since it made me think about the fish I had bought for my brother last Christmas. That fish died.

Please excuse another tangent, George, but I feel it is necessary. You see, I happened to be watching when my brother's fish died. It started swimming very oddly—like on its side. Its gills were not working in a consistently rhythmic way, and gradually the gills stopped moving completely. Then slowly, ever so slowly, the fish floated to the water's surface.

So here I am in your basement—now or then, for real or in a lie, what does it matter really? I am thinking about my brother's dead or dying fish (dying in the active sense as I am reliving it) and I am now on a mission: I must save the fish. I found fish food. I mistakenly dumped about half of it into one of the glass houses. It was amazing. Fish—disgustingly, brilliantly, brightly colored fish—started coming out and under from everywhere. I didn't realize how many hiding places there were.

It was exhilarating and nauseating all at once, if you want to know the truth.

I feel I should add, George, that it was hard for me not to remember, in addition to my brother's dead fish, my long-ago trip to Hawaii. I wouldn't swim in the water because the fish swim all around you there. To be quite honest, it made me very nervous. I was horrified, so scared that I spent most of my vacation out of the water. My mother told me that I was being ridiculous. My older sister made fun of me.

It is rather silly, really, to be afraid of fish.

George, this story is essentially defunct. There is no defined beginning or ending. To make matters worse, the moments in between, the moments that embody the story, are inconclusive at best. The fish cannot be made relevant and yet the fish are very important. I have visions of an ending in which all the fish die by morning because I overfed them in the middle of the night. I have other visions in which I am able to parallel the fish with myself, the story's narrator, who is lost and confused—who doesn't even have a home.

But the story has other problems. That is to say, there are other details that cannot be satisfactorily placed. For instance, there is the conversation I had with you, George, in the bar before you took me home with you. We had been talking about your fish (whom I had yet to "meet" and of whom you were very proud). And you said to me, "You know what they say about fish?" And I said, "No, what?" And then you said, "That a woman needs a man like a fish needs a bicycle," to which I replied, "That's not a statement about fish, that's a statement about women."

Very few conclusions can be drawn. To speak of the narrator as a separate entity, the one and only thing that holds true is that, for her, everyone is George—a person or people to whom she cannot relate. But, if everyone is George, then who is she? Who am I? Maybe we are all George, me, I, and her included. One would certainly hope this is not the case. Though, George, it does offer an excellent explanation for your aforementioned inflated ego.

To relieve you of any undeserving power or credit, George, maybe the whole idea should be amended altogether into the following and rather simple possibility: we are all fish. We are all fragile and delicate, and yet horrifying at times.

Yes, we are all fish, and so I think my analogy was accurate—you are a piranha. But George-the-piranha, you made a mistake: I am not a goldfish. I am not easily disposed of.

OK, so maybe we never had that silly conversation about the fish and the bicycles. But remember what I said about writers—that we can lie and get away with it? That we do it for effect? For the sheer stupid fun of it? So maybe I told a few lies—my reader will never know. I doubt that even you remember the specifics of our dates anyway.

You'll be pleased to know, George, that your story, this violation, is now complete. Regardless of when it started or when it ended, I have nothing left to say. If you're confused, if I lost you long ago, let me sum it all up for you: All I ever wanted was to have sex with you. All I ever wanted was a place to call home. All I ever wanted was one true moment.

Jess Stork Glicoes

This Message Will Self-Destruct after Your Last Paycheck

JESS STORK GLICOES works as a children's librarian. Previously, she was an art teacher, a museum guide, and a barista. In 2011, she was a winner in the Arlington Moving Words competition, and her poem was featured on buses in Northern Virginia.

D on prided himself on his cool, calculating manner, his quiet professionalism, and the way he could kill a man fifty-seven different ways using only a paperclip. But as he stared down at the incoming message, there were no other words.

"What the—?"

So this was it. Twenty-seven years of faithful work for a government that denied his existence, a tidy health care plan with a low deductible, a paid lunch hour, all gone. And without even the ceremonial, "Pack your boxes and we'll escort you out." Not that Don had an office in his line of work. Still…it was the principle of the thing.

The tiny device in his palm began blinking red as he stared at the screen. A quaint voice with a hint of a Southern American accent radiated from one of the speakers. "This message will self-destruct in twenty-eight seconds. Device will not be held responsible for any injuries that occur from the disregard of this warning."

They'd never had that clause in the old days. Don flung the device into the dumpster. It landed next to a pile of discarded spaghetti. Between the noodles, Don could still see the words. "Due to budget cuts and costly lawsuits involving loss of limb, your employment with us has been terminated." Then, the buttons lit up and the small black box vibrated, flinging noodles every which way. A bang echoed in the alley like the sound of popcorn cooking in a bank safe and the black device collapsed into pieces.

Don straightened his Italian-made suit coat and centered his silk tie. With an elegant gesture, he extracted a phone from his breast pocket and tapped the screen. His bank account appeared. He raised an eyebrow slightly. A depressing string of zeros blinked back at him. Silently, Don cursed his latest purchases, the nerve gas–dispersing wallet, the exploding cufflinks, and the new rocket launcher for the convertible.

He'd known the economy was on the rocks, but he'd had no idea it was that bad. He would have to cut back; perhaps no caviar for breakfast anymore. Still, the situation was not completely hopeless. It might take some time, but Don was confident. A stunning cover letter and a couple of kidnappings and he'd be back in work in no time.

Two days later, after several protected transmissions and one résumé sent by microdot, Don was forced to admit that the job market was depressingly slow at the moment. This would not be as easy as he thought. Governments were very suspicious of those willing to switch sides. And then there was that pesky noncompete clause in his previous contract.

Even worse, he was running low on champagne. He decided he would have to look outside his field if he didn't want to starve. With this decided, Don walked into the coffee shop near his apartment clutching the want ads.

He made the usual checks, looking for all the exits, noting profiles of each of the customers present, and locating several drop points where he could conceal microchips if needed. Then, he settled into an overstuffed chair with a nutmeg iced latte, shaken, not stirred.

He was wearing his gray pinstriped suit, having decided that the tuxedo was too formal now that he was unemployed. The rain splattered against the windows, mixing with the hum of voices at the tables. It was hard for Don to focus on the ads when all his training told him that he should instead be watching the baristas. Perhaps they were enemy agents. The hiss of the espresso machine didn't help, as it reminded him of a job in Brazil with a Russian agent back in '87.

Don forced his eyes down onto the paper and scanned the columns. There were a large number of ads for elderly companions and nursing assistants. He skimmed past those. After a nasty episode in Jamaica with a pretty nurse, he had learned never to trust health professionals or anyone who asked to take your temperature.

Finally, he came to an ad for a banking associate.

"Perfect," thought Don. He had lots of experience with banks, especially with Swiss accounts. It was a natural fit.

Mere hours later, Don was seated in the bank office with a completed résumé in his hand. Several high-profile assassinations and covert operations were bullet pointed with strong verbs in less than a page. It had been tough to get it down from two pages. He had to choose between disposing of a Bulgarian official and retrieving stolen submarine plans from Ukraine.

The office was a sterile room, sparse and tidy. A wood laminate desk and white walls. The bank manager returned from photocopying Don's photo id for the application. He'd chosen the New York driver's license, because he'd always respected a city that had a martini bar around every corner.

The bank manager was a solidly built woman, who liked pasta with pesto and had an affinity for collecting state teaspoons. Her desk was riddled with them. Don noticed that they were polished to a shine. She was clearly a woman who liked details.

"I'm so glad to see you've got a background in IT," said the bank manager. She smoothed Don's papers out on her desk. "That's great experience for a career in banking."

"Of course." Don smiled. He didn't know that blowing up a medical lab counted as IT work, but maybe the field was wider than when he had last checked.

"It says here that you, 'infiltrated a major network and eliminated key threats.'" She looked up and smiled. "My, that sounds like complicated technical work. I myself can't even get past rebooting a computer!"

Don nodded. He had a fair idea that they were talking about two different things, but had learned that when your opponent believes you, it's best to stay silent.

"And how do you feel that your specific qualifications could benefit us here at Brinkman Bank?"

Don pressed his fingertips together. He felt that this action showed people that he was sincere. It was often useful during interrogations along with a pair of pliers, a tool that is extremely sincere in its nature. "Well, ma'am, I feel that I've always been a person for thinking on my feet, and attacking any situation head on." This was not strictly true, as Don believed in attacking most problems from behind, but he felt that this might not translate well into the banking world.

"Wonderful!" The bank manager clasped her hands together. Don noticed that they were perfectly manicured with a red polish that matched the cardinal on her Ohio teaspoon. "I always like a go-getter." She glanced down at his paperwork. "Well, I've got a good feeling about you. I think I need someone with your qualifications. Plus, I have an immediate opening."

Don, of course, knew she had an immediate opening. He was the one who had disposed of the body.

"So let me just write this down…" She glanced around her desk. "Hmm, I seem to have lost my pen."

"Allow me." Don retrieved a pen from his pocket with a deft movement.

The bank manager took the pen gratefully and glanced down at her paper. "Now let's see here…"

Don smiled to himself. Excellent. A salary. His skills did translate. Lying and deception were the key to any profession.

The bank manager tapped the paper. "Here we are. I just need to sign here…" She clicked the pen, and a small whiff of gas sprayed into the air around her face. "Oh my, what…" But her voice trailed off, and her head thunked down onto the desk scattering all fifty states of the collectible teaspoons onto the floor.

He'd grabbed the wrong pen.

Perhaps there were some differences in the bank world. Don discreetly made an exit from the bank manager's office, pausing to retrieve his stunning one-page résumé from underneath the unconscious woman's head. He turned back once to survey the scene of his first interview. Perhaps this was going to be harder than he had thought.

Later that week, Don tried a funeral parlor, a nail salon, and a martini bar. But all the places he applied had either already filled their vacancies or he didn't fit the qualifications. He was surprised to find that half of the applicants at the nail salon already possessed PhDs, and that the funeral parlor required twenty years of previous experience. He of course had lots of previous experience with corpses, but the funeral director seemed unconvinced.

Don was almost ready to give up when he noticed a small Help Wanted sign at the dry cleaners near the coffee shop. Having now been reduced to eating steak that was not filet mignon, he decided that drastic times called for drastic measures. He strode in the door of Ramuel's Dry Cleaners with purpose.

The interview was remarkably short.

Ramuel turned out to be a former computer programmer, furloughed by his company a year before retirement. It was not his dream to run a dry cleaners. He stared at Don with deadpan eyes during the interview. Don could tell he hadn't shaved in two and a half days and that he was currently contemplating a turkey sandwich for lunch.

"Why are you wearing a suit?"

Don looked down at his gray suit with black tie and matching silk handkerchief. "Ah well, I had another interview, so I needed to look my best."

"Where was the interview?"

"Mimi's Nail Boutique."

Ramuel shook his head. "Fucking salon. I heard they hired an MIT graduate."

Don nodded. "It's a tough job market."

"What the fuck," said Ramuel with a dismissive gesture of the hand.

"Those were my thoughts exactly," said Don.

Ramuel looked him up and down with narrowed eyes. "All right. You're hired. Clearly, you're a jaded, cynical son of a bitch and I like that in a person."

Don said nothing. He often found it was best to keep a person talking.

"You can start tomorrow. I'll train you now. I've got a court date to keep so I need someone to watch the store anyways."

And that was how Don ended up behind the counter of a dry cleaners by himself on an early Saturday morning.

He'd chosen to dress down a bit, removing his silk handkerchief and loosening his tie just slightly. Business was depressingly slow. Don amused himself by examining the clothes waiting for pickup and profiling their owners. He felt a certain affinity to clothing racks, as they were headless, and Don had lots of memories with headless things. The only sound was the swish of the garment bags as he combed through the racks. The front counter was empty except for a cash register and a box of colored tags. A door to the right led to the back storeroom. It held more circular racks of clothing and the dry cleaning machinery.

Don looked out the window. The weather was damp. Any pedestrians on the street hurried through the puddles. Across the street, people cluttered the coffee shop, their animated faces showing in the steamed windows.

In a lot of ways, this new job was not unlike his old one. A lot of waiting. Don sat back on the stool.

In the silence, he heard a small click from the back room.

Don had previously been trained in a hundred and thirty-eight different types of combat, including the sudden appearance of inflatable pool toys. So when Don heard that click, he knew without a doubt that someone was in the back room, holding a .30 caliber pistol with their shoes untied.

Don turned on the television to a Spanish talk show. He fell into his old habits, scanning the room for anything that could be used to his advantage. All he found was a stack of metal hangers. Don grabbed one from the pile and cautiously approached the door to the back room. He started calculating the variety of ways he could detach various body parts using the machinery in the storage room.

It was nice to be doing something familiar again.

Crouching low, Don slid the door open a crack and slipped in. The back room looked empty, apart from three rows of racks, clothing neatly packed in plastic. Don heard the swish of the garment bags in the back corner of the room. Using the hanger like a boomerang, he flung it in an arc. It gracefully curved and disappeared around the rows of clothes.

There was a thud and Don heard the pistol clatter to the floor.

He raised an eyebrow. No one could be this sloppy.

"Perhaps you should tell me what you're doing here," he said. His words echoed in the silence.

There was more movement, as the person hugged the cement walls, sliding further into the back of the room.

"Look, I can tell that you're new at this, so there's really no point in continuing. Why are you trying to kill me?"

There was more shuffling, and Don caught a flash of a canvas windbreaker between the sleeves of the coats. He heard a flutter of plastic bags as the figure pushed past.

A voice echoed in the room. "For my résumé."

This was not what Don had expected. "Your what?"

"My job résumé," said the dark figure, darting to the left side of the room. Don caught a flash of blond hair. His assailant looked to be only about twenty with a pimpled face. A fake beard was plastered hesitantly against baby cheeks.

"The job market is tough out there, and it's impossible to get new jobs. I figured a hit against a seasoned intelligence operative might be enough to put me in front of the competition."

Don rolled his eyes. "Maybe you should try a career counselor."

The boy's squeaking voice came from his left. "Don't you know? In this job market, it's all about making yourself a more diversified candidate. I heard about a job in Oslo, infiltrating heads of state and stealing plans for solar-powered technology. They want three years of experience, and I've only got two. But with a bullet point on my résumé about killing you, they'll have to give me the job."

Don sighed. He could think of far more useful things to do with a bullet, several of them releasing him from this adolescent's irritating chatter. He was aware that this boy with his pimples was attempting to distract him while trying to edge around to a better position. Clearly, he was a bright young man, but he was no match for years in the field.

A pity. A bit of mentorship, and the boy could have been promising.

"Face it, old man, your time is up, and there's a new generation in the job market."

Don said nothing, calculating the boy's position from the echo of his squeaky voice against the cement walls. It sounded like he was near the back corner, but Don knew that the garment bags were throwing off the echo. Pressing his back into the doorway, he slid around the wall, using the rows of clothes for cover. His footfall was silent, his movement smooth and unhurried.

The boy continued, tromping around the edge of the storeroom. He was still moving closer to the doorway where Don had once stood. His voice carried back around the racks to Don. "You know what your problem is? You don't know about all the new tech. There's been millions of new gadgets just in the last month. Rocket-launching segues, ballpoint pens with GPS, wallets that disperse nerve gas…"

Don dug into his pocket as he turned around the rack of clothing. The boy was crouching in front of him, edging toward the doorway. With a fluid movement, Don extracted a simple leather wallet and pressed it against his assailant's face from behind.

As the boy flailed, Don straightened his collar. "I know about the nerve gas wallet," he said. "I own one."

In a few seconds, the boy collapsed onto the floor, and an expensive-looking pistol clattered across the waxed tiles. Don slid a hand into his victim's pockets and extracted a smart phone. His fingers flicked across the screen in practiced movements. An encrypted message about the Oslo job, no government affiliation necessary, appeared on the screen. Disposing of the body in the dumpster with a clank, Don quietly closed the door to the dry cleaners with a click. He shook his head as he placed the smart phone in his pocket. Puddles splashed against his patent leather shoes, as he walked farther back into the darkness of the alley. He composed a message to the contact in Oslo in his head as the shadows fell over his suit. He was back in business. Freelancing, it now seemed. He should have known. These days, getting another job… it was all about networking.

Madelyn Glist

N as in Never

MADELYN GLIST is a freelance television producer and writer in the
D.C. area.

My marriage ended at the Air and Space Museum in Washington, D.C. I was standing in front of a large model of Jupiter thinking how small Earth was in comparison to most of the solar system and feeling particularly insignificant, when Mitch turned to me and said, "I want a divorce."

I definitely didn't absorb it right away, because I said, "how do you think Buzz Aldrin and Neil Armstrong decided who would be the first to walk on the moon?" I was talking about the first lunar landing, an exhibit we'd just passed through, and I was preoccupied with how the astronauts on that mission decided who would be the first to take the giant step for mankind.

"It was decided before the mission," Mitch said, irritated.

"Really?"

"Did you hear what I just said?"

"Yes, it was decided ahead of time, no coin toss or drawing of straws involved."

"That's not what I'm talking about."

"What are you talking about?" I scanned the crowded exhibit room for Sophie.

"I—I don't love you anymore."

"What?" I said. "Are you serious?" I pushed Luke in the stroller and watched as Sophie studied Saturn turning her head to see it from all different angles.

"Mommy, there's Earth," She pointed to the model.

"Can you find Neptune and Mars?" I said hoping to buy some time.

"Yes, I am," Mitch said.

"There's Mars and there's Neptune," she said pointing to each. Done with the solar system, she walked back to the man on the moon exhibit.

I pushed Luke in the stroller to catch up to her while Mitch lagged behind. We reached a long wall of photographs of each Apollo mission and the astronauts on board. There was an enclave there and I stopped to wait for Mitch. A couple of French tourists walked between us and I pretended to be interested in the photographs. I happened to be in front of the Apollo 13 crew photo. Bad sign, I thought.

Mitch caught up, and I said, "Don't you think this is something we should talk about in private?"

The couple moved and Mitch stared at the astronauts of Apollo 13. "It can't wait because I can't live like this." Luke pulled at the straps of his stroller and I unsnapped the buckle.

"Like what?"

Luke jumped out of the stroller and ran to Sophie at the photograph of Neil Armstrong on the moon. I'd noticed earlier when we saw it that she was fascinated by the texture of the moon. I turned my attention back to Mitch and braced myself for his answer. Don't say, "I can't live a lie" or I'll throw up, I thought.

"I'm tired."

Tired? I didn't know what to say, then finally, I said, "We have little kids, what do you expect?" I stepped closer to the children, who were still captivated with the lunar landing photograph.

"I just can't do this," he said staring at Neil Armstrong. "I have to go—not going is not an option."

"Really, Mitch, this is serious. Let's talk about it later. Come on," I said.

"It's over," he said and then he walked away, leaving me with our two kids in front of the lunar landing. I felt for that moment like I was on the moon, some place other than Earth, because it all didn't feel real to me. It felt like outer space.

I tried to convince myself that I would see him at home, we'd work this out, but my gut said otherwise, and I reached for a bench near a seventies documentary; I keeled over. Richard Nixon flashed on the screen, and the narrator said something about the Watergate scandal and then former president Ford said, "We must go forward now together." I got up because

I wanted to go forward together now—as a couple, as a family, as before. I searched for my kids, and thought what if there is no together, how do I go forward alone?

I found Sophie and Luke jumping on a scale that showed how much they would weigh on each of the planets. Sophie would be fifty pounds on Neptune and Luke would be twenty pounds on Saturn. They giggled as they jumped on the huge scale. I reminded them that others were waiting and we still had to see the rocket ships.

"Rocket ships, yeah," Luke said. Sophie, far less excited, followed him toward the huge rockets downstairs.

I put one foot in front of the other, not understanding how he could be out of love. I still loved him, loved his smell, just a few days ago we made love.

It didn't make sense. Why would he just drop this bomb out of nowhere? When I looked down at the kids ahead of me on the escalator, my legs felt shaky and I had to hold onto the railing. I was relieved when it was time to get off.

I stood at the bottom of the rocket ships while Luke walked around them in awe.

"Where's Daddy?" Sophie asked as she reached for my hand.

"We're going to meet him at home. He didn't feel well." I waited for Sophie to ask more questions and my mind raced with other lies to tell her about his sudden departure, but instead she walked toward a multicolored biplane.

That is the last thing I remember before I fainted—the green, red, and yellow biplane shrinking out of my view and then everything went black.

I woke up staring into the face of a pimply teenager whose voice sounded like it was caught in an echo chamber. The engine of a rocket ship came into my view and I knew I was not dreaming but still in the Air and Space Museum, only now on the floor. My first thought was where were Sophie and Luke?

"You OK?" she asked.

When I actually managed to get to my feet, I realized there was a small crowd gathered around me. Sophie held Luke's hand and they looked terrified. I rushed to them and gave them a hug. Sophie cried and then Luke cried. I calmed them down and told them, Mommy was totally fine, despite feeling anything but fine.

I thanked the girl, then assured a security guard that really all I needed was some air. He escorted me outside and offered to call a cab. I told him I would call a friend and promised not to drive home.

I stood outside the museum with the kids and was suddenly overwhelmed with dread. This feeling was interrupted when Luke said, "Mommy, I'm hungry." I walked the kids over to a hot dog vendor and bought some pretzels.

I decided I was well enough to drive and set out to find the car. I was desperately trying to remember where I—or Mitch—had parked the car. I walked up D Street, then C Street, then Sophie turned to me and said, "Mom, I'm tired." The streets were all a blur and I couldn't remember where we'd parked. We rested on a park bench and I called the only friend I could think of who could bail me out. I called Renee.

Renee answered on the third ring, much to my relief, and over the noise of her kids in the background, I explained everything. She said she'd be right there. Renee and I had been through a lot in the fifteen years since she'd hired me for my first job on Capitol Hill, but never anything like this.

We walked back to the Air and Space Museum and waited for Renee in front of the twisted metal sculpture.

Renee's beat-up Volvo arrived about forty minutes, two pretzels, two hot dogs, and one ice cream cone later.

We all piled in the car. She just looked at me and said, "Has he lost his fucking mind?" I looked back at the kids to see if they'd picked up on her swear, but they were exhausted and had missed it.

"Do you have any idea what letter of the alphabet you might have parked on?" She turned down E Street.

"This doesn't look like it," I said. She hooked a left.

"It was near a Starbucks," I said.

"That's like saying it's near a parking meter around here."

"Thanks for doing this," I said.

"You can give me the nitty-gritty details when the babes aren't in the car," she said.

"I'll give you the nitty-gritty details when I know them," I said.

"Is this the time I'm supposed to tell you I never liked him?" she said. I laughed. She actually did like him.

"How'd he get home?" she asked as she turned down another street.

"Metro, I would guess. Didn't ask," I said. We fell silent because there wasn't anything to say and there was everything to say, but with the kids in the back we didn't risk it. She squeezed my hand and I almost cried right there in the car.

When we turned onto D Street, I saw my black SUV sitting right where we had parked it. Sophie clapped her hands in excitement. Luke sucked his thumb.

"Follow me back," Renee said. That's exactly what I did—I followed Renee's blue Volvo back to my neighborhood. I don't know if I would have ever made it home without her help.

She pulled up next to me at the stop light before my street.

"Call me tonight," she said. "I'd invite you over but Steve's parents are coming for dinner."

"Thanks," I said. She waved and drove off.

I had hoped to see Mitch when I arrived home, but his car was not there. I wondered how he got home—the Metro stop is not close to our house and the buses don't run very often on Sundays. I put Luke down for a nap. Sophie sat on the couch and flipped through some books.

I walked to the bedroom and checked the closet. Nothing was missing; it didn't look like he was going to move out. That calmed my nerves. I thought of his words, "I'm tired." Maybe he just needed a break, a vacation alone. I took a deep breath.

I didn't know what else to do, so I called Mitch's cell. I got his voicemail. I hung up. Just relax, he'll be back.

I sat with Sophie on the couch and watched *Finding Nemo* with her. Just as the sharks chased Marlin and Dorie, my cell rang. It was Heather.

"You are not going to believe this." She went on about how her boyfriend Carl's dog "shat" all over her kitchen cabinets. "I'm talking projectile diarrhea," she moaned.

"The white kitchen cabinets?" I said.

"Yes. What should I do?"

"Break up with him."

She laughed. "No, seriously."

"Where's Carl? Out of town again?"

"Yes."

"You're screwed. Admit it, that dog hates you. He rebels whenever Carl is away."

Heather sighed deeply and I knew she was gearing herself up to clean the cabinets. I debated if I should tell her, then it just came out.

"Mitch dumped me in front of the lunar landing today."

"What?"

"We were at the Air and Space Museum with the kids and he told me he doesn't love me anymore and wants a divorce. I haven't seen him since."

"That's crazy. I mean of all the museums that wouldn't have been my first choice," she said.

"Frankly, no museum would have been my first choice." I walked in the kitchen to make sure Sophie couldn't hear me.

"Holocaust Museum or Vietnam Memorial would have been better," she said.

"Why those?"

"You could have cried and fainted—no one would have thought twice."

"I did faint and no one really thought twice."

"Oh. You going to be OK? Seriously, this is awful—I'm so sorry. Come over, we'll give the kids pizza."

"That sounds real appealing given the cabinet situation."

"It will be sparkling clean by the time you get here."

"OK." As I hung up, I considered calling Mitch again, but before I'd made up my mind, Luke woke up from his nap and wandered into the living room, his hair stuck up in the back, the same cowlick as his dad. He looked so much like his dad; I thought, Mitch has left me with a mini-version of himself.

I walked into the kitchen to get the kids a snack and I called Mitch again.

This time he answered. I was shocked. "What are you doing?" My calm manner astounded even me.

"Nothing," he said.

"When are you coming home?"

"I'm not."

"I am utterly confused here. I don't get this."

"I told you, I don't love you anymore. I want a divorce."

"I heard you, but why?"

"You've changed." There was a long pause.

"I've changed? How?"

"You're not like you were when we first met."

"I was twenty-three when we first met. What do you want?"

"I want someone who'll mend my clothes. If I have a hole in my shirt, they'll mend it."

"You want a mother?"

"See, I knew you'd say something like that. You never listen."

"I'm listening."

"I want someone who'll take care of me. Someone who adores me."

"Who is she?" The word adore made me believe there really was someone else.

"There isn't anyone."

"How can you expect me to adore you after twelve years of marriage and two kids?"

"That's exactly my point," he said. I didn't know what to say, and after a moment Mitch said, "Look, I rented a place in the city. I need some time to figure things out."

"You rented an apartment? When? What about the kids?"

"They'll be fine." They'll be fine? Is he on Mars? Maybe the real Mitch is on planet Jupiter back at the Air and Space Museum.

"Where's this apartment?" And then my husband of twelve years said, "Thirty-one twenty-one N Street," then he paused and said, "N as in never." I think he thought he was being clever or he just didn't realize what he just said.

I waited for him to add "N as in never will I love you, never will I be with you, never will I hold you," but N as in nothing was said, and the line went dead.

Jessica Claire Haney

Out of Scale

JESSICA CLAIRE HANEY is a writer, blogger, and editor. A mother of two, she publishes MindfulHealthyLife.com, a lifestyle magazine for natural-minded parents. A former teacher, she is now a wellness advocate in schools and with Holistic Moms Network. Her writing has appeared in *Beltway Poetry Review*, the *Washington Post*, *Mothering*, *Hip Mama*, and *Have Milk, Will Travel: Adventures in Breastfeeding*. Find her at Crunchy-Chewy Mama.com and JessicaClaireHaney.com. "Out of Scale" is from her novel in progress, "The Unspeakable Passing of Clouds."

Could she have ever imagined herself in this position? Eight months pregnant at forty-two, clutching a list of birth supplies in her sweaty hand, and asking her friend to watch her boys after baseball camp because she was too tired to imagine getting through the afternoon with the two of them. And the two of her.

It wasn't that Melanie didn't want a third child. They'd hoped and tried, but, after six years and two miscarriages, and at her age, the unplanned pregnancy was a matter of significant ambivalence, even now. Although she told people the reason for planning a homebirth this time was because the first two came so quickly, it was something she looked into only because she didn't want to see her OB if she ultimately decided to terminate the pregnancy. Sarah, the midwife she called instead, was one of the more patient and accommodating people Melanie had ever met. Once Melanie got the ultrasound referral from Sarah and found out she was a full nine—not just five—weeks along, continuing with Sarah seemed like the only thing that made sense.

How ridiculous to have to park in the shade at 8:45 in the morning, Melanie thought, turning on the a.c. as soon as she started the car to leave the parking lot in front of the baseball fields. It must have gone up five degrees just since she'd left the house with the boys. Who the hell gets pregnant in November, she thought again. What a stupid season to be sexy and summer an awful one to be so big.

She considered going to Costco but decided Target was more likely to have everything she needed, and in reasonable rather than gigantic quantities. Sometimes Melanie had the sense when she entered a big box store that she was just a tiny speck that some giant could come flick away. During her first year teaching high school, she had lots of those moments in Kmart. A decade later, the hugeness of Costco took it to another level when she was newly postpartum. Her older son, Brian, was almost two when brother Curtis joined the family. In that newborn phase, Melanie's whole sense of size shifted, focusing like a camera lens on the smallest unit possible. Her nipple looked impossibly large in Curtis's tiny mouth, and Brian's previously cute toddler hand chubs came to look like padded boxing gloves. Those first few weeks, everything out of the immediate frame was blurry or just too damn big.

For a month after Todd went back to work, his mom helped in the middle of the week. That first Friday morning Melanie was alone, she was too scared to stay in. Brian would just do things to wake up the baby or bug Melanie while she tried to rest or get something done. Monday had been sunny, so they'd walked to the park in the neighborhood without incident and had nice snuggles before Brian's naptime. But when his grandma kept him in the house all day, Brian refused to nap, and Melanie worried he wouldn't sleep for her later on Friday if they didn't get out that morning. It was chilly and rainy outside and too chaotic at the soft play area to bring the baby yet. Costco seemed as good a choice as anything. They would stock up on some things so she could use Todd's time home over the weekend to sleep.

Baby Curtis was still falling asleep easily at that point, so the drive was smooth. But Melanie was unprepared to feel so impossibly out of scale once they got into the warehouse. For three weeks, her life had been distilled into ounces of fluid coming out of her and into the baby and back out again.

In Costco that Friday morning, she found herself yanking up maternity pants that didn't fit anymore and blinking in the brightness under a ceiling that was two or three stories high. In the cart she was nudging along slowly were two small children who expected her to know what she was doing. Curtis's car seat sat like a Weeble Wobble in the main basket, and Brian was strapped into the front, facing Melanie. After just a few minutes, he managed to pull his legs through and stand up on the plastic where his bum should have been. He refused to sit down and gave Melanie no hints toward negotiating. He just wanted her to pay attention to him. People always say, "He just wants attention," like it's a throwaway line—something that doesn't matter and should be ignored. But at that moment, Melanie understood exactly how raw and powerful that feeling was. She looked at her son's impossibly pained face and felt all the anger of every student who'd ever talked back to her, reeling from years of neglect, benign, or by necessity, or with malice. They all just wanted to be attended to. Who didn't?

Melanie almost wished she could still soothe Brian by breastfeeding. But he'd weaned over a year earlier. The few moms she had seen nurse two children of different ages had seemed like unnecessary martyrs to her until she stood there, under a thousand fluorescent lights, dwarfed under towers of cereal boxes, feeling powerless to make the heart of her child stop hurting.

And to make his throat stop screaming. There was no way she could finish this shopping trip. Having spent a solid five minutes stymied at the front of the store, bleary-eyed facing special offers on so many kitchen accessories, she'd only managed to get baby wipes and applesauce into her cart. Now some employee was going to have to put them back from where she left them on an endcap of toilet paper. Leaning her chest into Brian's standing legs and hooking them with one arm, she pushed the cart past the cash registers to the garage elevator. She lifted the car seat out of the basket as gently as she could, but between the jostling and the screaming, Curtis woke up. At least he didn't launch into a full-on cry, but he was clearly annoyed. Once she'd heaved Brian up and out of the cart and down to her hip and had maneuvered them all into the elevator, she bobbed her body and rocked the car seat with her foot until the ding told her she could stop. Melanie then hefted some forty pounds of people and gear and made her way through the silver doors toward the car.

She tried to get Brian into his seat first, before he could run away, with baby Curtis's face getting increasingly more pink and his cries more serious from his seat on the ground. But Brian did the stiff-board routine, and she had to karate chop his rigid body in half to stuff him into his seat. He shouted to make Curtis stop because he was hurting his ears. Melanie couldn't disagree. She just hoped Brian would keep his hands to himself and so fished out a box of raisins to occupy him after she clicked in the baby's seat. Curtis wailed the twelve-minute ride with a fervor she thought he ought to reserve for true starvation or hypothermia, but at least Brian busied himself chewing. When they got home, she grabbed them both bananas and *The Very Hungry Caterpillar*, and they sat on the couch reading while Curtis nursed.

Today, in Target, Melanie felt inordinately big and yet once again tiny. Her world was as wide as the trail of dirt her boys left and as wide as her generously expanded rear end. It seemed impossible to get out of her own mind's way. At the same time, thinking about her former students who had worked at this store, she felt inconsequential now that she would not be returning to the classroom in the fall. Without her there, the lives inside the school would go on as usual, but hers at home would be completely different. She glanced down the long line of registers with red vests, too many for this early in the morning when they only seemed to need three. Melanie wheeled her cart into the aisle of an older brown-skinned woman in a headscarf who she silently thanked for not making any small talk as she bagged all of Melanie's supplies.

As Melanie exited into the steamy parking lot, she felt so relieved that her friend had agreed to take the boys for a while after camp. This way she didn't feel rushed about driving over to the family-owned pharmacy where Sarah had told her they would have a good supply of what she called chux pads. For all the years Melanie had spent teaching Family Life and instructing high schoolers about pregnancy and birth—including some who had already experienced it—the actuality of what one needed to catch a baby never really made it into the curriculum.

The aisles at the pharmacy felt intimate. There was no room for passing on the left. Everyone had to agree to get along, to look at the Band-Aids while waiting to look at the peroxide. The cart was petite, seemingly half the size of the one at Target, and gray. When Melanie stood sideways for more than a minute looking at maxi pads, a thin woman with short hair and a green name tag guessed what she was looking for and motioned her over to the bladder control section where Melanie found the turquoise-lined underpads. Would they really be under a baby—her baby? And what would they be over?

Where in the house to deliver was still not something Melanie had seriously considered. The whole pregnancy had been a series of denials. She'd initially missed the fact that what she thought was a period wasn't, and then she kept expecting a miscarriage that never came. The reality of her boys needing to be cared for was yet another thing she neglected until Jennie had asked about her plans that morning, offering help but noting she'd be headed to the beach the last week of July. Melanie shuddered to think that the baby could come that early. At her sonogram in January, even mid-August felt too soon. If she went two weeks late, though, the boys would already be back in school. Not that she wanted an extended pregnancy, but it wouldn't hurt to have them back in their routine. And out of view.

Brian, despite his frequent talk of farts and butts, complained that his parents were gross, as was the imagined birth of his baby sister. Curtis said he wanted to say hello to the baby and to help put its diaper on. He was sweet, but he had no idea. Melanie knew that more conversation about the imminent changes would have been wise, but she just never felt like broaching the subject in detail. Or doing anything that made it feel too real until today when she had to get her supplies in advance of her thirty-six-week appointment the following day.

When did she get so jaded about parenthood? She initially loved it. As soon as each baby was reliably burping, predictably pooping, and showing obvious sleepy cues, she mourned the getting-to-know-you newborn period. It was like first dating someone and having no idea what they'd order at a restaurant, or how they would kiss, or what their first groping move would be. There was something magical about the unknown.

Even though the early days with two under two were hard—and maybe because they were—she had fantasized about another baby back then. She imagined how a third would come into a home of already-loving brothers who could entertain each other and even help a little. She envisioned the boys marveling over their sister (she always hoped it would be a girl), engaging in detailed and mature conversations about her dimples, and taking pains to ensure she slept well so that the whole family could sleep well. Melanie knew this was likely wishful thinking, but still.

When a baby was brand new, you couldn't really be doing anything wrong. Once a schedule started to establish itself, that's when every decision could be questioned. Melanie sometimes looked down on herself from above thinking she'd regret setting this or that precedent. The honeymoon lasted longer the first time with Brian because she was clueless about life with a baby, wholly unprepared even if she'd already been teaching Family Life for years. Second guessing was only intellectual. But once she'd seen him through babyhood and into toddlerdom, she knew what it meant to reap what you sow. Each decision about sleep routines or meals or snacks would come to bite her in the ass if she got it wrong.

And having the older child to consider complicated things, but since Curtis was more forgiving as a toddler than Brian had been, Melanie wanted the third to come soon. And beyond just wanting a new chance to start fresh, she also honestly wanted to give birth again. She never mentioned it to anyone, but long before she had any desire for postpartum sex, she craved childbirth like a hunger. She wanted to know she was minutes away from a life coming heavy through her legs, from where it had knocked against her ribs for months through its dark narrow passage to the open air where it would blink at its new surroundings.

That desire, though, had faded after two losses and more years of aging and more pounds that found their home on her increasingly saggy body. With a tired and dulled sex life, it seemed like a waste of energy for Todd to get a vasectomy or for her to go on the Pill. Had there not been such a warm and sultry air last Thanksgiving, inspiring her boys to camp outside their grandparents' door and leaving Melanie and Todd alone for the night, things would likely be looking very different right about now.

As she unpacked her birth supplies, Melanie thought about that long-faded desire for birth, which had dulled in some ways by the time Curtis was one and intensified in others. She was annoyed at Curtis's flailings and grabbing for her open nipple, but she didn't want to be done nursing forever. The cramping of the first miscarriage hadn't been nearly as intense as childbirth, but it did sour her on pregnancy for a while and wipe out the deep desire for feeling a baby's head pass through the birth canal, a desire she never mentioned to Todd or her doctor or any other mother. It seemed one of the more perverse feelings she could imagine until she was paging through a copy of a midwifery book when babysitting for a neighbor one night. There she saw photos of a woman supposedly having an orgasm while giving birth. Melanie felt like she was a teenager looking through porn while the parents were out. But the Ina May Gaskin book was just there on the shelf, next to *The Happiest Baby on the Block*. Melanie read some of the birth stories and realized a few things: she had been lucky to have such easy births, there was a whole birth culture world out there that she was clueless about and hadn't ever brought into her classroom, and she was not a pervert for feeling like birth was a sensual experience.

But after another miscarriage and a bronchitis-induced phase of contraception that went on until the night they were visiting her in-laws without having packed any condoms, Melanie had largely gotten past the expectation of a third child. Once its gestation was unexpectedly under way, a friend of Melanie's neighbor saw Melanie and her belly in the store and squealed with glee to find out she was having a homebirth. "I assume you've seen *The Business of Being Born*? And *Orgasmic Birth*?" she asked. Melanie said no, she just didn't want to have to rush to the hospital a third time.

"Oh my gosh, well you have to see them anyway," Elizabeth began, clearly so excited that Melanie was joining the homebirth ranks, she must have thought someone was getting a free toaster. "These movies will make you feel so good about your choice!" she said and went on about bonding with the baby and avoiding unnecessary interventions, adding, "And, well, the movie isn't really about orgasms—that was sort of just a marketing ploy, I think—but it does really show you how great birth can be."

Melanie just blinked at Elizabeth's enthusiasm and agreed to borrow the DVDs, which appeared on Melanie's porch the next day in a purple paper bag with green handles. It took Melanie a month to consider watching the films; she didn't want to watch them with Todd, and that disturbed her even more. The one Saturday the boys had three baseball games in a row, Melanie she said she needed to stay home to rest and grade papers. Instead she blasted through both films, fast-forwarding to make it through with a decent idea what they were about. The one made her worry about a C-section but feel grateful she'd avoided them so far, and the other made her feel like something really good was possible in birth but that she had to believe in it.

She still had her doubts about this baby, unclear what she'd do if offered a time machine back to November. Would she have had the sex, knowing she was going to get pregnant? Would she have offered a blow job? Would she have slunk her body back to push Todd out before he came? At least she wasn't mad at the baby or cursing it like that student she had her second year teaching. Melanie had taught plenty of teen moms but still shuddered when she thought about that girl and wondered where she and her progeny were today.

Even with all these questions, and even though she wasn't ready yet, she thought she could start looking forward to the birth, at least a little bit. The movies did make her excited for something different. She didn't know where it would be and hadn't rented a tub or even gotten a doula like Elizabeth suggested, but she kept thinking she'd find some time in the next week, once she had the supplies, to wrap her head around what she wanted.

Or maybe not. After accidentally knocking the smaller package of medium chux pads off the counter and onto the floor, Melanie squatted down like the yoga video lady suggested and felt like a balloon popped right above the pink donut where she imagined her cervix to be. Melanie stood up and a trickle of water changed her thoughts from "That was weird" to "You are kidding me that my water just fucking broke."

Melanie thought of the ticking clock in the birth movie and what she'd told her students: a hospital won't let you go more than twenty-four hours with broken water. She hadn't discussed that in detail with Sarah because neither of her other labors started this way, but she hoped that if things didn't move along quickly, Sarah would be clear about what to do. The clock on the stove read 11:02 a.m.

She looked around for her cell phone and saw it on the table by the door. She started to dash as best she could in that direction but was caught by a contraction. It was definitely not a "surge" like in the hypnobirthing book from Elizabeth. It felt like there were reins around her middle and someone was pulling back with a serious and hearty "Whoa!" After the contraction eased off, she walked to the table and unwrapped a chocolate before opening her phone to call Sarah.

She put the phone on speaker while savoring the sweetness and wondering if eating chocolate would help or hurt the greater cause. After the fourth ring, a rushed and breathy "Sarah's phone" was the answer. The voice might have belonged to Sarah's new assistant who Melanie was supposed to meet tomorrow, but it certainly was not the comforting deep tones she expected from her midwife.

"This is Melanie. I'm just thirty-six weeks and in labor. Who is this?"

The voice introduced herself as Stef, a doula who was just starting her training to be a midwife. "We're at another mom's house. She had the baby three hours ago, but the placenta hasn't come, and Sarah might need to go to the hospital with her. Where are you and what's going on?"

At the moment pain free but perplexed, Melanie asked, "When is it supposed to come?" wondering how such a problem was news to her.

"By thirty or forty-five minutes. Not usually more than an hour," Stef said and asked again about Melanie's progress and where she lived. Melanie asked, couldn't she just put Sarah on the line, or was the woman having a tough time? In the hospital, Melanie had been one of those women for whom the nurses, she later found out, had to ditch slower-laboring mothers. Now Melanie was the one looking for attention, negotiating for face time with her midwife. What would she have to say to get picked as important?

Finally Sarah's voice came on the line sounding hoarse. "Sorry, Mel," she said. "This has been a head-scratcher. No bleeding but I still can't leave her and if there's some reason this placenta is retained, they'll need to address it at a hospital. Tell me where things stand with you."

Melanie's middle started to tighten again. She spilled out as quickly as she could that she was home with broken water and a second strong contraction starting.

While she stood with her eyes closed, trying to take a deep breath, she heard Sarah say to her, "OK dear, hold on. We'll get you covered," and to Stef, "Somebody has to get over there soon. See who's on backup."

Sarah had to say Melanie's name three times before the contraction subsided enough that she could answer.

"Listen honey, I'm sorry this is happening—that you're going early and that I'm stuck here. But it's a first-time mom and we can't leave her without support or leave the baby with just the dad if we have to take Mom to the hospital. So I need you to hang tight, time yourself, drink water, and get ready. We know you go fast. Is your husband there?"

Melanie was done playing nice. "No, it's the middle of the damn day in the middle of the damn week. It's lucky enough I'm not picking up two boys from baseball camp."

"Yes, well, it's good that you're home. So here's what I'd like you to do," Sarah began.

Sarah hadn't gotten far into instructions when Melanie said, "Wait. Here's another one." She wished for nothing less than silence during the next contraction. This time she could not stop herself from moaning. It came from underneath her stomach, as though her womb were a kickball and the vibration of her sound and the tightening of her muscles traveled all the way around the rubber surface.

It stayed quiet on the other end after Melanie's moan tapered off. "What now!?" she shouted to the room.

"Well, it sounds like things are moving fast. Try to breathe into each contraction and in between get yourself set up in case the baby comes soon. You said you got your supplies?"

Melanie was already starting to walk back to the counter to pull open the plastic on the package of pads. Where the hell was she going to put them?

"Yes, I have them, but isn't there something else I should do? Can't you send someone?"

"Well, you can call your husband and if you want to call 911, you can do that. And we can stay on the phone with you if you want. We'll go through all our lists and try to get someone over to you, but I can't be sure who or when. I don't have my files in front of me; can you tell me your address before the next contraction?"

The tightening had already started. Melanie spit out the numbers and shouted "Get over here!" before pressing the red button to hang up. With one hand, she pushed on the phone on the counter and scrolled to Todd's number in her recent history. It went straight to voicemail, and she went straight to disconnect. When the pain subsided, she texted to Todd "Labor!" and pushed the phone toward the backsplash. The best she could hope was that he would read it and come home. She was not up for talking and certainly not writing anything more.

911? No, she couldn't deal with talking to them. And even if she did have a longer break between the next contractions, what if they put her in an ambulance? And Jennie brought her sons home to an empty house after their mother had delivered her accidental baby into the hands of a paramedic while they bumped along the road? She could hardly move from one side of the room to the other. Like hell she was getting into an emergency vehicle.

She looked toward the front door and saw that the deadbolt was unlocked. So if anyone did manage to get there to help her, they could just come in. Sarah has got to find someone, Melanie thought.

Where should she go? The family room floor was strewn with Legos, books, and a mesh bag of dusty baseballs, the living room was right by the front door. Anything else seemed impossibly far. Maybe she should try to pee before the next contraction, she thought, although she already felt a lot of pressure and was guessing she was probably beyond that stage. But it might not hurt to try.

Maybe she could get in the tub like Ricki Lake. It was probably totally gross, though. When was the last time she'd cleaned it? No, no water as long as she would be alone. Leave it to her to drown her own baby. Maybe that's where this all was leading: she didn't want the baby and now was going to manage to drown it and then what would happen?

She wanted to spin around or smack her hand against something to stop the shaking she felt in her nerves like an electric current. If she hadn't been so big or worried about a baby falling out of her, she'd have thrown a foot-stomping, maniac-dancing temper tantrum.

She hugged the bag of pads to her side, squeezing her forearm as hard as she could as she hustled awkwardly toward the bathroom. She was about to step over the threshold when the next contraction came with none of the warning of its predecessors and with a ramped-up sense of urgency Melanie didn't know was possible. It left as fast as it came having jolted her into a new state of consciousness, one that gave her marching orders to take the towel off the bar and lay it on the floor to be topped by several of the pads and then wash her hands. She obeyed and stepped out of her shorts and underwear.

Then Melanie got down on all fours and reached past her enormous belly to the place where it all began. Elizabeth had told her about a doula who, while expecting her first child, bragged that she planned to check her own dilation. Sarah said she wasn't in favor of checking her clients, but Melanie wondered if she could tell anything by reaching into the narrow space through which something much bigger than her fingers was anxious to emerge.

She hardly even had to enter herself. It was as though all her anxiety and concern had been about a mere fiction until that point when she truly understood she had created a person. A person with hair.

J. Howard

Who Were You When Kennedy Was Shot?

A D.C. area writer, J. HOWARD coordinates A Splendid Wake and teaches writing at Montgomery College. A 2016 finalist in the Moving Words competition, her poems have appeared in *MiPOesias*, *On Barcelona*, *Winners: A Retrospective of the Washington Prize*, *Whose Woods These Are: A Journal of the Word Works Residence at the Joaquin Miller Cabin, Rock Creek Park, Washington, D.C., from 1976 to 1983*, and *Teaching English in the Two-Year College*.

You asked Clare, the maid, if anyone would ever bomb the United States, and she said no, absolutely not, giving you that look suggesting that you were a strange little thing to be endured by your parents. In retaliation, you stepped on a crack in the sidewalk, secretly dedicating it to Clare, and the two of you continued walking towards the American embassy for a quick visit with your father, who smiled indulgently and assured you that no one would ever attack the United States.

Unconvinced, you continued to design bomb shelters each night before you fell asleep.

When your family had moved to Caracas, you had been told to be still if a robber ever broke into the house, but no one really told you how, so you practiced when you went to bed at night, focusing so intensely that you'd stop breathing for a while and your muscles would be clenched tightly, from your teeth to your toes. Designing bomb shelters, specifically a secret one that could only be accessed by you or your family, relaxed you, made you feel that even if robbers broke in, everyone would be safe. You'd fall asleep working on some problem in your plan.

Every morning you'd stand at the edge of the front yard, in those tan corrective shoes that you despised, holding onto your Hector Heathcoat lunchbox and your leather book bag, the bag that had your name, address, and phone number written inside in your mother's clear schoolteacher script. You didn't really need it since she had made you memorize the information almost as soon as you'd moved into the neighborhood, just in case someone tried to kidnap you en route to or from Campo Alegre, where, despite a hideous bus ride to school complete with the fear of vomiting all over everyone, you managed to be one of the strongest readers in first grade.

Years later, an older you would wonder how it was that you were such a star in the primary grades when you'd barely gone to kindergarten. An even older you would realize that being an early reader, in two languages, probably had something to do with it, though at the time, you were lonely in your reading group of one, even though you were reading third-grade readers which were much more interesting than Dick and Jane and their Spanish counterparts, Maria and Marco. The other students gathered in their circles near Mrs. Stutler. Occasionally a student would ask for help. You watched the drama of the walk, the attention Mrs. Stutler gave as she bowed her gray-haired head towards the child. You learned to pretend that you needed help.

And then, at home, you'd spread out the *Turpial* and read about war in Vietnam, trudging through sentences with words like "U.S. intelligence" and "boycott." While dripping a chocolate Popsicle all over the newsprint, you'd relax and forget about the trouble you'd just caused, or the freshet of chocolate pooling on the carpet. Soon enough, Clare would join your mother—each brandishing one of your father's leather belts—in a lively chase around the house, trying to get to you because, in a moment of anger—or maybe it was inconvenience—you'd called your mother an idiot for caring about the stain on the rug.

You were the kind of kid who took very quickly to climbing things, like furniture, concrete walls, and trees. Until your bike was stolen, you also took to bicycling all over the neighborhood without telling other people where you were going. "You could have been kidnapped," your mother would yell, her face turning red and then purple. "You can't take off like that! This isn't the United States!" Riding the long way to your friend's house so that you could look at all of the varied Italian modern houses or coast down a hill was too important to you, though you couldn't have explained why to your mother. You never divulged that you'd explored the ruins down the street, which you knew, because the house was worn down to rubble, that it was no doubt the birthplace of Simon Bolivar.

When pressed to confess your misdeeds to your father, you relied on the catechism you were learning from the old nuns at the church. "I was sinning, Dad. The devil took advantage of me." You'd say, while your father cast a confused look at your mother, who stood nearby, red-faced and unconvinced that the problem was theological.

You were fairly observant and noticed one tired Friday when Mrs. Garcia, the teacher next door, came into your classroom and whispered to Mrs. Stutler. You couldn't hear what they were saying, but you could feel somehow, that beyond the long window, beyond the pink and brown quartz of the hill next to the building, and maybe even beyond that, something was going on. You walked quietly with your classmates to the buses and noted that every single adult was lined up, from the janitors to the principal, watching the students climb on buses, which were not peeling away with the noisy energy of relieved students, but were parked at the curb, inert. Even Lucy Goosie, the third grader who made your ride miserable every afternoon on the bus with the greeting "Hello, Vomit Face," sat quietly in her seat.

The principal gathered the bus drivers and spoke to them, while the teachers watched the children, who returned their gazes or stared straight ahead. A few of the older students whispered among themselves: "Dallas... the president...Kennedy?" but gradually quieted down. Finally, the driver hopped on the bus, yanked the door shut, and drove away from the school. He wasn't taking the regular route, nor was he driving as quickly as he usually did. The bus seemed to be circling the city and dropping children off in an unfamiliar pattern. The phrase "Me llama Joanna. 33-38-51. Quinta Dahlia, La Floresta, Avenida El Seman," played in your mind, and you traced it over and over on your book bag until the foul smell of the refuse outside, mixed with the sour smell of end-of-the-day lunchboxes began to overtake you, and you hoped that a headache was all that you'd have that afternoon.

After driving past the embassy, unusually crowded with people in the parking lot, the bus rolled onto the Avenida and stopped, roaring and gasping, in front of Quinta Dahlia. You jumped off the steps and ran up the path to the door. As usual, you shook the knob, calling out "I'm home now, open the door," but you did not hear your mother or Clare reply, "Please. Open the door please." Instead, the door was already open and you walked inside. No mother stretched out on the chintz sofa reading *Ladies' Home Journal*. No Clare. Even on the afternoons that your mother went to some diplomatic function, Clare would be there, fussing with your brother or dusting the room. You dropped your book bag in the hallway and took your lunchbox into the kitchen. No one was there to remind you to put your lunchbox near the sink, not on the table, please, and stay out of the freezer. So you returned to the hallway, kicked off your shoes, and in your worn, gray anklets, slid down the cool tiled floor. Through the family room, past the concrete and tile bar where you used to hide from your mother, past Spooky, your cat, curled up on the brown rocker almost past the maid's quarters, you sailed until you heard the crackling of a radio tuned to a channel far away. You followed the sound to Clare's room and found your mother sitting on a chair next to the black Bakelite radio. Clare stood behind the ironing board, holding the iron, but the white shirt hung motionless from the board. You knew better than to say anything to them.

A man's voice, in English, emerged from that crackling static, announcing that the president had died. Clare sighed and crossed herself, gazing at her votive candles. Your mother's eyes watered up and she wiped them with the crumpled tissue tucked in her shirtsleeve. Neither woman moved, except to lean closer to the radio, which strained to bring the news from Florida. You pivoted silently and crept down the hall to your room, crawled into the closet with the wall safe, and felt something more intense than a spanking or feeling nauseous on the school bus begin to pulsate in your gut. Soon your head hurt, and you stayed in the closet, and would stay there until you heard your father shouting: "Where is she? She should be home from school by now. I'm going to drive back there and look for her."

You opened the door to the cool circulating air and ran to the living room, crying "Daddy! I'm here!" Still in his black suit, your father stopped hunting for the keys in his pocket and pulled you up into a hug. The sound of your mother's voice demanding to know where you'd been and the maid's clucking sounds seemed distant, and the pain in your head heard the rhythm of his heart, and you felt safe.

Margaret Hutton

The Heiress and the Radioman

MARGARET HUTTON's short fiction has appeared in several magazines, including the *Sun* and the *Chattahoochee Review*. She earned an MFA from George Mason University where she was named the Heritage Writer for distinguished fiction. Currently, she is working on a novel.

He lay on the floor for two days before they found him. "Dehydration, poor nutrition," the doctors said.

"A dizzy spell," he and Judith tell others afterward. It was true that when Judith broke her hip and went into the hospital Robert had little appetite. He may have skipped a meal or two. But, really, he can take care of himself. Except for one dreadful week, almost forty years earlier, they haven't spent a night apart. Surely it was natural, even a sign of his vitality, that her absence unnerved him a bit. At ninety-three, he's hardly a spring chicken.

Barring an unforeseen accident, Judith, who is ten years younger, will outlive him. His trip to the hospital uncovered the bad, but not terrible, diagnosis of bladder cancer. Bladder cancer means pain, he knows, but pain he can bear.

More upsetting news is that after the paramedics lifted him onto a stretcher, they looked at their surroundings and called social services. Robert and Judith haven't been home yet—they are now in a rehab facility with their cat, George, and a radio that Judith gave Robert long ago, while she gets physical therapy for her hip, and their apartment gets a "makeover. Fresh white paint on the walls, new carpet," the social worker, Freya, tells them. "It's quite spacious, you know. You're lucky to have such a big apartment."

"Where's all our stuff? My books?" he asks.

"My creative expressions?" Judith wants to know.

"A lot had to be removed," Freya says in a soothing voice, gently smiling. "You had a lot of stuff in there, and much of it was…damaged."

How will he remember what he's read? He could never remember until he saw the title on the spine and pulled it down from the shelf, or off the floor.

"Demeaned," Judith says. "We've been demeaned."

It isn't the first time. And then she finishes his thought. "The workers at George's vet. Remember what they called us? The dirty people."

EVEN WHEN HE WAS A small boy, his mother said, "You worry too much. You let go of one worry and pick up another. You reach for a worry the way other kids reach for candy."

Was that such a sin?

What worries him now is that his last thought in their old apartment before his spell was whether five one-hundred-dollar bills were still in a book on the shelf. He doesn't know why he went to look that day. The bills could have been there for months, even years. He found the book, all right, and the money, and laid both on a chair, then sat down to rest. The next thing he knew he was in a hospital. He's asked Freya to look into the matter, but she's said nothing about it.

THEY WARNED HIM. YEARS AGO, his family said, don't marry her. But they were married in early 1960, wintertime, and that summer his parents came to where they lived in Washington, D.C., for a visit. On the second day, his father said to him, "Leave now. I had no idea she was this crazy—why didn't you tell me? She'll ruin your life. You could still get an annulment. Your life was good. Not a thing wrong with it."

"Crazy is a strong word, Pa. She's very kind."

"You are living with a child."

He didn't have a response to that. All his brothers were married. It was no way to live, alone as he had.

They could hear Judith talking to his mother. "I went to Parsons to study art and met Isaac Soyer. He told my father, 'Judith's the only one in the class with any flair, but she's sick, and you need to marry her off.'

Then I took my portfolio to Edith Halpert's gallery in the city and sat at her desk. Mrs. Halpert looked at it and said, 'Live a little.' Three words. Then she turned and walked upstairs. I couldn't speak or move. I waited, sure Mrs. Halpert had more to say than three words. Then I followed her up the steps to a room that also looked out onto East 51st, a big plate glass window and Mrs. Halpert a dark shape against it. She turned to see who was there and then turned back toward the window. Turned her back on me. I went downstairs, gathered my pieces of art in my portfolio, and walked all the way home across the Brooklyn Bridge—"

"Judith," Robert called to her, knowing that the story had already gone too far, and where it was going next. His father's eyes were full of loathing for him.

"What, dear?"

"It's time for something to eat, don't you think?"

His father said, "Don't bother, we're leaving," and he went to pack his things. As he and his mother left through the front door, his mother said, "I'm sending you some recipes. You can't call that food," she said, "everything from a can."

Later, over their soup, Judith said, "I think your father is given to sporadic meanness." She has labels like this for everything. It's her primary—no, her only—means of organization. Then she said, "You didn't let me finish the story when they were here. That wasn't very nice."

"I know the end of the story. The end of the story is that we get married."

He hadn't wanted his father to hear the end, how she wanted to jump off the bridge, but didn't. Robert has heard the story dozens of times. She went home, closed the door to her room, but her father knocked. "What did she say, Mrs. Edith Halpert?" her father asked.

"She said 'to live a little.'"

"That's good advice. At the rate you're going though, you won't. We need to find you a husband."

AS A YOUNG MAN, ROBERT left Brooklyn and went to a university in Pennsylvania, where he got an F in organic chemistry, and though he had an A in another course—what was it, some kind of applied mathematics—this flunked him out and made him eligible for the draft. First he went to Camp Shelby and Gulfport for training, then to Tampa and other parts south to learn to be a radio operator. They did nothing for weeks it seemed, except fly to Cuba and back, playing. Nothing prepared them for flying from England over Germany, anti-aircraft missiles aimed at them. He was the only one on his crew to fly thirty-five successful bomber missions over Germany. Five or six times they almost lost their lives. Only once did they have to bail out when the plane was low on fuel, less than two thousand feet above France. "Worry-bird," the commander had called him then, when he was the first to ask what the pilot wanted the crew to do. Robert sent the distress signal, then pulled the red handle to open the door, and called out each man's name who jumped headfirst. He was the last crew member off before the pilot belly-landed the plane.

When he thought of it now, it was as if someone else had done those things: asked the question, sent the signal, opened the door, pulled his own ripcord.

He returned to the States, to Washington, with his love of radios, watches, clocks. He liked nature, so he got his degree in geography on the GI Bill, finished at twenty-nine. For ten years he lived on his own. Subsisted. Going to work each day, coming home to his room in a boarding house, eating with near strangers. Occasionally going for walks in the woods.

His parents, his Aunt Lois—not a nice woman, by the way—all thought he was queer. Couldn't talk to girls. Stuttered. W-w-w-would you like to g-g-g-g-o out sometime? But his Aunt Lois had had success with men like him who couldn't find love another way. She knew a girl in Brooklyn, so she set them up. They took a walk, ate supper somewhere you could dance. But Robert didn't dance, so they watched.

Later Lois asked Judith, "Did he talk to you? Because he didn't say a word to any of the others."

He knew she was sick, because she told him. She told him everything, including that she had a rich uncle who was going to leave her all his money. He had heard of this rich man. When Robert was in the war, hovering above death, Judith was only a girl of thirteen, living around the corner from his family in Brooklyn, though the two had never met. Later they put it together: her Uncle Mickey knew Aunt Lois; his Uncle Roger had worked with her Uncle Larry. Like dormant wires waiting a connection, they seemed meant for each other.

JUDITH IS SAYING TO THE nurse who's come to take his vitals, "My father was a gentleman, a machinist." Then about her mother: "My mother was educated, not an accent on her. She was an executive secretary for a munitions company—she knew what was coming and going before the big boys did—but then she met my father." Robert listens to her with the interest of someone who has never heard this story. "And she gave me dancing lessons, elocution lessons from Mother Superior at the church on the corner in Staten Island. I was so sad when those lessons ended for me and Marshall, my brother who was three years older. I cried. I remember she gave me her handkerchief and said, 'It's OK to cry.'"

At this point Robert interrupts and says, "What's missing from this story is she was a poor mother."

"Oh, no she wasn't," says Judith.

"Oh, she was, too." To the nurse he says, "She's in denial."

"No blaming. No shame, no blame. That's what we've got in the White House. Blaming doesn't do any good. It doesn't solve the problem."

"Yes it does. Face and accept and you won't do it. Remember Dr. Day, she said you need to face and accept."

"You're talking about things that are supposed to be private." To the nurse, she says, "See, this is all I get when I ask him for some help."

"That's not true. You know most of the time I keep quiet." What her mother had done to her, he didn't know. Judith was always told not to upset her father, who had a heart condition, but she could never avoid doing that. "Go in your room, express yourself with your art, your writing," everyone said. A father dying, that undoes you when the mother's no good. That's when she ended up in the hospital, when she was eighteen and left alone with her mother. An unbearable situation, along with the feeling she might have caused his death. When she went to the hospital in Vermont, she got to do all her "creative expressions." She was the youngest person there. "I thought they were all my mommies and daddies," she has said more than once.

Judith, with her white hair, her heavy-lidded blue eyes, her broad forehead, is wearing red today. Looking at her is as familiar as looking at his own reflection in the mirror, a conjugal phenomenon, he knows. What will happen to her when he's gone? She cannot care for herself. He is relentless in mentioning this to every person he meets at the rehab center.

AFTER MARRYING JUDITH, HE MOVED from a paper-pushing job at Commerce to a packing services company and then to the Defense Intelligence Agency. He knew he wasn't making a difference. At first motherboards excited him, but the future was in zeroes and ones and he had no interest. He only wanted to wire something together. He wanted to open a thing up to see how it worked. Fix watches. Tinker. He was tinkering all right, stacking paper clips on his desk.

One day he came home from work to an empty apartment. He called for Judith in each of their three rooms. His first thought was that she was out feeding the birds. That's the only thing she would do by herself. He felt for his set of car keys in his pocket and found the spare in a drawer; she would never try to drive. So he left the door unlocked in case she came back, and he set off through the parking lot and up to the grassy area adjacent to the reservoir—through hill and dale, Judith called it—then along the fence line, looking over the water. This is where they came most days. Canadian geese, swans—they fed them all, they didn't care. Treat all birds with respect, Judith would say. He passed two or three people on the walk but he couldn't stop them to ask if they'd seen her. He couldn't. Judith always had done the talking. He reached the end of the path and turned around.

Soon it was dark, and he found his voice enough to use the telephone. Calling her mother was out of the question. He called Marshall, her brother, in Florida. "Call the police, Robert. Do I need to come up there? Tell them how sick she is."

"Paranoid schizophrenic," he explained when the police said she would need to be gone longer before they filed any report. That still didn't get their attention. He'd begun to consider that she might have walked in the other direction, away from the reservoir, which would have taken her to the steep ravine above the river. What if she'd gone that way and tried to reach the water? Dear God, why hadn't he thought of that? He didn't sleep all night, waiting until it was light enough to look. Then he set out again, turning right instead of left, and sure enough, he came upon the river in no time. He saw clearly through the leafless brush and brambles to the water. They never walked this way, but how close it was, how easy.

He remembered then what it was like to have the antenna blown off their aircraft. He'd gone quiet in the center of the plane, alone in his compartment, closed his eyes, and waited for the dark to envelop him, his duty over. On that same mission he had turned his heated suit up to twenty, the maximum, only to have it short circuit—a surge of heat down the middle of his back and then nothing. Seventy-two degrees below zero.

He called the police again, right after he called into work, saying he couldn't come in. He'd already said a prayer: "Dear God, if you bring Judith home, I'll never go back to that job. I'll spend my life caring for her." He knew it wasn't much of a bargain, since it was what he wanted to do anyway.

She didn't have their telephone number. How had he left her so unprepared for something like this? He waited six days for her to be found. Six agonizing days when he was paralyzed with worry and fear, surrounded by her bottles of Elmer's glue, papers with found things stuck to them, bobby pins, leaves, bottle caps, bird feathers. She had a particular idea of keeping house.

Had he missed some sign? Caring for her depended on his ability to sense these changes in her. The night before she had woken up crying and he'd consoled her back to sleep, but then he'd lain awake himself. Maybe his own fatigue explained why he didn't notice anything out of the ordinary the next morning.

The phone finally rang. The police had picked her up in Arizona. "In the desert?" Robert stupidly asked. He couldn't imagine.

"What were you trying to do, give me a heart attack?" he said in an even, relieved voice when he saw her again. She had no memory of being gone; it was assumed she hitchhiked her way. "That wasn't me who did that. That was someone else," was all she ever said about the incident. There were more doctors, more medicines, more diagnoses. Theirs would be a life of books—just now they have Mark Twain on the table, Rosamunde Pilcher next to him—a life of feeding birds, of telling stories.

TODAY THE NURSE IS THERE to change his catheter—there is blood where there shouldn't be, and incessant pain. *Die Fledermaus* is playing on the radio. Judith starts up about where their money is. They have a niece, Judith's niece, who's supposed to be looking after things. They have maybe three hundred thousand dollars invested. They've been smart with money: they haven't spent any. There is only so much cat food for George they can buy, only so many cans of tuna fish they can eat, only so many glue sticks she can use. Oh, the doctors have cost extra, sure, but they have been savvy with insurance, his pension. They conserve. Judith is now talking about the money she was going to come into. Her uncle had made money in real estate, and his wife—she wasn't the most sophisticated woman, uneducated—they loved Judith. "But another aunt and uncle—they were going to kill Judith if I hadn't come into the picture," he tells the nurse, now wide-eyed.

"Oh, I don't think so," says Judith.

"Oh, yes, that's the kind of people they were. They got the uncle and aunt drunk and changed the will."

"Oh, no, Robert, don't say those things."

"She can't accept that," he says to the nurse.

And then Judith says, "We're waiting here to die. We're at your mercy. Robert, here, says what's the point?"

BACK IN THEIR BLINDINGLY BRIGHT, unrecognizable apartment, his life has been reduced to sensation and sound. Nothing hurts, but he can no longer open his eyes to take in the harshness of their emptied-out life, so many belongings gone. "Kindness," Judith is telling the nurse, whose name he can never remember, "a little kindness. That's how we've managed." There is Freya in the background, talking of money. The nurse holds his feet, saying, "They're still warm."

He has heard on the radio that birds adjust their tunes when they sing to each other in the city. Their lower frequencies can't be heard above the din of traffic, and tall buildings absorb high frequencies. They have to cast a new pitch somewhere in the middle. He relates to this. They are two strange birds, aren't they, he wants to say out loud. He remembers when he saw Judith at her door that first evening they met, he knew something was wrong. This pretty woman was smiling at him. Such a thing had never happened.

Soon, he knows, she will go and feed the birds, if only from the parking lot. The last thing he hears is her saying, "We are a country people."

Faith Reyher Jackson

Cedelia

New York native FAITH REYHER JACKSON, a professional dancer who for years served as headmistress of the Washington Academy of Ballet, left behind three fine sons, five grandkids, and several well-written fiction and nonfiction books when she died, in 2012, at age ninety-three. Her short story "Cedelia" may have been her greatest creation. Like Faith herself, the story's ten-year-old heroine is precocious, daring, vulnerable, and determined to be loved.

From the time she was eight until she was ten, Cedelia Jane Ronald could be heard all over Shipley when she wanted to make a big noise, and for those two years she did little else.

"That child found the one poor note in the whole world and the whole state of Kentucky and hangs on it," Parcy said. "I never knew a child in this life who couldn't sing some kind of tune, why did the Lord give her to us? Honey baby, come here and let me try to teach you a pretty song," but slippery Cedelia Jane was out and gone, her one note trailing her across the land. She sang at full bellow as she careened across the fields and hurled herself into the woods.

Once she swung on a branch that extended over the river and plopped herself into the water, not knowing how to swim, not caring, daring, daring the people in her universe to let her drown. She exhausted the family because she had to be watched all the time.

"Well, that bull call she makes ain't pretty," muttered the old woman, "but at least it tell us where she be—most o' the time."

"All of us but the one she's after, Parcy," sighed Cedelia's mama, Alys Husted Ronald. "If he wished, her daddy could straighten her out yesterday."

The heiress to a river barge fortune still was hopelessly in love with Hallam "Hap" Ronald, her handsome, wayward husband, who was twenty years her senior. But she also knew the current master of Shipley

Farms—which had produced its share of champion thoroughbreds over the years before Hap's boozing, gambling, womanizing father, "Booter" Ronald, had run it into the ground—would never be a doting daddy to his youngest. "It seems, however, that Mr. Ronald cannot be bothered with such trivial family matters."

"Yes, ma'am," agreed Parcy. "I tell you true, on heaven and earth, I never see a small girl so wroughted up."

Cedelia, hiding behind the door, heard them and sneaked away. She could be as silent playing Indian scout when she snooped on the household as she could be noisy when she had to blow off steam. There were days, like this one, when Cedelia rampaged and found it hard to slow down and walk, when running was not quick enough, when the wind was blowing too high to reach. "Wind! Wind! Come down," she called and felt it pushing her faster and faster to the rye field.

The rye, glistening and billowing beneath a morning sun, beckoned her in. Singing her hideous note, she gave herself up to a wild dance, running and trampling in wide arcs, loving the way the tall grain bounced back at her as she held her arms wide and leaped through it. She received a first class licking for damaging the crop, but she was not sorry.

"I had to do it," she said, "or bust."

Everything she did in her noisy calamitous way called out for Papa's attention: Please, Papa, notice me, love me, punish me. Papa paid her no mind. She would find him wherever he was on the farm and stand right by him while he spoke to a visitor or gave orders to one of his men. He never sent her away for he never seemed to notice that she was there. Cedelia did not give up. Beneath the hurt she had a well-guarded core of pride. Papa could ignore her but he could not deny that she was part of the same earth and sky. Like Papa, there was no other place for her than this thousand-acre spread in southern Kentucky that her great-great-granddaddy first had farmed: Shipley, with its crops and stock, and its partner, the Ohio River, the Ronald road to market. Seemed like she was born holding all of the secrets of her land and family, grief and good; she knew from first knowing when the house was in trouble, and when it was calm. Indoors, there was always Mama and Parcy, sometimes Ruby and giggly Jasmine, who told her "secrets" Cedelia did not understand. But mostly, there was Junius, houseman of all duties, which included bringing Cedelia to her tutor when he could find her.

ఌఌ

CEDELIA AND HER BROTHER, HAL-JUNIOR, tracked Papa as much as they could when he was not off to Louisville, or up River; it was as if the house held its breath till he came home. Cedelia learned the sometime whiskey smell of him, and she and Hal-Junior knew without being told, they must never speak of the woman, Esther, even to each other. It was wiser to pretend she did not exist, to pretend they never saw faces growing up with them with a telltale Ronald nose or chin. They had learned never to ask Mama where Papa was because it was too painful to see her go all pale and quiet. "I don't know," she would just say, and walk away from them.

Once, at supper, Hal-Junior tried to draw Papa out, which Cedelia thought brave. "Where have you been this time, sir?"

"On the *Shipley Belle*, son," his father answered kindly, referring to the once-stately stern wheeler that Booter had won in a poker game and had the rare good sense to hold onto. Hap Ronald continued to eat as if he were alone at the table.

When Papa was quiet like that, which was most of the time, Mama and Booter and Cedelia and her brother rarely spoke. When they did, it appeared to intrude on Papa's thoughts, and nobody wanted to annoy Papa—there'd be too big a price to pay. The food was served quietly; whenever a fork sounded too loudly against a plate, Mama would give a little start and Papa might frown, that is, if he heard.

"Drat!" Hal-Junior persisted. "If you were in Cincinnati, I could've come back with you, this vacation."

Cedelia knew Papa loved his son above all else, but he did not favor the talk just now.

"It wouldn't have hurt any, either," the boy said with his engaging smile, as if Papa were paying any real attention, "for my pals to see me come aboard."

Hap Ronald inclined his head, but did not answer.

"The *Shipley Belle*," Booter said, "could find itself to Covington without anyone at the helm."

"In your day, perhaps, sir. Whatever else I am," said Papa, his voice like steel, "I am not a gambler. The tables at Covington, Ohio, have never seen me."

"I think they have," said the old man, bitterly. The casinos had seen plenty of him back in the day, when he and Shipley Farms were both something to be reckoned with.

Cedelia Jane squirmed in her chair, trying to obey Mama's rule she must not speak out at table. This was too much for her. She knew every inch of their waterfront, she had often slipped into the *Belle* when the gangplank was down.

"Won't you take us with you sometime, please, Papa?" she said. "I've never been to Cincinnati, and slept on a boat. The little bedrooms looked so pretty—"

"Cabins," Hal-Junior corrected.

"Cabins," Cedelia repeated, "with the flowers and chocolates."

Her father stared right through her and went on eating.

Cedelia remembered the bright colors of the lady's kerchief she once had seen—red, orange, and blue—dropped carelessly on a chair in the *Belle*'s main cabin. Mama had never worn such a thing. Was it still there, the child wondered. She was bursting to tell what she knew, but she could feel Papa's rising anger and wisely bit her tongue instead.

"Someone," said Papa, icily, "should be able to restrain the girl from running wild, keep her out of private places, and raise her to be a lady."

"How do you plan to keep her locked up in this house," Mama said, "after she has finished her lessons—and very well too, Cedelia—I want to know? You gave her a pony, she has her own legs, and she'd rather be out of doors than breathe. What do you expect?"

Cedelia hung tight for his answer.

Papa left the room. Mama went out the other door. Cedelia found her way to bed. That was the way such evenings usually ended. Nothing much new in the House of Ronald.

❦

CEDELIA WATCHED MAMA WANDERING THROUGH rooms as if they could give up secrets, listened when she played her piano in a way that filled her with a torrent of confusion and sadness, just like Mama must be feeling. Then, she might begin to play with a lyrical serenity that made her daughter stand taller and smile. When Mama assailed the piano as if she were trying to find her way in an insane world, Cedelia would dash for Parcy's lap.

"Why does she play like that, Parcy?"

The old woman would rock and hold her close.

"I don't rightly know honey sugar. The Lord has ways of humbling us all."

Why, Cedelia wondered, did the Lord not humble Papa? Even a child could see how hurt her mama was by those children in the houses down by the creek, the ones that no one was supposed to recognize; and by her husband's "not-thereness" when he was most visible, and then the long times when he was just plain gone. But Mama never talked about them—at least not to Cedelia.

She, on the other hand, could not get the other Shipley children out of her thoughts. Day after day, she rode her pony, down past the little houses way over on the edge of the property and never saw anyone her age, only toddlers. Where were the children she remembered from when she was small, who came to the house and stayed most all day playing with her while their mothers worked? Had they seen her first and were hiding indoors? Wherever else she went at Shipley, someone was bound to stop work long enough to call out, "Morning, child, you enjoying your ride?" or make a little fuss over her.

What was it like, Cedelia wondered, living in those little houses which, years ago, Mama had ordered repaired and painted, grass sown, picket fences built to enclose the yards? Mama had even called in a plumber and well digger, Parcy had told her proudly back then, and made them run pipelines and tear down the privies, and then put in electric. Papa had taken some extra trips down River those times, Cedelia remembered, and her granddaddy had howled at the cost of "all that needless fixing up," as he called it.

"You spend money some awful goddam ways, Lady Bountiful," Booter had told Mama one day when Papa was gone. "Ain't it a mite ironic," he had sneered, "you dressing up the quarters for all those mammies and brats?"

"You may call it what you like, sir," Mama had coolly replied. "I call it keeping out the flies and mosquitoes and disease. You may have all the dengue fever you wish, but I am going to do everything necessary to keep my family—and, yes, all of Shipley's families—well."

Mama never let Booter draw her temper, no matter how angry she was inside. Cedelia was proud of her those times. Yet, the child thought, the cabins were awfully small for all the people in some of them, and truthfully, getting shabby again. Did Mama notice, or care anymore? Did any of those girls she remembered ever wonder what it was like to be her?

One day, she followed Papa when he was riding in that direction; he never noticed. Papa never walked when he could ride, he had so much to do. She wished he would take her on his rounds the way he did Hal-Junior when he was home on holiday, so she could understand better what-all he did. She had heard her uncle say Papa might be a hellraiser but he was the best damn farmer and horse breeder in Kentucky. Papa was her pride and love. He looked as if he had been born on that off roan. She trotted after him, her heart full of worship.

Up ahead, he dismounted and went into the third cabin. Cedelia pulled up in the shade and waited.

He was not in the house but a minute before he came out, still talking over his shoulder to the woman who followed him and stood in the doorway with a baby in her arms. Cedelia Jane Ronald thought she would dry up and be blown away by the storm in her head as she watched her father finish what he had to say, then put a gentle finger on the baby's cheek, and smile. A loving Papa-smile Cedelia prayed to receive. She leaned over the pony's neck and tried to cough or cry, but nothing came up.

Papa just mounted and rode off without looking around, not seeing her, but the woman did. She looked across the yard at her and Cedelia looked back. A long time. Then the woman walked over and gazed up at Cedelia on her pony.

"Your mama know you're here, does she?"

Suddenly there were several children standing with her and gaping at Cedelia, who had not seen where they came from. She stared back, frightened and newly shy, but held to her pride.

"I'm allowed to go where I want here, since it all belongs to Papa."

"Maybe," said the girl with the pigtail down her back like Cedelia's, and about her age; one of the very girls, Cedelia realized, whom she remembered. "But this is our yard," the girl said, "so you better get."

She stepped back and gave the pony a thwack across his rump; never having been so treated, he bucked and galloped away. Cedelia, unprepared, fell off. When she limped home, Mama went right up in smoke. Papa went to Louisville, where he had moved Esther and her children, Hal-Junior told her, and Parcy was sour with Cedelia for the longest time.

"Persons should stay where they belong and not get families riled up," she had declared.

"But I'm the one who was hurt," Cedelia said, in a small voice. "I'm the one who was hurt."

Ↄↄ

IT WAS IN MID-JUNE 1926, right after Cedelia turned ten, that she rode the plantation bell. "A full decade, miss, my, my," Mama had said to her on her birthday. "Maybe you'll cool down some, now."

Rather, she became more of a nuisance than ever, especially to her brother and his friend Oren, who worked on the place. They could never escape from her tagging along. Just when they thought they were free, there came Cedelia, panting and grimy.

Early in the morning of the Bell Day, the boys were stealing away when Hal-Junior heard a sound behind them and knew she was there. He slowed down and pretended to examine the new bell rope, cutting his eyes around to see how close by she was hiding.

The Shipley bell was situated in the place most convenient to reach quickly, to ring in case of fire, accident, declaration of war, birth of a son and heir. It hung from a strong, eight-foot post with an arm, like a gibbet, with a stout cord to reach up and pull, hard. The cord was attached to the bell clapper, which made a splendid resonance.

Hal-Junior saw the length of shiny rope from which the new pull was cut, carelessly left over a corner of the watering trough.

"You coming fishing or do you want to stay here all day?"

Oren had not heard Cedelia.

"Hold on, I'm coming." Hal-Junior picked up the rope, and imitated his sister's voice. "'Oh, Oren, I do love to swing.' Guess what we can do with this, Orry?"

"Burn your hands to pieces, you fool, that's what," Oren said, "or try to hold on when it slips away fast and skins you awful. Let's go."

"Look," Hal-Junior said. "It's easy to make a perfect seat to sit in. I'll just make a loose knot with this end and tie it to the bell cord, so: now throw the other end over the top, bring it down and fasten here, sort of like a noose, see? Presto! It will tighten around you as you start to swing and you'll be snug as a sausage."

"No thanks!"

He meant to untie the knot and free the rope, but they fooled around some more before going on to the river, beginning to laugh wildly, showing off to the hidden girl once Oren caught on, so Hal-Junior forgot.

Cedelia waited until she was sure they were not hiding to spy on her. She went over to the improvised seat and looked it over, doubtfully. She had to stand on tiptoe to grasp the cord at the top of the noose before she could give a little jump and slip her legs through it.

There ensued an ominously even bong-bong, regulated by the pendulum swing of the limp girl. The noose had drawn up tightly under Cedelia's armpits and lifted her too far off the ground to stop herself. She had vomited, fainted, and was covered with bleeding rope burns.

The boys knew immediately what had happened and ran back in terror to join the men already there. They helped spread hay under the arc of Cedelia's swinging body as two of the men, with a nod to each other, spat on their hands and jumped for the rope. Their legs, drawn up and clinging to each other, made a safe basket between them for Cedelia. Their combined weight immediately slowed down her swinging and pulled the rope right off the bell. They fell in a tangle—the man underneath dislocated his shoulder when he pulled back from the man on top, who rolled away fast, to avoid crushing the child.

ღ

THE BROKEN RIBS AND LACERATIONS mended too slowly for a healthy girl. There was no more one-note and chatter. Cedelia did not care anymore; Papa was furious with her: "Little fool, frightening the devil out of us, hurting others, what possessed you?"

Parcy came upstairs to Cedelia's room.

"I declare, the quiet round here is worth a whole lot less than the song. Honey sugar, get up from there this minute and come to Parcy, now, and she'll make you all the apple poly and custard sauce you can eat, that is a promise, and though it pains me for us all, I'll take all that note you can sing to me."

Cedelia lay quietly in her bed.

Mama sat beside Cedelia in the evening. She put cloths wrung out of lavender water on her daughter's forehead, held her hands and soothed her when she became agitated in her dreams.

One night Cedelia woke and opened her eyes a crack and saw Mama, who looked as if she had all she could stand, go out on the landing and call down to Junius as he crossed the front hall.

"You go in that room this minute and tell Mr. Ronald to get his gun and come upstairs at once and shoot his daughter. It will be kinder than what he is doing to her now. Tell him exactly what I said."

When Papa came, Mama lingered near the door to listen. He sat down beside the bed and held his daughter's hand.

"It's Papa, crazy D-D-Jane."

"Papa."

"The D's are for Darling-Dumb. You scared us all senseless, you know that, don't you? I couldn't come in here when I was so angry, and see you all cut up."

"Yes, Papa."

As naturally as the river meets the shore, the man could charm the sting out of a wasp.

"Little one, take it slow and easy, but don't stay in here too long. Get well soon, understand?"

"Yes, Papa."

"No more shenanigans, mind, you're a young lady now."

"Yes...Papa."

It was a whisper; she was slipping back into herself. He waited for a moment, but suddenly, as he walked softly to the door, her eyes opened wide and she was fully awake.

"Papa."

He turned around.

Cedelia looked at him across the room. Her voice was ageless, cold as Papa's could be. She spoke as if there were only the two of them left in the world.

"Papa," she said. "Would you love me if I was brown?"

Kelly Ann Jacobson
Alma's Afgan

KELLY ANN JACOBSON is a fiction writer, poet, and editor who lives in Falls Church, Virginia. She received her MA in fiction at Johns Hopkins University, and she now teaches as a professor of English. Jacobsen is the author of several published novels, including *Cairo in White* and *The Troublemakers*, and one book of poetry titled *I Have Conversations with You in My Dreams*. Her work, including her published poems, short stories, and nonfiction, can be found at www.kellyannjacobson.com.

O n the eve of her two hundredth birthday, Alma Hudgins settles into her rocking chair like an old cat might settle in the sunny spot by the window: bone by bone, until her two jagged shoulders settle against the wood and her thin thighs ease into the crocheted cushion. From her third-story apartment she can see the city spread out below her glass balcony door—the city that has grown up around her like a rampart, though whom it's keeping out and whom in is a question on her mind on such quiet Sundays—and though her eyes have glossed over, she can still see the Washington Monument across the water, one red eye blinking its presence onto her silk screen vision. Not yet relighted, though it will be; just that artificial lantern, and Alma, and the rare wheel whoosh on the dark street of her Rosslyn neighborhood. She is waiting for something, but what thing it might be or when it will come is yet to be determined, so she pushes off the floor with her slippered feet and lets them sail as far as they can, always returning to the same two depressions in the worn blue carpet.

IN THE LINCOLN TOWN CAR near the front of the line, Mary Lynne looks down at her black buckle shoes and tries to tune out the sound of her mother's sobs, loud heaves of air that remind Mary Lynne of the suction of a vacuum hose against her palm. Her stockings cling to her moist thighs and itch the bottoms of her feet; moving slowly, she sticks a finger behind her heel and scratches the sole while maintaining her steady gaze on the hearse running a red light a few feet away. Big Benjy, her father, sits pressed against the window, his thick arms leaving smears of sweat on the door whenever he moves to touch her mother's unresponsive leg. In the small oak coffin speeding down Wilson Boulevard, her older brother, Jonah, lies like a statue between the layers of plush red fabric. Mary Lynne wipes a drip of sweat from her forehead with her sleeve.

As they pass their new apartment, a solid brick structure far away from the neighborhood where Jonah lost his life a week prior, the girl happens to look up and see a face peering back down at her from the third floor balcony. It is an ancient face with crags as deep as tree bark valleys; Mary Lynne has never seen someone so old, except maybe one of the homeless men sucking down a cigarette under the blue liquor store lights. A dull red afghan with white stick figure men marching down the sides, some kind of Native American print, shrouds the woman's body and falls to the concrete base of the balcony floor, where it pools around her feet. When their eyes lock, the woman reaches out a hand as if to pat Mary Lynne's hair, and Mary Lynne feels a strange, soothing sensation rub across her otherwise burning forehead. Her eyes relax their gaze, and her ears tune out her parents' sadness and focus on the slow breaths escaping her lips. Then the old woman puts her hand down, and immediately a cacophony of noise and heat and sorrow crash back down on her. The town car turns a corner, and both the old woman and the new apartment building disappear from view.

At the burial they balance Jonah's casket over the hole, and the pastor says some words about him that sound nothing like the boy Mary Lynne remembers. Her brother was kind but wild, like a stallion, always sneaking out at night to roam the city streets with his high school buddies or making trouble for the girls who lived further east and walked around with their short skirts and high heels one size too big and always wobbling. He didn't take her along much—after all, she was only fourteen, too young for beer pong or the feel of a man against her back in time to a turned-up bass—but when he snuck back through the fire escape he would sometimes find her sitting at the kitchen table, drinking warm milk or snacking on a cookie while she waited for his return, and would tell her stories about his conquests or the crazy stunt he pulled on the Metro with his friends. In her half sleep he seemed like a demon or an angel, lit from the inside with a kind of fire she could not yet understand, and even after the time Big Benjy caught him crawling through the window and whelped him on the ear or the time they put him in jail for possession, she knew he would never stop. He couldn't... that was Jonah, and he lived for the adrenaline his wanderings brought him like a junkie lives for his next hit, at least he did until it pulled him under like a rip tide and spit him out on the street, bleeding and unrecognizable.

When her mother takes a turn at the casket, her hands full of dry dirt, Mary Lynne walks up with her and holds her mother's shaking hand. Her father doesn't come—his eyes are averted towards the sky, as if he's arguing with the Lord—so when his wife falls, the only person to keep her head from cracking on the pavement is stick-armed Mary Lynne. As she struggles with the weight like a piece of heavy fruit, the girl realizes that from this day forward, her family will remain as they are today: Big Benjy, absent even when sitting in his recliner sipping a Bud; Lila, vacant eyes staring into the wall as she analyzes her failures as a mother; and Mary Lynne, left to shoulder the burden of Jonah's passing. They will never again play Pictionary during the Super Bowl commercials; they will never again share a can of cola on the front porch of their old house as the bustling city day turns to dusk. Everything will remind her of him, even math class: four corners make a solid square, like their dining room table, but three make a triangle from which balanced objects teeter and fall. She will see him as the protagonist in *The Giver*, or later, Holden Caulfield in *The Catcher in the Rye*; her essays about these books will be situational, subjective, and insufficient, and she will cry while writing them.

After the funeral, they enter their new apartment as one might enter a mausoleum; it is not just the boxes marked "Jonah" that cause them to shy away from unpacking, but the ones marked with their own names. Who are these people whose names disrupt the blank, white walls of the empty space? Who is Benjy, or Mary Lynne? Instead of organizing the kitchen utensils or even throwing their clothes into the creaky wooden drawers,

Big Benjy hands Mary Lynne his credit card so she can order pizza and tumbles with Lila onto their naked mattress. The next morning when Mary Lynne quietly opens her bedroom door on her way to school, her parents are still asleep in their Sunday best.

TWO WEEKS LATER, ALMA PUTS a kettle on for tea and sets out two cups, then waits in her rocking chair until she hears the school bus spit the teenagers onto the sidewalk and chug its way up Wilson. Though she is three stories up, she can hear the fidget of a key in the front lock; she can feel the light feet dancing on the stairs; she can smell the remains of an uneaten lunch drawing closer and closer to her apartment door. She can even see Mary Lynne's hand running through her ginger hair, five fingers like sea creatures in fiery waves, and can feel the dizzy panic seizing the child whenever she thinks of returning home. Alma empathizes with her—after all, she has seen all that Mary Lynne has seen, and more—but the girl must come on her own, without temptation or encouragement. Then the knock comes, light as a branch against a window, and Alma eases herself up onto two untrustworthy legs and makes her way to the front door.

"Hi," the girl says when Alma answers, shuffling her feet. "I see you watching from up here all the time, so I thought I'd say hello. I'm your new neighbor, in 3C."

"So you are." Alma's voice creaks.

"I'm sorry to bother you, I just didn't want to go home yet and I don't know the area..."

"Not to worry. It's a pleasure, Mary Lynne."

"How do you—"

"I know a lot about you. Now come in, please, before the tea gets cold, I'll tell you all about it."

Mary Lynne hesitates, and Alma listens to her thoughts: *Mom and Dad will kill me if they find out I went in a stranger's house... but they won't. They probably haven't even gotten out of bed.* The girl takes a step through the doorway, and Alma heads into the kitchen to get their mugs. Mary Lynne sits on the saggy brown couch, empty for over fifty years, and presses her blue uniform down against the suede seat. Alma hands her one of the hot cups, her hands shaking so much that some of the tea spills down the sides, but Mary Lynne takes it from her and pretends not to notice.

"When you're as old as me," Alma says with a cackle, settling back into her rocking chair, "it's amazing when you can even get out of bed in the morning."

"How old are you?" Mary Lynne asks, then blushes when she realizes how nosey her question sounds.

"Don't worry, you can ask me anything and I'll answer, if I can. I'm two hundred, as of yesterday, though I like to hope I don't look a day over one hundred and fifty. What, you don't believe me?"

Mary Lynne shakes her head.

"Well, I guess I can't prove it; cameras had barely even been invented by the time I was born. But no matter… you'll believe me, soon enough. How are your parents taking the loss?"

Mary Lynne looks down at her loafers, tiny leather boats floating in and out of Alma's very limited vision. "They're not taking it well… and neither am I, though at least I get out of bed every morning. It's like the world went through the wash and all the color drained out."

Alma shifts her eyes behind Mary Lynne's so that she is able to see the world from her perspective, as if she is peering through a ViewMaster with only black and white reels. "I'm almost at the end of my rope," Alma says as she wiggles her arms out of her shawl and holds them up, "but I think I still have a few tricks up my sleeve. Now, child, close your eyes and think of your favorite memory of Jonah: not a recent one, nothing unpleasant, just the happiest memory you can dig up." Alma watches a young boy's face come into focus, ashen in the blurry, dark world of Mary Lynne's tainted memories, and then a small guitar in his hands. He sits on a swing in a park that must have been near their old house, since he and Mary Lynne are too young in this moving picture to have wandered far from home on their own, and strums the strings in soft chords as he croons an acoustic version of a song he taught himself. Mary Lynne sits on the grass, thick and hearty spring grass still damp with dew, and their backpacks are piled near one of the park bushes. "Very good, Mary Lynne," Alma whispers, "this is the one." Then, with a wave of her hand, she uses an imaginary paintbrush to wipe the grass first as if she's wiping grime from a car window. The grass slowly greens, a luscious green that would rival an emerald tree boa, and then the color spreads to the tree leaves and bushes. Then she takes her brush to the flowers, filling them with pink and purple, and the swing, rubbing in tarnished silver chains and black rubber base. Alma lovingly brushes over Jonah's clothes—his sky blue cotton shirt, the texture of his jeans, his brown loafers—before hesitating at his face. "Remember this," she whispers to Mary Lynne, the one watching from above. "Share this with your parents." Alma adds light pink into his cheeks, green to his eyes, and red to his thick Irish hair. Jonah smiles, and then Alma pulls them out of the memory like one would stop a video, the whole scene blurring and then turning to static.

THAT NIGHT, MARY LYNNE RETURNS home to find her mother standing in the kitchen furiously unpacking. When she hears her daughter enter the apartment, Lila runs to the door and lifts Mary Lynne with such force that her empty shoes remain planted on the hallway floor. "Where have you been?" Lila asks, kissing Mary Lynne's forehead and cheeks. "We've been worried sick about you! Your father went driving around the whole city trying to find you."

"I was here, in the apartment building, at my new friend Alma's house."

"Who's Alma?"

Mary Lynne takes her mother's hand and leads her to Alma's front door, then knocks and knocks again, but no one answers. They can't hear the shuffle of Alma's socks or the whistle of tea on the stove, so Mary Lynne tries the handle and swings the unlocked door open to reveal a bare apartment, stripped of all color except the red afghan spread across the floor. Mary Lynne takes two of the corners and places them in her mother's hands, then grabs the other two and walks them close enough to create a perfect fold. "Look, Mom," Mary Lynne says, holding up the afghan. "Look at the beautiful color."

Sinta Jimenez

Elephants

SINTA JIMENEZ is a writer, fine artist, and fashion journalist. Her short stories, paintings, and poetry have been published in several literary magazines including *Underground Voices*, *Otis Nebula*, and the *Sheepshead Review*. She founded the digital agency Social Buzz Pros and is the founder and creative director of AMIHAN Life. In 2000, she was a recipient of a National Association for the Advancement of the Arts Award in Short Story. She serves on the board for the Mid Atlantic Foundation for Asian Artists. Born in Manila, raised in Washington, D.C., she received her MFA from Otis College of Art and Design in Los Angeles.

S he ran away from home at the age of thirteen. She could hold her drugs but not her liquor and didn't drink anything except for tomato juice and water. She was into wearing her hair long and stealing punk records from shops on Barnaby Lane. Sometimes she stripped when cash was low. Sometimes she sang in the rain.

She had several boyfriends but her favorite had blue eyes, lean muscles, and a tattoo of a gun on his hip. His name was Crimson and he hauled furniture for a moving company and always had eye drops in his pocket. They had the same embarrassed laugh and loved to fuck stoned. She read to him from *Steppenwolf* and they swore to each other they'd never grow old.

Any concert, any gig, she always made it backstage. She fucked the rockers and roadies of most well-known lineups in the early '90s. Slash was her favorite headliner in the sack and a bass tech for Fishbone named Nacho was excellent with his tongue. It was rumored she had inspired half a song or two but, more or less, she was a groupie oddity who didn't care about sex or fame. Family wouldn't be the right word but maybe something like it. She went to Glastonbury for three straight summers and one year saw Keith Richards walking with one of his daughters, the one he had with the blonde American swimsuit model not Anita. She thought about the father she never knew, the father who didn't give her his last name. He was a musician too.

She had an old lover who she went to see when there was nowhere else to go. He was a wealthy banker with an angry-eyed Cantonese wife back in Hong Kong. In his youth he had been a dandy, yet his prettiness was artificial and up close one felt a little cheated, the same as with silicone tits or saccharin-based candy. He'd affected an accent while studying at Cambridge for uni and often lied that he was a half-Bengali son of a sahib.

"Yes, I go by Richard, Dick if you like, but my birth name is Pan-duranga," he said in a badly calculated move to bring pandemonium into their aching hearts. In actuality his birth name was Archie and he was from Missouri.

Archie wanted her to call him grandfather and sometimes he called her grandchild. Not even Daddy which can be sexy at times, she thought. But grandfather. But like the others she wanted his money so she tolerated the creepiness. To Archie what she was there for was fine and standard enough. Not everyone has a heart of gold but not everyone has money like his either, he thought.

It was after seeing Archie that she made her most reckless and tender love with Crimson. She searched the streets for him, for his smoking pro-file and long-limbed swagger that was part thug, part haute couture. She went to his friends' cramped apartments where he bounced from couch to couch barely conscious, lost in his stone, but radiant in a way that made her both hungry and loving.

"There you are," she said.

"Jungle love you're driving me mad, you're driving me crazy-y," he sang.

She looked at him slowly, lingering over his dark eyelashes and the angles of his face. The line of his cheekbone drew gracefully down to the wet, delicate suck of his mouth. Crimson's skin was smooth and dewy. He reminded her of the German model Veruschka. Crimson's body had the same slender strength Veruschka's boasted. Bodies like the arched Gothic doorways of solitary churches surrounded by tall grass in the northern windswept terrains of the British Isles.

"I'm your jungle love, am I?"

"And you're driving me crazy-y," he smiled.

CRIMSON WENT OVER TO HIS clothes and took out a colorful little paper bundle of mango-flavored beedies.

She put on *White Light/White Heat* and they smoked the beedies together, appreciating the smooth inhalation and sweet taste of the Asian tobacco. The afternoon had turned to evening outside her window and the lamps glowed on the street below.

"My grandmother used to smoke these. The smell of burning cigarettes reminds me of her. She was from India, you know," he said looking up at the spiraling smoke.

"Wot? You're Irish through and through, get the fuck outta here."

"Yah I am, both sides, mum and dad. But back in the day a lot of Irish went to India, for labor, soldiers for the Empire or to seek their fortune or whatever."

Crimson sat quietly for a moment thinking about his father, Jonny, who left India for England but was never able to get over his childhood in Asia and had still loved the occasional chapati for breakfast and almond nan-khatai cookies. Jonny's taste for India was stunted at that of an eight-year-old's but it's like that for anyone and their childhood. We hold onto those tastes, scents, cartoons, fads, games, and smells, no matter where they're from. Jonny was a deliveryman for the Royal Mail and was in a car accident four blocks from his home. Crimson's mother, Cairn, put her head and the head of his little sister Madeleine in the oven soon after. And because his mother didn't choose him too, at the age of eleven, Crimson was alone.

Crimson's mother never gave him hugs or praise. For his whole life it always seemed that he had to chase after her to be able to feel the softness of her body.

"Anyways, so me grandmother had an accent—she had that little Indian grandmother accent, no kidding," he smiled.

"Man, that's cool."

"Her name was Kathleen but she went by Latika. She'd tell me about it there. Incense and spices, and loads of different kinds of people worshipping all different kinds of gods, the markets, the mountains without end."

"We'll go together."

"Hell yeah, on a private jet that I'll fly myself coz by then I'll be licensed, a legitimate pilot."

"We'll have a bunch of kids, a whole tribe, and we'll take them too," she added.

"Everyone having chapatis and chai for breakfast."

They laughed and they laughed.

ONE DAY CRIMSON CAME TO her, looking weak and pale.

"I don't know," he said.

She undressed him and there were scars and open sores all over his legs. Her eyes swelled with tears. She had thought maybe he had been in a fight or a skateboarding accident.

"They just showed up, out of nowhere," he said.

SHE SLEPT ON THE CHAIR in his hospital room for several days. He mostly slept and was often too weak to speak but then he finally spoke to her.

"I got fired from work last week, when we got in a fight and I was too messed up to work my shift," he said softly, surprising her as she read a magazine.

"Oh hey, baby, don't worry about not having a job right now."

"No, I do. I got them to give it back to me. I made Sharon, the supervisor, cry."

"How?"

"You know she kinda likes to be in everyone's business and she'd said I should break up with you if you're always making me upset. But I told her I couldn't do that. Coz you're my sun, you know, and I don't want to live in the dark."

She stood up and held his hand.

"I'm glad you got the job again," she said.

"Anyways, make sure you call them for me, let them know, I'll be back soon as I blow outta here," he smiled.

The next morning he died from the staph infection.

SHE CRIED, HIS BODY, HIS body. His skin, she thought. His skin. I will never feel that skin again.

They were going to have a tribe, they were going to go to India and eat chapatis and smoke beedies.

The doctors drew some blood and ran some tests to make sure she was not infected as well. She was not. But it was then that she found out she was pregnant. She was fifteen and a half.

SHE WANTED THEM TO PLAY "Blackbird" in the delivery room but they played the wrong side of the tape and instead he was born to "Wild Child." The moment she saw him she realized she had loved him even before she knew him.

When they needed to prepare his birth certificate, they found themselves perplexed on which box to check for race. What are you, they asked, because they'd never seen anyone who had her eyes and her skin colored like heirloom gold.

"I'm Malinali and I want him to be named Cortez," she said with her haughty chin in the air, her body slightly stiffened with equatorial heat.

Because his eyes were blue, they checked White.

And how about his father, they asked, looking at each other sideways having made up their own thoughts about the answer.

"No. It's just me."

OK, they said. Just like they thought.

Her child was born several days after her sixteenth birthday, in the middle of November, in the secretive sign of Scorpio. But to her chagrin he had a cold Aquarius moon. Her mother, his grandmother, murmured in the warmest Portuguese, the Portuguese of Brazil, "Mmm so his love life will be erratic but he will value his friends deeply."

Their first night at home from the hospital she found herself suddenly terrified and was wholly convinced that her son would die in her care, his body was so fragile and she considered herself a crude creature.

"Minha filha, acalme-se," her mother had said.

"How can I be calm? I don't know how to do this," she cried, admitting fear for the first time since she came back home after running away. Fear was not easy for her to communicate, it was not part of the language of rebels.

"The goddesses are good. Come and kneel."

So while Cortez slept quietly in her bed, still wearing the soft knit cap given to all babies at the hospital, she kneeled with her mother before their voodoo altar, and prayed. They offered rainwater collected during the full moon, one hard-boiled egg, and white rice to Yemaya. In a special plate for their ancestors, she offered seaweed sprinkled with salt for her mother's mother, her grandmother who was half Japanese, half Afro-Brazilian. They burned two guardian angel candles, one for her and one for Cortez, that were washed in holy water and ancient hyssop oil. In the morning, she found that Cortez was alive and she was as much shocked as she was happy.

It had been humbling to return to her mother and her mother's home after finding out she was pregnant. Her mother, Isabella, had her own history of hard knocks but had always wanted more for her daughter.

"My life destroyed my face," Isabella told her.

It was true, Isabella's face had devolved greatly from its former beauty. Her feline eyes which had once swept up at the corners in a flourish of eyelash now hung sad and limp. Her skin which had once had such a brilliant sheen was now pale and dull. Even her hair which had been straight, strong, and black as obsidian, recalling her Indio blood, had thinned and lost its luster. Sometimes when Isabella looked at herself in the mirror she almost felt disfigured.

"Will it destroy my face too?"

"No, you're different from me, so things will be different for you. Too late in my life I realized it was a wonderful thing to be a mother. I know you and I know already you are thinking about all the things you want to do with your kid."

"Yeah," she said, a little embarrassed. The truth is she was happy, she was excited.

"Maybe I should've thought of you in friendlier terms, I was very harsh but it was because I thought I had to be—because we were alone. See, for so many years I was feeling sorry for myself about not having worked things out with your father. But I could've just been happy. I felt sorry for you too that you didn't have a father. I know Crimson's gone but you need to know children are stronger than we give them credit for. And they'll find joy if they're raised in it."

"Do you think I can make the baby happy?"

"You'll make each other very happy. The happiest you'll ever know," Isabella promised.

FOR TWO YEARS THE THREE of them lived together until she was eighteen. In those two years she stopped doing drugs and focused on art. Before running away, before the drugs, the boys, and the concerts, she was an artist. From the time she could pick up a pencil and crayon. Through old boyfriends, old hookups, old friends who were dating this dude or another in the music industry she began illustrating covers for bands on indie labels and music posters for local shows. The covers and posters led to a couple of invitations for group gallery shows at tattoo parlors, and she picked up some loyal and steady clients. She also started to do other freelance design projects under the artist pseudonym "Pirate Disco" and she made a steady living.

After she'd saved enough money, it was only right that she set out with Cortez to their own flat, for more privacy and a life of their own. She was nervous, though, she had to admit the night before they moved out.

"What'll happen to us, Mum?"

"Many adventures."

WHEN CORTEZ TURNED FOUR AND she twenty, mother and son boarded a ten-hour nonstop flight—Heathrow to Indira Gandhi International. To prepare for their trip she packed one duffle bag, put her hair in thin dreads, and allowed him to eat several spoonfuls of Nutella straight from the jar.

"Is it a reward?" he asked, his dumpling cheeks smeared with chocolate.

"Sure," she smiled with a shrug.

Afterwards she rolled and smoked one cigarette, on the inside of which she had written the names of their ancestors and spirit guides for protection on the journey.

On the morning of their departure she had the cab stop by her mother's home. She gave her mother their black kitten, Sabbath, to watch over. She fought the urge to cry as she walked away from her mother standing in the doorway holding Sabbath sitting forlornly in his cat crate.

"I'm going to miss Sabby," her son cried a little in the backseat.

"Me too," she said.

"Remember when he pooped?"

"Yes, he tracked it all over the house."

They hugged and under her breath she sighed, Poop Master Flash. Oh Sabby.

For the plane ride, she'd brought a portable CD player and they shared a set of earphones, one bud in his, one in hers, alternating the Ramones, Jane's Addiction, and Nusrat Fateh Ali Khan. He made one special request for Daft Punk's 1999 club hit "Around the World." She let him have both earphones for that song.

"Mummy, where are we going?" he asked on the plane.

"We'll have lots of fun," she replied cheerfully.

"Are we going to see the Ice Capades?"

She chose not to reply and feigned an exhausted sleep.

THEY TOOK THE KERALA EXPRESS from Delhi and ate fried savories and tamarind candy and drank chai and lassi in their cabin. In the old Vedic spiritual tradition, they were given bright marigold garlands to wear on the three-day journey to the south of the sacred subcontinent. In her right pocket she carried a laminated picture of Mahavatar Babaji.

"There is a saint, in the Himalayas, who is over five hundred years old," she whispered to Cortez as they looked out their cabin window to the eternal heat of Rajasthan. The sun simmered off the dry ground and its waves warped the horizon.

"Will we meet him?"

"Wouldn't that be nice," she replied, while rubbing the picture between her thumb and forefinger of the smooth-skinned saint with cheekbones high as the Himalayas.

All former selves and scenes were abandoned back in England.

FOR TWO YEARS THEY LIVED at the Bhakti Jyotish Academy. Their first several weeks were difficult with Cortez asking constant questions about the home they left behind, Sabby, and Grandma. He cried a lot in the beginning and it took over a month to adjust to the food and the heat. But before long Kerala became home just as London had been. Cortez giggled and played beneath ficus tree, divine as Gautama himself, perfumed with sandalwood. And she learned centuries-old Vedic astrology, her mind wrapping itself around the science of Jyotish, her body swathed in silk and sari.

She also learned devotional meditation. Just as she had loved music in her younger years of rebellion it was almost natural that she was most intrigued by how mantras and their simple repetition was healing—each and every syllable loaded with God, protection, and devotion.

"It is the very sound," her Guruji told her, "the repetition of it that brings us to Bhagavan, to God. Every syllable in every mantra is a prayer. So it must be repeated perfectly."

She worked hard to master the pronunciation of ancient Sanskirt, which brought such wealth to her spirit, she knew it was far more alive than dead, more alive than any other language being spoken around the world.

She became enchanted by spiritual sounds and spoken prayers and as fate would have it, she found the Salinger novel *Franny and Zooey* by accident in the ashram's library. Or rather Cortez had found it.

They had a new game with the shelf that held all the books left behind by tourists to the ashram. Cortez would hold a book in his hands and try to guess who had left it behind just by meditating on it.

"The American tourist left it."

"Which one?"

"The man who had the bright blue shirt from two days ago."

She remembered the man Cortez was talking about. It was her shift that day to guide the tours around the ashram. She had not thought so much of Americans because of Archie, but this young man changed her mind. He seemed sincere and curious, and curiosity was a trait she treasured more than any. She hugged him afterwards. He had enjoyed the hug, the saffron scent of her hair, the feathery thinness of her body. When he returned to the States, he would cradle that memory of holding her, think of it as a paradigm of the gentleness and warmth he experienced in India. Many years later, after he'd married and had a child, he named his daughter Kerala.

And through Salinger's Franny, she found out about the Jesus Prayer.

The Jesus Prayer, a most profound prayer for Eastern Orthodox mystics, is not a prayer of renunciation or repentance but of reunion—a return to the Godhead. Prayed by ascetics and monks, it is to be aligned with one's breathing and was known to be successfully prayed incessantly, even in sleep, by some ascetics and holy men under the influence of the Holy Spirit. It is at first a prayer of meditation, but when it becomes a part of the practitioner, the Jesus Prayer is called a Prayer of the Heart. A prayer that never ceases.

She was incredibly moved.

She wanted Cortez to learn how to throw his heart out to God, to Bhagavan. To return to the Godhead. She wanted him to master the prayers. She thought that because he was a child he would learn it faster and it would grow organically into the chemistry of his being.

Every night they kneeled together and prayed the Jesus Prayer and every morning they prayed the Gayatri Mantra with japa malas around their wrists.

"Cortez remember, when you say 'Lord Jesus Christ, Son of God,' breathe out. When you say 'have mercy on me, a sinner' breathe in."

"It's hard," he sighed with his face a little crumpled, fiddling with the red string at the end of his prayer beads.

His crumpling face reminded her so much of Crimson. Crimson had that same expression, the eyebrows drooping sweetly, the chin puckered. It had been a flirtation when Crimson had done it. A pouting appeal for her kisses and attention. She picked up Cortez and nuzzled the soft slope where his neck met his shoulders.

"If you pray it that way, it will become a part of you, it will never stop."

"OK."

"It is like the mantras, like the Gayatri we do in the morning. The sound of the words by themselves are magic. Guruji says that you can know how your heart feels through the sound of your voice."

"OK."

"Hey, remember when we watched that video of the Ramones at Lollapalooza? The 1997 one? And Johnny Ramone would hold up that sign that said "Gabba Gabba Hey" whenever he sang it?"

"Gabba gabba!"

"It's timing just like that."

"God will find me if I say it?"

"Yes, and the holy spirit inside of you will fly out of your body, through the eye in your forehead, through all the universes to the Goloka Vrindavan, the planet where God is."

Cortez loved to hear about the Goloka Vrindavan, about how it was supposed to be so beautiful, with no pain like when he was running and skinned his knee on the sidewalk. Guruji told him and the other children, in their classes with him, how in Goloka Vrindavan no one is ever sad. Sad like when he asked his mother what happened to his father and she said he was dead like John Lennon and he would never come back.

"There's a spirit inside me," he gulped. "Like a ghost?"

She smiled. She held his hand and put it on the bedpost, then the lamp. "See, everything we can touch and see has been created, so it can be destroyed, right? What would happen if you threw the lamp off the ashram roof?"

"It would break."

"That's right, kiddo." She moved his hand over his heart. "But in the inside of every living thing, a plant or a cat like Sabby, or you and me, there is the spirit, which can never be destroyed. It's in all of us but we can't touch it. It's what allows us to move and breathe, to be talking right now."

"What makes up the spirit?"

"God. Bhagavan. The Absolute Truth. The energy of God."

"How about sneakers? Is God in sneakers?"

"It took someone who was alive and had the spirit inside them, to make the sneakers. There's no spirit in the sneakers but even sneakers or buildings need the spirit. That's why it's the spirit that is most important. Praying helps us focus on the spirit."

"There's two worlds," he said solemnly and she knew that he understood perfectly. She thought to herself, this is why little Buddhas are found, why there is worship of children like the Kumari child goddesses, why she must teach Cortez now the incessant prayers. It's children after all who are closest to their previous incarnation and in that proximity have a higher learning potential for wisdom. That's why children have déjà vu more often.

"What happens if it's a person who falls off the ashram roof?" he asked.

"Guruji says the immaterial, the spirit still goes on. The person's body will die but their spirit will be born again, maybe as a person or a cow, or a banana tree."

"Who do you think Sabby was before?"

"I don't know. Do you have any ideas?"

"My best friend. From some other time we were best friends."

"You may be right," she said. She smiled at Cortez but suddenly felt sad and worried. There was still enough of the West in her to mourn death, long for the dead like Crimson, and falter when she spoke about transmigration.

She looked at Cortez and felt her mortality. She worried already about their leaving each other through death some day. Will they truly meet again, she wondered. The finality of death, the way she had believed in it until she had come to India, still rang and revolved inside of her, locking her like a wolf with a herd of sheep. She prayed that at least she live until he was old enough to take care of himself. In a world of war and calamity she knew that the end could be coming soon enough, but she prayed for his life, that he experience enough of it to enjoy and grow. She felt guilty knowing that the end of this world would not be the end of life eternal and to cling to this life in any way would only bring depression and fear. But every mother's hope is for her child to see old age, a long, prosperous lifetime of karma burned.

SOME NIGHTS, WHEN SHE HAD a hard time sleeping, she would smoke Kashmiri hashish bought from her friend, a Khareshwari yogi baba who had taken a vow to stand and had not sat or laid down in over seven years.

The Khareshwaris were as well known for the potency of their hashish as they were for the deformities they suffered from their atrophied feet and legs. They used slings to keep themselves steady when they slept and would speak about the importance of smoking chillum as a tool of meditation.

"Do you miss the other place, amma," her son asked as she smoked by the window of their room. The intonations and habits of England had left him and were replaced by those of India. Brazil had been the same for her.

"I was born in a hot country. Now I'm in one again," she said to him.

For weeks after this conversation she meditated on her early memories of Bahia, before she and her mother left, and dreamt in Portuguese. She remembered how her friend Isla, back in London, had come back from holiday with her family in Costa Rica and had seen turtles give birth in Tortuguero.

"So, these big bloody turtles go swimming all over the world, from the South Pacific to the Atlantic. They go 'round with their mates, swimming about, to beaches in Thailand and all this, but when they give birth they swim back to where they were born. Scientists put these tags on 'em and they track where they go so it's no lie. They've got to give birth on the same beach they were born. Strange fuckers, like they couldn't find a decent spot on a beach wherever they happened to be," Isla exclaimed.

Back then, like Isla, she'd also thought those turtles going back to where they were born were wasting their time. But it's only natural, she thought, it cannot be helped, like the monsoons returning every year or the sun coming back to rise in the morning. At some point you have to go home.

AT THE BEGINNING OF THEIR second year at the Academy, the face of her son finally began to take a real form, the chubbiness of childhood vacating his cheeks. She saw for the first time how they resembled each other right after she'd had her first elephant bath.

Her long dark hair still wet, she saw him playing with other children at the Academy's garden. They had the same delicate jaw line and unobtrusive nose. They both had a beauty mark on their cheek. She'd had lovers who had kissed this freckle and later in his life, when he grew up, he would too. Yes, he was lighter, his hair the color of Saharan sand, a color right next to Crimson's blond on the color palette. And Cortez had his father's eye color, blue stones recovered from the deep, cold center of the ocean. But there was just the slightest upturn at the corner of his eyes, shaped by his eyelashes, just like his mother and his grandmother.

She found their resemblance beautiful and understood clearly, without her earlier anxiety, the things that don't end at the physical death. The cycles of rebirth. The never-ending lifetimes. The cup changing but the tea inside staying the same. There was nothing to mourn. No one ever died, no one ever really lives.

On his forehead, on his third eye, was a red vermilion powder dot. She walked through the stone walkway, passed a bronze statue of Vishnu, and went to her child who was sitting by several aloe plants.

Later they would remember the following incident fondly, recollecting the same scents and sounds of India as though the moment she grasped the infinity of life had been a holiday sequence or memorable birthday party caught on videotape:

She put her nose to his, her third eye to his, their eyes so close together it was dizzying, and said, "Cortez you could've been my mother in another lifetime."

To which he replied by smacking her ears with both his hands. "Namaste." Peace.

Jeanne Jones

Spark

JEANNE JONES is a lawyer and writing teacher in the Washington metropolitan area. Her work has appeared or is forthcoming in *Barrelhouse*, *theEEEL*, and *1:1000*. She was a finalist in NPR's three-minute fiction contest judged by Ann Patchett. She received her master's in writing from Johns Hopkins University and lives in Hyattsville, Maryland with her husband and two children.

We sat in the same silence, but we didn't know each other yet. We were in St. Patrick's Cathedral in New York City, looking at the crypt that held the tomb of Pierre Toussaint. I didn't care about Toussaint. I barely recognized the bust of the Pope. I know now that you were there with your wife, Myra. I like to imagine you then, talking about the glass in the Lady Chapel, the walk back to the hotel, what you might have for dinner. Any of those things. I was alone. I know now I was waiting for you to find me, but back then I imagined myself on a grand adventure. My first trip to the city on my own. I peeled back the foil from a packet of chocolate spread and ate it with my fingers right there at Toussaint's tomb. Then I left the church and wandered the streets alone.

It was then I decided this adventure sucked. It suddenly seemed a misguided trip. Who wants to be alone in their midtwenties—the prime of everything—in New York—the prime of everywhere—alone and stealing packets of chocolate from the hotel?

I hated New York then, but I like to think back on it now. I like to imagine that I walked right by you. I imagine Myra turning her head to watch me pass, thinking to herself, *That woman is beautiful.* Or maybe, *Who is that gorgeous young thing? Thank God my husband didn't see her. How could he resist?* She would be right. You couldn't resist me. But not yet. There was not a hint of me in you yet.

A YEAR LATER: THE FIRST time we finally met. I was back in New York, trying to find a way to move there. I thought that I could be someone in that city. You were there for a conference. We were crossing the river in one of those commuter ferries. I was reading a pamphlet someone handed me on my way in. It said, "Why Islam?" It said, "Learn the Basics." It told the seven noxious things Muslims must avoid. One of them was magic. One was consuming the property of an orphan. You asked me if you could have a few of the almonds I was eating. You were starving; you were seasick. I offered them. Your fingertips touched the palm of my hand when you picked them out. I knew then my life had changed.

These were the first words I said to you: "You would not make a good Muslim. In the twenty seconds I have known you, you have done two noxious things."

You said, "I am known for that." You smiled at me.

Weeks later, when I was in your entryway, your wife's cat glared at me. It made me uncomfortable to be stared at like that, as if she were going to report to Myra what she had seen; this cat was a preschooler who couldn't wait to tattle.

Many people believe that cats are proud, self-conscious, wise. I am not one of those people. Still, she watched me like that until I left. So I did. But I bent down and whispered to her. I said, "Tell Myra he is magic. I know that he is magic. And tell her he is mine."

I went to sleep the night after visiting you, and all I could think of was the universe, every star, every planet, the whole wide blackness. Once, all of the matter and energy of the observable universe was concentrated into a tiny little dot, the size of your eye. And then, in less time than it takes you to fall asleep at night, it expanded. It became what it is today. Forty-six billion light years in radius.

On those nights, so much of it was swelling inside me. I could feel the atoms, the stars, the galaxies, and the dark energy moving around, pushing me down into the mattress. I could never sleep, and when I got up, I had to climb out from inside the mattress. I used to call your name first when that happened. But it's the dark energy that scared me. It makes up ninety-five percent of the mass-energy density of the universe, even though no one knows what it is. And so much settled inside me at night. It curled up like a bowling ball inside me. It wouldn't go away until I removed your doubt.

So I made a plan. I wrote it out. It included getting rid of Myra. I wrote that I would write you love letters; I would bring lunch to your office. I would kiss you every day. I would start with your eyelashes, each tiny feather that keeps out what might hurt you. I would spend an hour on your neck. An entire hour. I would fix your coffee, with lots of cream and no sugar. This plan made me feel better. It helped me fall asleep.

A DREAM: WE ARE EATING garbage behind the dumpster next to the little park off K Street. We are hiding, even though no one is looking for us. It feels better to hide like that, in a place where it would be so unexpected to find a scholar and his girlfriend. You are wearing a suit and a yellow tie that has a little diamond pattern on it. I am wearing a short dress. I feel like a kid. Kissing you makes me hungry, you say. So we eat garbage right there from the dumpster. A pack of crackers someone had thrown out, a few chips. You draw the line at old French fries. I would have eaten them, though. It feels good to shove things into my mouth. I start screaming. He's mine, he's mine, he's mine. I want the city to know it. You want me silent.

I do what you ask because kissing you makes me feel like I felt that time my father made me spaghetti. The noodles had stuck to the pot and he told me to pull them off with my fingers. So we scraped them off with our fingernails until we had a fistful of noodles, and then my dad poured cold sauce all over our hands and we stood there in the kitchen, laughing and slurping them out.

Kissing you is even better than that. I stick my tongue in right when the homeless man comes by, humming "The Battle Hymn of the Republic." He stops the song right at the part where the snake is getting crushed under the hero's boot. He says, "Well, lookie here. Didn't know you was using my spot." We give him his spot back. As we walk away, I follow behind you, and a streak of light comes in between the two buildings and lights up your white hair. It surrounds your head like a halo. I tell you the story about each blade of grass having an angel that whispers to it, "Grow, grow." You say, "Stop being so foolish. I have to get back."

You are an angel to me. I whisper, "Thank you for protecting me." You get in a taxi. I still see you like that sometimes at night. I see your face when I'm lying in my bed, and your hair is all lit up like that angel you were. And I still whisper to you.

I LIKE TO TELL MYSELF this is a journey I am on. I am discovering my limits and myself. I used to see a therapist for a while, before I met you. She spoke in Zen koans, which I found to be not very useful.

"Then go home and think it over." That was her favorite thing to say to me when I told her I didn't understand.

Live with cause and leave results to the great law of the universe. That was the one I liked to repeat over and over. I can't actually remember if she told me that one, or if I read that online. It has a certain soothing effect. I found there was very little I did without cause.

Here is a story I like: There was this Zen master who lived next to a family with a young girl. The young girl got pregnant and the parents blamed the Zen guy. But all he said was, "Is that so?" Still, he raised the child and fed it milk and whatever. Finally, the girl couldn't stand it anymore, and she told her parents that the real father worked at the fish market down the street. The parents went to the Zen master and told him the truth. "Can you ever forgive us?" they said on their knees. But all the Zen master said was, "Is that so?"

Most of the time I feel like I have a wicked heart. I am a Disney villain, dressed in silver and black robes, slinking around the back of your house, peeking in your kitchen window. Other times, I feel like I'm the innocent one. The girl in the short dress trying to eat a banana without you noticing me. But sometimes, I'm just sitting on top of my mountain, saying, "Is that so?" over and over again.

MY DAD TOLD ME HE was lonely once. We were in the car on the way to the Peter Pan restaurant. He was being forced to pass a car on the right, and he was cursing. He didn't understand why people didn't follow the basic rules of driving a car. *It's so fucking easy*, he was screaming. *A kindergartner can get a license for Christ's sake.* I was ten and knew I couldn't pass the driving test, but I didn't say anything. We pulled into the Peter Pan parking lot. They gave you so many French fries with a cheeseburger at this place. He had promised me a chocolate milkshake as a reward. And all those French fries. But he started crying in the parking lot, and we never went in. He said he was lonely and that's why this all was happening. I didn't know what he meant. I was sitting right there next to him. I started telling him knock knock jokes. I told him the one where, after the other person asks, "Who's there?" you say, "Did you forget me already?" I did this to remind him I was sitting right there. I said, "You're not lonely. There's Mom. There's me." He turned around and drove us home. I should have said, "Is that so?" But I didn't know that one then.

I DIDN'T START OUT TRYING to cause you trouble. After the ferry ride with the almonds and the Muslim edicts, I pretended all was normal. The ferry stopped, the people crowded and jostled to get off, and I gathered my bags. I had a lot, so you offered to carry one for me. You asked where I was going. When I told you, you mentioned that we could probably share a cab.

I love thinking about that cab ride, even today. Our love is like a movie to me, and that cab ride is my favorite scene—the part in the beginning where anything can happen and everything will change. I felt your hand next to my leg; I felt your hand touching my leg. I slid away from you a little and still I felt your hand. Suddenly, I knew it was deliberate.

I remember the hotel room—sheets the color of butter, little bars of soap like fingertip sandwiches, room service on silver trays with tiny glass bottles of ketchup.

You said, "I am at your mercy. I am an old man. Look at me."

I didn't know what to say, so I said, "The Statue of Liberty is old too, but people still love to look at her."

You said, "That makes no sense."

I looked at your skin, how it fell over your knees and hung around your elbows. To me, it was beautiful.

I said, "You are beautiful to me. I will call you 'My Old Man.'" You didn't like that, but I loved it. You were my old man. You will be my old man forever.

MY FATHER WOULD LEAVE ME paper clues sometimes. It was a game we played where I had to search for him. The clues would be in obvious places—in the refrigerator, taped to the bathroom mirror, beneath his hat, which was inexplicably sitting on the dining room table.

The first time we played it, I was thrilled. It was hide and seek for grown-ups, and he was including me.

When I found him, he told me he used to play this with my mom, but she didn't want to play with him anymore. He asked if I would always play. I said that I would.

He had my stereo on so loud I could hardly hear him. I wanted him to hide again, but he said we hadn't finished the first round yet. He was lying on my bed with my white, hairy gorilla pillow behind his head.

I turned down the music so that I could hear him, but he told me that part of the game was to touch nothing in the room that couldn't talk back.

He said, "You can only touch things that talk."

I touched my gorilla pillow behind his head.

He said, "You're not playing the game right."

I sunk my fingers into the matted hair and found the cord. I pulled it.

The gorilla said, "Give me a banana and I'll be your best friend." I laughed at that, but my dad got angry. He grabbed my arm and I fell down on him. He turned me over so that my face was buried in the gorilla's chest. The gorilla now smelled like Old Spice. The whole time it was happening, I was so mad about that smell. The way it changed my pillow, and I didn't even see it happening.

When my dad dropped asleep, I sprayed my gorilla with Windsong, which was the perfume my mom wore whenever they went out at night, which wasn't very often, so there was lots of it.

I walked out of the room and left him there, asleep in a mist of Windsong, with the radio still playing.

BEFORE I MET YOU, I used to think my very best day was my first day of school. So silly now, to think that. My mom picked me up right in front of Stephen Girard Elementary. She was standing there in her black-and-white checkered coat and red heels waiting for me. I ran up to tell Mrs. Bunch.

She said, "Wow! Your mom looks just like Jackie O!" I waved to who I thought were all my new friends as I walked across the playground and ran straight into my mom's coat.

The wool scratched my face and I stuck my hands into her sleeves so I could feel the satin lining on my arms. She pulled me away from her and looked at me.

She said, "My bright girl, my little spark. I'm taking you for a special treat to mark how grown up you are."

I wanted to go to the fountain in the city where the cold water sprays out of a woman's fingers and I could stick my feet in and splash. I wanted to swing on the green plastic swing that bent when I sat on it. But my mom took me to the Rittenhouse Hotel in the Square, so we could have tea. The clear brown liquid in my china cup looked like the soup broth I had to eat when I was sick. I took a small sip and pretended I liked it. My mom taught me how to hold my pinky out when I held the cup, and we laughed about being fancy. We rode home on the bus, and I put my head on her lap.

The wool scratched my face again, so my mom said, "Wait. I can make this better." She took off her coat and laid it on top of me. The light green satin now covered me like perfume, and I closed my eyes and fell asleep.

The next day, and the following thousand days of school after that, I rode the bus home like everyone else. My mom never took me back to the Rittenhouse. When I asked her about it later, she told me to stop asking. That kind of trip never happens twice.

Still, I told my new friends about the Rittenhouse, and how my mom was kind of famous and how she wore real satin, but no one wanted to hear it. In notes, they told me they hated me. Notes they tore up into tiny pieces of paper and put into one big folded piece of paper that said, "Shut up." The little papers flew all over the bus when I opened it.

The bus driver got angry and made me sweep it up while the bus was still moving. People thought it was funny, but I thought I held my balance pretty well.

ON THE DAY WE RETURNED from New York—you by train, me by bus—I told you I wanted to see you every day.

Your reaction surprised me a little. You said, "I'm married." That seemed like the kind of thing you should have told me going in.

I said, "I understand. But I am undeterred." I have a certain ferocity of spirit when I find something I want. That is what my English teacher wrote on my eighth grade report card, and I sort of agreed with that, and now I wear it like a tiara.

You were not difficult to locate. You did not live that far away.

I showed up one morning, only to spy on you. And I saw her. The person I now know to be Myra. She was older than I had imagined she'd be. Short, straight hair, glasses attached to a chain (Know that I will never do that. No matter how bad it gets), wearing flat brown shoes and a suit at least one size too big and the color of wet clay. Clearly a woman out for comfort. I have to admit, at first it infuriated me. She had given up. She was taking you for granted.

When she drove away in her sensible car, I knocked on your door. You answered it holding a half-eaten bagel. You hadn't showered yet. You tried to swallow, but you were shocked.

I said, "Surprise!"

You said, "This can't happen."

I said, "But it's happening."

You said, "I'm telling you—I'm not sure how you figured out where I live—but this can't go on. You have to leave. I told you I'm married. My wife just left, for Christ's sake."

I said, "Well, you started this, you know. And now here I am. Put down that bagel. Look what I brought you!" I held up a bag of cronuts.

You said nothing.

I said, "Cronuts!"

"You have to leave now."

"But you said you loved them. Remember?"

You said, "Well, I don't love them anymore."

I wanted to see your bedroom. I wanted to get you in there and kiss your whole unshowered, unshaven self. I wanted to lie on your sheets with you, bury my head in your pillow. I pushed past you and started walking up your stairs.

You ran behind me and grabbed my arm. Your voice was low and trembling. You said this very slowly: "Get out now."

I walked back down your steps and acted like I was walking toward your door, but I made a sharp turn and headed into your dining room. I laughed as you chased me. "This is fun," I shouted. "A little early morning exercise!"

You lunged for me, but I dove under your dining room table, and I crouched there, with the cat. You put your hands on your hips and looked around the room. I imagined you planning your next move to capture me. I liked being your priority, your only concern. In that moment, I felt responsible for everything inside you. I wished I could have stretched that moment out forever.

You ran your hand through your hair and took a deep breath. I imagined being that breath, filling your lungs and moving your heart.

I said, "I am inside you now." You looked at me.

I said, "Admit it. I am inside you now."

Still nothing from you. A much different version of you than the guy in New York.

"I'm in there now. You have to admit it. Admit it."

You said, "OK. I admit it."

"That's better," I said. I crawled out from under the table. I kissed your shin, the hair tickling my face. I said, "I knew it," and I left.

THE NEXT TIME I SHOWED up, it was only Myra and me. She answered the door, in a similar version of the outfit she had on the last time I saw her, without the shoes.

"Hey, how are you," I said, staring at her hair. I found I couldn't look into her eyes yet.

"Hello," she said. Her tone was not unfriendly, but it was expectant. She was understandably waiting for further guidance from me.

I froze. I realized too late that my zeal had once again overridden my common sense. I said the first thing that came into my mind, which admittedly wasn't that good.

"My name is Cassie and I'm collecting for the Save the Whales charity here in the area."

"Save the Whales? In Maryland?"

"Well, wildlife in general," I said. "Whales are generally an easy sell. But all wildlife. Like, for instance, what's your favorite animal?"

She said, as you possibly know, the platypus. I felt my chance had truly passed since even I realized I couldn't work with that, but when I looked at her, it was not an unwelcoming look she was giving me, so I pressed on. I said, "May I come in and tell you more about me, this?"

There was this moment of absolute silence, like a beat, a pause in a song that seems to last one second too long. She spent that moment looking at me. I noticed that her eyes were rimmed in red, as if she'd been crying. She recognized something else in me then. I am sure of it, because she stepped back a tiny bit. She created a space for me in the doorway.

She gave me this opening, so I took it. I squeezed by her and stepped inside. The foyer smelled strongly of coffee and floor wax. I looked up to see the framed pictures on a dark blue wall. In my fervor during the last visit, I hadn't paid attention. But there they were, these frozen moments of your life before me. I felt her at my back. I turned around.

Now I was in the foyer looking out at her by the door. This made me feel stronger. It gave me an outsized and probably undeserved sense of power.

She said, "What is this about?"

"I'm not sure. I was wondering if Professor Stig was home?" It felt like I was using a term of endearment for you.

She said, "I should have known." And then she said, "Christ, so you're one of those, are you?"

"One of what?"

"The moony ones. Coming around here, mooning over the professor."

"I am not a fan of the moon," I said. "It's too insignificant. There is so much dark energy out there, why would anyone waste a minute on the moon?"

She rolled her eyes. She said, "You know, students like you are a dime a dozen. There's one every year."

I have to admit, that stung a bit. I wasn't a student. But I acted as though it did not matter. I looked down at her unshod feet. I said, "Why are you wearing nude nylons?"

"What kind of question is that?"

I told her it was a fashion choice question.

She looked me up and down, but she said nothing. We stood there, facing each other.

I said, "I guess you were mean to me so I was just being mean back." Her shoulders dropped which I recognized as the universal symbol of giving up. I remembered those pictures, so I turned around and walked directly to the blue wall. I found a photo of what looked like Myra with fifty pounds and fifty years gone, standing next to you—my old man in a much younger form—and a girl of about ten.

I said, "Who took this photo?"

Myra said, "I think my brother took that one."

"You look pretty here. Is that your daughter?"

She said, "That's Cymbeline."

"And Cymbeline is your daughter?"

"And Cymbeline was my daughter." She put her glasses on and came over to the picture. She looked at it closely. She said, "She was so young here."

"She has a great spark here."

She looked at me and then turned back to the picture. She said, "You know, you're right. Cymbeline's spark could light an entire fireworks display."

"When you think about it, any spark could do that. Fireworks are pretty touchy."

She said, "You're right about that. But not everyone has one."

I said, "I think I do."

She said, "Well maybe that is the reason why I let you pass."

"I don't think I'll have any tea, after all. Tell Professor Stig I've been here."

She said, "I'm not going to do that."

WHAT ABOUT MY MOM? WHERE was she through all of this? It was a joke between my mom and me, sort of.

After my dad died, my mom started drinking more. What started out as a glass or two of wine with dinner became bottles and then vodka and probably sleeping pills. I'm not really sure. I only know that if I caught her at the right time, before she got too bad, we could have a conversation. If I caught her too early, she wouldn't speak at all. But right when the second glass of wine warmed her cheeks, she would say, "I'm sober as a widow right now," and I knew we could talk.

It was on one of those occasions that I asked her if she knew about Dad and me.

"Do you mean did I know he was diddling you?" She laughed. "I knew. Of course I knew. The whole neighborhood knew."

"The whole neighborhood?" How could that be?

"That's right. The whole goddamn neighborhood."

"You told people?"

My mom put her elbows on the table and rested her chin on the shelf of her hands. She was smiling at me as though I were still a child and she had to explain about Santa Claus. "Cassandra, get real," she said. "You didn't really think this was yours and Daddy's little secret, did you?"

"I wasn't telling people."

She stopped smiling. "No, of course *you* wouldn't. You wanted him all to yourself, didn't you? *I* told people, Cass. Me."

This conversation was not going at all like I had imagined. I had planned for something completely different. I had nothing to say.

"You can't mess around with another woman's man and think there won't be consequences, Cassandra. It comes back and burns you every time." She stood up and went to the sink. She began to wash the dishes from dinner. She said, "Give me a hand with this. Why am I always telling you the basic things a daughter should do? I can't remember a time when this wasn't the case."

I got up and picked up a dishtowel. I folded it in a square and set it on the table, and I walked out the door.

THROUGHOUT OUR AFFAIR, SHORT AS it was, I never did anything mean to you. I never lied to you, tied you up against your will with a hotel sheet, poisoned you with second-hand smoke, forced you to watch Fox News, required you to listen to me pontificate on Spinoza, or made false promises to you.

If my calculations are correct, and I believe they are, you did all of those to me. So I hope you read this as a message.

I looked up some information on Spinoza, and he said that everything that happens *has* to happen the way that it does. Things only *look* imperfect, but really, they are perfect. So if this "situation" of ours seems unfortunate to you, it is only because of your inadequate view of reality.

THE NEXT TIME I SAW you, you were sitting in your backyard, reading the *New York Times*, and drinking a cup of coffee from a little metal tray that was set right beside you. There were crumbs on a plate along with your coffee cup, and a glass ashtray with one cigarette in it. The leaves from the tree shaded you from the sun and made shadows on your face. You looked like you were auditioning for the role of Elderly Sick Man in a French movie. I opened the iron gate that put me on the path to you.

I walked up to you and said, "Surprise again." I think it worked. You jumped in your chair as if waking from a falling dream and gave all the indications of surprise.

You said, "I don't know how to make this more clear to you. Leave me alone."

I said two things to you in return. Number one: If you are going to love, love openly. Number two: what makes you think I am here for you? I came to see Myra.

Presumably, this is what sent you into a frenzy. You jumped up from your seat, knocking over your little tray of Frenchness in the process. The coffee cup and saucer hit the ground, the cup broke in two, the crumbs scattered.

You said, "Why are doing this to me?"

I said, "Why are you doing this to me?"

"This was a one-time thing. I told you that in New York. You are the one with issues. You need to sort it out. Sort it out and stop dragging other people into it."

I said, "Is Myra here?"

"No, she is not here. You need to leave."

I said, "I have a box of tea for her. She loves tea. I don't trust you to give it to her, though. I'll come back tomorrow."

You sat back down on your chair. You put your head in your hands. I walked back up the path, through the iron gate, got into my car, and left.

WHEN I WAS YOUNG, THERE used to be a television program I would watch all the time. On this show, there was a beautiful woman who lived in a suburban house with her husband. She had all of these magical powers, but she never liked to use them because they made her husband unhappy.

She was beautiful and kind and filled with purity. She thought that all she wanted was to live in this house and make dinner for her husband.

I used to imagine this woman was my mother, but she didn't know I was waiting for her to find me. I was magic too, and we had somehow become separated. Once we found each other, we would live together and be happy and do our magic together and have a wonderful life. Until that happened, though, we were doomed to a life where we knew something was always missing.

HERE IS A STORY THAT might help you. Myra told me this story on one of the afternoons when I visited. You know, after I gave her that tea, she started letting me come over whenever I asked. I've decided to change my plans about getting rid of things that might be in my way. Nothing is really in my way anymore.

On this afternoon, she made me tea and we both took off our shoes and sat in those big, soft chairs that you have in your living room. I sat in the burgundy one and Myra sat in the green. Her cat jumped up and sat on my lap and let me stroke her. Myra was letting her tea cool off. She nibbled on a sugar cookie and told me this story:

There once was a shy little boy who was loved and protected by his family. He never wanted anything in his life. His parents seemed to anticipate his every need. He grew up surrounded by love, completely secure and happy. One day, this family went for a picnic near a forest. The little boy went collecting leaves and got terribly lost inside the forest. A very hungry wolf was in this forest, and he was thrilled to see the plump boy. When the boy saw the wolf, he covered his head and cried. He said, "Do not hurt me." The wolf attacked the boy and ate him up.

There once was also a little girl who did not have it as good as the little boy. Her family did not love and protect her. Because of poverty, or work schedules, or inadequate child care or whatever, they had to leave her alone for most of her childhood and because of this, the girl learned to take care of herself. She knew how to mix formula and learned how to cook eggs, how to make macaroni. One day, this girl got lost in the same woods and came upon the same hungry wolf. He was thrilled to see another child. When the girl saw the wolf, she grabbed the knife she always kept on her for protection and fought back. She did some damage to that wolf, but eventually the wolf won, and he ate her up. The end.

I was shocked. Both of the children die in this story. I told Myra I thought that was a horrible story.

She said, "Not if you look at the story from the point of view of the wolf."

I said, "Who wants a story from the point of view of the bad guy?"

"He's not a bad guy," Myra said. "He's just a wolf in the world, being the perfect version of a wolf. And the children were just being perfect versions of themselves."

When you look at it that way, everything in this story is perfect.

Dini Karasik

Ghosting on the Rio Grande

DINI KARASIK is a writer of Mexican and Irish descent whose work has appeared in several literary journals, including the *Más Tequila Review*, *Kweli Journal*, *Bartleby Snopes*, *The Butter*, and *Literal Magazine*. Her story "Amalia on the Border" was a finalist in the *Texas Observer*'s 2013 short story contest judged by Dagoberto Gilb. She is founding editor and publisher of *Origins Journal* and the recipient of a 2016 Arts and Humanities Council of Montgomery County Individual Artist Award.

Lupita stands at the stove stirring a pot. She's wearing a white Playtex bra, a terry cloth robe, and gray polyester pants with an elastic waistband. Her skin is clammy. The space heater is on high and she's still warm from ironing clothes in the back room where the windows are all nailed shut to keep out the *mojados* who cross the river and sometimes steal from her. A garden hose. Laundry on the clothesline. Fruit from the lime and fig trees. She can't prove it, of course, but all she needs is for them to break in and take her inventory of used clothes, which is basically like robbing her of all her money.

On her feet are a pair of Dr. Scholl's she found at the bottom of a barrel at *la ropa usada*. They still had the tags on them and even though they are a size too small, she bought them. They only cost a dollar. She had planned to resell them, at least for four dollars, but when she tried them on, they didn't hurt too bad. They are the wooden ones with a single strap and buckle that fits over the top of the foot. The strap pinches the bunions on the sides of her feet but she figures that they are leather and they will stretch.

Lupita places three sticks of cinnamon into the boiling water and moves the pot to another burner. *Té de canela*. Cheap and flavorful. It makes the house smell like Christmas, which she hasn't celebrated since the fire sixteen years ago that took Joe and the girls. She heats a flour tortilla on the open flame of the stove and then another, charring them a little and scraping off the black flakes before placing them on a small plastic plate. She pours the tea into a cup and stirs in a tablespoon of sugar. Of the four chairs at the table, only one sits flush with the floor. She chooses it, scraping its metal feet across the linoleum and sitting down to slather butter on each of the tortillas. When she bites into one, butter dribbles down her chin. She wipes it away with the sleeve of her robe.

She finishes getting dressed, choosing a thin, dark sweater from a tall stack of clothes leaning against the dresser in her bedroom. A column of women's capris neatly folded from light to dark obscures her view of the mirror leaning against one wall, so she puts them on the bed in neat rows in order to get a good look at herself. The sweater hugs the rolls of fat around her middle but she decides to wear it anyway.

Down the hall, she arranges a new pile of infants' clothes on top of a mound of dresses and jumpers and pajamas in the second bedroom. There is a small closet full of baby blankets: fleece, crochet, macramé. There are crib sheets. Hundreds of them. Some crisp and new, others the color of dishwater. The edge of a twin bed peeks out beneath a heap of tiny shoes. A chair, a nightstand, and a bookshelf without books are buried beneath the hoard like lost artifacts. The room smells faintly sweet; clothes cling to their aromas, even years later. Lupita takes a deep breath. With one foot, she kicks aside a bundle of cotton swaddles that has fallen to the floor and turns off the light.

She gathers her pocketbook and keys and tears several large plastic bags from a bolt she keeps at the front door. She leaves her house and sees that a storm is coming. From inside her pocketbook, she roots out a silk scarf with a drawing of the Eiffel Tower in the center and a thick silver border, a steal at two dollars. She ties it around her head to keep her coarse gray hair out of her eyes.

The winds are kicking up dust from the dirt yard and disturbing the tiny pebbles in the gravel driveway. It's a good thing she changed her shoes, not that she's crazy enough to wear sandals outside in the dead of winter. Highs in the fifties today. Freezing cold, by her standards. Keds on her feet now. No socks, though. That's the one thing she never buys at *la ropa usada*. Well, socks and underwear. Bras, yes. Nothing wrong with that. It's not like she can afford to go without, not with her enormous bosom.

It's Wednesday morning and *la ropa usada* always gets in new shipments on Wednesdays. She's running low on winter inventory and if she doesn't get there early, she'll miss out on the best things: silk blouses, cashmere sweaters, wool coats, and puffy jackets. Incredible what the wealthy throw away. If she stocks up now, she'll have plenty to sell at the flea market before the days grow warmer.

Lupita eyes her rusty old Civic, her only worldly possession—aside from the nightgown she wore to bed—that wasn't destroyed by the fire. The tire on the driver's side looks a little low. The bodega isn't far. Just a mile down the road. She'll deal with the tire later.

The jumbo garbage bags she carries under one arm flap like black flags in the wind. She wrestles with them as she forces them into the hatchback. The hinges groan when she finally slams the door shut.

She prefers the summer storms that roil out of the sky after a long, hot day, dropping rain and cooling the sun-baked streets. She swears she can hear sizzle when those first droplets hit the ground. But on days like today when the sun hasn't once broken through the cloud cover and the world seems to be missing its shadows, it seems as though summer will never come. She thinks of her twins, Perla and Paloma, who on sunny days sat on the front stoop, crisscross applesauce, opposite one another, casting shadows, one a mirror image of the other. Seeing the flat, gray world around her only reminds her that they're gone.

She gets in the car, puts her pocketbook in the passenger seat, and arranges a thick phonebook and two small pillows underneath her. It's the only way she can see over the steering wheel. The engine starts after a few tries and she puts the car in drive.

The streets are empty. At least compared to how they used to be when people would come from across the river to buy things from her. That's when she had the stall at the downtown *mercado*, which closed years ago, along with the Woolworths, the Hotel Hidalgo, the Plaza Cinema. Now the place is a ghost town. She makes half as much selling clothes at the flea market as she did at the *mercado*, and now she has to compete with the viejas who come from across and buy up all the clothes in bulk, sight unseen, and take it back to Mexico to sell in the streets at a fraction of what she charges.

Her most loyal customers won't cross the bridge anymore. There's always an excuse: the cartels, the Border Patrol, too few pesos. It's no wonder her house is full of inventory. Still, she could use more.

She rounds the corner to *la ropa usada* and parks at a broken meter. She'd park in the garage two blocks down, but the car doesn't go in reverse anymore; that she found this spot is Joe's doing, she's certain. He knows her back has started to ache, that it's not so easy for her to drag bags full of clothes to the car. A close parking spot is his way of looking out for her. His messages don't come often but when they do they are almost always helpful.

Every now and then he sends her more personal messages. Like when she was at the H.E.B. recently trying to decide between bistec and chicken and one of his favorite songs came on, the one that goes "I'll light the fire, you place the flowers in the vase that you bought today..." She knows that's him saying, "Buy the *bistec, amor*. You know that's my favorite." Or when she's driving and "Oh Sherrie" by Steve Perry comes on the radio. When she first met Joe, it was popular. It hardly ever comes on the radio anymore, but when it does, Lupita knows right away that Joe is sending her a message, reminding her that he loves her.

It's early yet and she knows she'll have to wait for *la ropa usada* to unlock its doors. When she doesn't get there in time, she misses out. It happened to her last week when she overslept and arrived midmorning. Nothing was left but miscellaneous linens and summer clothes—shorts, blouses, spaghetti-strap dresses. Though she'll often buy off-season if she finds something that would've looked nice on the twins. Denim shorts. Swimsuits and exercise clothes. Once, she found two wedding dresses, not the same but similar enough had they wanted a double wedding. They would be in their midtwenties by now, probably with children of their own, so the clothes in the second bedroom are really for the grandchildren she imagines. These clothes are not for sale. The living room, dining room, hallways, and master bedroom are where she stores current inventory, and right now she needs to stock up on men's slacks and overcoats.

She presses her face against the glass door, clutching her plastic bags, her pocketbook slung over one of her shoulders. The lights aren't on yet. The words "*ropa usada*" are painted in white block letters across the middle of a large picture window behind which, years earlier, the coiffed mannequins of Avelina's Boutique stood in a neat row modeling the latest in border town couture. *Dresses for Any Occasion*, was the store motto. She bought Paloma and Perla's first communion dresses there. Lacy and smooth, a layer of tulle underneath the sheath. She can still hear the swish of the dresses when they walked, the clicking of the twins' white patent leather shoes on the cement floor of the church. She can feel the crisp but forgiving fabrics as she gathered the girls in her arms to kiss them on the plums of their cheeks. That was before that fancy treaty the U.S. signed with Mexico. Before the insectlike invasion of eighteen-wheeler trucks going back and forth across the border. Before the disappearances and killings on the other side. Before the fire that took Joe and her Pearl and Dove.

Lupita thinks she sees movement in the back of the bodega. She taps on the glass with her car keys. It must be close to nine a.m. There's no answer. She walks to the end of the row of abandoned storefronts, clutching her plastic bags, and squints as she looks down the road at the bank clock. She can just make it out. It reads 8:50 a.m. and she wonders if the owner is running late. She heads back to the storefront and stands beneath its tattered awning as the first raindrops begin to fall.

It rained a slow and steady downpour the last night she and Joe spent together, sitting in the kitchen, conspiring to surprise the twins. It was drafty, cold, and they left the stovetop burners on to warm up as they settled on their plans. They had saved enough and would drive to California for Christmas, take the girls to Disneylandia, visit all the *primos* in East Los where she was born and raised. They turned out the lights, went to bed, kissed each other good night.

That Christmas, all the relatives wound up coming to Texas instead, to attend the funerals, to help her get back on her feet—which took years, not days. No one realized how long it would take for her to recover from the shock, for the insurance money to come through, for Joe's police pension to kick in. One by one, they all went home.

They still call or send Hallmark cards on holidays, but no one comes to visit. Lupita doesn't mind. It's easier this way. There's really no place for anyone to sleep anyway. The rooms are all full, stacked floor to ceiling with supply. And they would just try to talk her into getting rid of everything. They don't realize how much money she stands to make. She has some real treasures, too. Silk dresses and vintage coats. Men's dress shirts and three-piece suits. Sweaters of all styles in a variety of fabrics: wool, mohair, alpaca. Crocheted scarves and French berets, which sell like hot cakes in the winter months.

She raps on the door again. Nothing. Then it finally hits her that no one else is waiting to get in. She looks up and down the street. Not a soul. Then she hears the sound of church bells. It takes her a moment but she remembers: it's Christmas Day.

After the fire, the church raised some money to buy her food and clothes, but the funds to rebuild the house came from the insurance company after a lawyer helped her file the right papers. Juan J. Cielo, Esq., that was his name. She saw it as a sign: *Cielo.* Sky. Heaven. That was the first time Joe pointed her in the right direction. Why hadn't he signaled that the store was closed today?

She gets in her car and drives home. There's no traffic, of course, because it's Christmas. How could she have forgotten? The rain is coming down hard when she parks. She finds an old newspaper in the backseat, covers her head, and walks as fast as she can back to the house. Once inside, she peels off her wet sweater and leaves the soaked Keds by the front door. The room is dark, the windows blocked by mounds of clothes. The light bulb in the overhead fixture burned out long ago and she can't quite get to it to put in a new one. She pulls a long-sleeved shirt from one of the piles and puts it on. It's faded pink and has small lettering on it. She moves to the kitchen where she can see and tugs at the front of the shirt to read what it says. *Life is Good.* She smiles. Joe again. Reminding her to take it easy, the store will be open tomorrow.

Rhea Yablon Kennedy

Digging to Switzerland

RHEA YABLON KENNEDY's work has appeared in the *Washington Post*, *Civil Eats*, *O the Oprah Magazine*, *Tablet Magazine*, the *Forward*, and the travel anthology *Whereabouts: Stepping Out of Place* (2Leaf Press). A resident of Washington, D.C., Kennedy loves to garden and bike in the city. She is also an English faculty member at Gallaudet University and a collection of pixels at RheaKennedy.com.

*A*liya dug the hole. She dug the hole like eating vegetables. She worked at that beach sand like Pete said she should, just in case it really was true. In case she could get to Switzerland.

So far, Aliya only saw water. She scraped the hole deeper and deeper with her pink shovel, and with each big scrape, the bottom filled with water. In the water, small creatures in shells wriggled. They looked like tiny Easter eggs—oval-shaped and colored the lightest purples and blues and pinks like mints at the diner.

"In Switzerland, they got so many kinds of chocolate," Pete said from his beach chair, looking out at the water, watching Mama hold Davie on her hip. "You know that, Muhammad Aliya?"

Aliya nodded. Well, she knew it now that Pete told her. The sun felt hot on her face. She could see the sunbeams streaming through her eyelashes and onto her cheeks like white and yellow ribbons.

Pete slurped a sip of beer and smiled. Then he fit the can back into the beer-shaped pocket in his chair. The can was covered in a fuzz made of tiny water drops. Pete was looking not that much at Davie, more at Mama. Looking, really, at Mama's bottom. Pete's brown hair, long for a man and bleached in the sun, blew around his face. Mama called his hair shaggy.

"Delicious, creamy candy bars," Pete continued. "Sometimes it comes in brown bars like what you're used to in Maryland, but sometimes? You will not believe this, Ali. Sometimes, they're ivory white. Or in the shape

180

of little pyramids and swirled red and white."

"Oh."

"Oh is right. I once saw this guy—biggest, beefiest sonofabitch, just sucking away at a pack of those pyramids in a fancy beer bar—they call them *brasseries*, you know—spending a good five minutes on each one, like they were tiny pieces of heaven. Sonofabitch sat there savoring each one."

Pete turned to Aliya now. "Anyway, enough about that. You're about to learn all of this cultural stuff in kindergarten next year," he said. "You're about to get mighty cultured, indeed." Pete held up the beer to her like making a toast.

The big wave hit fast. Aliya could hear the *shhhrit* from way up on the beach. She looked up to see Mama stumble from the smack of the wave, her legs bending to one side. Aliya gasped and scrambled her feet against the walls of the hole and put her arms at the top, ready to scoot right out of that hole. Then Mama held out one hand. Her legs straightened. She balanced.

Aliya panted. Her mouth turned down to cry, but she didn't. That would be silly.

Mama was looking at Davie and smiling like, *Wasn't that fun? You weren't scared at all, right?*

No one had to save Mama, at least not right now.

And what was Pete doing? He was laughing. "Nice one, Ada. Them killer waves'll getcha if you don't watch out!"

Mama gave him a look, is what Grandma would say.

"Love ya, Sweet Cheeks!" Pete said.

It seemed like half the time Mama was looking at Pete that angry way, and half the time she was happy with him. That left Aliya wondering how she should look at him, but usually she had no reason to be mad.

When Pete shouted, a brown pony far down the beach looked up. Aliya hoped the pony would come closer, but at the same time she hoped it wouldn't. She crouched down in the hole.

There had been signs on the road that Mama helped her sound out: *Caution* (that was the hardest word), then

Wild ponies bite and kick. Do not feed.

"How goes it, Ali-yoop?" Pete asked. "You still in there?"

"Good!" Aliya answered, extra loud from inside the sand where she crouched, so Pete would know she was still there on Assateague Island, not halfway across the world yet.

This far down, anyone walking by would only see part of the digger. When Aliya stood up, her hair showed, flying around now that it was dry, and her greenish-brown eyes, and her shoulders that glowed with a lobster-red burn. What they couldn't see were the places that stayed white where her floaty jacket always sat, or the one foot that twisted when Aliya forgot to turn it the right way, making the toes point to the opposite foot like they were trying to start a conversation.

More digging, more diner mint creatures. Pete was taking a nap. His chin sat on his chest and the orange brim of his Orioles cap covered his face. Aliya checked on Mama and Davie. Yes, still there, looking like the flamingos Mama showed Aliya at the big zoo in California—birds with bodies like cotton candy with skinny legs and long, slim necks. Yes—the way Davie looked clinging to Mama's hip in his fat swimming diaper, sucking his thumb, looked just like that. Then a small head—their mother's head, with its slim neck and hair the color of light wood pulled back into a ponytail—at the top, always looking around. While the waves jumped up at her feet like puppies.

❦

COMPARED TO THE FUNERAL, WHERE everything had smelled like a basement and everyone said "Bless you" and "I'msosorry," and stared at Aliya's shiny black shoes facing in different directions, the zoo was much better. Aliya had been only three, but still she remembered it. She saved the memories when she was three, remembered when she was four, and now at five she understood some of them better. She remembered spoonfuls of something perfectly sour and sweet. That was frozen lemonade melting in her mouth. And the trolleys that went by and the microphoned voice talking about how these flamingos got their colors from a special food the zoo gave them. It made them just as pink as feeding them shrimp, but at a bargain. "Ha ha!" The lady's voice in the microphone laughed at her own joke.

All of the faces at the zoo smiled when they looked at Mama, her tummy like a pillow in front of her, and little Aliya holding her mother's hand.

Aliya always felt like she was about to cry there in California, even when she forgot for a minute that Daddy fell one day, and then he was gone. At the zoo, swinging buckets on cables carried people above the animals and the tanks and windows that kept them in.

☙

THIS WAS THE RULE: YOU can't go back outside until you finish lunch. Aliya didn't like the rule. Davie didn't know the rule yet, but he didn't like it either. He turned his head from side to side so Mama had to follow his mouth with the little spoon of applesauce.

"Mama?" Aliya said.

"Yes, sweetie?"

"What's sonofabitch?"

Pete looked up from the book he was reading on the bottom bunk. Aliya kept her eyes on the PB&J sandwich on squishy bread on the small RV dining table in front of her. "I heard it...somewhere."

The inside of the RV smelled like their dirty laundry and the floor of the campsite shower. Aliya wanted to sit in the fresh breeze that blew over the picnic table and tent Pete had set up out front. She could work away at her sandwich there. She wouldn't get distracted and wander off. She could do it.

Pete's book was thick and had a monster with tentacles on the cover. Aliya had opened it once, saw the pages covered with tiny words and no pictures. Aliya and Mama's book cover showed hands around a sword's golden handle. Inside, along with the words, were drawings that Mama would show her, pictures of Narnia and the Prince and four daring children in socks up to their knees and a faun.

Mama looked up at Pete fast. One of those looks, her mouth pulled tight almost like a kiss.

"We're not going to talk about that right now."

Pete looked back at his book.

"Mama, will you read me *Prince Caspian*?"

"After you finish eating. And if you do some of those games Miss Chelsea taught you. The jumping and picking up the ball on one foot. And if you get ready for the museum fast. Now finish your sandwich."

"But the peanut butter is sticking to my mouth!"

Davie started to cry like he had the hiccups. "Aheh aheh aheh," Davie said.

"Eat," Mama said.

∽

THIS WASN'T A MUSEUM. ALIYA could tell right away. It had a big metal anchor and posters of wild ponies on the walls and a shallow pool with ambling horseshoe crabs. Real museums had dinosaurs and touch screens. Everyone knew that. Aliya did touch the horseshoe crabs, but she got bored with that. They were easy to catch.

Aliya was in the shop looking at horse dolls and stuffed lighthouses with red and white stripes when she heard Pete's voice.

"You buy a desk or something for your school or your office, and it's supposed to last thirty years, right? But what they don't tell you is little things will go wrong. A bolt will pop out here, a screw get loose there."

Pete pointed one finger in the air. He leaned on the counter. The person he was talking to was a lady in a tan and blue park ranger uniform, with dark hair pulled back tight in a bun.

"That's where I come in. Fixing that industrial furniture so it will last. My company's sent me all around the world for it. Our clients see their investments last for generations."

The lady nodded. Pete smiled at her.

"Not as long as a state park, though. What you have here, what you work for, that lasts forever. It's a beautiful thing."

Aliya suddenly knew that Pete shouldn't see her. So she hid behind a tall display with cards that had pictures of shells and beaches on them.

"It is a great place to work. A little sad sometimes, though. The shore keeps eroding, and that's not fun or easy to explain. The real challenge is keeping visitors in line, though!"

"Yeah?" said Pete.

"Oh my God, yes. An Assateague Spanish Red walks by and you wouldn't believe how badly they want to feed and pet it. It's like Justin Bieber just walked onto the beach."

Pete laughed. The lady did, too. "We visitors are some naughty bastards," Pete said.

Suddenly, Pete looked. Right at Aliya's hiding spot, she thought. When he turned back to the lady, he turned his hand so his palm was open and his fingertips pointed to Mama at the crab pool with Davie.

"Now the woman you see there, she's the real star," Pete said. "Runs the show at a school back in Bowie. Behind the scenes, of course. Giving out visitor passes and all of that, keeping the principal's calendar. My girlfriend. She's something."

That was when Aliya remembered the binoculars. Mama had pointed them out as they walked into the museum, two big metal faces with holes like eyes. They swiveled to look out at the tan grasses and some low green trees and a big stretch of flat water, and Mama said you could see a single blade of grass if you looked through them. Aliya wasn't sure why she needed to see a blade of grass so far away when there were plenty growing right out in front of the museum, but she was still curious. So out she went through the big glass doors, onto the porch of the sort-of museum. It was what Lucy or Edmund or the Prince would do.

The metal face was higher than Aliya had expected. Luckily, she found a step right near it. She touched the hot metal and put her own face toward it. No grass. Just dark. Just then, she noticed a man coming toward her, big like a teddy bear, with one hand out. The other hand came down on her shoulder. It was heavy and warm. That was all she noticed before she heard Mama's voice.

"Aliya?" Mama was almost screaming. Her face looked tight and mad. The hand was gone. Aliya ran to where Mama stood nearby, forgetting to watch how she moved, making a mix of a limp and a horse's canter.

The big man's eyebrows went way up into his forehead, which was wet with sweat. His face would look kind, Aliya thought, if he didn't look so surprised. Then the man did something strange. He told Mama he was sorry. So sorry. He didn't mean to do anything. He had this quarter for the binoculars. You can't see anything without putting a quarter in, and… But the man didn't get to finish explaining.

Because Pete was there then, and everything moved fast.

"We got a problem here?" Pete had run out so quickly that the big glass museum door was still wide open. "He touch you?"

"What the hell is this?" The man said. His eyebrows were down now, but his face was red like a dark sunburn. A woman with big shoulders and a round belly like the man came over, and she looked at the man like she might yell at him.

"I'm warning you: Don't mess with my family," Pete said.

"OK, OK," the man said. He had his hands up, palms open like he was about to play Miss Mary Mack. "Can't you give a kid some damn change?"

"I don't know—can you?" Pete pushed the man's shoulders. Pete was taller, so he only had to bring up his hands a little to do it.

A few grown-ups and kids had stopped to watch. No one said anything. Aliya could hear the grasses moving out on the water behind her. She had just wanted to look at them.

Then the teddy bear man, who was really just a fat, sweaty man, started to turn away, toward the parking lot, his hands still up.

"I'm out of here," the man said, loud enough for the whole crowd to hear. Then, quiet: "Like I give a fuck about that slut and the gimp."

Pete's face got red. He pulled on the man's shoulder this time, jerking him back toward the crowd.

"The fuck you say?"

Pete made a fist. But the fat man was quick. He made a fist faster and hit Pete. *Fap!*

Pete threw his punch, but it went into the air. The man had stepped back. Then a tall man from the crowd grabbed Pete's arms, and Pete was jerking his shoulders from side to side like a caught fish.

It took two people to hold the fat man's arms.

Back inside, Aliya felt her mouth pull down at the sides and her face went hot. She cried and cried, pulling in short breaths. Crying, crying, crying like a baby. Her head felt light. It was hard to see. The lady from the counter, with the tight hair, was kneeling in front of her, brown eyes with long eyelashes looking right at Aliya's eyes. The world came back. The lady was really a girl, maybe a high schooler. A tiny gem sparkled from the side of her nose. The girl was saying "Shh, shh. Everything's OK."

Mama was holding something on Pete's eye and shaking her head. Mama's face was a mix of anger and something like a smile.

ぐゝ

PETE WAS TALKING ON MAMA'S phone. When it rang in her beach bag, he had opened it and started talking like it was his own phone. He said that she was "indisposed at the time" and "This coming Tuesday?" Yes, he would surely let her know. And "Likewise, you have a good afternoon yourself."

Pete shook his head, leaned back in his beach chair, and put his hands behind his head. He watched Mama pick up Davie from the sand, her bottom in the air, with a smile he used sometimes where he smiled out of just one side of his mouth.

The afternoon beach trip was different from this morning. Now when Pete took out a new beer, instead of pulling the top to make a hissing sound, he first lifted his sunglasses to put it on his cheek, where a bruise circled his eye like a purple and blue moon. Aliya had heard men say her mother was beautiful, wording it in different ways with different kinds of voices. She wondered if Pete was saying something like that in his head.

Finally the hiss came, then Aliya watched Pete bring the beer to his mouth and take a long, gurgling gulp. Watched like she hadn't before, seeing if she could find something new about him. Pete swallowed, then pursed his lips like something tasted sour but so good.

Maybe Pete was right about the strange things he said. Like that the teenagers watching their phones as they walked around the mall were idiots, they didn't know what life was. Or that Miss Chelsea didn't visit to play. What else would someone do with a big ball and bright red and blue blocks? There was something strange about the visits, Aliya knew. Pete said it wasn't really playing but that she had to do it anyway. It was to get her ankle stronger and her toes forward, strong and straight like a pro soccer player. Pete said people should be straightforward with kids.

Pete spotted the little creatures this time, and told Aliya about them. "Cute little guys," Pete said. "Little soft-shell beach clams. You know their whole body is called a foot? And those kind can't even get their whole foot back in the shell sometimes."

The sky was turning blues and grays with some red streaks in it. Pete watched Mama move Davie up the sand when a big wave came, then sit down again, the baby plunking down with a bump and Mama pretending to lose her balance, throwing her legs up in the air with a "Whoa!"

Pete smiled with that strange half smile. *At the museum, he called us his family*, Aliya thought.

"But why?" Aliya asked. She climbed out of the hole and wiped sweat from her forehead.

"Why what, Aliya?" said Pete.

"Why are the soft-shell beach clams too big?"

"You still on that? They just... well, they get too fat and full of themselves," Pete said. He gave her a serious look that Aliya hadn't seen before. "Now you go on digging. We don't have all the beach time in the world, you know. Give ol' Pete some peace."

The hole got skinnier as Aliya dug. If you could pick up the hole right now, and hold it in the air, it would look like an ice cream cone. *Could you pick up a hole?* She thought about asking Pete, but then remembered the serious look.

Aliya tried to shovel out more space to make the hole wider at the tip of the cone but the sand felt heavier there. So she just dug down, deeper and narrower, until she could feel the sand scratch her shoulders from both sides. The floaty jacket Mama made her wear was too big for her to move right.

"Pete, will you take this off?" Aliya asked, pointing to the puffed shoulders of the jacket.

"Well, why not?" Pete said. "This far up the beach, even a tsunami's not gonna get you." He held out one hand. Aliya looked at the hand and held her hand up to hold it and—*whish!*—it was gone. "Gotcha!" Pete said. The second time, Pete kept his hand there and Aliya held it, but her legs did most of the work. When Pete pinched open the clasp, she felt like a clam busted out of its shell and she forgave Pete for taking his hand away.

Where was the fat man now? Aliya wondered. What if he drove up next to them in his car when they went out for firewood, or walked by on the beach? If Aliya saw the man, she knew what she would do. "Mother fucker!" Aliya would say. Then Pete would look at her, and he wouldn't spot the man. Pete wouldn't have to think about how he didn't hit the man back.

When the jacket was off, Aliya sat in the sand between Pete's ankles. She felt the little hairs on Pete's legs tickle her shoulders and liked the feeling of having them on either side of her. The sky had deeper colors now. The waves came closer to where Pete and Aliya had set up their chair, towel, and digging. Some waves came up past them, leaving some water in the hole and puddles nearby it. Some families were packing up their towels.

Then Pete's legs were gone.

Mama stood there with drops of ocean water sparkling along her legs and arms. Her eyes glowed clear. She held Davie's hand, and Davie twisted away, reaching for a gray and black bird that skittered by them. He giggled.

"How's it going, honey?" Mama asked.

"Good," said Aliya and Pete at the same time. Pete looked over at Aliya for a minute, almost angry, and lost his balance for a second. Then he chuckled.

"My two beach bums," Mama said.

Pete was squatting at the cooler now, raking his hands around the ice.

"Two beach bums? No way. We're here holding down the fort. Am I right?"

"Uh huh," Aliya said. She tried a one-sided smile.

"What's wrong with your face?" Pete said.

"What's wrong with *your* face?" Aliya said. She giggled and ducked down in the hole. She stayed crouched, waiting for Pete to laugh. He didn't.

Then Aliya was up in the air, flying on her mother's arms, and then she was on her mother's hip like when she was little.

"How is my beautiful, industrious girl?" Mama said. Mama pushed a kiss into each of Aliya's cheeks like they were thumbprint cookies.

Then Mama froze and looked at Pete. "Peter, where's her life jacket?"

"Kid wanted it off," Pete said. He was holding two beers over the cooler, letting them drip icy water down. He pointed his chin toward the mouth of the hole. "It's over there."

"That is to stay on. You know the rule," Mama said. "Look how close the tide is to where you're sitting!"

"Ada. Jesus." Pete stood up and stood on the other side of Mama from where Aliya sat on her hip, and talked right into Mama's ear. "What do you want from me?"

Mama put Aliya down and pushed Pete down onto a puddle in the sand. The next minute, Aliya and her jacket might as well have gotten to Switzerland. Pete pulled Mama onto his lap, and she made a pretend "Ew!" and said the sand here was all wet. Pete said he'd show her all wet, and Mama turned around to face him. They kissed and Aliya looked at the sand. Davie sat down with a thud, his thumb in his mouth and one finger up his nose.

"Hey, Hot Stuff," Pete said. "You got a call today."

∾

FINDING THEIR WAY ACROSS WET sand when the sun had gone down was hard for adults. Especially tonight. Mama walked lightly for a few steps, then lost her balance a little and stamped for a few steps, and then walked light like a bird again. Aliya felt a chill and it was hard to see.

After a shower and a hot dog, Aliya was happy to climb up to the stiff bed at the back of the RV. Through the narrow windows, she saw red and orange campfires, small as cigarette butts. She could smell them, too: sizzling burgers and burnt marshmallows. She liked knowing people were out there.

Mama kissed her own hand with a big *mwa*, then reached her fingertips up. Aliya squirmed over until her cheek met the kiss.

The big map opened with a whoosh. Aliya kept her eyes closed. "You sure they need you tomorrow? It's the summer, for Godsake," Pete whispered. He would look at the crackling paper while he drove, following a line he drew. Only Pete knew why he made the turns and loops that he did.

Mama said the grant, state officials. Dr. Givens needs her. Logistics won't work out themselves. They should go first thing. Tomorrow. Yes, unfortunately. Sorry, honey.

Pete knew she ran things over there, he said. No problem. *Capisce. Entiendo.* Aliya felt a warm balloon of pride in her chest and a sinking sadness in her stomach all at once. Tomorrow. No more digging, no way to see if she would get to anything beyond more water and big-footed clams.

∾

THE MAN HAD FOUND THEM after all. Despite Aliya's careful watch. The man, or someone like the man with short fur and a bear's ears, was walking toward them on the beach. Pete didn't see him, and though the fat man tramped closer every second, he didn't see Pete either.

The man said something without making a sound. "Gimp." His lips made the word without realizing, like he was singing to himself, but like he hated the word, or like he had something bitter in his mouth. Each time, a pop at the end. "GimPAH. GimPAH."

The man got closer, but Pete was still rolling in the sand with Mama. He pulled Mama's hair and growled. *Rrrruff!* Mama's face turned angry. But then Mama was laughing, because Pete was playing with her hair, like the strings on a puppet. *Ruff! Ruff!*

Aliya woke up to a glowing window. A dog barked a few campsites away.

She had to finish the hole. She just knew she had to. This was her plan: to scratch at the sides until she could get a better angle, to dig faster. Both Mama and Pete would see she could do it. She would make up for Pete's punch in the face and Mama's worry about her limping little girl. She could get to Switzerland, too. Or at least a little closer.

Aliya knew where it was. Just over the dunes in a straight line from the campsite.

Mama lay curled up on the bottom bunk, with Pete next to her on his back with his mouth open. He made low, dragging noises. Davie's crib blocked the usual way out, but Aliya climbed around it.

"I'm going outside," Aliya said, in a whisper. No one answered.

Aliya's feet ground through the sand and avoided the stones and grass expertly. She had to be smarter than other people when she walked, she knew. She had to understand both the path of her good foot and how the turned foot would fall. There was the bathhouse, there was the red piece of wood, there was the low fence blocking people from walking on part of the sand. There was the old juice container, full of water and tiny, squirming worms.

Pete and Aliya and Mama and Davie had passed this before.

હ

"IT'S LUCKY I FELL BELLY up when he knocked into me," Mama had told a friend on the phone. Her face shone from the tears on it, but she smiled. "If not, then David Junior... I can't even imagine." Her only wish, she told the friend, was that her husband could come back for one day to see their beautiful baby boy.

Aliya had tried to remember that day, but she just recalled his face twisted and the sharp, tinny smell of blood. Now Aliya wasn't sure if she was remembering that day, or remembering that memory, like going back to watch a video of herself. The word for it—the what happened—was something like anyour or amoor. Amoorism?

Grandma had been happy that Aliya could visit and see their beloved zoo, but she wished under better circumstances. Grandma laughed a little at her joke, then cried. Her daddy used to love to go to the zoo when he was a child in San Diego, Grandma said. Aliya saw herself, a little girl, doing the same thing her father had done as a boy. Later, he went to live in Maryland, and now he had died. Sometime later, maybe when she was four, Aliya knew the same would happen to her, too. But when would she fall down?

Pete had told her that those worms were mosquito larvas. "Larvae," Mama had said. That must have been yesterday, though it seemed like a long time ago.

∽

AT THE FUNERAL, THEY HAD walked out of the crowd of skirts, stiff pants, and a dull green carpet to the moment Aliya remembered most about the day: Her mother looking at the sky, her hands shaking as she brushed Aliya's hair with her fingers, the hill of her belly hugging her daughter through a smooth, black dress. It was a sky full of thick strokes of pink and orange, like it was painted with three fingers, with a sun big and bright sinking. The sun looked like it would burn through the buildings on the horizon and keep on going. But instead the buildings swallowed it.

Back home, Aliya would come to Mama with a drawing to enjoy or two Legos to pull apart. Mama would look at things but not really look at them, like she was still watching the sun.

How could mosquitoes, with their straight, striped bodies and tiny wings, have ever been those squiggly lines?

۷۵

ALIYA WALKED ALONG THE BEACH for a long time before her stomach went tight. She saw nothing but flat sand everywhere. The bright sky had faded to a gray blanket of fog, and a cold wind hit her shoulders. A shard of lightning cut the sky. Then thunder. Where was the water? And the hole? Where were the blue and red umbrellas and the towels and chairs? Aliya would be happy even to see the fat man and woman now. A cold drop on her shoulder. Another one hit her head and started dripping down through her hair.

"Aliya? Where are you?" It sounded like Mama's voice, very far. Aliya felt excited for a minute. She had gotten so far from the campsite. By herself! And now Mama would know it, and pick her up, just Aliya and Mama, and carry her back.

"I'm here!" Aliya screamed it, but her voice sounded tiny. It went nowhere. Or maybe Mama would be mad at her—if they ever found each other with their voices so far apart.

Then another voice, Pete's, higher than usual, louder than Mama's. A Pete-shaped smudge appeared and moved like his steady walk, but faster. "Hey Muhammad Aliya? Ali-yoop?" the smudge said. "Aliiiiyaaaa…"

Pete didn't see her, but he would soon. The smudge got closer. Aliya felt her heart lift up like it had tiny wings and thump back down and then lift up again. She stood still and watched the smudge coming like a dark worm, through the howling storm.

Caroline Langston

The Silent Stars Go By

A NATIVE of Yazoo City, Mississippi, CAROLINE LANGSTON is a convert to the Eastern Orthodox Church. She is a widely published writer and essayist, a winner of the Pushcart Prize, and a commentator for NPR's *All Things Considered*.

O n the night Serena called to say that she would be coming home for Christmas, the year that Daddy got sick, Jody and I were alone in the house. It was a weeknight in December, the year of the Bicentennial, school was almost out. The town Christmas parade on Main Street, always the first Monday in December, had taken place so long ago it seemed like only a memory. At the public elementary school where I was in the fourth grade, we had already had our party, at which we had sung Christmas carols and cut angels from squares of pink and brown construction paper, then decorated them with trails of gold and silver glitter over lines of Elmer's glue. Now they were posted in rows on the bank of windows that filled one whole side of the classroom, and whenever Jody and I drove by at night, they stood out in the dark like a flock of luminous birds.

That night, we were alone in the house because Mama was still at the hospital and Davis had gone off in Daddy's truck without telling anyone where he was going. I could not go to the hospital because a sign in the lobby said that Visitors Must Be At Least 12 Years Of Age. Someone had to look after me, and the lot had fallen to Jody. Jody was twenty-three years old and had recently come back from Berkeley, California—where, he said, you could eat food that was not "this plastic stuff," and there was more than one kind of lettuce available at the grocery store. Well, why don't you just go on back there, my mother always said, if you don't want to eat what we have in Mississippi.

That night, though, Jody dumped a can of Franco-American Spaghetti-Os into a saucepan, lit the gas stove with a wooden match, then ran two glasses under the sink tap and handed one to me, its cool circumference damp and streaming. "What about ice?" I asked.

"Europeans don't use ice," he said. "Besides, Lila, it's cold outside. Why would you want ice anyway?" I had never thought of it like that before.

We ate at the kitchen table from cereal bowls, sitting under the yellow overhead light holding folded slices of white bread in our hands. All around us the house was dark and still, and when the telephone rang, both of us actually jumped. When I ran into the hall to answer it and it was Serena, suddenly the evening was transformed. "It's Serena!" I yelled to Jody, and put down the phone's heavy black receiver. Barefooted, I ran up the stairs to Mama and Daddy's room where the other phone was and sprawled across the quilted taffeta bedspread, and grabbed the blue princess phone off the bedside table while Jody got on the phone downstairs.

It was unimaginable: Serena was coming home for Christmas. She *would* have taken the Greyhound bus, she said, but what with the baby she was worried about getting sick all those hours on the road—"So Jimmy got me a plane ticket from Kansas City," she said. Jimmy Landry was Serena's husband. He was a Catholic from Louisiana, Mama said, and that was the reason that Serena was having a baby. The Monday before Christmas, Jimmy was going to drive her to the airport in K.C., and then on Christmas Eve come down to Mississippi all by himself to be with them—"since this'll be the baby's real first Christmas."

But until he arrived, she said, we had four days where everything was going to be like it was Before, when it was just us, and Mama, Daddy, and Davis. We were just going to have fun, and make it a special Christmas on account of Daddy being sick. "Did y'all put up the Christmas tree yet?" she asked.

We had not. Weeks ago Mama had dragged out from under the stairs the tattered Holsum's breadboxes that held the strings of colored lights and ornaments, but they still sat untouched in the middle of the linoleum den floor.

"I'm afraid we've been kind of preoccupied," Jody said. "We've all just been worried about Daddy."

"Daddy is going to be all right," Serena said, and we believed her; we could hear her insistence coming through the line across the thousand miles between here and Kansas.

"Tell him I'm getting there as fast as I can," she said, and rattled off the flight information to Jody. "See you Monday, then," she added, and until I heard the purring of the dial tone, I didn't even realize that she had hung up the phone.

I ran back downstairs without bothering to straighten out Mama and Daddy's bedspread. Jody was standing in the hallway, loitering the same way he always did, but now the house was filled with radiance: Serena was coming home, and there were only a couple of days before she arrived.

We abandoned the cereal bowls on the kitchen table and immediately set to work: Jody whipped out his wallet to see how much cash he had left over from his last paycheck as the assistant manager of the Acacia Theater, and when he saw that he had enough, we lit out for the Jitney Jungle in Mama's Chrysler New Yorker to buy a Christmas tree. Standing in the cold in front of the store, in the pool of fluorescent light cast through the plate glass windows, we ran our hands over the delicate branches of scotch pine, fir, and cedar, until Jody pointed to one, a cedar, and the shivering bag boy in his bow tie and shirtsleeves helped haul it into the trunk.

At home we dragged it through the driveway and into the den, in which the heavy bed where my father had lain for months before going to the hospital still sat, carefully made. Feathery cedar twigs scattered behind us. Somehow Jody found the red iron Christmas tree stand and tilted the tree into it. When we stepped back, the tree looked just a tiny bit lopsided, but Jody said there was no way he was going to go look for a saw at this time of night.

We started to decorate the tree: Jody unrolled the heavy strings of colored lights, checking to see that there were no burnt-out bulbs, then wound them carefully among the skinny limbs. Then we lifted the mirrored red, green, and silver balls from their egg-carton boxes and threaded them with hooks to hang on the branches. I dropped one onto the floor, where it shattered open to show its silver-mirrored insides. "Don't worry about it," Jody said, kicking the broken pieces out of our way for now. He said he would clean it up later. After that came the crystal angels with their garlands and trumpets, risen from between the flat layers of a *Clarion-Ledger* newspaper from last January.

"Do we want icicles?" I asked, pulling out a hank of silvery strands from a box that pictured snow-capped mountains and said "ninety-nine cents."

"No, I think it looks tacky," Jody said, and so we left them off. Serena wouldn't like them anyway: Too artificial.

It was way past my bedtime. I fell asleep in my clothes on the den sofa during the WLBT 10 o'clock news, then woke up during the Johnny Carson show when my mother finally walked through the door. She had gotten a ride home from Daddy's nurse who was getting off her shift. "You put up the Christmas tree!" she said to us, surprised, clapping her hands, her eyes lit up, and for a second you could see that she had once looked like Serena. Turning to me she said, "But what are you doing still awake? Go on off to bed right this minute. Now, scoot!" To Jody she said, "I can't believe you let her stay up until all hours of the night like that," but Jody only folded his hands in front of him and looked at the floor. "I'm sorry, I'm sorry," he said, though I could tell he wasn't.

Later, after I washed my face and brushed my teeth and Mama came to tuck me into bed, she kissed me on the forehead and said, "Your father says to send you that, and to tell you he'll be home for Christmas."

During the next few days, that was the hope that hung in the air around us: If he was well enough, they were going to let Daddy out of the hospital for Christmas. As though Serena's telephone call had been a kind of unexpected herald, everyone in the house got excited about Christmas in a way that was different from any year that I could remember. Jody still sat around all day long in his place on the living room sofa, reading his film and French philosophy books, but he kept the Christmas tree lights plugged in even during the daytime and sang along with his Roxy Music albums on the stereo, out loud, until Davis came home and told him to cut them off.

On Friday afternoon, Mama left Jody at the hospital to sit with Daddy and said that she was going to Meadowbrook Mart in Jackson; she came home late in the evening with a trunkful of identically wrapped presents from McRae's, all with gold stamped seals bearing the McRae's logo. I took the thirty dollars I had been saving in a coffee can in the closet and bought little presents for everyone at Abraham's, the Lebanese department store downtown. Even Davis was affected, and Saturday morning brought out a decorated canister of Christmas spiced tea that one of his girlfriends had made from cinnamon, instant iced tea mix, and Tang. The can was covered in red and green felt and had the cutout of a reindeer on it, along with glued-on sequins that spelled out "DAVIS" in gold and silver. "You want a mug?" he asked as he stood at the kitchen sink running water into the copper teakettle. "It's good."

Serena was coming home, Serena was coming home: I played it over and over again in my mind the same way that at one time I had thought about Santa Claus. *Five days until Serena comes. Four.* I had not seen her since her wedding more than two years ago: Serena was tall and stiff and elegant in her long lace dress and the Baptist church filled with Jimmy Landry's relatives who looked just like he did, with black hair and milk-white skin so pale that it appeared blue. She had married a boy from the ROTC even though she had been a student radical at Sophie Newcomb: "Gone over to the other side," my father called it, shaking his head and chuckling. She had taught kindergarten to ghetto children in the St. Thomas projects, and once, when Richard Nixon came to New Orleans, Serena had somehow ended up getting arrested—a word that still made my mother drop her voice and whisper whenever she told the story. People Serena used to run around with were now on the run from the FBI and lived other lives somewhere out in the country.

My family told these stories again and again; Mama, Daddy, Jody, and Davis passing them back and forth like worn game chips, that had been passed to me so many times they were also a part of my memory. But I had my own memory as well: Way back in the reaches of my own recollection, I remembered being held in her arms against slippery satin the night of her high school graduation, the stadium lights shining down on her long blonde hair that was parted in the middle. Now she was going to have a baby of her own.

When Monday morning finally came, my mother was already back at the hospital and Davis was still asleep from having stayed out all night at a party at the lake. When I walked into the kitchen in my nightgown hungry for a bowl of cereal, Jody announced it was we who would be charged with picking up Serena.

Within an hour we were dressed and ready, the December air tingling against our skin. Midmorning sun fell in slanting rays across the fields of dead cotton stalks that stretched the sixty miles of highway to Jackson, which were broken only by tiny towns and leaf-shorn stands of trees. In Flora we stopped to go to the bathroom at the whitewashed Billups gas station which had hundreds of cheap stuffed animals for sale, hanging from the ceiling inside. When I came back from the ladies' room with the wooden key paddle in my hand, Jody had bought cups of instant hot chocolate for both of us; the scalding water burned my tongue but the Styrofoam cup was warm within my hands. "We'll get lunch later, after Serena gets here," Jody said.

When we finally arrived, the Allen C. Thompson Airport was lit with the glare of windshields and chrome, and filled with the bustle of Christmas travelers. It was a familiar ritual to me from all the times I had gone with Mama and Daddy when Jody was coming home from Columbia, or when we were sending him back there, before he dropped out and went to Berkeley and then came home to stay. Jody checked on Serena's gate and we drifted down the concourse through the river of families who moved past in groups, talking and laughing, carrying shopping bags of presents marked with the names of department stores I had never heard of, like Goldwater's and Maison Blanche, whose very names seemed to trail an air of distant glamour into the echoing concourse.

There was nothing, though, that could look as brilliant as Serena did when her face appeared in the jetway door, framed by the crowd around her. "Serena!" I shrieked. Her eyes searched and caught us, and then she was bounding down the carpeted aisle ahead of everyone in front of her, all of whom turned and seemed to take note of her with the same amazement I felt. She was wearing a blue jean skirt and a loose gauze blouse (why wasn't she cold?) that was embroidered with morning glories and which skimmed lightly over her belly that was just rounding, as though she were trying to stick her stomach out. She was wearing clogs that thudded on her feet, and her still-long blonde hair whipped back when she finally reached me and bent to crush me against her. "Lila Lila Lila Lila," she said. I could feel the energy that was in her long arms, and sense myself being swept along by it.

I twisted my face to the side and said, "Can I touch your stomach?" and she laughed and said, "Of course you can," and it felt like the curved rind of a hoop of cheese. The she straightened up and, less exuberantly, clasped Jody, who then turned and asked, "Are there any bags you checked?"

"No, I got it all in here, " she said, pointing at two tote bags looped over her shoulder. "Can you believe?"

"Well, let me take one," Jody said, and slung one of the bags over his back. That was something Daddy would do. I had never thought that before, that Jody could be like Daddy. We walked back up the concourse; all of the people were happy, talking and sparkling, but we were the sparkliest of all. Serena walked fast up ahead of us, her long hair swaying in the back, her arms swinging at her sides. "Let's sing, y'all," she said, then even started to, in her high voice that sounded like a icicle or a silver bell: *Christmas is coming/The goose is getting fat/Please put a penny in the old man's hat.* I wished that I could have had a kindergarten teacher like her.

"If it's a boy," Serena said over her shoulder, out of nowhere, "we're thinking of naming him Ezekiel. That or maybe Tristan."

"Listen, do you want to get something to eat before we drive back?" Jody said. "We're hungry." It was afternoon now. I had forgotten that my stomach was rumbling.

I looked at Jody. A while back he had cut off all his hair, which had been long ever since I could remember. Sometimes when I wasn't thinking I looked at him and was surprised all over to see it short.

"Where would you want to go?" he said.

We stood in the brown asphalt parking lot in front of the airport, the high buzz of a jet taking off in the background. "Let's do something special," Serena said. "Let's go to Primos Northgate. We're all adults now, aren't we?" A second later her eyes fell on me and she laughed and said, "You too, Lila," and patted me on the head. I beamed.

Primos Northgate was one of the fanciest restaurants in town—a vast cement and tinted glass labyrinth of convention rooms named after Con- federate themes, a bakery, and a dining room that filled the parking lot with Cadillacs and Lincolns at noon and every night. It was the kind of restaurant my parents went to only rarely, on special occasions like their anniversary, and I was thrilled. When we pulled through the wrought iron gates that fronted the massive building on North State Street, Jody swing the Chrysler New Yorker under the covered driveway that shielded the entrance, and then ran around the front of the car to open the doors for Serena and me. When had he ever done that before? Jody ran to park the car and then, following behind Serena, we swept through the double plate glass doors.

Though it was late for lunch in Mississippi, the dining room was still filled with the tinny din of conversation; white-haired old ladies and businessmen in starched shirtsleeves still sat over white oval plates of country-fried steak and oysters Rockefeller, ice melting in the glasses of tea before them, even in December. I was already thinking of the fudge pecan ball, a specialty of the restaurant, that I was planning to order for dessert. All of the people in the dining room were acting Christmas—jovial, and colored lights twinkled from small trees set here and there throughout the space. This was the finest place to me, the social summit of the world I knew. Serena stepped to the lip of the dining room and beckoned to the hostess, saying, "Could we please have a table for three?"

Then I noticed something else I had never seen before. The people in the Primos dining room were glancing up from their bread plates and their butter knives and were looking curiously at Serena: at the long blonde tongues of her messy hair, the morning glory shirt that clung a little too closely to her stomach and breasts. They did not look at all dazzled by my amazing sister, but instead seemed to demonstrate a combination of embarrassment and pity, as if Serena had done something horribly wrong, but just didn't know it.

Seeing their reactions, part of me wanted to jump forward and yell, "Y'all quit looking at her." But just then, just as unexpectedly, I instantly knew that I was filled with embarrassment too, and would have given anything at the moment for Serena not to look the way she did. In this outspoken and independent family I had always been told we had, I knew in that moment that I was a traitor.

The auburn-haired, beehived hostess motioned with the three heavy menus in her hand for us to follow her. Suddenly, as though she could judge our reactions, Serena wheeled around and pointed across the Primos lobby to the tiny cocktail lounge and said, "Can I ask, would it be possible for us to eat in there?"

"Of course," the hostess said, probably relieved, and led us into the enclosed room that, in the one or two times in my life I had been to Primos Northgate, had always been a source of satisfaction for me: a little window-less jewel box of dark upholstery, mirrors, and light glinting off shelved amber bottles. Because we were Baptists and Baptists were not supposed to drink, for me to actually be in that dim room was all the more exciting, and I was glad we were hidden from all the scrutinizing eyes outside. We sat in the curvy French chairs, and the hostess left us with the menus. Jody wondered out loud whether the gumbo was any good. I said that I wanted to have the Chicken Supreme.

We were alone in the lounge except for the black bartender who wore a mustard-colored jacket and a medium Afro and who leaned against a steel refrigerator that hummed into the silence. "May I please have a scotch and water?" Serena asked.

Instantly Jody frowned. "Are you sure it's all right," he said, nodding at her belly, "for you to have something like that?"

"Once in a while won't hurt a thing," Serena said. "Really."

Hearing this Jody decided to order a bourbon on the rocks, and when I said, "How come I can't get anything?" Serena asked the bartender for a Shirley Temple, and wordlessly the bartender brought one to me, a clear-pink concoction speared through with maraschino cherries on a toothpick. Serena said, "Let's toast, y'all," and we all put our glasses together and she said, "To Daddy."

"To Daddy!" we echoed, and each of us drank. And then the afternoon started to become very strange; the high excitement of the hours till then fell, and it was as though the day were a thread being slowly spun out from a spool. Serena started talking—about everything, it seemed: the way that sunset looked on the Flint Hills of Kansas, all of the things that the Head Start kids she taught had to go without ("Some of them don't even have pencils, for God's sake. It's as bad as Mississippi."), what it was like to wake up each and every day and be married to Jimmy Landry.

Jody did not understand, she said. There was no way that he could understand. A waitress in a frilly apron and a hairnet brought our lunch on the same white oval plates, and a gold wire basket filled with cornbread and rolls, but still Serena kept on talking, her voice becoming ever lower and measured, as if she were determined to get out whatever it was inside her.

Jody leaned back in his chair and looked at her intently, sloshing the ice cubes around in his drink. He was not paying attention to me. Neither of them ate much of their meal. I, on the other hand, quickly finished my plate, along with the fudge pecan ball, which was as delicious as I had expected, but I could not share it with them because they were not listening. Instead I simply sat there waiting, and as Serena ordered another drink and Jody did in turn, I thought about Mama waiting the long hours in the hospital with Daddy and how this was somehow the same.

How many hours did we sit around that table, in the middle of that room's windowless shadows? All at once Serena and Jody inexplicably started to giggle, breathing hard into the starched gold napkins that until a moment before had lain on their laps. Then something turned and I could tell that Serena had started to cry instead, and that was when Jody took her by her gauze embroidered arm and said, "I think we should probably go." They fumbled between them for the money to pay for the check the waitress brought in on a little black tray; at last Jody pulled out my father's Bank Americard, which Daddy only rarely used. I could not imagine why Jody had it. He signed the credit card ticket with a flourish and then we both helped shepherd Serena out of the door. "Don't cry, Serena," I said, reaching my palm up to stroke the back of her hair. "It's all going to be OK."

By now it might have been midnight outside for all I knew, and I was startled when I saw that it was still daylight. We put Serena in the front seat of the Chrysler New Yorker, then crawled through the afternoon Christmas shopping traffic with all of us silent and the radio turned up on the FM rock station, WZZQ. Finally Jody arrived at Delta Drive, the wide boulevard that ran past dilapidated markets and exhausted neon motels, then shot a straight two-lane line of highway deep into the country.

It was the road we had driven on that morning. But now, in the weakening afternoon sun, the fields seemed not merely the worn end of a decaying season, but something more permanent, eternal, and vast. Suddenly this too reminded me of Christmas, the Christmas we had sung about in school: *A cold winter's night that was so deep.* I knew now what that meant.

The light was truly falling now, and we were driving into its emptiness. When finally we drove through the crossroads that marked the far edge of our little town, Serena reared up from where she had settled quietly against the seat, and said as though she had awakened, "Jody, Jody, please take me first to the hospital!"

And that was what Jody did: Drove down Main Street, the artery that split our town in two, and pulled the Chrysler New Yorker into the dark parking lot of the Good Samaritan Hospital, which was white and long and low and seemed to steam through the night like a ship. Serena got out and slammed the door (wasn't she cold in that morning glory blouse?), and we clambered up the cement stairs behind her, and through the heavy plate glass and metal doors, and into the linoleum lobby, right up to the sign that said Visitors Must Be At Least 12 Years Of Age. "May I help you?" a nurse in a white cap behind the registration desk said, and Serena said, "It's my daddy, I've got to go see my daddy," and right at that moment Jody looked at me and I looked back at him, but it was already happening, the nurse was already pointing through another set of metal and glass doors ("We'll be back in just a second"), which were opening before them and just as quickly again they closed, leaving me alone.

Christmas came to me then, under that fluorescent lobby light. *Above thy deep and dreamless sleep the silent stars go by.* I could see nothing in that antiseptic hall, just the gentle flash of colored bulbs on the miniature plastic Christmas tree that sat on top of the registration desk counter.

Daddy was never going to come home again, I suddenly knew. In another few moments I saw Serena coming back again, framed inside those glass doors, collapsed against Jody's shoulder. I rushed to circle my arms around her and bury my wet face against her waist, and tell her to shush, and even at nine years of age know enough to lie and say that everything was going to be all right, truly it was. Hadn't Serena herself said so?

Barbara F. Lefcowitz

The Pink Suit

BARBARA F. LEFCOWITZ (1935–2015) was a professor of English at Anne Arundel College in Maryland and taught at the Writer's Center in Bethesda, Maryland, where she was a guiding light. A poet and fiction writer, her books include *A Risk of Green*, *The Wild Piano*, *The Queen of Lost Baggage*, *Red Lies and White Lies*, *The Politics of Snow*, *Photo, Bomb, Red Chair: New Poems*, and *The Blue Train to America*. She was the recipient of grants and fellowships from the Rockefeller Foundation, the Maryland Arts Council, and the National Endowment for the Arts.

I've never told a soul before: you, reader, are the first to know that for over twenty-five years I, Mrs. Arlene Schramm Duley, have had in my possession the pink suit that the late Jacqueline Kennedy Onassis wore that day in Dallas. Bloodstains, the little black velvet collar, buttons and all, though I don't know what happened to the matching pillbox hat.

I suppose she never included the hat when she sent the suit out to be cleaned. Back in 1963, my father, the late Henry J. Schramm, owned a dry-cleaning store on 7th and F Streets, less than a mile from the White House. It was called Congressional Cleaners and my mother and him—her name was Matilda Schramm—did indeed take care of lots of congressmen's suits and shirts. They would give personal attention to each customer's clothing, as if they were grooming a poodle or piping frosted roses on a wedding cake. Mamma would iron some of the collars and ruffles by hand. Not at all like today, when you're lucky if your skirt shows up on the computer. Mrs. Kennedy—to this day I can't bear to call her Mrs. Onassis—would send Daddy all of her outfits. Mamie Eisenhower had recommended him to her. In fact, he went all the way back to Eleanor Roosevelt, though she never fussed much with clothes. I remember as a kid how once she came into the store herself and how I stared up at her, feeling a little bit sorry that she was wearing this flowery cotton smock-like dress instead of the shiny purple silk gown I imagined a president's wife would wear. I think she smiled at me but I'm not absolutely sure.

When daddy died of a sudden heart attack in 1969—Mamma had passed away two years before—my sister Jeanette and me went through the store, contacting customers, cleaning up, doing inventory, all those sad postmortem chores. If I hadn't tripped on a torn place in the old tan linoleum back in a dark corner of the store, I would never have found The Suit, which was hanging like an empty skin inside a plastic bag that was stuck to it in several places because of the heat. Immediately I knew it was the suit, I can't explain why, it's just that I had that certain feeling. And I snuck it home, making sure Jeannette didn't know, hiding it inside a garment bag way in the back of a closet in the attic of our house in Wheaton, so my husband and kids wouldn't suspect nothing. Of course, I did cut through some of the plastic and, sure enough, there were the bloodstains still on the suit, though they were considerably faded.

Did I feel guilty? Well, in a way, yes, I've got to admit it. But I also felt I had been blessed with a special privilege; maybe responsibility is the right word. You see, Mrs. Kennedy and I were the same age almost to the day, and from the first time I saw her picture, I adored her. My Mary Ellen was born a few weeks after Caroline and my Kenneth two months before John-John. To top it off, I too had a miscarriage, the same time she gave birth to poor little Patrick who died of Hyaline Membrane Disease. Though I'd never heard of that disease before, I couldn't get it out of my mind no matter how hard I tried. Hyaline Membrane Disease, even now it sounds terribly important and scary. I guess I was luckier than her, though, because when I miscarried I never had to look at the lost baby. Oh, how I cried for her then, and so many times later.

Unlike some of my friends, though, I never tried to look or act like her. How could a short plump woman like me even pretend to look like a goddess? How could Arlene Schramm Duley, born 1930 in Baltimore and raised on Farragut Road off 16th Street in Washington; a commercial-track graduate of the now-demolished Central High School and wife of George Duley, branch manager of a Peoples Drug Store; Arlene Schramm Duley who, except for one trip to New York City when I was eleven, had never been out of the Washington area, let alone to a foreign country; Arlene Schramm Duley whose greatest talents are baking snickerdoodles, embroidering guest towels, running up simple dresses on my old Singer, and doing some china painting—how in the world could I be so uppity as to pretend I looked and acted like Mrs. Jacqueline Bouvier Kennedy? Besides, I was perfectly content with my life, dull as it might sound. I never even kept a scrapbook of her pictures like my friend Betty Walsh did. Every single picture and news article she could lay her hands on! I guess I'm just not that kind of person; I don't even have no pictures of my own kids' graduations or the time George and me rented a place in Ocean City. One time we considered going all the way up north to Maine, a place called Ogunquit where George's cousin has a house, but we were afraid it would be covered with ice, even in summer.

Just to pick her brain, I once, in a real cagey way, asked my daughter Mary Ellen (she was taking courses at the community college) what she would do if she had secret possession of the pink suit. At first—would you believe it—she said she didn't even know what I was talking about. When I explained, she just laughed. "Oh that pink suit. With the little black velvet collar? It's nothing but a cliché." When I pressed her further, she said it was trite, out of date, and she couldn't imagine for the life of her why I asked about such a dumb thing. Still I wondered what to do with it and back around 1978 approached the Smithsonian about donating the suit to them, but I guess they thought I was just another one of those crackpots, like all those weirdos writing books about assassination conspiracies. They never gave me an answer even after I went there in person, suit in hand, all nicely wrapped in a fresh plastic bag and tied with pink ribbons. So back it went into the attic closet nobody ever opened. I myself actually forgot about it after a while.

But then I heard back in May 1994 how sick Mrs. Kennedy was. I could hardly believe it when she died so suddenly; just a couple of hours after I arrived in New York on the Greyhound to stand outside her apartment house with lots of other people. Don't ask me why I went, I just had to, that's all. I didn't even get to see Caroline or John-John or that paunchy bald guy, whatever his name is, her lover. I did, though, get to see the hearse on the way to Arlington Cemetery after standing four hours in the hot sun. Just to glimpse it for a few seconds. I think I saw one of Bobby's sons, the one with lots of curly hair, and another nephew, not the kind of sleazy guy who got in trouble last year with a girl down in Florida, but maybe Teddy's son, you know, the one who had cancer. I also saw Hillary Clinton, but to be honest, I don't like her one bit. Much too uppity, as if her mother never taught her the proper way to be a woman. Yes, I know, it's the mid-1990s and like Mary Ellen tells me, oh, Mother—in that mocking way of hers—things have changed. Even so, I'm entitled to my opinion, right? So what if I'm a cliché. What Mary Ellen and Hillary don't realize is that they themselves are clichés, just a different kind of cliché.

It was when I went to Arlington the next day and placed a bunch of roses on Mrs. Kennedy's grave that I realized that now I really did have to do something with the suit. It just didn't seem right to keep it hidden now that she was dead. Just leaving it on her grave with all the flowers and notes was one possibility, but the park police would probably remove it right away and put it in the trash, not even bothering to donate it to Goodwill or the Purple Heart. If only I had more imagination! Like I had when I was a kid!

Some lady with bright orange hair was kneeling over President Kennedy's flame, so close her dress almost caught fire before a guard ushered her away. Something I had seen once on TV crossed my mind: how in India the widow of a dead man has to throw herself into the flames when he's cremated. I forget what they call it but I thought it was pretty awful. Why should the wife have to die just because her husband died? I'm no libber, as you know, but that really seems unfair to women.

Well, one thought led to another and I decided I would sneak back at night with the suit and toss it, all bunched up, into the Eternal Flame. I could just see it burning up, the flames leaping higher and higher and little shreds of pink wool soaring over the Potomac like a great storm of cherry blossoms, or better yet, like what happens with the fireworks on the Fourth of July. And then the suit would be gone, one last great salute to Mrs. Kennedy, and my conscience would be free. Yes, it was exactly the right thing to do.

The only problem was I couldn't get anywhere near the flame when I drove to Arlington a few nights later. I could see it all right, glowing in the warm distance. All the tourists had left and it was so peaceful and quiet I could have stayed outside the locked gate all night. But the park police got suspicious and told me to leave. Maybe they thought I was carrying a bomb in the plain Giant Food sack I had stuffed the suit in. For a minute I tried to explain my mission, but I could tell the man just thought I was another of those nut cases on the loose from Saint Elizabeth's. So much for the great wild flames and pink shreds soaring over the Potomac! And there I was again, wishing I had some imagination.

If only I could consult Mrs. Kennedy herself, I remember thinking. Sure enough she would have some bright idea of what to do with the suit. Not that I believe in any afterlife. But it did cross my mind that she must be very busy catching her husband up on all the things that happened since he was shot. Just think: he never heard of Lee Harvey Oswald or Jack Ruby or the Warren Commission or how Bobby was assassinated or about Chappaquiddick and Mary Jo Kopechne, or Watergate or how Vietnam finally ended or how Ronald Reagan ended the Cold War or all the nasty stories about him and those Mafia women and God knows what else. Would she tell him about that awful man, Aristotle Onassis? I hoped not.

I guess I would never have thought of the solution if Mary Ellen had not complained to me over the phone (she's married now and a mother herself) how the stores had no summer skirts that looked right on her. Either they were too short—unfortunately she inherited my fat legs—or too long, all the way to the floor as if you were going to a ball. Could I run her up something on my old Singer? Of course. And while I was at it, having chosen some real nice cotton with daisies on it, why not make a few nips and tucks on the pink skirt, add an elastic band and an extra panel so it would fit me and wear the darn thing myself? How crazy that I hadn't thought of doing that a long time ago. Now the jacket was a real problem, there wasn't much I could do with that, but the skirt would be perfect.

Naturally, I didn't tell a soul that my new pink skirt had been remodeled from Mrs. Jacqueline Bouvier Kennedy's skirt. The bloodstains I concealed with a clever little sash. I don't think I can possibly express to you how great I felt when I wore that skirt. Tall, rich, beautiful, clever, every bit as worthy as the late Mrs. Kennedy. Like I was wearing a brand-new skin. Soon I began to feel that way even when I wasn't wearing the skirt, like I really had created for myself a new skin. I didn't even care that nobody seemed to notice, not George, bless his heart; not Mary Ellen or Kenny; not Betty Walsh or any of the girls I went bowling with. Not even the teacher of my china painting class at the Y. But, like I said, I didn't even care. What was important was that I myself noticed.

So when later that summer there was a special show at the Smithsonian about the Kennedy era called "Camelot Revisited," I didn't even blink when I saw on display the pink suit, complete with the little black velvet collar and buttons. Not one blink. Because I knew it was no more real than the silk roses that supposedly stood for the roses she was carrying thatdayinDallas.

Fiona J. Mackintosh

Penitentiary

FIONA J. MACKINTOSH is a British writer living in Washington, D.C. Her short stories have been published on both sides of the Atlantic and have been longlisted for Plymouth University's 2015 short fiction prize and the Heekin Group Foundation's Tara Fellowship in Short Fiction. Her flash fiction "On Warren Ward" won the TSS Flash Fiction Competition in November 2015. You can follow her on Twitter @Fionajanemack or on her blog Midatlantic, http://fiona-midatlantic.blogspot.co.uk/.

I.

THROUGH THE LOCKED SCREEN DOOR, Thelma looks out into the dark front yard. Theirs is the only house on the block where the porch light isn't on all night—waste of electricity Perry says. As Thelma pushes open the screen door, a sliver of shadow disconnects itself from the darkness and darts inside, with a flick of tail against her leg. The cat is in. The newspaper bundled in its lurid orange bag has been laid gently, precisely, across the exact center of the mat. All Thelma has to do is bend to pick it up.

Thelma's always woken long before Perry. The minute the first bird starts up in the tall trees at the bottom of the yard, her eyes open and she's pitched into the day. She wakes to every nagging worry that had been in her mind when she turned off the light. Perry is the opposite. He sleeps like their dog Mustard used to, with dreams so vivid that they make his legs twitch.

Even though he isn't there, liable to wake at the least little noise, Thelma moves quietly. It's a habit. Nora's upstairs in her old room, but she sleeps like a hibernating bear. Always did. It used to be a devil of a job getting her up for school.

She has to heft up the front door by the knob as she closes it or it'll wear on the linoleum, which annoys Perry. It annoys him even more if she suggests he fix it. He always says he'll do it, just as he says he'll clean out the basement and put down proper flooring and build them a powder room down there. But that's Perry. Since he retired from the carpentry business after his first heart attack, every hour is his to spend as he pleases. Meanwhile, Thelma does the cooking, cleaning, shopping, and laundry, takes the car to be serviced, balances the checkbook, and picks out birthday cards and gifts for his family as well as hers. Somehow it never occurs to him to help, not even when she was working eight hours a day as the receptionist at the veterinary clinic and sometimes even a half-day on Saturdays.

It's her own fault. She let it happen. Nora's always saying, "Pack up and come and live with me for a while, Mom. It'll do the lazy bastard good to have to look after himself for a change."

But the one time she tried it, she'd spent a week of precious vacation time picking up after Nora in her one-bedroom walkup in Brooklyn. "Just leave it, Mom," Nora would say when Thelma put newspapers in the recycling bin or hung up a pair of jeans on a pants hanger. When Thelma came home, pushing open the front door with her rear end as she slid in her large suitcase, Perry had looked up from his chair with undisguised relief. He even made her a grilled cheese sandwich for dinner. As she ate it, he admitted he'd been wearing the same underwear two days in a row because he couldn't make head nor tail of the dials on the washing machine.

She keeps the main light off in the kitchen, just flicking on the small fluorescent bulb above the sink. She can see the sky turning milky gray above the Beltway, which hums out of sight beyond the end of the yard. All those cars now where there was nothing but woodland and a stream at the bottom of a steep embankment. Where Nora and Joe played and later likely went to smoke cigarettes and hide from their parents. The teenage years. Not a time she'd volunteer to go through again.

Waiting for the teakettle to boil, she looks into the dark living room, thinking for the thousandth time how tired she is of the same old furniture. Nora and Joe's wife have given her ideas—putting up a picture here, buying a sectional, getting rid of the bulky TV set on its ugly stand. But it all means spending money. Perry told her to go ahead long ago, but she's never been able to do it. She's afraid it won't end up the way she hoped and it'll all have been for nothing.

Regrets come either way—whether you do a thing or you don't.

II.

AT THE FOOT OF THE hospital bed, Nora plays with the gizmo for changing the angle. Perry says, "Higher. No, too high."

He's grumpy today, a good sign.

"Where's lunch? It's noon, isn't it? Not that it'll be worth eating."

"You made short work of that corned beef hash yesterday," Nora says, now rearranging the items on his tray table like she's playing chess with herself.

Perry's bed is the one closest to the door. Behind the curtain his roommate breathes heavily in his sleep. The light changes in the big urban sky outside the window, but the artificial light in the hospital is always the same. You can't tell what time of day it is or even what season out there in the staccato, keyboard clatter of life. It's like walking through a denser substance than air. Every noise is muffled, even the endlessly ringing phone at the nurses' station.

Thelma says, "Someone's been putting the paper on the mat every morning. I think it's Ricky Mullin."

Perry moves his legs in the bed.

"He'd better keep his distance if he knows what's good for him."

Nora pulls a chair up to the bed and sits down.

"Why you guys didn't move after that business I'll never understand." Perry is indignant.

"Why should we? Why should that criminal drive us out of our own home?"

Thelma fiddles with the clasp on her pocketbook.

"He tried to apologize when he got out, but your father wouldn't have it. He turned his back when Ricky tried to shake hands."

"Don't blame you, Dad. He was always trouble, even before the PCP and crack and whatnot. He asked me to a dance once in high school. No way I was that desperate."

There are footsteps in the hallway and then a doctor is in the room, holding a buff file against his white coat. There is a tiny shaving nick on his smooth young face, high up near the ear. Thelma wonders how old he can possibly be.

"Hello folks. Mr. Hood, how are you feeling today?"

Perry shifts in the bed, trying to sit up straighter.

"Better, thank you, Doctor."

"That's what we like to hear."

The young medic looks at each of them in turn.

"Well, we've had a look at your EKG and your angiogram and things look pretty good."

Thelma lets out a breath.

"As you know, we've put a stent in that one artery and all seems well there. You may also have had a touch of angina so we'd like to keep you in for another day or so for observation to see how the meds go. But we'll get you back home as soon as we possibly can. All right?"

Again the doctor nods his head at Perry, Thelma, and Nora in turn, and in unison they all say, "Thank you, Doctor."

Thelma goes to Perry, and he lets her take his hand. She feels the carpenter's calluses on his palm, still there after ten years of retirement.

"Looks like you've got to put up with me for a while longer."

There is moisture at the corner of his eyes. On an impulse, she kisses the thinning hair on the top of his head. There is a rattling of trolley wheels and a cheery aide with some sort of Asian accent calls, "Lunch, Mr. Hood! Meatloaf today—yum yum."

Thelma and Nora go down the shiny-floored hallway to call Joe from the pay phone. Empty IV stands and blood pressure machines cluster in corners. Thelma sits on a hard chair in the waiting area and fumbles in her purse for her long-distance card and the scrap of paper with her pass code on it.

"I'm going to tell him not to come now Dad's doing better."

Nora stands in front of her, her hands working inside the pockets of her red wool coat.

"Of course you are. Why put Joe out? He has a life."

"Oh Nora, that's not it. You're just closer is all. It's a long way to come from Houston. And you must get on home now your dad's on the mend. I can cope, really."

"Maybe so, but I'm not leaving till Dad's back on his feet. Especially with Ricky Mullin hanging around."

III.

SHE'D BEEN SITTING AT THE kitchen table with the paper spread out in front of her, leaning in to read her horoscope. She'd just glanced at her watch—9:15 a.m.—wishing Perry would wake up so she could start the washer. That's how she knew exactly when it happened.

It was a splitting of sound, like the inside of her head had exploded. Perry shouted a filthy word she'd never heard him use before. Rigid, she sat at the table, eyes wide, staring and staring like looking hard would yield an explanation. Then the second explosion, her ears still ringing from the first, and she heard Perry yell, "That bastard's shooting at me!"

Gunshots. They were gunshots. She leapt up.

"Perry! Perry! Are you hurt?"

His head appeared round the door at floor level. He wriggled into the kitchen on his stomach, his face red. Getting up into a running crawl, he barreled into Thelma and knocked her down into the space between the fridge and the kitchen cabinet, whacking her leg against the metal sill on the bottom of the fridge. A line of blood oozed through her beige pants. Perry's chin was wedged against her shoulder, pressing her cheek to the linoleum, which didn't feel as clean as it should after all her scrubbing. She could smell his morning breath as he panted against her face and the iron tang of sweat from inside his pajamas. Her knee throbbed.

"Where is he? What if he comes round to the patio?"

Perry waved his hand to shush her. From outside in the street, they heard a woman's scream and voices shouting.

"He's crazy!"

"Shit, he's got a gun!"

"He's heading for the Mandelbaums! Someone warn them."

They heard the commotion move off down the street, but Perry kept her down on the floor for another half hour till they could hear not just the sirens but the actual cackle of police radios outside the house. When they hauled themselves upright, Thelma nursing her knee, she saw a large urine stain on the front of Perry's pajama bottoms. His face flushed a dark red, and she was ashamed she'd let him see she'd noticed.

By some miracle, Ricky Mullin didn't kill anyone. Irv Mandelbaum, short, wiry, and all of seventy-five years old, had come roaring out of his house and smashed Ricky to the ground with a two-by-four and kept on hitting him till the cops came. Thelma saw Ricky's beaten, bloodied face as he was driven away in the patrol car, his eyes wide as a sunburst with whatever was happening inside his head.

She tried to tell Perry it was the drugs that'd made him do it, made him get his father's .44 Magnum out of the locked gun cabinet and go after everyone on that street who'd ever looked at him crossways. But she wasn't sure she believed it. Mrs. Berwick, whose son was a cop, told them Ricky had scratched the names of his intended victims onto his bullets.

"See!" Perry said. "That's premeditated right there! That punk wanted me dead, Thelma. He aimed through the damn wall at the exact place he knew I'd be in bed. Drugs had nothing to do with it."

Ricky got just five years. Perry was furious.

"For attempted murder? What a farce."

He still went down to the Legion every day for his card game, but now he always drove away from the Mullins' house even though that was the long way round. When he'd go with Thelma to Walmart, he jumped at every loud noise. Once he broke away and left the store running, and Thelma had to pretend to believe him when he said he thought he'd left a window open at home. She learned how to wake him from his nightmares without him realizing. She'd pretend to be asleep as he sat up in bed, wiping the sweat from his face with his pajama top.

Thelma felt safe as long as Ricky was locked up, but when she heard he'd been released, she kept thinking she heard noises and turned the radio down to listen. She couldn't get away from the image of him hunched over a table painstakingly scratching HOOD onto his bullets with a rusty nail.

Ricky came back to live next door with his elderly mother. She came round one day when Perry was down at the Legion and told Thelma Ricky had gotten sober. He was going to meetings twice a day and was deeply ashamed of what he'd done. Perry didn't believe a word of it. He installed extra locks on the doors and windows and made Thelma keep the blinds closed on that side of the house. But there was no way to avoid seeing Ricky once in a while, sitting on the porch swing, smoking or tinkering with the engine of his truck, his hands black with oil. Thelma brought up the idea of moving, maybe to one of the bright airy townhouses they were building near White Marsh, but Perry wouldn't even consider it.

"I'm not going to let that miserable bastard think he can intimidate me. This is my house and I'm not going anywhere."

IV.

SOMETHING FLINGS THELMA AWAKE FROM a dream of trying to run through water. As she hurries into the living room to the ringing phone, she can still feel the panicky drag of it on her legs. She knows before she picks up what the call will be. She's known since the day Perry fell forward in his chair, his face blue around the edges, his eyes wide with fear.

"Mrs. Hood? I'm Staff Nurse Collier on the coronary ward at St. Joseph's. Is there anyone there with you, Mrs. Hood?"

"Is he dead? My husband?"

Nora's coming down the stairs, struggling to get her arms in the sleeves of her bathrobe. The voice on the phone carries on as if Thelma hasn't spoken.

"Is there someone there, Mrs. Hood?"

"My daughter."

"Good. That's good. Mrs. Hood, I'm afraid I have some bad news for you. At about 2:45 a.m., Mr. Hood went into cardiac arrest. We tried our very best, but I'm afraid we weren't able to save him. It was a massive coronary attack. If it's any comfort, I don't believe he suffered, or not for more than just a few seconds."

When she hangs up the phone, she sees her daughter's face.

"Oh sweetheart."

"My daddy's dead!"

Thelma sits on the stairs and holds Nora as she wails and sobs. After a while, they move to the kitchen where Nora slumps over the table and cries as Thelma makes hot chocolate and toast.

"As if I could eat right now."

Thelma takes a bite herself, but her throat closes up on her when she tries to swallow.

"I won't call Joe till morning. His morning, I mean—I always forget they're an hour behind. Might as well let him sleep."

Thelma sends Nora back to bed. She sits on at the kitchen table nursing her cooling mug of chocolate, watching the black square of the window turn gray and then a watery beige and listening to the never-ending white noise of the Beltway. Scenes bubble up. Perry scooping her up outside the courthouse after their wedding and calling to her brother to take a picture. The time they stained that old chest of drawers together. Perry lying in his TV chair, Joe and Nora in their pajamas wedged in beside him, one under each arm. The newspaper cuttings he'd pin up on the corkboard in the kitchen for her to read. The "backseat driver's license" he made for her, even had it laminated at Kinkos.

He's never coming back to this house. Thelma pushes back from the table, and as she wipes the kitchen rag round the rim of her cup, another picture surfaces. Perry on the night of the shooting sitting on the edge of their bed, weeping as he stared at the two ugly dents in the wall where the cops had dug out the bullets. She'd put her hands on his shoulders and bent to press her face to his, but he'd pushed her away and told her to leave him the hell alone.

V.

THE NIGHT OF THE FUNERAL, Thelma doesn't go to bed. She's alone in the house. Joe and his wife flew out from BWI immediately after the reception, and Nora caught a ride with Perry's niece up to New York.

"You sure you'll be all right, Mom? I'll stay if you need me."

"It's OK. You'll lose your job if you don't get back. I'll be fine."

She dozes on the sofa, keeping an eye on the green numerals of the VCR clock. When she sees 4:30, she gets up and unfastens the locks on the front door. Looking through the angled blinds into her dark front yard, she sees the newspaper delivery guy drive up the street at a snail's pace, flinging papers from side to side through his rolled-down windows.

Thelma's paper hits the mailbox and skitters to the ground, half on the sidewalk, half on the lawn. The car fades down the sleeping street and for a while, there's absolute silence, not even a dog's bark or the distant rattle of a train heading north to Philly.

Thelma waits, rubbing her arms for warmth. No more than five minutes go by before a figure slides out from behind the yew hedge between her yard and the Mullins'. It passes under the streetlight, and she sees it's Ricky, barefoot in an undershirt and sweatpants, rubbing one eye with his knuckles. As he bends to pick up her newspaper, she flips on the porch light and throws open the door. He stops dead in his tracks.

She steps out onto the porch like it's a stage, trying to remember to breathe. She hasn't the slightest idea what to do now. Ricky looks up at her from the lawn, his eyes wary, his hands slightly away from his sides like he's showing her they're empty. He waits for her next move.

"Hello, Ricky," she says.

He blinks, and his mouth opens and then closes. For the first time since the incident, he's just a skinny young man with sleepy eyes who needs a shave.

"Mr. Hood and I forgive you, OK?"

They look at each other for what feels like a long time till Ricky drops his gaze. He bends to pick up the newspaper. Thelma holds out her hand, and he tiptoes up the cold porch steps to give it to her.

"Thank you."

He nods and moves away. Halfway down the steps he turns. If he wants to hurt her now, there'll be no one to see.

"I could mow your lawn for you maybe? Same time I do Mom's?"

His voice has a morning gruffness. Her grip on the rolled-up newspaper relaxes.

"Sure. That would be good."

Then she watches Ricky Mullin pick his barefoot way across the grass to his own house.

The cat emerges from behind the planter and strolls towards her, meowing. Thelma follows it inside, the screen door creaking shut behind her. She turns to switch off the porch light but changes her mind. Might as well leave it on till the sun comes up. The cat jumps up onto the couch and circles and circles and curls up to sleep. Thelma slides the newspaper out of its plastic cocoon and it plops onto the coffee table. She'll read it later. There's no hurry. Not for anything. She might start sorting the things to go to Goodwill or maybe she'll go back to bed. In the dark room, the air around her feels thick and buoyant like water, like formaldehyde, holding her lightly, kindly, upright and in place. She takes a step forward like a swimmer walking chest-high in the ocean and stands up on her toes in her old bedroom slippers, poised and willing to sink, float, or swim.

Caron L. Martinez

Black Ice

A native Californian, CARON L. MARTINEZ earned her degree in English from Williams College before a career in diplomacy led her to serve at the U.S. embassies in Quito, Ecuador, and Mexico City. She earned a master's degree in organizational and social psychology from the London School of Economics, and her MFA in creative writing from George Mason University. Currently, she is a professorial lecturer at American University in Washington, D.C., where she has taught writing since 2008.

*Y*ou are driving him to his four o'clock guitar lesson at the start of the commuter rush through town, the slanted afternoon sun relentless in your eyes. Thirteen years old, he slumps in the passenger seat, silent for so long that the sound of his voice actually startles you.

"Mom. What do you think of this song?" The first time in two days he has communicated with more than a grunt or a shrug. Even now he does not look at you, but fiddles with bass and volume controls, his fingers deft, a young sound engineer.

You hear techno *pops* and *booms*, and from the fog of your own memories comes a remembrance of a party in the '80s, your sophomore year at Bates, when a certain Clifton from Scarsdale couldn't have come up with your name if he'd been given a list. Yet you gyrated near him all night—a dance floor stalker—just trying to attract his attention.

"Sounds so familiar," you say slowly, "they're Swedish and sing by the syllable since they don't actually speak English. Red Balloon? Huge hit when I was in college." A quick roll of the eyes shows how utterly clueless you are as usual. His low sigh, whistling next to the air vents, confirms your ignorance. Your stomach lurches, pulse rises. You've said the wrong thing.

"It's Fall Out Boy. New band. I just thought you'd like the beat."

You consider arguing. You know this song is not new; could prove it if you cared to. Even now he regards you somewhat curiously from the corner of his eyes wondering how you are correctly singing along with the words of this "new" song. You remain quiet. You often don't. But you do now, because later this evening you will have more important clashes with him and you will need every shred of calm you can conjure. This is called "picking your battles." All of the books about teenagers advise it.

He's nasty to his younger brother and sister. You blame it on the same hormones that are causing the persistent shadow over his lip and his penchant for forty-five-minute showers. He only yearns to exist within the pools of blue light shining forth from computer screen or television. Criticizes everything you make for dinner. Can't understand why you won't replace the cell phone he's lost, twice. Has been booted from the gifted and talented classes because he doesn't do the work. You are so tired of hearing about his wasted potential that you are nasty to the teachers who do take the time to call you. Fidgets with the zits on his forehead even though you've explained he'll create permanent scars. The acne kit he begged you to buy from the infomercial sits unopened by the bathroom sink.

A part of you wants to shake him. Another part wants to hold him, to rain on his impassive, upturned face the tears of your frustration. A part of you feels the failure of being this child's mother. You know for a fact that any other female between the ages of twenty-five and sixty-four in your town could do a better job. You consider the past.

HOW ECSTATIC YOU WERE WITH this newborn baby. How, in the midst of sore nipples and sandpaper eyes and episiotomy stitches you dragged yourself to the edge of the bassinet just to marvel at his cocoa perfect skin, his fluttering eyelids, his miniature fingers clasping and unfisting in sleep. How in your besotted madness you flirted with waking him up when he miraculously slept more than five hours straight, just to remind yourself of his beating compactness against your heart.

In those days you read his mind, anticipated his wishes, distinguished the hunger cry from the hurt cry from the cry of being-exhausted-yet-not-quite-able-to-go-to-sleep. How he screamed like a wounded animal at age two when your husband dragged him away, down the hospital corridor, and back to a waiting car and an empty house after you'd introduced him to his newborn brother. How you cried for being the source of his first betrayal by a woman he loved. And knew it would not be the last.

Fast forward here to thirteen and you are changing his sheets. Under the mattress you find a DVD: *Increasing Your Pleasure: The Couples' Guide to Better Oral Sex*. You've heard all the rumors about the spike in oral sex as an alternative to intercourse, how young people sign abstinence pledges until marriage only to go oral like crazy. *Today Show* experts claim that kids brag about having it performed on them while riding the school bus home. A part of you is impressed your son is consulting outside resources, and you wish that same skill would transfer over to his homework. Upon questioning, he confesses to boredom in Home Ec leading him to flip through the issues of *Good Housekeeping* strewn about the classroom, and yes, the alibi is solid. There's the ad for this very videotape in the classified section at the back of the magazine.

You and your husband overreact, but you realize this only in hindsight. He is grounded for a month—more for the deception of stealing a check out of your wallet and forging your signature to pay for it than for his understandable and age-appropriate interest in the subject matter. He doesn't understand your distinction, barricades himself in his room, and, once you pop open the lock with a screwdriver, after pounding your fists to a pulp on the six-paneled door, you discover he's climbed out of the second-story window, and is gone.

You imagine all horrors, including the delight of the cruising child molester whom you are certain just happened to be on *your street* as your son headed up the cul-de-sac. Or you envision him hitchhiking to a bus station putrid with urine and the odor of fast food, all fluorescent and abandoned, before you remember your town has no bus station: it is unadulterated suburbia and there is no lurking downtown just waiting to engulf him. You call him on his cell phone. As if, having just run away, he would answer.

Your husband goes to sleep, but not before instructing you to lock all the doors. Proclaiming that if your son wants to live the drama of an escaped outlaw he should have to spend the night in the dampness of the nearby park, or your front lawn, and own his decision. You despise him for the obvious good sense this makes and your certainty you will not be able to stand firm to allow the just consequence to unfold. Besides, your husband forgets you are convinced your son is already halfway from D.C. to Philadelphia. You also hate for the neighbors to see him in a dew-stained heap on your lawn as they leave for work the next morning. You glower at the side-reclining hump that is your husband, and curse at the snoring soon emanating from his side of the bed.

Your seven-year-old has cried herself to sleep; the eleven-year-old, pale, stayed up with you until midnight. A few more hours pass. In the quiet of a moon-marked darkness, your son attempts to open the locked front door, delicately rattles the brass knob. Then a tentative, but clearer, knock. Finally, a pounding. Relief for his return is tempered by fears that, unable to get in, he will run again, this time for good. Your husband continues to snore. Should you let him in? Which male will you betray? You are spared from this decision as you hear the protesting slide of the downstairs double-hung bathroom window—the one too swollen with age and rot to close and lock properly.

You make no apologies for your gratitude that replacing this window has slipped to the bottom of your to-do list for years.

FAST-FORWARD FOUR YEARS: HE IS seventeen. You exist in the kitchen together, carefully, silently. Your emotions are just beginning to subside after discovering and raging about concert antics over the weekend—beer, overcrowded cars, curfew deadlines thrown away. It's his senior year, and he is consumed with feelings of invincibility, of "almost" being eighteen and "almost" in college, of forming part of a snotty social caste at school.

You search, and fail to find, topics for discussion, even light ones, as you sauté the garlic for the enchilada sauce. He says, "Mom, listen to this song." A few violins, some minor chords, the thick *thump-thump-thump* of the rapper bass line. You marvel at how he's always been drawn to the minor keys, a fact you attribute to your fighting off months of morning sickness to the recurring soundtrack from *Phantom of the Opera*, and your commuting in the car to the strains of Enya until swollen with expectation, you lay down to await his arrival on the first day of spring. A heavy-hearted voice, thick with anger and regret, sings *Would you have had my face/would we be in this place/teaching you to ride a bike/show you all the things I like?*

"It's called 'Happy Birthday,'" he tells you.

It isn't profound, but it is accurate: the learning to read, the toothless smiles, the first day of school. The rapper's pain is your own: neither of you have appreciated the perfection in the ordinary, the transcendent joy of all those sloppy, everyday moments. Memories of him as a little boy wash over you with the pulsating rhythm. Before you know it, your eyes burn. Where has that little boy gone? He is as much a memory to you as the rapper's unborn child in the song is to him.

Your son coughs on his turkey sandwich and demands, "Are you crying?" You deny it. He chews, swallows, and downs a swig of the Red Bull you forbid him to buy but he does, occasionally, anyway. "You are so lame."

You add cumin to the garlic and he asks if you are keeping onions off one half of the enchiladas. You nod. He finishes his sandwich, yet you know he will still be hungry for dinner. He watches while you slice the black olives. He takes more than a few. You make him stand up then—he is taller than you are—and put his arms around you in what can only be classified as a tenuous? Try spiritless, hug.

"What's wrong with you?" he asks.

"I don't know where the time has gone," is all you can manage.

"OK Mom," he says, "but what do you think of this song?"

YOU'VE TAUGHT HIM TO DRIVE. Met endlessly with teachers. Discovered cigarette lighters in his room that he swears he uses only to fuse the knots on his lacrosse sticks. You like him best when he is on the field, running with the grace of a long-limbed deer. He can't argue and run at the same time, and he's at least fifty yards from the nearest bleacher seat.

Girlfriends come and go. He seems to like best the ones that don't mind frequenting your basement, even with the younger siblings making periodic, deliberate appearances to offer Bagel Bites and soda.

"Clarissa likes you. She says she loves our family." You observe the parade of Girlfriends with purposeful dispassion.

You find the condoms in his dresser drawer. You watch yourself react from a distance, as if you have been scripted by a Movie of the Week. As if you have been waiting for this moment your whole life. Which of course you have not. You leave the condoms there, unopened, just as you found them. You don't know if they represent wishful thinking, or a rare effort at planning ahead—a skill foreign to every other aspect of his life.

You think back to a discussion of girls you had when he was fourteen and in ninth grade and Jezebel—not her real name, but might as well have been—asked him to be her boyfriend. The hussy—asking him—and unbelievably he cares about your opinion; wants to know what you think. You swallow and say, "What's Jezebel like?"

"Intense," he replies, and you don't know what that means but have decided what point you want to make anyway, so you begin, willing your voice to stay neutral.

"Could be a big fat chance to be in the dog house. Often," you say.

"What? How?"

"You know, the whole, 'why didn't you sit with me at lunch? How come you said hi to Brendan before you looked at me during science? Didn't you remember it's our third-week anniversary?' Having to do something or be somebody and not really remembering to, and so always having her mad at you. It can be a lot of pressure."

You berate yourself for living in a household where the mood turns on the whim of just one person, and that person, inexplicably, is one of the children. No alcoholic mother or abusive father here. You're as typical as any well-meaning, falling-short modern family in America could be. Yet the five of you dance to whatever jumbled-up tune your one son is playing—his is the emotional compass you follow. His default mood runs to shades of angry: with subtle variations such as impatient, rude, and sarcastic rounding out the daily offerings. The pressure of college applications and still-low grade point averages, speeding tickets, detentions, scraped bumpers, finite amounts of allowance, community service and futile groundings: the tension explodes, rebuilds, re-explodes. Then, on his own internal clock, for however short a time, he is fine. Wonderful even. Expansive and generous as he downloads a song or five for you to listen to, weigh in on: "Here's

one. Celtic alternative." It's a peace offering, a bridge, and you accept it
with the relief and self-loathing of the abuse victim.

On this night the band is called "Enter the Haggis," and they're exuber-
ant, contagious, like James Galway on speed. Soon you are stamping and
clapping as your youngest finishes her fractions sheet and your fifteen-
year-old writes about the ways Vietnam could be compared to Iraq, and
you place a lemon in the chest cavity of the chicken you are so late this
early evening to roast. When your husband walks in he notes the careful
happiness all around; as your seventeen-year-old keeps time with the can
opener, and plays you more tracks from the Haggis band, bestowing on all
of you a smile so broad his face can hardly hold it.

A few weeks later and winter feels as if it will never end. His car is in
the shop as they investigate why his oil turns to glue and the dashboard
light flashes constantly. You decide to take the Old Van out to pick him
up at Merchant's, your husband's voice an echo that morning wondering
if anyone has "bothered" to drive the Old Van in the frigid temperatures
of the past week. As you could have predicted, your son is disgusted you
have come to collect him in a car older than the sum of his siblings' ages.
He declines your offer to let him drive home and slinks as far down in the
passenger seat as is possible given his long legs.

You take the shortcut by the park because of his loud claims of starvation and limited ability to endure This Stupid Van. By definition, your
route is a street less traveled than your town's main drag and the lack of
traffic this yields is a good thing. But as you approach the stop sign and
the intersection beyond, your brakes fail to engage and you begin to slide.
Gliding past the remaining two houses on the block, sliding over the black
ice the afternoon sun melted, then abandoned to the return of the frigid air,
slipping straight for a main road with its constant supply of afternoon rush
hour cars and heavy trucks rumbling by on their way to the construction site
a half a mile farther on. If you were in a cartoon you would be doing those
wild large reverse cartwheel circles with your arms as you are propelled
off the edge of the cliff and the silent warm air holding you close for just a
moment before releasing you to the pull of gravity and looking down as if
in a parachute on the miniature landscape below, your own breathing the

only sound; but here is your son croaking, "Mom. MOM! What are you doing?" and the fact is there is nothing you can do, and he knows it and you are out of ideas and there is a curious panicky freedom in that brake which will not respond and everything you experience in that moment is out of your control. You sail unannounced, unanticipated, unstoppable in a perfect 360-degree circle of blue metal and chrome, into the intersection, the easy centrifugal motion of the van in contrast to the vise grip of your hands on the steering wheel, as useless to affect your fate as the brake that will not respond to your touch. Your son is silent, gripping the dashboard in front of him and so stunned and you begin to shake with such violence that you feel like a Parkinson's victim at the end of her life—a panicked palsy—and your son watches this and his helplessness is anger because he has never felt so unsafe with you.

The van stops, facing the wrong way and leaning into the ditch as the enormous, illogical serendipity of that moment—that you were not crushed together, bleeding and dying in that moment together, looking at each other through the shattered glass and heaving metal and twisted sounds for the last time together—envelops you then and makes it impossible to breathe. You never even thought to pray.

Yet. You are both alive. That is his voice, thin and attempting a tone of authority, saying Mr. Hove in Driver's Ed told them it was always possible to throw a car sliding on ice into park or reverse, or slam on the emergency brake and didn't you know that Mom? Didn't you know what to do? DIDN'T YOU?

You will your trembling hands to turn the steering wheel heading north towards home and not a half second later, rumbling in the opposite direction, is the half-ton truck. Grimy windshield from the salt and sand, dirty headlights and gray striations of old snow splashed Spirograph-like, geometrically wispy, on the truck's side windows and doors. Anonymous workers who, for the difference a second makes, might have been standing at this moment on the road just beginning to jam up with gawkers and Good Samaritans shaking their heads with regret but telling the cops and ambulance drivers: "They came out of nowhere. They never even stopped." You look at the clock. 4:07. That could have been the time your friends, all shocked and stunned, refilling their coffee cups at the reception after your funeral, whispered, "It could have been any of us," as, simultaneously, they would for their own sense of safety have searched for reasons it was somehow your fault. Because an accident of timing is just too terrifying. No one would get up in the morning if this complete failure to manage your own destiny, much less protect your children, were so completely unattainable.

You sneak a look at your son from angled eyes. He is glowering, pale. For once you are certain what he is thinking. There is so much barely concealed fear and fury in his profile that something in your core begins to fizz, and melt, and drain right off your body, leaving you as limp as a laundered sheet on the clothesline. You struggle to say something, anything, but all that comes out as you shake your head is a kind of wondering aloud at how sorry and shaken up you are.

You reach out to touch his hand in the afternoon glare reflecting off the dashboard and you find his upper arm instead. It is a man's arm. Under his sweatshirt you feel the curve and tension of a bicep that could not possibly belong to him. You sense how little you actually know about him, starting with his strength. You hadn't noticed.

There is no music; he offers no possible soundtrack for this moment, and you drive the rest of the way home in silence.

Cynthia Matsakis
In the Fable of My Life

CYNTHIA MATSAKIS is a therapist living in Greenbelt, Maryland, who uses expressive forms: poetry, journal writing, painting, bead work, mask making, sand tray, and ritual.

Who can recall the particulars of passion? Slowly I have learned I enter into desire the same with any man. It's my body after all. Still, I can remember the first time you kissed me, the fullness of your lips, the narrow tip of your tongue. I was afraid at first to write about you. To remember you I thought about the day before the day before, but found there was no context. Without you there were only the words... In the beginning I want to say something about the images. They are in the air. Listen. I want to say I am in the center of a fall reaching in all directions down. I can remember writing lies in my diary; can only be certain of details: the blue shadow cast by headlights, a slight swelling at the back of my tongue. I can almost feel your hands on me.

BEFORE YOU I WAS THIRTEEN. In the front yard, under pine trees, I wore short shorts and lined my eyes with blue shadow. Down by Shaker Lake where the boys are.

Who can recall the particulars of passion? I wait while others speak. When I was a girl, I want to say, when I was a girl, I liked a boy, any boy for a while. I liked a boy to brag about. Still, I can remember the first time you kissed me. Listen. You had on a blue shirt, top button undone. The thin white edges of your fingernails were neatly trimmed. Your hands were tan. You touched my face and turned me toward you. I could feel your breath on my cheek, the pressure of your thumb. Your fingers moved with the shadow shapes of trees as you lifted my chin. My head was braced by your arm. I let go, felt the fullness of your lips, the narrow tip of your tongue moving into my mouth.

Sure, I'd been kissed before, at the front door good night, or in the movies after popcorn, but when you kissed me, narrow shadows of your fingers moved over me. We were in the backseat while Wayne drove faster. I wasn't ready. I was watching Wayne put his arm around another girl. Wayne's elbow was skinny. He had a pack of Marlboros rolled into the sleeve of his T-shirt. Later, you said it was all your idea; you had planned the whole thing. Because I was Wayne's girl before that night. We had been fighting. No, I never cared that much for Wayne, but the thought that I had hurt him, and could somehow make it up to him, had appealed to my imagination. And that night I had waltzed out; when Wayne arrived, I was smiling. I remember. I was barefoot, in the front yard, in the half light. I was almost shy, swinging my white sandals by their straps, and I never saw that other girl, not until I reached for the handle of the car door. A redhead. She was Nadine, Wayne told me. Of course he was nervous. Sliding in behind the wheel, he couldn't look at me straight for laughing. But not you, sitting in the backseat waiting.

You didn't flinch when you spoke to me. You had dark close eyes and high cheekbones. And you were taller than Wayne; looking into the car, I could see how tall you were.

Later, when you said, listen, the trees were moving fast as we drove faster. You said I shouldn't waste my time being angry with Wayne. We were in the backseat when I felt you lift my face. I wasn't ready for the fullness of your lips. "Forgive me," you said, "since this was all my idea anyway." And you liked my hair long, you said. Then your tongue moved into my mouth.

RANDOLF CHARLES KETT—A FIVE-FOOT TEN-INCH, hundred-and-fifty-pound, fourteen-year-old boy. Middle class. Your father was a history teacher, your mother a nurse. You grew up on World War II stories, grinned too much, and disliked authority. You wore Gant shirts, liked to surf, fist fight, and come to see me every single summer afternoon.

It was the year that the palm tree finally grew tall enough to reach my window. I could hear the fronds scratch at the glass. I had to arch my back to stop you from kissing me. Your fingers were on the inside of my blouse. I tried to slip out from underneath you, but the muscle of your arm tightened. You held me a moment longer, then lifted yourself away from me.

I felt a dry heat color my cheeks and neck. I was afraid at first to speak and laughed instead. You looked out the window, then back over your shoulder at me.

I said, "Do you want to go for a walk or something?"

You said, "No."

I said, "Look Randy, we've got to think of something else to do."

You said, "I was happy doing just what we were doing. Weren't you?"

I said, "How about eating something? We could bake brownies."

You shook your head and kissed me again.

"But listen," I said, as I leaned back into your arms, "don't touch me anymore. You know I can't let you touch me like that, so why do you keep trying?"

You smiled at me. "I try to touch you," you said, and stopped to kiss me, sliding your hand inside my blouse and rubbing your thumb across my stomach until I moved. Only a little, but I did begin moving to the rhythm of your hand rubbing me. "I only try to touch you," you said, "because you want me to." Then you grabbed my wrists and pulled my arms out from underneath me. I fell back onto the bed laughing as you lay half on top of me.

But it was a long time before you tried again to put your hands on me. You would lie near me, and I would move myself up against you, trying to get closer. We kissed so quietly sometimes I could hear the palm tree press to my window, hear the fronds ruff up the glass, hear the sliding sound of stiff leaves when the wind blew. And then I wondered if you were waiting for me to ask you, to invite you, to touch me again. And I don't remember when, but one day, when you finally let your fingers slide up against the fleshy part of my breasts, I remember how I let myself lean into the palms of your hands.

Randy is the boy for me—do da do da
The one and only can't you see? Oh da do da day

SOMETIMES WHEN I AM ABOUT to wake up I feel the dark thread of my mouth pull open, hear my breath turn backward, and reflecting on the still surface of my eyes, I can dream your face into my own.

If I were a man, could have been a boy, could have been you, hands knuckle deep in the pockets of my jeans—I would have leaned against my car. Easy like. One foot crossed in front of the other. Casual. That's how I picture you, smoking your cigarette slowly, looking fearlessly into the group of boys who are circling you. One of them pushes his head forward, makes a kissing sound with his lips, then opens his mouth wide and says, "I asked you what you waiting for?"

"Yeah," a couple of the others join in. "Yeah, what're you doing?"

You think about the chain behind the driver's seat. Wonder when to reach in through the open window as the tall one moves toward you, one step, "What's your name boy?" he asks.

"Randy," you say, "Randy is my name."

"Listen, we don't want to rush you Randy, so we're going to give you till ten, right? And if you're not out of here…"

It's now, you decide, and yell loudly as you grab for the chain. You are facing them then, waiting for your friend Mike to come back out of the store. You bend your knees. You can feel the blood pump into your neck. Balanced on the balls of your feet, you are slowly swinging the chain. When Mike appears, you jump into the crowd. They don't expect you. Jump back, all of them. Now, you move with your shadow, feel light scale your spine, let it go from the knuckles.

boy for me do dah do dah—the one and only can't you see
Randy—I cannot think of you without remembering myself.

DOWN BY SHAKER LAKE WHERE leaves make red upon the sand, we were children really. I wanted to drown myself in brown water. You chased me over the sandbar when I ran into the lake, pulling the water back with my hands. You grabbed my ankle. I floated until you loosened your fingers, then I dove down to where you found me. Pulled me straight up in front of you. We smiled at each other. And with your hands running along my naked waist, you made a low sound somewhere that I searched for with my tongue. I remember you in details: your narrow eyes and your full lips opening the shadows.

GOING STEADY WAS NOT YOUR idea. "There are these rings," I told you, "with two silver hearts joined by a diamond chip."

"That's just stupid," you said, and lifted your arm from around my shoulder. I must have gotten out of the car. I don't remember you leaving, only the trail of gravel behind your car floating in the air like a wedding veil, as I pressed my hands so hard against the screen, red squares were pinched into the soft skin of my fingertips. *one and only can't you see.*

I WAS SCRUBBING THE STOVE with a blue soap pad when three of your friends came to the house. It had been a while. This was already summer vacation. I had taken a trip. I had tried to forget all about you.

"Randy's got a new girl," somebody said.

And I said, "So what? I saw plenty of boys while I was gone, and I started drinking too."

"Yeah?" one of your buddies said as he offered me a cigarette, "I bet you learned a lot up there."

"I could teach you all kinds of things," I said, and leaned forward for him to give me a light.

"OK," he answered and grabbed my wrist, like I was going to waltz with him to the bedroom. I let him pull me to my feet, but we didn't make it out of the living room before we both started laughing. That's how I remember it, laughing so hard we sat right back down on the living room floor. And you drove up then, in the new car your father had bought you that August. You came into the house, looked around at your friends and then at me.

"You're just in time," Scott said, "Cindy was about to show us what she learned while she was gone."

And although I don't remember your exact words, I think you said, "Show me." Anyway, you didn't stop at the bedroom door, laughing and winking over your shoulder like Scott had done. Not you. You didn't flinch. And when you closed the door behind us, all the other boys were gone. All the other boys were long gone. I got my ring that day, laced hearts and all.

I REMEMBER YOU IN THE rain. All through the summer and halfway into fall—it will rain in Florida, in the afternoons mostly. I remember when you took your shirt off and held it over my head like a leaky umbrella. I looked at you standing straight as a tree, with both your arms raised up; and I remember that I ran my finger along the thin line of hair from your chest down to the middle of your belly, before you let that shirt fall slowly down over both our heads.

But sometimes it could really storm. Raindrops as heavy as marbles pelting house fronts and the car roof, with palm trees bending and flexing in a wind so thick with water, you couldn't make your way through it. Had to angle over onto the gravel shoulder of the road, and when you cut the engine, I couldn't breathe; it got that hot. I rolled the window down, and rainwater spilled in on us.

"It's a flash flood," you said, grinning.

"I can see that."

"Can't blame me for a flood," you said, as you reached over to roll the window back up. And when I protested, you added, "If you're so hot, why don't you take your clothes off?" I grabbed your hand to stop you, and you pulled my arm around your neck, you caught my tongue in your mouth, and sucked it while the rain wet our hair and our shoulders.

WAIT. WAITING FOR YOU ONE time, I whispered the word *wait*—again—*wait.* I am waiting. I have waited. Waiting for you I learned to weigh the tension in my chest, control the muscles in my throat. I could pattern my breath and hold it when necessary. (*hep 2-3-4*) It was a discipline. Speak cautiously, I told myself. Do not form words without first considering their meaning. And in this way I grew closer to myself. Waiting for you, I grew closer to the woman I am today.

It is difficult to imagine myself, in the narrow room, sitting in the yellow light. These are the memories I cannot reach easily. Feeling, at first, only an irritation, a buzz under the skin growing unbearable, like waking insects inside my thighs. I would have to take a walk.

"If Randy comes," I would say to my mother, "tell him I went out to get cigarettes."

"Oh, is he late again?" she would ask, as I let go of the screen door, listened to it bang once, twice, three times.

I don't know where you went, when you went away from me, Randy, but I do know you are not fully imagined until you are imagined gone.

Suppose I had forgotten you, and the chance that you might knock on the door, say how sorry you were? Suppose I had forgotten you then? I was young enough. But there was always an excuse. Like when you told me you had hired on as a diver down the coast. That's where you'd been. "Made good money too," you said. Then you pulled out a bag of loose sea shells; told me you'd found them for me on the bottom of the ocean. I noticed they were varnished already, but I liked that you had taken the trouble to lie.

Randy in daylight, you were a tall boy in dark glasses. I'd look for you in the school parking lot. Sometimes, you'd be there in the distance looking back at me; sometimes not. I never knew what to expect. Listen, I'd get calls from your friends asking me for dates. That's how I'd find out we were separated. Sometimes I accepted just to make you jealous, and sometimes just to get drunk. One of your buddies, in particular, he used to tell me what a fool I was, but whenever he tried to touch me, I could feel the rum climb back up the sides of my throat.

YOU WERE A SON OF a bitch, Randy, and now you're dead. Maybe nobody cares what really happened. Maybe it's enough to say you were a boy who never grew old. One boy. That's all. The last time I saw you was on Christmas Eve, we were under the tree, with my whole family celebrating in the next room. We were so quiet, my mother thought to call through the closed door. "Are you still here?"

"Yes." We said it together. And I remember how I felt it, the inside of my own body, I could feel it. But the slow stroking was only a drum beat; the slow stroking was only an echo of my own pulse. I don't think I said I'll miss you. I know I didn't say don't go.

RANDY, I WAS AGAINST THE war. Of course I was against the war, and when you left for Vietnam, I left for California. There were your letters.

The jungle was a wall of green you could not penetrate. A new friendship. A fear of the dark.

"Suppose you've heard," my mother scrawled across the top of the newspaper clipping. It read: TAMPA BOY KILLED IN ACTION. No. His father threw himself onto the grave weeping, she wrote. The funeral was on a wet day. It was predictable. You can set your watch by the rainfall in Florida.

No. I had not heard. You were running ammunition up a hill when you were stopped. The article said you were brave, but you were just a boy. Even at nineteen you had a boy's room, a brown plaid bedspread with matching drapes gathered over a desk with a lamp whose shade had a cowboy painted on it, a cowboy roping a steer. How often had I lain down on that brown plaid spread and taken you deep inside me, but still I did not think to say—Don't go.

It was sweet when you kissed me, Randy. It was soft. Under the oleander trees, we would pull in late at night, and walk barefoot down to water warm as air. We would wade waist deep in the bay with phosphorus lighting the lines of our bodies and falling like sparks from our hands while we stripped and watched our clothes fill with stars and float far away from us. Still I did not know how I would long to recover you. How I would spend hour after hour trying to draw your face, your eyes. They were close in. Your eyes were like two simple flowers opening onto a field of light. Now the rain is spent with faces I had forgotten. I want to say who cares to recall the particulars of passion? Still I can feel my breath turn backwards and I can almost hear how you said to me. Listen, if anything should happen, while I'm gone I mean, well, don't just marry anybody. No. You didn't flinch. I shot a man today you once wrote, I saw his face fall in.

AT FIRST I HAD TO stop myself from thinking of you, and then I stopped without having to think. Filled in the empty spaces... I've been so busy all these years.

I only happened to visit the Vietnam Memorial because we live here in Washington. I'm married now. There was a protest, a march against the next war, and I went with my family, my daughter and my son who was fourteen that year. The age you were when I met you. I decided on a whim to look for your name. It was almost by accident. I mean it wasn't a pilgrimage for me, except that when I finally found your name, I don't know how to say this, but it was raining, and when I saw your name, it began to really storm. I could barely see my hands reaching through the thick air.

Again and again my children called to me from over their shoulders, but I couldn't leave it. I wanted to scratch it off the fucking wall. That's what I wanted: to squat down, pick up a rock, and scrape your god damn name off of that terrible dark stone. And when I say listen. Today, I mean. Right now, at home in my garden—with the petunias opening their sails of color in a spray of rain—it is because I cannot stop thinking of you.

ONE BOY DEAD IN THE fable of my life; who can recall what part I played in yours?

Lily Meyer

Wellfleet

LILY MEYER was born and raised in Washington, D.C. She studied creative writing at Brown University and the University of East Anglia, where she received the Curtis Brown Prize for best dissertation. She works at Politics & Prose.

We sat cross-legged, knees touching. The sand was hot on the bare backs of my thighs. Della had recently given up shaving, and the hairs on her shin glittered with salt. Rosie was crying behind her sunglasses. "It's stupid. She's never going to give a fuck."

"Her loss," I said. Della hummed in agreement.

"She told me she's still in love with Lucas."

Della shook her head. "Lucas is still in love with me. And he's a douchebag."

"Fuck Lucas." Rosie's voice snagged. "He's awful. Carmen told me he never makes her come after they have sex. If she doesn't come before he does, fuck it. He just falls asleep."

"He was the same with me. I used to do it myself. He never even watched."

"She told me I give the greatest head. You know what she said once? She said if she could be all the way gay she would, just for me, but she can't." Rosie pushed her aviators onto the top of her head and wiped her eyes with the inside of her wrist. As she replaced the glasses she took a long, shuddering breath. "No more fucking straight girls. I'm done."

A seagull circled us, cawing, then flapped away toward the dunes. I wrapped an arm around Rosie. "I thought Carmen was bi."

"Bi-curious," Rosie said miserably. She dropped her head onto my shoulder.

"Do you love her?" I asked.

"No. I think so." She sighed. "Yes."

"That counts for something."

"Not if she doesn't love me."

"Sure it does," Della said. "Every time you love someone it stretches you out inside."

Rosie snorted. I burst out laughing and Della joined in, rolling her eyes. "OK, not like that. Like you learn how to do it better. How to love better."

"How to fuck better," I continued. "Well, not for you."

"You know what, someday when Tony and I have sex, it's going to be great."

Rosie sat up. "When's that going to be, on your wedding night?"

"Or if I ever convince him the Virgin Mary doesn't care if we bang."

"You actually think you might marry him?" I asked.

Della nodded. "I think anything that ends in us fucking."

"Go back to what you were saying before," Rosie said. "How love stretches you out like a vagina."

Della tossed sand at her. "When I started dating Lucas freshman year, I didn't know shit."

"That's why you were dating Lucas," I told her. "That and the free weed."

"Didn't hurt. But I'd never had a boyfriend before in my life. It was just, oh my God, this hot guy wants to have sex with me and he wants to talk to me? We must be in love. Except all our conversations were about what happened in his head. He wanted me to get him. And I did, I always understood what he was talking about, and it seemed like we had this amazing connection, and I loved him for it. But I never talked. I only responded. Half the time it seemed like Lucas was talking to himself and I just happened to be there. When I broke up with him I remember thinking, The next guy I'm with, I want him to understand what's in my head, too. And Tony does."

"You're just saying that being in relationships makes you better at relationships," Rosie said.

I held up my palm like a crossing guard. "I don't think that's true. I think I'm worse at relationships than I used to be."

"Well, you're nuts," Della said. "You used to be normal and now you're insane."

"I know." I tilted my head back and looked at the saturated blue sky. "You know how long I'd been with Gabe before I told him I loved him? Not that I'm with Gabe."

"Yes, you are."

"Gabe is not my boyfriend. Gabe and I are not officially exclusive. For all I know he's fucked every hooker in Thailand by now."

"While emailing you every five seconds about how much he loves you?" Rosie said. "Shut up."

"I'm just saying, he could have. Anyway. The first time I told Gabe I loved him was the sixth time we slept together."

They stared. Waves crashed on the sand. "The sixth time?" Rosie echoed.

"Yep. And this is me and Gabe, right, so the sixth time was literally the sixth day. As in, the first time we had sex was a Wednesday, so this was the Tuesday."

"You know it was a Wednesday?"

"It was a Wednesday."

Della shook her head. "See? Insane."

"You know how we decided to go to Mexico together?" I said.

Rosie pushed her sunglasses up again. "I forget."

"It was three weeks before graduation. Gabe was over, and we'd just had sex and we were talking about our, you know, our thing. How great it is, and how much we were going to miss each other, and he just said, I can't say goodbye to you in three weeks. I can't do it. And I said me neither, and so we got on Expedia and Kayak and what's that one, Student Universe, and we looked to see where we could both afford to fly, and it was Mexico, so we bought tickets."

"That's nuts." Rosie was smiling now. "That's so romantic it's disgusting."

"That's not disgusting. It was disgusting when we both got the shits from eating fried cactus at a street cart in Mexico City."

A wave licked close to us, leaving streamers of seaweed. "Tide's coming in," Della said. "We should go swimming."

I looked down the beach. Umbrellas fluttered in the distance, candy-striped and tipped to the sun. There were no clouds in the sky, no figures approaching. We had walked forty-five minutes from the parking lot. "We should go skinny-dipping."

Della bounced to her feet. She held out her hands, hauled Rosie and me off the beach, saying, "Last one out of her suit's a rotten egg!"

I laughed, tugging at the knot of my bikini top. "You're such a fucking camp counselor." We ducked out of our halters, shimmied our bottoms off, left them piled on the sand like burst balloons as we lined up giggling, linked hands, counted to three, and ran.

The ocean was cold on my feet, cold up my thighs and my belly. Rosie dropped my hand as I plunged underwater. I popped back up and grabbed her hand, dragging her with me. "Motherfuck—!" she spluttered. "It's freezing!"

I splashed her. "Welcome to the East Coast." Her boobs floated pale as moons below the surface. I looked down at mine, made out the blue veins running up from my nipples. "The water's so clear today."

Della swam toward us, her neck arched high. "Why is swimming so much better when you're naked?"

"'Cause your tits float," Rosie said instantly.

"They float anyway."

"No, they feel floatier without a bathing suit," I agreed. "That's definitely part of it."

"And it's less cold somehow." Rosie was squinting toward the horizon. "What's on the other side?"

"I think Portugal," Della said, standing. The water lapped at her shoulders.

"Isn't Portugal warmer than here?"

"Maybe not in the north bit. I don't know anything about Portugal."

"It's amazing how much we don't know," I said. "Don't you think? We just graduated from college. I thought when I graduated from college I would have read more, I'd have more ideas about how the world works, but I don't know shit. I'm completely clueless. When I was in Mexico I kept thinking, here I am in this country directly south of mine, this country whose language I speak more or less fluently, and I don't know anything about it. I don't know Mexican history, politics, literature, nothing."

I kicked onto my back and floated, the sun stamping white circles across my vision. My mouth was full of salt. Rosie was saying, "Maybe that's why I keep being such an idiot with Carmen. I don't know anything yet."

"That's part of what I meant," Della responded. "Obviously Carmen isn't as horrible as Lucas, she's not a drug dealer or a complete egomaniac—"

"You think Lucas is an egomaniac?" Rosie said. "I kind of think he's a sociopath. Aren't they supposed to be super charming?"

"He might be. The point is, Carmen's not comparable to Lucas, but she's been jerking you around for months, and that's never really happened to you before, right?"

"No, it hasn't."

"So maybe next time you'll know better, or you'll be able to protect yourself, theoretically."

"But then how does that fit with the more room for love thing?" I asked, still floating. "Because I think that's true. Two years ago I don't think I was capable of loving anyone as much as I love Gabe."

I let my legs drop to the soft ocean floor. Rosie was drifting next to me, eyes closed. "How much is that?"

"I love him so much I could choke. It feels like I'm going to puke half the time, or like my rib cage is going to explode. I can feel how much I love him in my finger bones."

Rosie opened her eyes and pushed herself vertical. We were standing in a triangle now, just our heads above water, slick as seals. Every wave forced me onto my toes. "You make it sound awful."

"It's a good thing." I felt water trickling down my forehead, into the hollow next to my right eye. "It's painful."

Della spat into the ocean. "What isn't? It's painful for me that Tony and I have this huge gulf between us, that he believes in God and I can't, and that might wreck our relationship, but I still love him. And meanwhile Lucas goes around hurting people and saying it's because he loves me, and that's painful, too."

"Well, it's painful for me that Carmen goes around not calling me for weeks and saying it's because she was with Lucas and then still expecting us to have sex. And it's painful for me that I do it."

"But next time." The seawater was nipping at my eye now, inside the corner. Gabe was eight thousand miles away. I didn't believe myself as I said, "Next time we'll know what to do."

"Or the time after that."

"Someday," Della said as I squeezed my eyes shut. They felt dry under my lids, but when I opened them water streamed out and the salt sting was gone. Through my wet lashes the ocean shimmered pine green. Della was facing the horizon, but Rosie was watching me. There was a black ringlet flattened against her cheekbone. I reached out and pushed it behind her ear. She touched my hand as a wave rolled by, and we drifted together in the current. Her mouth was softer than I expected. She held onto the small of my back, our knees and stomachs brushing together as we kissed.

When it was done I saw Della looking at us, blushing. She smiled and flicked a bit of water our way. Rosie and I watched her for a second, and then I dove underwater, swam to her, came up and kissed her. She tipped her head and sucked at my lower lip, her eyes closed. Rosie was swimming toward us already. Della and I bumped noses, laughed as we lifted our faces apart. Rosie surfaced and we held our hands out to her, linked arms again, and the three of us splashed up to the beach, naked and dripping, together.

Nicole Miller

Mack's Misery

NICOLE MILLER has published essays in *New Letters* (Dorothy Cappon Prize, 2014) and *Arts & Letters*; her short stories have appeared in *The May Anthologies*. She has an MPhil in Victorian literature from Lincoln College, Oxford; a PhD in English from University College, London; and an MFA in creative writing from Emerson College. She is a scholarly reader for *The Oxford English Dictionary* and teaches literature and writing at Politics & Prose, Grub Street, and Kingston University (UK).

Summer, 1983

WHEN MACK BOYLE'S MOTHER LEFT, he and his father Otis moved from Egg Harbor, New Jersey, to New York City, where Otis could thump his fist on the trading desks of Wall Street. Happy, a bouncy six-year-old, gold-and-black cocker spaniel mix with protruding temporal lobes which made her wobble when she walked, came too, though Mack wondered how she would live away from the ocean, with fewer rooms, sofas, and wall-to-wall carpets. They lived on the twelfth floor of a building with a doorman, right off Washington Square Park. Within two weeks, Otis hired a Puerto Rican babysitter named Rosa. Her eyes were black reef, ogling under electric blue lids. When Mack played with the Masters of the Universe, Rosa's lids puckered and slid open like mollusks to follow his movements.

The sitter didn't say much, but switched on the television and let the Spanish soap operas trill all day long. She sat on the leather sofa with her knees wrapped around a step ladder and a platter of metal bowls on her lap. She wove shiny ropes of dough with her salami-pink fingers while keeping her slow eye on Mack. At quarter to five in the afternoon, Rosa popped open the two top buttons on her nursemaid dress, and swung her arms into a little housework. She turned off the television and polished the screen with spit and her apron; she lifted the rug and swept the dust and dog hair on the floor under it; she blew away the crumbs from the kitchen counter into the crack between the appliances; and then, like the cartoon of the hippo on tiptoe, she sidled to the window and gingerly unlatched the child lock in order to smoke while she babbled to San Juan on the house phone.

This was Mack's first summer in the city before he turned ten, entered fourth grade at St. Osbert's, and donned the official navy school blazer, armband, and green striped tie. He took home a couple Math and French tests but didn't do well on them and ended up being put back a grade. For French, he was put back two. He was destined to sit with the second graders who were half his size.

Mack hated the tests and counted down the hours until he could unlatch the door for his dad and Rosa would leave. She was scared of dogs, which meant that Happy had to stay in a crate in Mack's bedroom and wait for him to enter with snacks: peanut butter 'n' beef jerky sandwiches, cheesy goldfish dipped in jam, dog bones that Mack had rolled secretly into Rosa's wet bread.

All summer long, Mack missed his mother—her pale moon face and midnight hair, her tea-rose perfume and long, powdery hands; the strange birthday cakes she used to make for him, stuck with live flowers of the kind he could never eat, like buttercups and sweet peas, because they were poisonous to the taste. He always knew she was approaching from the soft jangle of her earrings—hoops set with orbits of smaller stones—and sometimes fringes of coins, like a belly-dancer's belt, that glittered around her neck. When Mack was a baby, just the flashes and leaps of gold around his mother's face were enough to pacify him. He used to grab at the earrings while she darted her head playfully, until one day, absorbed in a shouting match with Otis while Mack was coloring in a book near her lap, Mack reached up and managed to catch one of the hoops and pull it right through his mother's ear. Blood and gunk streamed out; Odessa swore at her son, and Otis rushed her to the emergency room. When the bandage came off, the rip through the cartilage made a clean split. After that, she only wore a stud in the shape of a tiny jeweled fang that poked up from her nose.

Otis was probably wrong to take Mack out to buy chocolates for his mother's birthday, as he knew Odessa wouldn't turn up. They went out on an important errand to the Upper East Side at the French confectioner's. The shop had a marzipan castle and white chocolate lake in the window.

Inside, Mack bought rose and violet crèmes, all nestled in a black heart-shaped box. He noted the crystallized candy petals of pink and purple and envisioned his mother eating these. He dared not ask the confectioner whether they too were poison, but he lay awake many nights wondering.

The night of Odessa's birthday, Mack put on a polo shirt, long shorts, a clip-on bow tie and clean socks; he flossed the string cheese from his teeth, and waited. He pulled a book she had given him when he was eight off his action figure shelves: *The Swiss Family Robinson*. It was not very interesting when he had read it before, and had doodled skulls and eyeballs in the margins. As the hours ticked on, the apartment grew quiet: his father turned a Lionel Richie record on in the sitting room, and the air conditioner rasped under the music. Mack was stumped by chapter 3, and punished himself for daydreaming by pulling out strands of hair from the top of his head and making a nest of the pieces on his pillow cover.

The ritual of waiting went on for three nights, after which time, Otis came in to tell Mack "the whore wasn't coming," and he could eat the chocolates if he wanted to. Mack now had champagne truffles packed into a pair of zebra pumps that his father was going to give to Odessa along with the heart box Mack had bought for her. He placed both, with stuffing provided by the ripped-out pages of *The Swiss Family Robinson*, in the hairy pillowcase, and threw the sack to the back of the closet.

After this disappointment, Otis gave Mack money to buy a silver pocket television set at the electronics store which he now watched in his room. Originally, his interest had been catching the program *Crocodile Jocks*, but in the dead heat of the summer, he discovered World Federation Wrestling, and with his He-Man action figures, copied the movements of the giant men in bumblebee tights and satin capes as they hurled into each other and slingshot their bodies across the ring. After WWF and public programming for the hearing-impaired, Mack stayed up for the female mud-wrestling championships that started after midnight.

Otis never chided his brooding son, and Rosa did not know what the child did after she left to make him sleep during the day—nor did she care. If Mack got up later, she had even less work to do, and could devote herself totally to the Spanish game shows which came on before the soaps. At night, Otis came home and yelled down the phone to lawyers, scratched out forms, and snapped his pencils between oaths. Waiting for the shouting to stop and the silence to begin became a hunger for Mack. The wired boy woke up just to stay up, to reach the point in the day when Rosa was gone, Otis was preoccupied, and he could retreat to his room without being disturbed. Then, he made a tent of his covers and pulled up the antenna on his pocket-size silver screen.

Mack still took his cocker spaniel for walks, but they were shorter now and he avoided the park. They could spend hours playing "I spy a pigeon" through the tube from a used-up roll of Brawny, but Mack was aware that on the palm-size TV, which only had reception at the apartment, there could be a match or a lady in a skimpy leather body suit that he would miss. When they ventured beyond the canopy of the building at Washington Square, Happy still veered towards the topiary where they used to go; each night Mack jerked the other way, always slightly harder than the last time, towards the concrete curb.

Something in him hated dragging Happy towards the stinking trash cans and the fire hydrants, the fenced-in stumps and flowerless stalks, but he did not stop doing it, and when Happy started to wander towards the greener areas with her rooting rubber nose and knobby head, Mack pulled back, sometimes choking Happy to make her give up.

There was no point going anywhere in New York. The city was filthy, and Mack started to see the dirt in everything from the mold-green uniforms the doormen wore, to the tattered awnings and steamy windows of the local shops, to the yawning cellars which opened at street level from the restaurants that smelled of rotting fruit and dead fish.

Mack had gained weight; he was nine years old but almost one hundred pounds now. It was probably because he walked less, and lay in bed more, filling his bowl with corn pops in apple juice several times each night, and sucking liquid sugar tubes until his teeth turned purple and orange when he woke up in the morning. He was going to start a sport at his spiffy new school in the fall—St. Osbert's was the private city school, where there wasn't a lot of choice in teams. He could only do indoor sports or ball games which were played on a fenced-in rooftop. His father promised to practice touch football with him in Central Park when the weather got cooler. Mack liked going to the Metropolitan and looking at the Greek statues with marble genitalia and cowering at the killer bees and giant tarantulas which sprung from the 3-D screens at the Museum of Natural History, but his father only took him twice.

Sometimes Mack wished to meet other kids; and sometimes he grew greedy for more time alone. He waited through the weekend for his father to go to work on Monday, and ground his teeth when Rosa left late. A couple of times, he tried to lock the door to his room while Rosa was there, but when she couldn't turn the knob she hurled herself against the boards and screamed, "No close this!" He discovered that he could push his wicker dresser against the lock, though, late at night, when his father had fallen asleep in front of the sitting room TV. Safe from intrusion, Mack explored the dirty channels to his heart's content, and pored over the *Sports Illustrated* swimsuit issue he had found in the trash. He kept a sketch pad under his bed and started life-drawing.

At last August closed in and Mack pined for the ivory shore of Seven Mile Island where he used to swim and chase sand sharks, and meet other kids at the barbecues on the dunes with the brindled grasshoppers. When Mack took Happy out for her last walk of the summer, New York reeked: the humidity clung to everything, browned the air. When the trash collectors went on vacation, the leftover garbage sacks split open; roaches skittered over the cartons of curdled milk and bags of soiled diapers. Storefronts were stapled up with metal gratings: nothing to see in the whole East Village but CLOSED signs and balloon-word graffiti. Occasionally, an illuminated bus skidded by on Fourth Avenue—empty, except for a driver and vagabonds who nodded off in the blue plastic chairs, leaning into their laundry carts.

On the last night of August, Mack walked Happy to Washington Square and let the dog off her leash to cavort in the ashy grass. There were no squirrels to see, but sometimes a black rat scuttled by, or a rumpled sparrow flew down from the lit-up arch. There was nothing to play with—no ball or toy, but there were some flies in the dusk, landing on the lampposts, and in her few moments of freedom, Happy started to leap and snap at those. These were a dirtier version of the lightning bugs that Happy had chased down with Mack on Seven Mile Island the summer before; Mack had been the one to point out their different colors to his father. He trapped his specimens in jars and proved the abdomens were green, pink, and yellow, like wax bottle candy. It was harder to find virtue in houseflies, but Mack had been studying them too. When they got caught in the organza drapes of the sitting room, he noted that their shiny backs were at one with ginger ale and club soda cans, and their iridescent wings like the materials that had been draped over the manikins in the Garment District of the city.

On this particular night, Mack felt like buying himself a slice of pizza but it was too warm: the cheese on the pies at Famous Ray's had congealed. He decided he would not tie his lonely girl to a mailbox where she would yelp and cry while he bought bubble gum and magazines. No, not tonight.

When meandering too far towards one of the stone benches, Happy got whacked by a mumbling old lady who had made a mattress of all her bags, and was calling out, "Basta, basta!" Mack swept his girl up and out of the park and she responded by settling her paws around her master's neck. In this fashion, he carried his curly lamb out of the square.

When Mack got upstairs, his father was wrangling on the phone and banging a stapler against the table. A stack of bills and receipts flew in a blizzard to the floor. Mack crept into his room. He made Happy comfortable in a harem-court of cushions on his bed.

"I have a treat for you, darling! A treat fit for a princess."

The black heart had not been touched since the day in June when Mack pushed it to the back of the wardrobe. The perfume of the lining still lingered, but Mack now loathed the smell. The crèmes were engraved with a "V" in sugary curlicues. Mack bit into a piece, and spat it out. It tasted like detergent.

Mack dumped the dark chocolates onto his bed. The box had several layers, and had been packed so carefully that when he poured it all out, there were dozens of fondants. He was glad now he never gave them to his mother, that she never came to pick them up. There was a lady, "a *real* lady" said Mack to his spaniel as he nuzzled her, "who deserved them more."

"Sit, girl, sit. Give me your paw." Happy sat down and waited.

"Here, pretty baby. A chocolate for you." Mack gave her one, and she gobbled it up.

"Give me your other paw." Mack gave her a second, a third.

"Now roll over." Happy was golden tonight, and Mack loved how she listened to him. Her eyes followed his every gesture as he took a chocolate and hid it behind his ear, and slipped it under the pillow, and threw it in the air and one, four, five, six…snap!

Seven, eight, nine.

Snap. Snap. Snap.

"What a beauty! Do that again!" Happy wiggled her paws, and Mack dropped the smooth morsels in her mouth, from one foot up, two feet up, three. He had good aim, and what a super catch she was!

"That's enough, girl," Mack whispered when his father rapped at the door.

"Maxwell, we need to discuss something. Can you come now?"

Otis looked beat. He had grown stubble, and smelled of Camels and beer. His temples were clammy, and his hands shook when he blotted the sweat with a handkerchief. He was wearing boxer shorts and a sleeveless undershirt with mustard stains which showed the salt and pepper hairs on his chest. This was hardly the father who had coached his son's baseball team in Egg Harbor in the spring of '82.

"Put Happy in her crate, so she doesn't scratch at the door. I'm supposed to watch you do *somethink*, so you don't get up from the table or *nothink* funny like that."

Mack already knew what this was about, and he didn't want to do it.

"All right, give me one minute."

"One minute, Maxwell. Sixty seconds. I'm counting."

Mack stroked his dog. Her eyes were filling with milky goop and her stomach was gurgling. Mack couldn't bear to lock her up, so he kept her out, and put her back on the bed.

"You're too nervous, girl. I'll only be a little while. I have got to do something for school, and I'll be back."

"Mack, put the pooch in her cage." Otis bellowed from the table. "You don't want her getting into your socks, or chewing your good school shoes—I can't buy another pair for you, if she does. Your mother's suing me for every penny I got."

"Yeah, Dad."

But the boy looked at his brown-eyed girl, with the speckles of white around her nose and her long matted ears, and he couldn't bring himself to do it.

"Won't you be a good girl," Mack lifted up one of her ears, gently, and breathed into it, "the best girl in the world, and just lie here on the bed until I come back?" He made her sit, then produced another violet crème from under the pillow.

"There's more where that came from. But you've eaten enough tonight. We're saving the others for another day, when I teach you how to bring Pop his paper in the morning."

Mack looked back at her sitting majestically with her large blonde head aloof and her paws stretched out: a sphinx, watching him. Then he shut the door from the outside, until it clicked. Once he lumbered to the table and sat down, his father began to lecture.

"Mack, these tests—the French and the Math. The school's sent them back. You can't fail in this school, Mack. It's Catholic. I'm paying for it. If you don't get in, you're going to the local PS school with the hoodlums. They don't even speak English there. They'll beat you up, son."

This was no pep talk, and Mack hung his head. He had no idea how to take these tests. He didn't even understand what they were asking.

"St. Osbert's sent a letter," Otis fumbled for his smudged glasses and read out a passage, "They mean business. Listen—"

Dear Mr. Boyle,

If you see your son doodling on the page, we ask that you confiscate his pencil until such time that he is ready to resume his efforts in a serious manner. Neither Mr. Potato Head nor various outstanding parts of the human anatomy sketched into the margins will be received in good humor a third time.

Mack sighed.

"That's it, no more pictures—you need to use words, kiddo."

Otis chuckled at the sketches. The nose with nose hairs, and the earlobe with beauty marks were pretty good, and remarkably true to life.

"Tell you what, Mack, if you get into this school, you can use the studio there. I saw it myself: lots of skylights and a big kiln for firing pottery, and all the papier-mâché, clay, and charcoal you could ever want. OK?"

The last thing Mack wanted to do was take this test, again, to spend the rest of the night struggling to spell and remembering his times tables, but he knew he had to do it.

In silence, he opened the twelve-pack of Twinkies his father put out in front of him, took the booklet of pages with small bubbles for answers and began to work his way through them.

After a while, Mack could hear Happy whimpering through the door. He saw her paws slip through the crack, and her liquorice nails scratch against the parquet.

"You put that dog in her cage, Mack?" asked his dad, without looking up from his paperwork.

Mack said, "Yes," though his eyes shifted uneasily, and he bit his lip. He thought a few times that he should get up and check on Happy, but when at last he launched out of his chair, Otis laid a hand on his shoulder. "Do this for me, Maxwell. Think of *me*," and that kept Mack down, and brought his son's eyes back to his paper.

After the first hour the sounds went away. Happy retreated from her station behind the door; Mack could no longer spot her paws or hear her nose bumping against the brass knob. All was quiet. Two hours later, when Mack finished the test, and turned to go to his room for bed, Otis grabbed him and gave him a bear hug—the kind he used to give when Mack ran home for his baseball team or got his lines right (or right enough) in the school play when he was cast as the boulder or the troll.

Mack felt warm all over, and proud; he had done something for his dad, more than for himself, and he was ready to sleep tonight and to start next week at the preppy academy where the boys wore blazers, armbands, and ties. It was an hour away from the start of September and the air was changing in the city; there was a new briskness, a faint edge to the heat that cleared a spot in the mind. Mack could distance himself from that lost boy who watched the racy late-night channels, and took his dog to the trash cans for a walk. He was past all that now.

When Mack opened the door to his room to go to bed, his coverlet was wrinkled but empty. The lights outlined his pin-ups, the antenna of his small screen, a football helmet he hadn't used yet, but where he stashed Lemonheads and jawbreakers; some twelve stories below a car put on the breaks, a distant squeak. There was a smell like the abandoned corners of Washington Park in the air.

Mack didn't see Happy anywhere.

"Come here, girl. Come here, my princess," called Mack.

Mack spotted a tail poking out like a feather duster from under the bed.

"Aw, you are playing hide-and-seek with me. I'll find you!"

He began to jump up and down on the mattress, expecting her to scurry out on cue. Again no spaniel appeared. With every bounce, thimble-size chocolate papers began to fly: all mere shells without the chocolates. Mack picked up the heart-shaped box and shook it: not even the rattle of a single piece. Finally, Mack flopped down, poked his head through the skirt, and peered into the shadows. When he groped, his hand found Happy's neck, then her collar. When he tried to pull her out, she growled.

"Come on, girl. Don't be mad with me. I won't be away from you that long ever again."

Mack slid to the floor and crawled like a fat caterpillar in his baggy pajamas, until he was under the bed too.

Mack nudged the cocker spaniel with his toes, kicked her lightly, and then harder.

When he felt his foot hit the ridges in her back, he stopped. This was not right. He was afraid of hurting her, and under his foot she was shivering, murmuring, whimpering.

When he wrapped his arms around her, her grin was ghastly: the gums showed, speckled with black. She bit at the air with a slack, snapping jaw, chopping away like the city cranes which scoop up rubble and dribble silt from their interlocked teeth.

Mack cradled her. Her fur crumbled and her muscles were loose; she was like a rug unraveling in his hands.

"It's all right, girl. You'll be all right. You're sick but we'll make you better."

Happy whined and shuddered—and after a few minutes Mack saw that it was the shuddering which made her cry out, as if small explosives were going off inside of her.

Finally, there was nothing to do but wake Otis. Mack believed his father would know what to do next. But he didn't. When he flapped into the room with his greasy robe and toe-worn slippers, he shook the dog, and pulled out strands of his own hair the way Mack had learned to do. He even called up the number he knew his wife was at, living with the dentist who did the gold fillings for the residents of Stone Harbor, and barked down the receiver to get the name of the veterinarian they used to go to. After fifteen minutes of pacing and swearing, Otis and Mack took off for the twenty-four-hour emergency clinic on the Upper East Side. They wrapped the limp spaniel in a lady's raincoat that Otis pulled out from the hall closet, and carried her to a taxi between them, swaddled like a child. When Otis stretched his hand to shut the car door, Happy bit it—the first and only time she ever bit anyone in her life—so hard, that Otis punched his knuckles through the cab ceiling, and scratched his hand on the grate. Blood splattered his tan robe with beet-colored streaks.

At two a.m., the father and son sat together on the vinyl chairs at the clinic and filled out forms. When Otis went to get a tetanus shot, Mack watched the door to the examination rooms open and close and owners walk out with their bulldogs in casts, cats in calico blankets, and iguanas in neck braces, to take their pets home. But the door didn't open for him. Happy had been rushed to the back, "an urgent poisoning case." They had given her an emetic and pumped her stomach. When they asked what time Happy might be released, the clerks only frowned,

"You know that chocolate's a killer."

At last a petite blonde in a white coat came out and called Mr. Maxwell Boyle, owner of Happy Boyle, into the examining room. Fear made Mack's movements heavy and slow; he would have waited for the floor to rise and tip him to his destination rather than walk there himself. Just as he saw the gleam of the metallic operating table, he turned to the side and threw up the Twinkies that had helped him get through his placement tests. In a great flurry of paper towels, Otis was ushered in to accompany his son.

"Mr. Boyle, I am Dr. Finch." Otis stepped forward, but it was Mack she was addressing. With the sweetness of a sad Shirley Temple, the veterinarian took Mack's pulpy hand in her spiny fingers and squeezed.

"I've been sitting with your beautiful dog, *Happy*," she said, "for the hour since we operated. What a fighter she is! A truly brave spirit. I've injected her with something which makes her feel less pain, but she will not close her eyes to rest. We figured out she was looking for you."

"Oh," said Mack and he could say nothing more as he studied the floor, a rash prickling his neck. Though he could not articulate what he had done, he knew in the pit of his stomach that this was all his fault. He thought of the mud-wrestlers and the cheated walks by the trash cans instead of the park and the way he had buried everything which reminded him of his mother in a pillowcase at the back of the closet. His thoughts swarmed, like so many flies around him, buzzing and insisting and whining.

Look what you've done; look what you've done Maxwell Boyle; you fat stupid, black-hearted boy!

The fairy-like doctor took Mack to Happy's table. He could hear her moaning softly; her breathing was strange and staccato. He recognized her and yet with her weeping eyes and dull coat she seemed to him like a different animal: he did not know her.

"It's not Happy," he said to himself. "This is another dog. They've changed her with somebody else's. We're being tricked."

"Here she is," said the vet. "She will hear you if you talk to her."

"It's not Happy," Mack grunted as he balled his hand. He thought of hitting the vet, who was smiling at him through her lip gloss, but some motion from the table distracted him.

Without warning, the sack of loose curls and fur on the table twitched and shifted; the drooping tail quivered and the eyes rolled and showed the whites. Not understanding what he did or why he did it, Mack stroked the spiky whiskers on her soft snout and with a jerk, pinched them between his fingers.

Mack reached over Happy, and covering the bloated gourd of her body, bundled together her paws which were splayed like sticks touched by autumn frost. Unyielding, suddenly, her legs; her muddy jaw clenched over some eternal bone. The gurgling at her throat subsided; her pink nose darkened to blue.

Mack pulled harder and harder at the whiskers, wanting her to feel. He managed to snap a few of the brindled strands from her lip. Stiff on her face, these curled in his palm, shivering threads of life.

In the lady's jet rain slicker, they carried Happy's body to the checkout window where cremation was arranged. As they pulled her off the table her back legs flopped and her bladder let go a puddle of cream soda. Otis grabbed a jar of cotton balls from the sink and began mopping it up, in a frenzy of swearing and tears. Mack stood motionless, though his insides seemed to be waving, flapping, careening at volcanic speed.

At three a.m. that night, instead of mud-wrestling or comics or taping together the ripped-up pages of his *Swiss Family Robinson*, Mack stood in the middle of the curled chocolate papers and rammed his head repeatedly against the wall. "Poor girl, stupid boy," he said with every smack against the paint until he grew drunk with his own pain, and the words came out in insensible stutters. He kept going until the blows printed a rosette of blood on the whitewash, and the wiry hair of his forehead became matted and wet. He dumped the candy out of his new helmet, put it on and closed the gate over his face. He rammed until he felt dizzy and dropped off at last to sleep on the shaggy rug in front of his mirror.

In the morning, Otis took his son for stitches, and so the stupid boy from Egg Harbor, New Jersey, started his career at St. Osbert's with a turban of bandages on his head. Whispers went round the fourth grade that Mack Boyle had a mean left hook—had decked a Harlem deli man for a canister of fireballs and a drawer full of quarters. When the bandages were removed, his head had a dimple in it where the hair never grew back, but started to recede. So began the fear and respect for his early gruesomeness—the cruel, wounded face that unnerved the skinny quarterbacks into dropping the ball into his hands; the grampus body which swelled with every year until the uniforms had to be tailored for him; the perverse test-taking skills that involved finding a new fold in his torso or limbs which could fit a French word or math equation. He tapped an uncanny pipeline to lewdness which brought *Penthouse* and *Playboy* to his peers and gave him the power to seduce the first Catholic school girl in the boys' bathroom at a New York city all school-square dance at age twelve. But above all it was his pout that made them quake—the pout which came to be known as "Mack's Misery" though it always boded torture for somebody else—as he grabbed the most sensitive parts of his victim's anatomy and squeezed, with insatiable fury, the impulse to quell another boy's blubbering and tears.

Amanda Miska

Sam and Dee

AMANDA MISKA is editor/publisher of *Split Lip Magazine* + Press. She received her MFA in creative writing from American University. Her fiction and nonfiction have been published in or are forthcoming from *jmww*, *Storychord*, *Five Quarterly*, *matchbook*, *Hippocampus Magazine*, *Atticus Review*, the *Prairie Schooner* blog, The Rumpus, *decomP*, *BULL*, *Little Patuxent Review*, and elsewhere. She lives and writes in the suburbs of Philadelphia, but you can find her online at http://www.amandamiska.com/.

*A*fter Sam leaves Delilah, she decides to cut off all her hair, telling the barber to shave the sides smooth and leave the top longer so it can still fall over her eyes, allowing a little room to hide. As the hair falls to the linoleum floor, inch by inch, she remembers how Dee would curl pieces around her finger as they lay in bed. She would wrap Sam's hair around her pinky and trace it across her upper lip like a brush on a canvas. Sometimes she would tug the front pieces hard—like reins—to pull Sam close and kiss her.

ຕ

ONCE THEY MOVED IN TOGETHER, they talked about never moving anywhere else ever again.

"Not even from this bed," Dee said with that wicked grin of hers. Her incisors were a few centimeters shy of vampire fangs. Sam would offer herself up as a willing victim for that smile.

They were about to celebrate their seven-month anniversary. After finishing a bottle of wine, Dee had confided that on the night of their first date, she had slept with her ex.

Sam felt betrayed: she'd had this feeling about Dee. She was the kind of person you'd never get tired of. They had kissed for half an hour in her stairwell, Sam's back pinned against the mailboxes. Sam couldn't wait to see Dee again. She couldn't even sleep. But while she was lying in bed with a heavy pulse in her throat, reliving every detail of their evening, Dee had gone to fuck Kim.

"I didn't know then. I wasn't ready for you."

"You were horny and didn't think I'd put out on the first date."

"Maybe."

And then she grinned and started to kiss slowly down Sam's stomach and all was forgiven, or at least forgotten, for now. Sam's mind went blank. She only felt nerve after nerve coming alive like little wildfires beneath her skin.

In high school, Sam had played the violin. It was small and quiet like her. She quit once she went to college, but she never sold the instrument. It slept on the top shelf of their shared closet. When she was alone in the apartment because Dee had to work a late shift at the consignment store she managed, she would sometimes get out the violin and play songs she still knew by heart. She dragged the bow across the strings softly to avoid irritating their neighbors. One night, Dee came in and she was still standing by the window, playing a sonata. The moonlight fell across her face, emphasizing the shadows beneath her cheekbones.

"You look like a painting," Dee said in her ear, wrapping her arms around Sam's waist and pulling her close so her breasts were against Sam's back. Sam set the violin down on the windowsill and allowed herself to be turned, to be touched, to be kissed. She didn't ask why Dee was an hour late or why her cheeks were warm and flushed when it was freezing outside. There was a reason for everything, but she didn't need a reason right now. She just needed a body next to her in bed to keep her from shivering.

Dee was excited, rough with her, hands pushing under her skirt, lifting her up by the back of her thighs. She lifted Sam right up to the windowsill, forgetting about the violin resting there. Dee's hand bumped the violin's neck, and it fell to the floor in a cacophony of scraping strings. She left it on the ground and hiked Sam's skirt up to her hips and knelt down. All Sam could think about was the awful little song the violin had played on the way down, like something from a horror movie right before the oblivious heroine is about to die.

Sam did things with Dee that she had never done with anyone else. It wasn't necessarily that she felt safe with Dee, the way it was with old married couples looking to spice things up, but that she felt in danger of losing her every second. She wanted to please her. So she let Dee tie her up with old silk scarves, one delicate wrist to each bedpost, one fragile ankle against the other. Dee was an expert at tying knots. Sam knew she could not escape, so she just lay there with her eyes closed, breathing faster and faster.

"I want you to fight," Dee said as she took a break from kissing Sam's breasts.

"But I like it."

"But I'd like it more if you struggled a little. For me."

When have I not struggled for you? was the thought that Sam swallowed down.

Sam didn't consider herself a good actress, but she tried whimpering a little, straining her arms until the posts creaked. She wondered how many other times these scarves had caressed skin that was not hers. Not just in the far-flung past but in more recent days, when Dee had no reason not to be home but texted Sam to say she was going to be late—again.

Sam's thick, wavy hair was getting to be unmanageable, taking hours to dry in the open air. She had started putting it into two wide braids which she wrapped around her head and bobby pinned. At night, she would remove the pins, letting the braids unravel. Dee loved to watch her do this and was always a little put out if she did it and went to bed before Dee got home from work or wherever she had been. Sometimes Sam would awaken to Dee's face between her legs after she'd already been asleep for hours. She didn't mind it, although sometimes she just wanted to stay in whatever dream she was having. Because the dream was simpler. The dream didn't leave her entire body spasming. The dream didn't expect anything in return.

ꙮ

THEY DECIDED TO THROW A New Year's Eve party with all of their friends at their apartment, which they'd just rearranged and redecorated together. Kim showed up in a short sparkly dress—she was dating Alexis, another one of their friends and didn't seem to find it at all presumptuous that she could be there.

"I told her it was fine," Dee said as she chopped celery and carrots.

"When did you talk to her?"

"She emailed me. To ask." Dee never looked up from the vegetables.

"You could've asked me first."

"I thought you were done with all that."

Sam was quiet. She was composing herself, dragging a spoon slowly through a bowl of sour cream and spices, around and around. Dee set down her knife. She walked over to Sam and put her hands on her face.

"You trust me, right?" she said, forcing Sam's gaze to meet her own.

Sam nodded after a brief pause. Dee kissed her, taking her lower lip into her mouth gently. She knew just what to do to end an unwanted conversation.

The two of them carried appetizers out to the table. They were playing some '60s French records of Dee's. Everyone held a bottle of beer or glass of wine. White lights twinkled around the windows.

Dee and Sam split up to talk to their groups of friends, introduce friends-of-friends. Sam sipped champagne, even though it was early. She watched Dee toss back glass after glass of Pinot Noir, until she finally just carried the bottle around, swaying her hips to the music as she walked. She stopped to talk to Kim and Alexis. Sam tried not to stare, but she couldn't help it. She had a vision of the two of them in bed, wrapped up in each other, all naked limbs and sweat and tangled sheets. Or maybe it was more of a premonition. When Dee talked to Kim, she kept touching her. Brushing her hand. Leaning into her side. Alexis didn't seem to notice (or care). Sam didn't blame Kim. Dee was a little like a virus that swam in your bloodstream, leaving you a little sick all the time, while also being the only medicine that could make you feel better: poison and antidote in one pretty package. By eleven thirty, the room was a collective buzz of alcohol and voices. One of their neighbors, an amateur magician, had started doing card tricks and disappearing acts. Sam was feeling a little sick, so she edged her way through the crowd down to the hall bathroom to take an aspirin. She noticed the door to the bedroom was slightly ajar and she heard giggling, followed by hushing.

She tiptoed closer.

She'll find us.

But doesn't that make it more exciting? Dangerous.

She knew that voice, of course. Dee was in the habit of convincing people that being terrible was great fun. Sam had suspected all along that Dee was being unfaithful, but she talked herself out of accusations because she didn't have proof—only intuition. Her gut instincts had always been strong. She just had trouble with the follow-through.

There was a soft gasp and a low hum, the liquid sound of mouths opening and closing. Now, Sam tiptoed backwards and turned into the bathroom. She closed the door and stood before the medicine cabinet, hands perched on the sink edge to hold herself steady. In the mirror, she looked fragile, but she knew that she wasn't. Dee didn't. Dee didn't know her at all—her body, yes, intimately, every crevice. But not the beating, bloody heart of her. She'd never tried.

Sam swallowed two pills down and sipped water straight from the faucet. She scrunched her hair and applied her bright red lipstick again, blotting it, and then applying one more coat. She smiled at her reflection and rubbed a speck of waxy red from her front tooth. She flipped off the light and walked out.

By the time she returned to the living and dining area, Kim was sitting with Alexis on the couch. Ron, their magician neighbor, was standing before Dee with a deck of cards. A crowd of partygoers surrounded them. Sam stepped closer. Dee picked a card and put it behind her back.

Ron shuffled the cards, cut the deck, shuffled them again. He threw them up in the air so they drifted down like unwieldy snowflakes. He caught one. The rest scattered on the parquet floor. The audience was quiet.

"Is this your card?"

He turned it around. It was the queen of spades. Dee gasped.

"Yes! But…"

She went to bring her card in front of her, but it was a joker, no longer the queen of spades she'd originally pulled. An impressive sleight of hand.

The crowd clapped. Ron bowed. Dee handed him back his card.

Just before everyone broke up, Sam cleared her throat.

"I also have a trick I'd like to share with you all. If you'll gather around the table."

Dee gave her a questioning look, which Sam read as *I didn't know you could do magic.* Sam shrugged at her as if to say *There's a lot you don't know about me.*

The table was covered in half-drunk glasses, plates of crudités and dip and bread and assorted cheeses. There were small vintage vases full of flowers and several candelabras, all resting on top of an old lace tablecloth, like something out of an entertaining magazine.

"I will now pull this tablecloth right out from under everything," Sam announced. She raised her arms dramatically. The room was quiet. Kim and Alexis had even come over to watch.

Sam grasped a corner in each hand. She counted aloud to three and pulled.

There was a quiet second and then the sound of crashing glass onto the wooden table. Wine flowed like blood, making rivulets down the corners and across the floor. The candlesticks tipped over, starting several small fires that grew when they touched the alcohol. Sam stood there, holding the tablecloth, watching, not moving, while the guests scrambled for towels to soak up the liquids and pat down the flames.

"What the fuck, Sam?" Dee said, hitting the table over and over again with a dish towel.

"I lied."

Sam opened the tablecloth up, wrapped it around her shoulders like a cape, and stepped out of the apartment into the bitter winter's night. As she walked down the street to the Metro station, destination unknown, the church bell began to chime, people shouted from balconies, and fireworks set off distant car alarms. It was a new year.

Roberta Murphy

Shu. . .ush

ROBERTA MURPHY was born and grew up in Wales. She has published stories in numerous magazines, including the *Georgia Review*, the *Harvard Review*, *Feminist Studies*, the *Laurel Review*, the *Greensboro Review*, and several times in *Nimrod*. She received an NEA grant for fiction writing and recently completed a novel for young adults.

*W*hen the final notice came in June, we were all at sea, as usual at nine o'clock on a Saturday morning. Grandma was wearing my dead Grandpa's best burgundy waistcoat and Sunday shirt over her blue- and white-striped pajama bottoms. She'd let me plait her red hair into a pigtail. "I spy whales on the horizon," she said in a rumbly voice as she squinted through an empty toilet paper roll. It was a joke she'd made up because Wales was our country's name. Grandma's big bed was our merchant ship, and we were bound for the Barbary Coast.

I said, "Any mermaids in sight, First Mate?"

I was the ship's Captain in the fancy jacket my father used to wear to take my mother Bronwen dancing before he got lost in the War. I had his silk scarf tied around my waist to hold my poker sword.

"I spy a mermaid on yon coral reef, Captain Meggie," Grandma said.

Great-Aunt Lilac sat on her single bed opposite Grandma's. Over her nightgown, she was wearing the silver Lurex blouse Bron had no use for anymore. Her hair was loose to her waist. It was gray and scraggy, not like a mermaid's, but the paper flowers from the dining table vase made it a bit better.

She was pulling at the flowers, saying, "The wires are sticking into my head."

"Don't!" I shouted. "You'll ruin yourself as a mermaid."

"Stop it, Lilac," Grandma said, "be a sport. Don't spoil Meggie's game."

Grandma was a sport. She was forty-seven years old, but she could play better than any six-year-old. Better than Patti Parry, my friend down the street that I'd quarreled with yesterday over who'd learned the most, her at school or me at home.

"I can read the whole of *Treasure Island*," I said.

"Get away, you fibber," she said. "I've seen your mam reading it to you."

"She just helps me with the big words I don't know yet."

"There's a ton of things you don't know. I bet you can't even say the dooty two times table. One two is two, two twos are four—"

I slapped her mouth, and we started pushing, and screaming, and tugging hair. Grandma came into the street and sent Patti home. "Come inside, love," she said. "I'll play with you."

Now Grandma was steering the good ship *Adventurer*, using a round tea tray for the wheel and bouncing her bottom to make the bed rock. I stuck my little finger in my left ear to make the sea noises come. Grandma pulled my finger out. "Don't, lovey," she said. "Remember that's our secret." She was afraid I'd get into the habit and do it in front of people who shouldn't know, like Dr. Howells.

"Jolly Roger ahoy, Captain," she shouted. "Long John Silver at the helm."

"Yo, ho, ho, and a bottle of rum," Bronwen growled as she dashed through the door of the back bedroom we shared, waving the bread knife. She wore an eyebrow pencil moustache and beard, one hoop earring, and her normal hair, black corkscrew curls that looked like a pirate's already. She jumped onto the bed and joking attacked me.

Grandma made her arm into a pretend blunderbuss and fired and Bron shouted, "Aargh!" and fell back on the bed.

"No one takes my Captain," Grandma said.

That was when the front door knocker banged. A voice called through our letter slot, "William Davies, clerk of the Town Hall, here. Open up, please, Mrs. Johns."

"He's brought another notice," Bron said.

"Keep quiet and he'll throw it into the passage, like he did the others," Grandma said. "We can say it went out by mistake with the rubbish letters."

"Mrs. Johns," Willy Davies shouted louder, "I bear an official notice for your daughter, Bronwen Pugh, and I'm instructed to hand it to her personally. It concerns the matter of your granddaughter Megan Pugh's school attendance."

Bronwen got up off the bed and went to the stairs.

"Don't accept that letter, Bron," Grandma called after her as she ran down. "Tell him Meggie's not going to school for another year. She's registered as anemic."

"She has to take it," Aunt Lilac said. "She could go to jail for refusing a Town Hall notice."

I jumped off the bed and ran to the window to see if Willy Davies was putting handcuffs on Bron. They were standing in the street, Willy Davies looking astonished. He'd never seen Bron with a moustache and beard before. He'd only seen her on weekdays, in lady's makeup, going to her typist job. He was holding an envelope out to her.

"Don't take it!" I leaned out of the window to shout. The poker slipped from my sash and fell. It crashed onto the pavement between Bron and Willy Davies. He jumped away, swearing, "Flaming hell!" and Bron screamed.

"What happened?" Grandma said. "I hope my brass poker didn't break."

"Willy Davies is going away. He threw the letter on the ground. Bron's picking it up."

"*Daro!*" Grandma said. "She never listens."

Bronwen came upstairs. She had opened the letter. "You've lost the battle, Mam," she said. "Ronald Lambert himself has defeated you. Listen to this." She stood up straight, stuck out her chest, and read in a stern voice:

Dear Mrs. Pugh,

Our new truancy officer for Avon Fach, Miss Heulwen Humphrey, has brought to my attention your failure to enroll your daughter, Megan Pugh, in school last September 1st although she had reached her fifth birthday in May of that year. Five is the mandatory age for school attendance. Parents can be prosecuted for noncompliance.

"Ahem!" Bron said in her own voice. "Cardiff jail here I come."

Apparently, Megan was excused on the grounds of anemia. Miss Humphrey and I concur that this is insufficient reason to keep her out of school. There are many children in attendance with worse ailments.

"No wonder they're worse," Grandma said, "with his niece for their teacher. And who is this new busybody with a name like a circus elephant? Dai Dote was the truancy officer. He minded his own business. What happened to him?"

Unless you present her for admission to Standard One on September First, 1949, we will have no option but to issue a summons. The child has already missed an entire year of education.

"It's signed Ronald Lambert, Superintendent of Schools."

"Superintendent of Bullies," Grandma said. "Why doesn't he summons his niece for indecency? She showed her knickers to little children."

"She couldn't help that. Her skirt rose up when she fell."

"And what sort of teacher falls down in the classroom? There are rumors Miss Lambert is too fond of the bottle. She shouldn't be in charge of young children. Even Lilac would make a better teacher than her."

"Oh, no, I could never be a teacher," Aunt Lilac said. "I don't have the brains."

"That's my point, Lilac," Grandma said.

"I don't mind going to school," I said. "I want to show Patti Parry I can read more than her. Maybe I can read more than the whole class."

"You're not strong enough yet to go among children carrying those 'worse ailments.' You might catch one," Grandma said. "We'll go to see Dr. Howells straight away. He'll stand by us."

"Ronald Lambert won't accept anemia anymore," Bron said.

"No, but he'll have to accept something more serious. Wash Meggie's hair. Put her best dress on her. *Hurry up*, Bron. Surgery closes at noon."

In the scullery, while my mother washed my hair and sang "Sweet Polly Oliver," I played the game I'd discovered four months earlier. When she'd wiped soap out of my left ear with the washcloth's tip, her singing had vanished and instead I heard sounds like the sea at Barry Island, only faint and faraway. Shush...shu...ush...shush. Jiggling my finger made the noise much louder.

That first time, in March, when I told Bron, "I can't hear your voice when you shut my ear," she said, "What are you talking about?"

I put my finger in my left ear. "Say something."

She did, and I could see her lips moving, but I could only hear the sea sounds. I took my finger out. "What did you say?"

Bron stared at me. "Oh, my God," she said, and she shouted, "Mam, come quick!"

Grandma and Aunt Lilac came rushing into the scullery.

"Meggie's going deaf. She says she can't hear with her right ear."

"Don't be daft," Grandma said. "Why would she go deaf all of a sudden? You're playing a game with us, aren't you, lovey?"

I put my finger in my ear. "Speak, Grandma."

As her lips moved, I jiggled my finger. "I can only hear the sea," I said.

Bronwen pulled my finger out. "We have to tell Dr. Howells. Meggie might need to see a specialist."

"A specialist will send her to the deaf school in Brecon," Aunt Lilac said, "where they teach sign language. It's a boarding school, so she can't come home every day."

"Hold on, hold on," Grandma said. "Just hold your horses, both of you. No one's sending Meggie anywhere. This isn't serious. It's a leftover effect of the 'flu she caught in February, when she was weakened from that bout of measles at Christmas. Aren't you hard of hearing yourself, Bron, when you have a cold? Let's wait and see."

"Wait to see what, Mam?"

"Lilac's right for once. A specialist might send her to that school fifty miles off. You don't want Meggie sent away from us, do you?

"I don't want her to go deaf, that's for sure."

"She won't, I'm telling you. Haven't I always known what's best for our family? If your dad had heeded me and not taken the night shift at the colliery—"

"Oh, lord," Bronwen said, "here we go again."

"And if Davie hadn't joined the Welsh Fusiliers like I told him not to—'Pretend you can't see straight, Davie,' I said—you and me wouldn't be widows today. I'm not allowing another loss in this house. Who knows what might happen at the deaf school? Meggie could have a fatal accident there. An epidemic outbreak could kill her."

"I won't go!" I shouted. I grabbed the bowl of water Bron had washed my hair in and threw it on the scullery floor. "I want to be alive!"

"See, Bronwen, the state you've got her into? Come to me, my treasure. Lilac, fetch the mop. I'm asking you, Bron, to wait only until Dr. Howells petitions the Board for another year's reprieve. Soon as we've got the release—a couple of months, that's all it takes—we can see a dozen specialists if Meggie's hearing doesn't come back, as I know it will. Don't make a snap decision you might regret all your life."

"I give up." Bron went off to fret in the bedroom we shared. I followed her upstairs. We had twin beds, and she was sitting on hers, crying. When I sat beside her, she said, "I don't act like a mother, do I?"

She was twenty-four, old enough to be a mother, but it was true, I did feel more like she was my big sister, judging by other mams in our street. She never said, "You must do this," or "Don't you dare do that," or "If you don't stop whining, I'll smack you into the middle of next week."

"I'd rather have you than a different mother," I said, and she put her arm around me and cried a bit more.

"But I don't act grown up, Meggie. How can I in this house? Your dad always stood up for me. He used to say, 'You have to learn to do it yourself, Bron. What if I wasn't here?' And now he's not here. Why did he go off to the War, Meggie? We'd only been married six months. I miss him so much!"

I didn't miss my dad like she did because I'd never known him, but I did wish I still had him. "Tell me another story about him," I said, "before he went to the War," and she said, "Sit on my lap and *cwtch*. I'll tell you how he walked across the ledge of the Pontsarn viaduct on a dare from his pals. They were a wild lot, and he was the ringleader. As he climbed up, my heart was in my mouth…"

NOW, WHILE BRONWEN WASHED MY hair for the visit to Dr. Howells' office, I played the game. Opening and closing my ear as she sang, I turned her into a mermaid, the words of her song coming to me on the surge of the waves, "*As sweet Polly Oliver lay musing…*shu…ush….*a notion she took…* shu…ush…*her dead brother's clothes…*" I liked this part. I took my finger out. "*And off to the war, sweet Polly, she goes.*"

At breakfast, Grandma told her new plan to Bronwen.

"Ronald Lambert won't swallow that," Bron said.

"It runs in our family. In case you haven't noticed, your Aunt Lilac's a victim. Suffered for forty-odd years, haven't you, Lilac?"

"I do get flustered," Aunt Lilac said. "Aspirin calms me down."

"And how did this tragedy come about? Our mam let go of Lilac's hand to test plums on the greengrocer's stall, Lilac toddled into the road, and under the wheels of a milk cart she went. The doctors saved her life, but she's never been right in her brain since then."

"I've heard this story. What's it got to do with Meggie?"

"You've heard it, but you haven't harkened, have you? It's about neglect. Mam should never have let go of Lilac. A thoughtless moment, a ruined life."

"My nerves do play up," Aunt Lilac said, "but my life's not ruined."

"That's not for you to say, Lilac. You don't know any different."

"Where are they?" I said.

"Where are what, my pearl?" Grandma used the voice she saved for me, like the tenderest slice of roast beef, the ripest peach.

"My nerves. I can't find them." I squeezed my fingers and moved my arms up and down, jerking my head. "How do I make them play with me?"

"Do that in Dr. Howells' office," Grandma said, "when you hear me say 'bad nerves.' Can you do that for Grandma?"

"I'VE RECEIVED ANOTHER ONE, HUW." Grandma took the Education Board's letter from her purse and put it on Dr. Howells' desk. "It's Ron Lambert, the big boss, hounding me this time. Threatening a summons, can you believe it?"

As Grandma spoke, she was stepping backwards, holding my hand, so that when she said, "We're throwing ourselves at your mercy again, me and Meggie," we'd reached the sofa Dr. Howells kept "for patients who might faint when they hear the bad news," Grandma had said. She sank onto it, her best blue summer coat falling open to show her scoop-neck white blouse, her wide, floral patterned skirt, and her legs in shiny nylons. She looked lovely with the flowers on her skirt spreading out, like the picture of the lady floating on water in *Tales From Shakespeare* that Bron read to me.

"Rest, Meggie," she said, pulling me down beside her. "Walking tires you. You're still anemic. Read the letter, Huw, and we'll discuss our next move."

Usually, Dr. Howells gave Grandma a compliment about how fine she looked, but today he was frowning. "I don't need to read it, Eira. I got one myself yesterday. Ron Lambert's ordered a second opinion. My word isn't trusted anymore."

"Never! There's an insult! The whole town knows what a good doctor you are. You won't take this lying down, I hope."

"Eira, you're not beguiling Dai Dote anymore. This new truancy officer is a woman, and she's calling your bluff."

"And I'm calling *her* an interfering cow. Who does she think she is, judging whether Meggie is fit for school or not without ever setting eyes on her? This child could be wasting away in her bed, too weak to stand up, for all that *woman* knows. Anyway, something new has developed. Meggie's showing signs of bad nerves, Huw."

Grandma said this last sentence in a voice like people use to say, "Passed away, poor thing." She clasped her hands together, crossed her legs, and leaned towards Dr. Howells. I could see down her blouse. She was wearing a white lace brassiere. A long red ringlet, come loose from her bun, hung down on her neck, making me remember the ladder Rapunzel made of her hair for the prince to climb up.

"Eira, please." Dr. Howells took off his glasses and rubbed his knuckles across his eyes. "Don't do this. Have mercy."

"*You* have mercy, Huw. You know our sad story." Grandma told it to him again. "Meggie was just a baby when we lost her dad in the War. I'd already lost Owen in the colliery cave-in. She has no father and no grandpa, and as for the aunt and uncle she *might* have had, the pneumonia epidemic robbed me of my twins before they were one year old. You don't forget that *double* tragedy, Huw. You had to sedate me for months. You came to see me every day, didn't you? We sat on the parlor sofa. I had to keep the curtains drawn because I couldn't bear sunlight... I was only twenty-one, Huw."

All the time Grandma was talking, I was acting bad nerves like she told me to, but Dr. Howells hadn't once glanced at me. His eyes were fixed on Grandma. "Those pale green curtains…a filmy light…like being in a dell," he said. "That chartreuse robe that shushed when you walked. It felt like silk…"

"You and me got very close. 'Best friends,' we said, both of us being married. And you made me a promise, didn't you? Now I'm begging you, Huw, don't put my precious child in jeopardy. Get her another year of home care so I can build her up. You'll have my heart's deepest gratitude."

"You're a persuasive woman, Eira," he said. "After all these years, I still…"

"I do too, Huw. 'It's forever,' we vowed, 'even though it can never become real.' Do you remember?"

"As if it were yesterday."

I'd heard the story before too, how Dr. Howells led Grandma "out of the woods," where she was wandering after my baby aunt and baby uncle died. Cwm Woods was near our town. Bron and me went nut picking there in summer. Grandma never went with us though. Probably, she was afraid of getting lost again. I would be.

I got bored with doing bad nerves and nobody taking any notice. I stuck my little finger in my left ear to entertain myself while the talk between Grandma and Dr. Howells continued. When I closed my eyes and jiggled my finger, a cavalcade of seahorses pranced out of the waves, their foamy manes sparkling in sunshine. "Come with us, Meggie," they whinnied. Then they disappeared. Grandma had pulled my finger out.

"Answer Dr. Howells when he speaks to you, lovey."

"I'm asking if *you* want to go to school, Meggie," Dr. Howells said.

"Not to the deaf school in Brecon. I can hear. I can stop the sea noises whenever I want to."

"The sea? What sea?"

"Barry Island is in my head. Seahorses come to me. They speak to me in horse language. Nay-eee-nay-eee," I whinnied through my nose at Dr. Howells.

His eyes went big behind his glasses. I thought my imitation had amazed him. I did it again. This time, I hee-hawed and snorted as well, and pretend galloped, rolling my fists like pounding hooves. "Boom, boom! Hee-haw! Nay—"

"Stop!" Dr. Howells said, loud and sharp. To Grandma he said, "How long has she been having these fits? She sounds delusional. A psychologist, maybe—"

"Oh, no, Huw! There's nothing wrong with her brain. It's only a slight deafness in her right ear. It makes her hear funny noises."

"Put your finger in your left ear, Meggie, and listen to the question I ask you."

With my ear plugged, I watched Dr. Howells move his lips. When he stopped, I took my finger out. "You looked like my goldfish," I told him.

"Can you repeat what I said? I'll give you a treat if your answer's correct."

"Can I guess?"

"You didn't hear me ask how old you are?"

"The waves were too rambunctious." I'd learned a lot of big words through reading with Bronwen.

"How long have you known about this, Eira?"

"Not long. Since she had the flu in February."

"Four months, and you haven't consulted me."

"I was waiting until we settled the school board matter. A few months would make no difference, I thought."

"And since when are you qualified to make such decisions? Do you have a medical degree?"

"I don't like your tone, Huw."

"Like it or lump it, Meggie needs to see a specialist. This may be serious." Dr. Howells reached for his pad and pen. "I don't understand you, Eira. You come to me with trumped-up ailments to keep the child at home, and about a real affliction, you don't say a damned word. I'm writing you a referral to a good man I know in Cardiff. Partial deafness won't keep her out of school, mind, so don't try to wheedle him."

"I never *wheedle*." Grandma stood up. "I tried for your sympathy, Huw, that's all." She was fastening her coat. "But you have none left to give me."

"It has worn thin, Eira, I admit, since it's started to threaten my livelihood. Now, Meggie's deafness might qualify her for the Brecon school if it's degenerative, so you'd better prepare yourself for that." Dr. Howells stood up and walked around his desk to hand Grandma the referral. "Tell my receptionist to make your appointment."

Grandma slipped the paper into her pocket. "What about Meggie's nerves?"

"Give it up, Eira. I can't risk my career any further, not to mention compromise whatever integrity I have left."

"You promised me once I could always count on you."

"Not to abet negligence regarding a child. Not to break the law."

"Right, Meggie." Grandma tucked my hand into hers. "Let's go. There's no help here." As we passed Dr. Howells, she said, "Breaking my heart doesn't matter, I suppose."

"I'd have to find it to break it, Eira. See to that appointment straight away. Goodbye, Meggie." He patted my head. "You'll like school, I'll wager."

"I'll be finding a new doctor, Huw."

"I think that's the right move for both of us." As Grandma led me out of his office, he called, "Next!"

All around the walls of the waiting room, the chairs were packed with coughing men in miners' caps and crying babies in their mothers' arms. Grandma flounced past them, and past the receptionist's desk.

As we stepped out into the street, I said, "I won't have to go to that Brecon school, will I?"

"Over my dead body."

"What if the deaf doctor in Cardiff says I have to?"

"He won't be having any say." Grandma drew the referral paper from her pocket, crumpled it into a ball, and tossed it into the gutter. "Tell Bronwen Dr. Howells says there's nothing to worry about, all right? She'll believe it if she hears it from you."

"I'll be going to ordinary school though in September."

"At least it's only up the road. You'll be coming home every day."

"I don't mind going to school," I said. "I'm ready."

My grandmother bent down to press her cheek against mine and whisper in my ear. Most likely, she was calling me her treasure, her pearl, but she'd got my deaf ear by mistake. All I heard was, "Shu...ush."

THERE WAS A NEW TEACHER in Standard One. Miss Lambert had been taken away, "for treatment," people said, and Miss Rose had replaced her.

She was young and smiley and she moved graceful and light like a fairy. You could never imagine her falling down.

"You're an excellent reader, Meggie," she said in front of the whole class. Later, when we were doing sums off the board, she whispered, "We'll have to work together on your arithmetic, won't we? You're having a bit of trouble adding up."

At the end of the first week, the nurse came in to examine us. "Nothing to worry about, children," Miss Rose said. "It's routine. The School Board requires it."

Nurse Bevan wore a white coat. She had a stack of papers in her hand that Miss Rose said was our "personal information." Grandma wouldn't have liked that. She walked around the desks, looking in our hair for nits. I didn't have any. She tested our eyes for glasses. I didn't need them. Then she examined our ears.

"You can't hear in your right ear, can you?"

"Not since last February. I could before."

"Have you been examined by an ear specialist? No? Well, you should be. There's a very good one in Cardiff—"

"My Grandma thinks it will go away." I said this fast because I was thinking of the deaf school again. "She says it's temporary."

"Does she, indeed? It states on your form that you and your mother live with her. Does your mother agree with Grandma?"

"None of us want me to go to the deaf school in Brecon. That's why Grandma didn't take me to see the specialist like Dr. Howells told her to."

"Ah, I see...and who said you'd go to the deaf school?"

"Aunt Lilac. She lives with us, too."

"Well, Meggie, it seems there are mistaken opinions in your house. I'll pay your family a visit. They shall hear my opinion, backed by the school board."

Bron took me to see the Cardiff specialist. "Why miss a day of work?" Grandma said, "I can take Meggie," but Bron said, "I want to look after my own child. No need for you to come with us, either. You seem to get confused about what doctors *really* say."

Our first appointment with the specialist was a "consultation." He asked a lot of questions, sitting in his big leather chair, and I answered them all, and at last he said, "Sounds like the measles caused it. Come back so I can run some tests."

"Will you be sending me to the deaf school in Brecon?" I asked him.

He half frowned, half smiled. "Where'd you get that notion? No, my girl, that's for children far worse off than you, and it has a waiting list as long as I'm tall."

"You're great at imitating a horse," Bron said as we walked along Cardiff High Street. "Now it's time for treats. We've got two hours before the train." We were going to the National Museum in the Civic Center, and for tea at the posh Café Royal.

Gigantic shops lined Cardiff High Street, "department stores," Bron said, and there were crowds of people on the pavements and a lot of cars and buses going up and down the wide road. Behind the shops, among lawns and flowerbeds, was the Civic Center. All the buildings were white stone. Bron told me what they were as we walked past. "That's the National Library of Wales. That's the Office of Cultural Affairs."

"Which one is for the government?"

"We don't have a government, Meggie. The English Parliament rules Wales. We're a subject nation, like you and me and Aunt Lilac at home. Not for much longer though."

"What do you mean? Is Wales going to war with the English?"

"We lost that battle a long time ago. I'm talking about Grandma, not England. I'm standing up to her…at last. Like your dad always told me to. Here's the museum."

As we went up the steps to the entrance, she said, "I've already won my first victory. We've come to Cardiff on our own."

"I'm surprised Grandma let us come without her. Why did she?"

The entrance hall of the museum was a circle with a fountain in the middle and marble statues standing about. A marble staircase led up to the next floor.

"She knows she went too far," Bron said as we climbed the staircase. "She made you lie to me, Meggie, about what Dr. Howells said. That was a bugle call for me. I had to put a stop to her before she did more harm."

"Grandma would never harm me. She loves me...and you."

Bron put her arm around me. "'Course she does. And we love her. I'm just growing up, Meggie. Here's the room with the British Romantics."

On the walls were a lot of paintings in gold frames. "They're reproductions," Bron said. "Copies, that means. But they're still grand, aren't they?"

I could only nod my head. I was too astonished to speak. I'd seen plenty of paintings in books Bron brought from the library, but I'd never seen them huge and hanging on walls before, and the scenes of nature, and the figures in the scenes, all looked so real, except the colors were more extraordinary and fierce than in the real world, at least what I'd seen of it so far.

I crossed the room to a painting of the ocean. It showed a great storm. You could see the dark, scary waves rising high, like mountain peaks with silvery tips, and the black, rain-stuffed clouds rolling down, nearly joining with the water. In the middle of all this, lifeboats were tossing about, the people inside them hunched up and clinging. The sky and the sea were so massive they made the boats and the people look *dooty*, and you didn't think they'd escape. I looked at the name next to the painting to see who could have made it. The plaque said J. M. W. Turner, *The Shipwreck*.

Bron was standing behind me. "Are there more paintings by J. M. W. Turner?" I asked her.

"Not here," she said. "There are plenty in London at the Tate Gallery. We'll go one day. The real painting of *The Shipwreck* is there."

"Can I buy a postcard of it in the gift shop?"

"If they have it. We'll buy one for Grandma as well. She likes tragedies."

We went into all the museum rooms, and we bought postcards in the shop. For Aunt Lilac, I got one of a clown with a lopsided face. The painter's name was Picasso. Bron told me how to say it. "He's famous for doing things differently from painters before him. He was daring." Maybe he's not right for Aunt Lilac then, I thought, but the clown was nice. Perhaps she'd laugh...or smile at least. Then Bron said, "We've done a lot of walking. Are you ready for a cream tea at the Café Royal?"

"I am. I'm starving."

On the way to the Café Royal, we passed the Palais de Dance. "My friends at work come here on Saturday nights," Bron said. "Look at these photos of the inside. It's plush, isn't it? They're always asking me to join them. Maybe I will."

"Grandma might not let you."

I was hoping she wouldn't. I didn't want Bron to go dancing. I didn't even like her talking about it.

"I won't be asking her permission, Meg."

"But you've already been dancing, with Daddy. Why do you want to go again?"

"Because I miss it, and Daddy's not here to partner me now."

"So who would you dance with?"

"Oh…some nice man who asked me. I'll have to send my Lurex blouse to the cleaners."

"But it's part of Aunt Lilac's mermaid costume."

"That game's getting a bit wearisome, don't you think?" She took my hand and we walked on. I was glad to pass the Palais.

"We could put a shipwreck in it. That might be thrilling."

"Can you see Grandma and Aunt Lilac rolling about and falling off their beds onto their bottoms?"

Trying to see it made me laugh. I'd been thinking myself that the pirate game wasn't fun anymore. We'd played it too long, and it was true, what Bron said, Grandma and Aunt Lilac couldn't frolic. I hadn't known that about them until I started school. "Off you go to frolic, children," Miss Rose said every day at recess, and out we rushed to play hide-and-seek and What's the Time, Mr. Wolf? and Last Man's Feet Off Ground.

"Grandma still likes the game. I think Aunt Lilac hates it though."

"It's time for the underdogs to revolt. We must be audacious like Picasso."

Bron had been speaking strangely here in Cardiff, and acting differently, all lively and excited. For the first time too, it struck me that she knew a lot: about books and big words, and now about paintings.

"How do you know so much?" I asked her.

"I only know a *little*, Meggie, but I was a good scholar. I studied hard, and I was always top of the class in English."

"Why aren't you a teacher instead of a typist?"

"Because I left school at fifteen. Grandma needed me to earn money.

After your grandpa died, we were hard up, with only his accident compensation to live on."

"Grandma could have gone to work and kept you in school."

Bron looked at me surprised. I was surprised myself. Like her, I was thinking and saying new things.

We came to the Café Royal. Inside, a man in a black suit greeted us. He called Bron Madame, and me Young Lady. A waiter in a white shirt and black tie led us to a table. "The à la carte tea for two, is it, Madame?" he asked Bron.

"Yes, please. I hope there's plenty of clotted cream. My daughter loves it."

"I shall bring you extra, Madame." He was a young waiter, and he was looking at Bron as if she was clotted cream. I stared at him and he put his eyes down and went off.

"It's nice having a day out together, isn't it," Bron said, "just the two of us? Next time, we'll go to the castle and look round the posh department stores."

Soon the waiter came back, pushing a trolley laden with scones and pastries and a tea set decorated with red roses. He was smiling at Bron and pointing at a big china jug.

"Spread your napkin on your lap, Megan," my mother said.

"Yes, Madame."

Tanya Olson

o camerado close!
o you and me at last

TANYA OLSON lives in Silver Spring, Maryland, and is a lecturer in English at University of Maryland, Baltimore County. Her first book, *Boyishly*, was published by YesYes Books in 2013 and received a 2014 American Book Award. In 2010, she won a Discovery/*Boston Review* prize and was named a 2011 Lambda Fellow by the Lambda Literary Foundation. Her poem "54 Prince" was chosen for inclusion in *Best American Poems 2015* edited by Sherman Alexie.

dear Mr President my first plan
was *swim to Cuba* since they were the enemy
closest at hand imagine that journey
103 miles 61 hours stingrays jellyfish sharks
the only way anyone ever has made it
is locked inside a cage but I
was determined to try armed only
with the heat banked inside
my fiery fiery bones
                    but that evening
we got your letter Mr President and I
nodded along with the sympathy until I read
No act of violence no matter how heinous
will halt the spread of freedom have you seen
how they die a wash of flame then the gentle
drift down a strange town's street before they settle
into the lungs of someone they
never even knew

or the ones who char abroad
and return as sticks stacked in a hold
given to families who grind them down
and grind them down until all that's left
is a handful of dust the person who wished most
to hold them whole just one more time again
must cast across the water into
a suddenly meaningful breeze
                              which leaves me to wonder
Mr President what would have happened
if I had said *Don't Go* surely a boy
can hear his sister's *Don't Go* through the white noise
all around surely he listens for the *Don't Go*
inside each *Thank You For Your Service*
behind the *Active Duty Boarding First*
but I never said it *Please Don't Go* I guess
no one else did either
                              my next plan started
with a *Leaves of Grass* somebody left on the bus
did you know Walt himself came to Washington
after reading in the paper his brother
had been shot at Fredricksburg he stared
into wounded face after wounded face
until George was the one looking back
when George got better and returned to war
Walt stayed to help the other hurt boys
write their letters home in one he called grass
the beautiful uncut hair of graves can you imagine
writing such a thing Mr President can you imagine
reading it Walt stayed and wrote and stayed and wrote
until he had a terrible stroke and this time
it was George who came to fetch Walt
and tenderly bring him home

                                   writing is all
Walt had to get him through the war and writing
is how he came to realize every last molecule
of every dead being lives still in existence somewhere
that every face he saw he'd see in some other face again
at first I kept all his letters in a box
tied it shut swore I wouldn't read them until
he came home safe turns out Mr President
he had signed each one *Now You Stay Sweet*
made sure he left out the ugly
                                      we hold so tight
what we wish to keep a sailor's knot a mother's grip
swear there is no life without it think of
Jackie crawling back along the trunk to grab
that lump of Jack's skull she's so sure
he'll need it again I visit them when I visit him
how they rest framed by Baby Patrick
and the one they only called Daughter
                                          mornings
I glimpse him standing there in his mirrory echo world
he tries to talk but his voice won't work
each week he's dimmer fading sliding farther away
my final plan Mr President my last grasp straw
the day's first word will be his whispered name
a wasp upon the tongue

Abbey Mei Otis

Party Doll Surprise Attack

Abbey Mei Otis is a fellow at the Michener Center for Writers. She previously worked as the program manager for the D.C., Creative Writing Workshop. Her work can be found in places like *StoryQuarterly*, *Barrelhouse*, *Tor.com*, and *Superficial Flesh*.

Can't remember if I was nine or ten when the sex robot fell from the sky. Just after my sister ditched, when Mom was twenty-four-seven plugged into her chair, plugged out of her grief. My brothers were left to watch me, Floro and Bello, scarred princes of the scrounge and salvage, which pretty much meant I was left to watch myself.

We were cul-de-sac kids, born in the burbs, sprawled into the sprawl. We lived in the master bedroom of a house so identical to every other house it didn't matter what it looked like. Two-story foyer with water ripple-rotting down the walls. Burns on the ceiling. Flagstone façade that dropped off in chunks and beaned you. The burbs had been spiraling down for sixty years. Hiding holes for sea-rise refugees and space rejects. Shame-shaded wastelands ringing the city pretties. Our lawns were neat because the grass was all dust. Our streets were clean because there was nothing to throw away. City dwellers flew overhead in their decked-out cars, looking down even less often than we looked up.

My brothers had not been home for a week and I spent every morning waiting on the front step, imagining each head that rounded the bend to be one of theirs. That day I was hunkered against the heat, scarfing a pseudosnacker, pink flavor, licking spilled frosting off my shirt. The burbs in summer are the cracked eggshell colors of the houses, the flat dog-belly tan of the dust, the worn-out gray of asphalt and sky. The streets smell like carpet glue.

Dark shapes came round the bend and my heart leapt. 'Til I realized there were not two but three of them. And how short they were. And that they were Corry, and Leave Alone, and Scram Pha. Skinny boys with scabby elbows, chests concave (though so was my own), mistrusting eyes dark and long lashed. *Never judge a burb boy by his eyelashes, babydaughter,* my mother told me. *I did, and look what I got.*

The three plowed up the street, Corry trying to keep up with Leave Alone, Scram a cool step behind. Leave Alone would have barreled right past my house but Scram hopped up on my curb.

"Hailo, we saw it fall. Saw a body." He flung a pointing finger toward the west end of the neighborhood, where a century before the man had run out of money to build houses on spec and so just quit. Now half-framed colonials speared out of the ground, weathered whale skeletons. They would have been declared hazardous if anyone had felt like making declarations. Instead they became our playground.

"We think s'in one of the houses and we're a find it."

Things fell from cars all the time. Tumbled down from the skyways, burst through the flat clouds. Crumpled-up computers and blipping baby toys and food wrappers that shrieked as they fell. The trash we shrugged off like weather. The treasures we crowed over like manna from citygods.

"You'na come?" Scram cocked his head so far one jug ear touched his bony shoulder.

I had never seen a body. I couldn't have imagined, back then, what it meant to fall. I jumped up, snagged for just a moment on the thought of my still-absent brothers, and ran after the boys. Down one curving street and then another, across cracked-up bleached-out lawns. Past houses and houses, identical fat white houses, torn-up walks and sagging vinyl and garages with the roofs kicked in because time wore heavy boots. After three streets we were wheezing and the houses were slack jawed and vacant. This one without windows, this one without a roof. Then no siding, then no Sheetrock.

Then only bones. The bare frames of squat McMansions, their two-by-fours gray and wormy, their foundations crumbling. Something obscene about them, half-birthed but decrepit. Like fetuses left to yellow in jars. The walls were ghostly, permeable, revealing everything. Pipes and wires speared up at strange angles.

We clambered through one and then another, scanning the ground, swinging on the framing. It gave me a nervous thrill to twine in and out of the splintery pine beams, like I was tracking dirt through the soft vessels of someone else's dream. The houses, the neighborhood, everywhere I had ever been my whole life squirmed at my footfalls, breathed out, we do not want you.

And we asked, So?

↢

I WAS THE ONE WHO found it. The body. Crumpled between cracked valves from which copper piping had been looted. One glimpse and all the motion went out of me. Because it wasn't a body. Not quite. I opened my mouth to call to the others and found my voice had fled. I wanted to turn away, bury it deep—but Scram came up behind me.

"Ossht!"

Which made the other two hop over. *Oh! Woh-woh!*

None of us, then, knew really what it meant to fall.

Amid the rusty pipes in the unfinished bathroom of the half-built house, we squatted and stared at the robot's broken form. Naked except for what must have been a gauzy robe, jewel-bright turquoise, now shredded and bunched around her neck. Her skin luminous brown like it was lit from within, like she would be hot to the touch. It was a glow that people lose when they die, but this thing kept it even now, even shattered.

She looked so human my breath caught in my throat. Something made me think of when my mother shooed us from the room and filled the enamel tub. I never left all the way, peeked through the cracked door, watched her tilt her head back, eyes closed, sluice water over her bare breasts. Mom never looked so happy as when I was gone.

This body, she didn't look happy. Her white eyes were way open and bugged out like some restraint had snapped inside her skull. Her blonde hair much lighter than her skin, snarled by the wind into a single mat that puddled on the concrete. Her wrists and elbows bent the wrong way. One of her legs must have hit the framing as she came down because a beam was splintered and her left shin was missing. Her knee ended in a raw haze of wires, plastic-coated viscera that looked gray until you got close and realized they were every color.

Scram got up and ran through one of the unfinished walls, came back holding the shin. "This is a very serious matter." He shook the foot at us like a gavel. "I want you all to do what I say." He shoved the foot right up in my face. Its toenails were painted, hot pink.

He broke the spell and we all quit genuflecting, crowded up around the body. Her torso was punctured by two lines of pale dots, which were, I leaned in and realized, the nub ends of her pseudo-ribs, driven through her skin by the impact. Corry and Leave Alone crouched together, giggling over her chest. Her breasts lay long and blobby like something inside them had burst and was seeping away. Her nipples, large and dark, spooned strangely over jellied flesh. Corry reached out a single finger to press her tit like a button, then snapped his hand back. Leave Alone fell over laughing.

I moved to one of her flung-out arms and realized she was missing a hand as well as a foot. This one wasn't ripped but smoothly severed, the edge dark and puckered like someone had sliced through it with hot wire. Unthinking, I reached out to stroke her wrist and recoiled. How utterly like skin it was—supple softness with strength underneath. Yet I could see her severed wrist, the mass of wires, no bone no muscle no blood. I reached out again and managed to clasp her wrist, and the realness made my eyes grow hot.

"Hailo, cmere." Scram crouched at her foot. "Cmere lookit this."

I dropped the wrist and walked to him. Scram was two years older than me and I liked it when we got close enough so his arm might brush mine by accident. I knelt and he pointed, "Look."

Between the robot's legs there was nothing. No vagina or skin or hair, just a wide square hole. Her illusion of humanity ended in a gaping plastic port that extended up inside her into darkness. Something in my brain clenched. My stomach roiled. Later my brothers would teach me that those kinds of robots are left empty there so you can plug in whatever apparatus you want, but at that moment a blank terror was blotting out my brain. I was shrinking, the night was encroaching. I squeaked and Scram grabbed my knee. "*Shh.*"

No idea why we had to be quiet but I shushed. And thrilled at his hand on my leg. And we crouched together and stared into terrible shadows.

"Oh man." Leave Alone nudged her with his toe. "We should take her back to our fort."

Corry snorted. "How we gonna move her, dummy? She's not walking anywhere."

"We could carry her." That was Scram, standing up. "I bet. If we all helped."

We stared at the body for a moment. "Yeah," I said. "Yeah. Snot like we can leave her here." Which was true though no one knew why.

"Cmon," Scram tugged one of her arms, "help me."

We joined him. Terrible to feel her loose weight move under my palms. Her body bent in too many places, a bag filled with broken pieces. Eventually we hoisted her onto Scram's back, Corry and Leave Alone bracing her on either side. Her leg dragged on the ground. Her head lolled on Scram's shoulder. Her breasts smushed into Scram's back. I wanted to cry.

We started out of the house, tiny steps, wobbling. Her robe fluttered behind her, gleaming turquoise amid the dust and concrete. "We should get her some clothes," Scram announced. "She can be our queen."

∽

THE FORT WAS AWAY FROM the whale skeletons, away from the homes, in a gully where the power lines used to run. Against two real trees we had piled up branches and boards and the door off a wheelie car. It had started out as a place to hide the things we stole. Crinkle packs of food and broken tech bits. One time Leave Alone made off with a whole case of gel candy from someone's front room store. We gorged ourselves for three days until we all shit glowing green. There wasn't much that made it to the burbs that was worth stealing. Sometimes we nabbed photographs, old music players, dug up the only tomato plant in the yard, somebody miss it, please, someone. Miserly place, wouldn't even let us be criminals.

The robot we dumped outside the fort. Scram groaned as her weight eased off him. Propped her up against a real tree and straightened the shreds of nightgown around her body. I tried to close her eyes but her eyeballs bulged like balloons when I pushed the lids down so I left her to gawk.

She gawked as we dragged a dirty skirt out from the fort and covered her legs. She gawked as we draped tattered plastic around her like a smock. She gawked as I twisted her a crown out of TV cable.

Scram and Leave Alone went off to search for rocks. We were going to build a second room for the fort. Corry and I stayed to dig a circle in the dirt. I scraped the ground with a piece of window frame. Beads of sweat crawled down my arms. As I dug, I stared at the robot's leg. Her skin was butter smooth and dry.

"Yeah," Corry rocked back on his heels, "I think she's beautiful."

I stared at him. "Shut up."

"What? I do."

I couldn't think of what to say to this. "Huh. You would."

"What's that mean?"

"Nothing. Don't talk to me."

"What?"

But his mind was on the robot, I could feel it, on the little band of belly flesh that showed every time the breeze lifted her smock.

As we worked, the boys looked for excuses to touch her. Corry kept brushing his arm along her ankle as he dug. When Leave Alone came back lugging a hunk of cinderblock, he heaved it down and staggered, catching his balance by grabbing her neck. Scram kept adjusting her crown, her shawl, brushing his fingertips over her collarbone. Their sweat rubbed off on her, left smudges bright on her poreless skin.

§

IN THE DISTANCE THE DEEP-DOWN hum of scooters, and my ears perked. My brothers, maybe, on some late-night errand that had dragged into morning. I didn't understand what my brothers did then but I knew it was important. I knew bad things would happen if they messed up. I knew they stayed awake when everyone else grown-up was plugged into games.

About once a month Bello blitzed out on too many tabs, forgot his rule about not letting me on his scooter, pulled me onto his lap, and roared onto the highway. *Vroom.* He talked as we sped, "You scared yet, Hai-girl?" His spit flecked my neck before the wind whipped it away. "You gotta get scared sometime." *Vroom.* "How about now?"

He steered with one arm, the other around my waist, the scooter careening crazily across the empty road. My front was numb in the wind but my back against him was warm. His fingers dug so hard into my side that the next morning there would be four parallel bruises. Warehouses and empty lots flew by. *Vroom.* I bit the noises back so hard I tasted blood. "How-about-*now?*"

Eventually he veered around and dumped me on the outskirts of the neighborhood. If I closed my eyes I could still see him speeding away, dark dot on the static country of my eyelids.

↝

I MOUNDED THE DUG-UP EARTH. Scram and Corry slung down big chunks of cinderblock, pried like molars from the McMansion foundations. Every so often I pressed my mouth to my arm, tasted sweat. Feeling my muscles move, it made me happy in a way I couldn't name.

Sometimes when Mom was plugged in I would touch her. Drape her arm over my shoulders, lay my head on her knee. It made me nervous and safe at the same time, to feel her body without her. Here was weight, here was warmth that couldn't leave me, even when all the rest could.

When our stomachs' knuckling could no longer be ignored, Scram dove into the old fort and pulled a phakecake from under a board. It was squished flat but the metallic icing still shone. Divided into quarters, one for each. Scram got the back wrapper, I got the front. Leave Alone and Corry split the cardboard tray, licked it until the paper sogged.

As we ate we asked the robot questions. We had a big metal ball bearing from the construction site and we set it on her sternum. If it rolled off her left side that was yes. If it rolled off her right that was no.

"You have to be very polite," Scram told us like he'd been doing this for years. "You have to say, O Queen, first."

"O Queen, will I marry someone rich?"

No.

"O Queen, will I ride in a skycar some day?"

Yes.

"O Queen, will my uncle who lives in the basement die a horrible death that makes his dick shrivel up and fall off?"

No.

"O Queen, will there be plastipatties for dinner?"

No.

"Yeah that's a big lie." Leave Alone stood up and prodded the robot's thigh. "She's tilted to the right. It's always gonna fall this way. This is stupid."

He went back to piling rocks. I stayed by the robot and asked her more questions in my head.

Are my brothers OK?

No.

Will I ever get out of here?

No.

I picked up the ball bearing and hurled it at her throat, hit her so hard that her head bounced and flopped to the other side.

∽

AGAIN, THE DOG-GROWL OF SCOOTERS, whistles, and hacking laughter. "Kid-kid-kiddos! Lookit! That's a big doll you got there, little boys. Sure you can handle it?"

Almost I spun around to say I wasn't a boy but my thumping heart kept me staring at the dirt. "Whatever," Scram mumbled, tearing up a real leaf with his nails. The scooterjocks revved and skimmed away but two whiny trails remained, wound closer to us. They cut out right by our fort and I finally looked up. Against the white sky, a squat gnarled silhouette and a lean restless one. I knew those shapes. Floro, Bello. They were back.

More than double my age. Both short, though Bello was just barely taller. So different except they were always together and even now I can't picture them apart.

Bello stood thumbs-in-waistband, bouncing on the balls of his feet. So tense, secondbrother, like the clothespin holding space and time together.

Like if he relaxed for a second reality would come flying apart. Floro didn't bounce. Floro was poured out of concrete. Thick bull neck and prettyboy face. He lunged forward and grabbed me around the waist, flipped me upside down so my feet stuck up over his shoulder. "What you looking at, babysister? What, huh? Think we brought you presents?"

The world swung wildly. I could feel the sugar roll sliding back up my gullet. I clenched my teeth. Firstbrother smelled like grease and sweat and something strange, a cloying darkness that clung to my nostrils. "What? What?" Then he caught sight of the robot. "What do you know. Hailo's finally playing with dolls."

He dropped me. I stayed face down for a moment, breathing in the warmth of the dirt. Waited 'til my ears didn't ring. When I looked up Bello was right over me, bouncing, bouncing. His face was blank but he thrust out a hand to pull me up. I ignored it.

"You shouldn't of left me."

Bello's eyes narrowed a shade. He wrapped his arms around his torso like maybe it would still his body but he kept bouncing. Silence, and then he nodded. "Yeah. I know."

I stood up. I charged at him and rammed my head into his gut. Bello took it noiselessly, held me at arm's length. "Hailo. Hey. We're here now. We're back."

"What-ever. I'm not stupid, you won't stay." I twisted out of his hands. "You know you won't."

Bello took a deep breath. Chewed his lower lip. His eyes like embers burning up the things he couldn't say. Apologies for what they had done to me. Forgiveness for what I would one day do to them. All he said was, "Probably not."

"Hey broh, come check this out. This worth anything?" Floro beckoned, bent over the robot.

"Not for sale," Scram blurted.

I scuffed a pebble at him, "Shut *up*." It bothered me when other people weren't afraid of my brothers.

Bello shook his head as he walked over, "Neh, they're dropping all over the place. Cheap partydolls. Somebodies up there must be breaking some rules."

We watched my brothers skate their hands over the robot. Scrunch up her shirt and prod her belly. Yank her hair and stare at the back of her neck. My scalp prickled. Bello lifted her severed wrist and flapped it at Floro. "See? They cut out the memory."

"Huh, ladybot." Floro sucked in his breath. "You been through hell."

Then Bello knelt in front of her, tugged off the balloon skirt, and plunged his hand into the hole between her legs. His arm disappeared up to the elbow. His eyes got the blank look of someone concentrating hard on something he couldn't see. "Ha, ha," Scram said weakly. I didn't want to be watching but I couldn't look away.

Floro squatted near the robot's head, fingers rapping a manic beat on the flesh of her neck. Her head trembled.

It must've only taken a minute but time felt like it was being shredded like Scram's real leaf. Bello withdrew his arm. Shrugged and scratched his scalp. "Everything's fried. Told you. Let's go."

They walked back to their scooters. Floro collared me as he went by, scrubbed his hand through my hair. "Come party with us tonight, baby-sister? We are taking it eas-*ay* tonight, you bet."

Through the crook of his arm I saw Bello staring hard. He was either examining my bone marrow or he was a thousand miles away. Then he twitched and shook his head like he was unsettling flies, "We'll be around for a while, 'K Hailo? Maybe get you some new clothes."

I wanted to press up against them. I wanted us to lie together in our pajamas while I traced my fingers over their scars. I wanted them to try and scare me. One more time. Go on, just try. But they kicked on their scooters and whined away toward the neighborhood.

❧

IN THEIR WAKE WE SAT around picking scabs, drawing lines in the dirt. I didn't want to look at anyone. The robot was gummy with dirt and other people's sweat. In the distance a bus swooped down bearing tired bodies home from the recycling plant. Through the quiet there came a tiny raspy noise. Corry twitched, "What was that?"

We strained but heard only the vanishing hum of the bus. The sun was backing down. The house frames combed long blue shadows through the dirt. Scram stretched arms over his head. "Probly my stomach. I'm going home."

I didn't move. Home sat in my mind like a hungry hairless animal. I fed it only when I had to. Just when I'd made up my mind to stand, *there*, again the noise, as though it were right by my ear. Leave Alone whooped, "It was her!"

He pointed at the robot.

The four of us froze and watched her. She was utterly motionless. Her head drooped. Her eyes bulged. The shadows of the real trees lay across her sunken belly. We stared until my neck pinched.

"Don't be an idiot," Scram said, kicked dirt at the robot and hiked off toward the neighborhood. The other two followed him, poking each other, shooting scared grins over their shoulders. I stood but couldn't make myself leave. I decided to stamp the floor of the fort down flat. I swept out the real dry leaves that had fallen. There was a leaf on the robot's chest. I flicked it off and my fingernail grazed her breast. Touching her curled my stomach so I forced myself to grab hold of her shoulders with both hands. I leaned down and rested my forehead against her forehead.

"What do you know?" I whispered to her. "You're *trash*. You're not going anywhere."

The robot brought her handless arm up to pet my shoulder and murmured, "You smell so good."

I would have screamed if I'd been a screaming type girl—instead I just fell backwards, gasping, my skin lit with fear. The robot's arm fell down limp again but her face twitched. Her distended eyeballs rolled. Her lips flapped like they were trying to escape her face. Her shoulders twisted and the cloth we had draped over her fell away.

"Oh dear!" she giggled, "I seem to have lost my shirt!"

Her voice came from her head but not through her mouth. Full of all the sweet things I had never eaten. Her legs knocked against each other. I realized she was trying to cross her ankles. "I have been bad, haven't I?" Her feet snaked back and forth. "You might have to punish me."

Red waves were breaking over my brain. The world had narrowed to a dark alley with her lipstick prints on the walls but I could see light at the far end and I throttled toward it. Reaching back I groped for the cinderblocks the boys had uprooted. My fingers clutched at one as big as my head. I cradled it in both arms and stood, took a step toward the robot. The wires in her severed arm flexed and fluttered. I hoisted the ancient cornerstone over my head. My biceps screamed. "My!" Her eyes lighted on everyplace but me. "How strong you are!" And I slammed the block down on her face.

Her head collapsed inward. I threw my weight onto the block, crushing the circuitry of her brain. Like crushing honeycombs. I backed off and let the block roll away. Nose split. Lips all over her face. I squirmed my body under the block and heaved it up and again brought it down on her head. Her skin broke into rubbery fragments. Her eyeballs popped and dissolved. Her head a misshapen mass of pale plastic and wire. I ground the paste of her skull into the bark of the real tree.

Then I took the block again and smashed her sternum. I smashed her breasts into the dirt. I smashed her severed wrist until you couldn't guess where arm ended and earth began. I smashed her pelvis and her kneecaps, grated away the fake softness of her skin until she was only a pile of parts, shattered wafers of circuitry and pulverized filaments. I smashed until my muscles wept, until I couldn't inhale without shrieking. Then I collapsed on the mound of remnants, curled around the block, spat out a mouthful of slime. There was no blood. Course there was no blood.

It was dark. The sky was starless but car lights zipped overhead. I stood up all shivery, turned and ran home. If you saw me then you might've thought I had no idea where I was going, but I knew with each step my foot was headed for the ground.

❧

UP THE CURVING STAIRCASE WITH the rotting boards, our room door was open. My brothers sat on the floor, winding the clockwork of their crazy. I stopped in the doorway to watch them, my heart thudding in my throat. Floro hugged his knees to his chest. Bello leaned against the wall, legs splayed out. Tabs trashed about them like fallen petals.

"—nothing left." Floro spat out the words. "And what about us, think we're still pink slick? Think we still ooze when they squeeze?

Bello rubbed a hand over his face. "Nah. We're not dolls."

Floro sprang up. "Want to find out?" He leapt to the other side of the room and came back holding a knife.

Their eyes were glassy. A tendon flexed in Bello's foot. Floro knelt and laid the blade against Bello's lip like a steel mustache. "How about I slice your lips off?"

Bello grinned against the knife edge. "You are such a clown."

"You think? You think I'm joking?"

"You're always joking. Ha ha ha."

"Funny, yeah sure. Here's a good one. Fill a body with plastic, what do you think happens? Huh? We're the punch line, littlebrother."

"OK," Bello shrugged, "for real you want to find out? Here." He thrust his fist out between them. "Cut off my hand."

I stepped into the room. They didn't turn to me but Floro waggled the knife hello. "There's a patty on the windowsill for you, Hai," Bello called. With his other hand he reached out and pulled Floro's knife to rest on his wrist. "I'll show you. Cut off my hand."

I curled up in the window to eat, the frame digging into my tailbone. The yards outside were going shut-eye dark. I sent the fibrous lumps of patty efficiently into my stomach. Food has always seemed like the least pleasurable thing you can still yearn for. In the dark corner Mom was in her chair, plugged in. I didn't look at her. I watched my brothers across the room. They crouched together, staring at Bello's wrist like angels would pour out of it. Floro's hand trembled. Silence clogged everything.

Floro did a dismissive *psh*. "You're a plastic person, littlebrother. Like the dolls, like the rest of us."

"Not yet. You'll see. You coward. It'll bleed." Enough hope in Bello's voice to break a window. "I know there's some left."

Oh, my brothers. The ones who taught me not to be afraid of hate. In the dim room they glowed blinding like green balls of fire. Bathed in this light of theirs I could feel a new kind of love. The kind that gives you x-ray vision, that lets you see into the future. If they didn't slit each other open, they would die protecting me.

Floro's hand trembled again and Bello snapped, "*Do it*." If he were a fuse he would be lit, if he were a particle cannon he would be firing. "I'll *strangle you* if you don't."

"Yeah? You'll strangle me if I *do.*"

"How'd I strangle you with one hand?"

"Ha!"

"Ha!"

They laughed like they were heaving cinderblocks at each other. The knife pressed a shallow valley in Bello's skin.

The green fire lit them up, showed me what they would find. Sparks and wires, filaments and honeycombs. Inside Floro too—I could see the petal-thin cogs of his brain. The tik-tok mice running, running, turning the wheel of his lungs.

The pressure would burst my eardrums. There was too much of this, always the same thing. I got up and brushed by them on my way out, left them frozen, straining against, against.

చ

I SETTLED CROSS-LEGGED ON OUR stoop and rested my chin on my hands. In the darkening even the burbs look pretty, the way a shipwreck is beautiful at the bottom of the ocean. The houses swim black-black out of the blue-black night. If I raised my eyes I could catch the blinking of cars flying overhead. Red-white, red-white, through a star-spangled sky. I watched for a moment and then turned my eyes back to the houses. My arms ached from lifting the block. I wrapped them around my skinny chest and felt something warm pulse through me. Not happiness. More like satisfaction. Funny how dropping something heavy can feel just like clutching something close. We in the burbs—we didn't need any kind of robot. We had all been pushed out the car door. We fell the thousand feet, we hit the ground, we got up and kept going.

Virginia Pye

The Lemon Man

VIRGINIA PYE is the author of two novels, *Dreams of the Red Phoenix* (Unbridled Books, 2015) and *River of Dust* (Unbridled Books, 2013). Her award-winning short stories have appeared in numerous journals, including the *North American Review*, the *Tampa Review*, the *Baltimore Review*, *Failbetter*, and elsewhere. Her essays and interviews are online at the *New York Times Opinionator*, Literary Hub, The Rumpus, *The Nervous Breakdown*, and other sites. Please visit her website to learn more: www.virginiapye.com.

Sara's new Italian sandals have heels that she knows no sane American tourist would risk on cobblestones. Yesterday the Roman shoe salesman assessed her calves with an unreconstructed male gaze and subsequent nod of approval—as if her legs had been put on this earth for his pleasure, which she knew was also wrong in every possible way and for which she now pays the price in a sore back.

Had she even thought about her legs like that in months, perhaps years? she wonders now. The children grab at her skirt and shoulder bag as her husband hurries on ahead in the wake of the tour guide. Sara answers her own question: on a rocky path in the Roman Forum, an American woman jettisons her sensible shoes and doesn't have a clue which way to turn.

"*Gelato,*" her son Graham says, for the umpteenth time.

"*Gelato,*" little Emma repeats.

They buzz around her like the bees in the Boboli Gardens that morning. Emma was stung, something so shocking to her that her eyes welled up with indignation more than pain. Sara longs for such shock, although she suspects that the itching and burning afterward would hardly be worth it.

Under the shadow of a cross that rises from the ruins, as if Christianity itself were a monumental afterthought, she saunters toward the tour group, drawn not so much by the sights as by the sweat beading routinely, handsomely, on the guide's brown neck. At the back of the group, her husband Richard appears rapt, his whole being hung on the guide's every stilted English phrase.

"I can't do this anymore," Sara whispers.

Richard wheels around, letting the crowd go ahead to the next sight without him. "What? Why? We have to keep up."

"You go on."

He looks perplexed yet sincere, as if seeing one more ancient pile of rubble will solve everything. Sara thinks he wants them to carry on by simply going forward.

"I'll wait in the shade with the kids. We'll meet you outside the Colosseum."

"Here, take some euros."

"What for?" She gestures at the ancient olive trees, the dry landscape, the spiky weeds poking through stones unmoved for all time.

"Get the kids something from the snack carts," Richard suggests, then turns to them. "What do you think, guys, you want some *limonata*?" His accent hurts Sara's ears, he's trying so hard. She knows she is being uncharitable, but perhaps, she considers, that's part of who she is now.

Their children huddle, deciding if their longing for *gelato* can be satisfied by *limonata* instead. That's the question, isn't it? she thinks. Can one high and desperate hope be satisfied by something else instead?

Sara's husband gives her coins from his jangling pockets. He is generous, always has been. It makes her wonder how they'll resolve things. Amicably, she suspects.

Graham reaches his sweaty hand into hers for the money. Coins fall to the pebbled ground. Richard tells him to cool it and to pick up the change.

"All right, you guys," he adds, "I'll see you in half an hour over at the entrance to the Colosseum. Help Mommy find me, all right?"

Then he looks at Sara and presses her purse against her hip, ever mindful of the notorious Roman pickpockets, although their family stands alone on the path. He lowers his voice and leans in closer. "You seem a little out of it. The jet lag must still be getting to you. I'll take the kids later at the hotel so you can nap. But stay alert now, OK? Don't get lost." His expression is as searching and mystified as when he gazed up at the Sistine Chapel ceiling earlier in the day, Sara thinks, although nothing about her is so awe inspiring.

She nods slowly, noncommittally, the latent teenager in her unwilling to offer more. Richard then turns and scurries up the trail. The children and Sara watch him go. She tries to picture that this is how it will be from now on.

Over the past week, their family has stumbled into dark medieval churches looking for the finger bones and femurs of saints, the preserved bodies of bishops still in their robes, their wax faces surprisingly plump considering there's nothing inside. The bodies are hollow, eviscerated, and yet people kneel before them and close their eyes.

Graham pulls on Sara's purse and jolts her back to the moment. "Euros, Mom. We're dying of thirst."

For an eleven-year-old, he has the presence of someone much older, she thinks, packing all the punch his father lacks. Somehow Sara knows her son will be all right. And little Emma will be too young to remember. She will try to recall her parents together from snapshots on trips like this one—the picture this morning in front of the fountain in the Boboli. Their separation will mix in her mind with that first bee sting and the Mediterranean heat, all mysterious and conveying a pain that startles, but eventually subsides.

Graham takes the coins and grabs Emma's hand. They dash off up the path. At least they have each other, Sara thinks.

"Slow down," she shouts after them. "I need to keep you in sight."

"Don't worry, Mom," Graham shouts back over his shoulder.

"Yeah, Mom, don't worry," Emma copies.

Her voice rises and tangles in the olive branches where the sparrows twitter at midday.

As Sara meanders after them, she notices off to the side of the path a flight of ancient steps leading up to nowhere. At the top, a young Italian couple stands close together, their arms around one another. What a romantic sight, she thinks, the woman with summer in the folds of her dress. Sara pauses and gazes up at them, prepared to smile and sigh, then move on. The young man wears sleek black pants and Sara notices the way his browned forearms and the back of his neck glisten in the sunlight. The girl rises on her toes to reach him and Sara can understand why.

As they kiss, she notices how the young man's hand curves over the young woman's hip. It presses down her side and disappears into the fabric between her legs. The small purple, embroidered flowers on the white background are crimped against his outstretched fingers. Her skirt will be wrinkled, Sara thinks and quickly realizes that she is the only one who cares.

Any initial thought that this was a tame moment vanishes as the girl lets out a throaty laugh and squeezes the man's shoulder in a clawlike grip. He does not smile and, what's more important, does not remove his hand from between her legs.

Sara stays frozen on the path, enthralled. Then she glances down at her new sandals covered now in fine, ancient dust. Something about them on her is as outrageous as the kissing couple, she thinks, and lets out a surprising laugh. It's far quieter than the girl's, but every bit as guttural and real. Sara then rubs the toe of the sandal against the back of her leg, which feels cool and smooth and firm.

When she looks up again, the couple has moved away from the steps and across a ledge overlooking a deep archeological pit. To get there, Sara figures out that they've slipped around a low rope barrier and entered an area where tourists aren't allowed. She can't help wondering what they think they're going to do out in the exposed sun with occasional groups of tourists drifting by.

Without thinking, Sara heads off the central path and up the stairs, too. Each stone step is high and as she ascends, her skirt catches air and flares out. She senses heat billowing around her, but her thighs feel damp and shadowed and secret beneath the light fabric.

When Sara reaches the top step, she realizes she is exposed, her purpose there unclear. But when she looks across at the couple, she sees that they haven't noticed her. They stand, locked in an embrace at the edge of the cliff beside the pit. The man has bent his dark head into the woman's neck and appears to be feasting there. Her neck looks startlingly white against his black hair, and then Sara notices his actual lips and open mouth as he kisses the woman's skin. The wetness of his tongue on her cool neck, Sara thinks. That's all she thinks, because it is a thought unto itself: attention must be paid to that tongue and those lips and the press of his body against hers, his hand at the small of her back, pulling her towards him, her dress hiked up and the lovely raised violets smashed.

Sara looks away and still can't fathom what they think they're doing. They can't make love there on that cliff, can they? she wonders. Or do people do that in Italy, because it's Italy? Perhaps, like her new sandals, allowances are made for such things—sex and passion woven blatantly into everyday life. This is foreign territory where we Americans are clueless—at least this American, Sara thinks.

When she looks back up, they are moving on again. The man has the woman's pale hand in his and he's steering her across the ledge. Sara spots a grove of olive trees in the near distance and imagines that's where he is taking her. The rocky ground appears to give way to soft grass there. He will ease her down into it, or perhaps she will pull him frantically to join her.

Sara can feel the young man's hand, the force of it pressing against her thighs. He pushes her back, hair outstretched like a virgin's on a sacrificial slab. Only nothing about the couple is virginal, and certainly nothing about Sara is either, which is why she wants to step over the rope barrier, teeter across the precarious ledge, and join them in the partially hidden incline that has no doubt been used for this purpose since time immemorial. Only in her own country, in her own stark and dull life, would someone hesitate, Sara thinks, as she hesitates. But she would do it, she tells herself, really, she would.

Only then she looks back and realizes she can't see the main path that leads to the *limonata* carts or the plaza where Richard will be meeting them. Sara can't see the kids from here. She scrambles along the rocky hillside, clomps hastily down the stacked steps, and stumbles onto the trail again.

Her greatest fear in this moment is that Richard will have left the tour early and discovered the kids alone by the snack carts with Sara waylaid off in the bushes. Her absence, she thinks, will prove something undeniable about her. A recklessness and irresponsibility that show she is a bad mother. Richard has recently accused her of being untethered. He doesn't know the half of it, she thinks.

In the days before their trip, Sara lost the car keys three times, accidentally shut the cat in the garage overnight, forgot to pick up Graham from soccer again. She left a flame on under an empty pot and kept the water going in Emma's bath until a gray cloud appeared on the dining room ceiling. Richard may never know the details, but he grasps the overall effect: she's lost. And wrong. All wrong.

Sara slows down on the path and tries to consider the truth. She has been leaving for some time now, so much so as to be already almost gone. It's a wonder she's here at all. But she is a mother and a mother needs to be present. She needs to watch over her kids who, she reminds herself with another jolt, are nowhere in sight. The thought of her imminent and justifiable punishment rises before Sara: he will get the kids if she doesn't get her shit together.

She hurries up the trail and pushes through the turnstile that leads out of the Forum, glancing at the souvenir and snack carts that circle the cobblestones. And look, she thinks, there are her children, bent over their drinks, the long, serpentine straws curving into their mouths. As she approaches, she hears the happy slurping, the pull of the syrupy liquid to their lips.

Then Sara realizes those aren't the sounds at all: instead of satisfaction, the burbling noise is crying. She dashes forward and crouches down in front of Emma. Her daughter's face is red from the sun, but her cheeks are dry. Sara turns quickly and sees the last thing she expects: Graham's face streaked with tears. She grabs her son by the wrist, not meaning to frighten him, but he lets out a cry and drops his drink. Acid yellow liquid spills onto the cobblestones like urine.

"What's wrong?" Sara asks. "Did a bee sting you, too?"

Graham's narrow shoulders heave and he tosses himself against her. Sara rocks back on her heels and lands on her butt on the hard cobblestones.

"Graham," she says, starting to scold him, but something in his shaking body stops her. Sara tries to peel her son off her chest so she can see him better, but he won't let go.

"Emma," she says over his shoulder. "Tell Mommy what happened."

Her daughter bows her head lower toward her drink and lets out an old lady's worried sigh. It's not like her not to talk, Sara thinks.

"Did you spend all the money that your father gave you? Is that it? You can tell me. I won't be angry with you."

She rubs a hand over Graham's hair and he flinches.

"Children," Sara tries more seriously, "If you won't tell me what's going on, I'll have to ask one of these grown-ups here." She spreads her arm towards the milling strangers, not one bit sure her meager Italian could do the job.

Her son yanks himself away and shakes his head hard.

"Oh, for God's sake, darling, it can't be all that bad," Sara says, her voice harder than she intended. She knows she shouldn't have wandered off, but can it really all that terrible? Her boy is fine, she tells herself as she reaches for him again, but he steps away.

Graham wipes his cheeks with his forearm and looks at her, pausing for what has to be dramatic effect. "You don't know, Mom," he finally says. "You'll never know."

Sara can't help it, but she laughs, not a lot, but enough. She tosses back her head and actually chuckles. She wants to tell her eleven-year-old that he can't possibly understand the extent to which no one will ever know. No one will ever understand. The cruelty of her own laughter dawns on Sara a little too slowly and she stops abruptly. The children watch her, worried, perhaps even scared.

She suddenly feels exquisite sympathy for these small people, although in this moment it is hard to grasp that they are hers. Her son's words, spoken so defiantly, seem foreign to her. She simply doesn't get their meaning.

Sara looks past the children and the Colosseum recedes into the distance just as the cobblestones that fan out rise into a wall around her and her children. She thinks that they are disappearing before her eyes down a tunnel. She must reach for them before they are sucked away.

This is crazy; the heat's getting to her, she thinks, as she looks over at the man who runs the *limonata* cart, as if he can help bring her children back to her. Gray stubble shades his face and his eyes are hidden under a plaid cap. She decides he is the culprit who harmed her child. But then he smiles benignly down at a little girl who stands beside her mother, politely waiting for her drink. Sara notices the mother holds her daughter's hand and she thinks, That should have been me. I should have been that mother.

So if the lemon man didn't do it, Sara wonders, who did? A young Algerian in an NYU T-shirt leans against his souvenir truck, his head bent into a GameBoy. Under the shade of an ancient tree, the ubiquitous matrons dressed in black shake their heads at some long-repeated tale. A blond Northern European family sits wedged together on a bench, eating their healthy lunches.

Which one of these innocent-looking people stole my son's change, Sara asks herself, or tried to sell him something illicit, or yelled at him needlessly? Which one is a pervert or a pedophile, a nightmare come true? It had to have been the lemon man, she thinks again, although now he is whistling as he unloads bright lemons from a wooden box.

She decides she will interrogate him nonetheless in a language he can't understand. She will shout at him and blame him and insist he explain why this country of fine wines and routine epiphanies has not moored her more successfully to her family and life. Give me back my boy, Sara will shout, when really it is herself she wants returned.

That's when her husband steps into her line of sight. He looks plain and well-intentioned, familiar and somehow right.

"That was fascinating," he says, nodding over his shoulder at the Colosseum that has come into focus again.

He leans forward and offers a peck to the air near Sara's cheek. Instinctively, and for no good reason, she leans toward him, too.

She looks down at Graham to try to understand what has happened between them while his father has been gone. Her son stares up at her with an adult expression, one that shows he has things under control now. He surreptitiously wipes away any sign of tears.

"Everything all right?" Richard asks, glancing at each of them. "Is something wrong?"

"No," Graham says firmly. "We're good. Mom bought us some lemonade. Mine spilled, but it's no big deal."

Graham offers a manly shrug. He is protecting her, she realizes. Something bad has happened and he is covering it up for her sake. Something has come between us, something terrible, Sara thinks. Then she realizes that something is her.

Richard looks to her for an explanation, but she is at a loss. She looks to Graham and after a long moment, she nods in agreement with her son that they are fine. Graham and Sara have made a pact. In one brief moment, her son has become fully grown and capable of deception, as well as great sacrifice and love.

But, Sara reminds herself, I am his mother, and not his accomplice. Now is the moment to speak up, to set things straight. The voices of strangers, the wings of birds flapping as they rise to the triumphal arch beside them, the chatter of birds as they settle on the cross that casts a shadow on the path, the guides explaining significant moments in history to interested tourists, the calls of the street vendors: Sara must speak above it all.

And yet she stalls. She's not sure what she would say. She stands frozen and feels nothing until Graham steps forward and takes her hand.

"Let's go, Mom," he says.

Sara looks down and wishes she could go forward.

"All right, then," Richard says as he takes Emma's hand. "We've got just enough time to catch the last bus of the day."

"We're coming," Graham answers for his mother as he starts to pull them forward.

"Richard," Sara finally says. "Wait."

Graham looks up at her, his face dark with adult betrayal. He tries again to pull her onward, to march them into the future he assumes is theirs.

Sara turns to her husband, opens her mouth, and begins.

Pam Risdon

Sara's Way

PAM RISDON has written a dozen short stories and self-published a novel, *The Harder They Fall*. She lives with her husband in Alexandria, Virginia, where she shares the responsibility of their photography business.

S ara's eyelids fluttered as the shadow of a raven crossed over her and its squawk startled her awake. The sun was teetering on the top of the ridge and about to cross the line from sunset to dusk. The hammock had stopped rocking, and she sleepily lifted her head to check on Mark and make sure he was still sitting where she remembered before she drifted off. He was backlit and his head looked round on top of his shoulders. He swatted a gnat and settled, waiting patiently for Sara to wake up and let him know she was ready to make the walk back down from the bluff to home.

Sara was groggy and not ready to crawl out of the hammock. She laid her head back on the warm spot where it had been for an hour or more. Sara drifted back into that place that's not quite consciousness. Her body felt numb and detached and she dreamed. As the sun set, the air stirred as usual and her face grew cold and it woke her. Sara stared straight above, watching the colored leaves of late autumn move and rustle. As her vision came into focus, so too her thoughts formed and discerned the day, date, and time, and she remembered it was a week ago that the call came and he was gone.

That unwelcome feeling of dread washed over her, and she wished she could go back to just seconds ago when Mark was sitting in that chair and everything was as it should be. Sara's face contorted, for the thousandth time it seemed, and her cheeks grew hot. Tears streamed out of the corner of her eyes. Her sobs filled the woods behind her, crescendoing into a wail. She smeared her face dry with her sleeve and abruptly pulled herself up and out of the hammock. Her legs felt weak as she lost her footing and skittered to one knee. Her left hand broke her fall and landed on a sharp rock that punctured her skin, leaving a small divot. The cut was a welcome distraction; even with the pain, it helped her think of something other than her missing husband.

Mark disappeared on a hike, on a trail he wasn't familiar with, and the thought of him actually getting lost sent rods of rage through Sara's mettle. Each minute of each day that passed, Sara became more obsessed with every detail that the fellows in his group could recall. Sara waffled between happy memories from when they first found their farmhouse, how excited they were to have finally made the decision to actually buy the place, change their life for good, and the tragedy of the day she woke up alone there.

Mark and Sara were lifelong suburbanites. In their former life, they had lived in a cramped condo just outside the city. Mark wanted a close-in spot to commute from and once he retired from his government job, both his and Sara's fantasy of moving to the country filled their conversations. Once Sara found the house, over long and exhausting Internet searches, it didn't take them long to sell everything they considered tired and worn out and make the move two hundred miles southwest to the mountains. Sara liked to recall the house when they first discovered it. Its state of disrepair and dilapidated appearance is laughable now. She wondered what in the world either of them was thinking, buying such a run-down shithole. There wasn't even a kitchen, for Christ's sake. For the first four months, they cooked on a Coleman camping stove in the living room on his father's handmade tool chest, the one he had dragged all the way back from New Zealand just before he died. As time passed and the renovations were completed, they fell more in love with their new surroundings and felt a sense of accomplishment over each bit of progress made.

Mark was a trooper, sanding floors and putting up new drywall over the wooden walls that had been stained almost black. Sara helped as best she could, painting and sanding and doing most of the gardening, a chore she both loathed and cherished at the same time. Five years later, you wouldn't have thought it to be the same place. The house was white then, white metal siding, all stained with country dirt. There were no shutters either, and it looked like a woman without her jewelry. Strange, the things your mind settles on, Sara thought as she stumbled back down the worn path from the bluff. She didn't know why she had decided to walk up there tonight. She had this feeling she'd lost something and just kept walking around the place looking for it. Oh yeah, now she remembered, it was Mark.

Sara never enjoyed being alone, not for long anyway. She had grown so dependent upon Mark over the years. *He's her left arm* all right, was…such an awful thing to have to say…was. But she can't go there. Not yet. Is, is, is. "He is still here," she said aloud, and looked around as she crossed the road to the garden gate. Sara hated the idea of being in that house without him. The space didn't feel the same, all that quiet. He was never quiet, always blabbing about something, the bird he saw or the next lunar eclipse. That was the entire point of the camping trip, to see that damn blood moon. "Goddamn it," she yelled and pounded her fist on the kitchen counter. The waves of anxiety clench her guts. Again her mind went back to the same questions. *Why that trail? How could they let him go alone? Why would anyone let someone walk back to a spot he was unsure of, alone?* To get his phone no less, how stupid, stupid fucking cell phone. I'll call it again, she thought, then remembered there was no service there anyway, but maybe he's made it to an area where there might be service now. It had been an entire week and he just may have made it out to a clearing. Sara dialed Mark's cell phone again for the hundredth time, hoping there was some chance he might be here, still on this Earth, looking at the sky, as he loved to do. It rang and quickly went to voicemail, as they do when they're out of range, and she listened very carefully to her husband's voice as if maybe somewhere in that same message there was a clue planted, a secret to where he was and that if she listened really hard, she just might hear it this time.

There's no cure for this feeling, she thought. She couldn't drink it away, although she'd tried. She can't take any more of those sedatives they gave her, although she wanted to. She could only hope and pray, even though she didn't believe, and wait. She'd kept a log of all the phone conversations she had had with the police and their efforts in the search. She'd kept a diary of her observations of what she'd seen while walking that trail three days ago looking for Mark. Everything was so ordinary and so surreal at the same time. She wandered around the empty house, up and down the stairs, washed clean clothes, and swept the porch for no reason. She scoured the history of Internet searches from a week ago on the computer, hoping for clues to things that don't exist. Sara looked through Mark's dresser drawers—for what, she was not sure. She emptied out boxes in the middle of the floor and then scattered the contents into the corners of the room. She could find no comfort in anything and, if she did, she immediately felt guilty for having a pleasant thought, for what was there to be happy about in any minuscule way; her husband was missing.

As the sun's last light faded to night, Sara inhaled deeply and hoped that something would bring her relief from this misery. Maybe a phone call would help, but she decided against it. Her mother had called her every day except today. Sara figured she too has grown tired of this waiting for some news, good or bad, and has given up on calling. As Sara sat on the couch, she stared at the phone, trying with all her might to will it to ring. *Ring, damn it*, she said to the phone, but it wouldn't, for there was nothing to tell. There's a deep patch of dark forest that has swallowed up her beloved and no one on this earth could tell her where he is. Her eyes closed, like the night closing in, and she laid her head back on the cushion. She was terrified of falling asleep, death-sleep. *It's the same? No it's not.* The bottle was calling and she took a Valium. She knew she shouldn't, but she couldn't stand it any longer. Then a drink, yes a shot of Mark's bourbon would help, then another. The medicine dissolved into the liquor and the warm safe feeling of inebriation replaced her terror.

Sara's eyes sprang open to the darkness. She was disoriented and cried out, "*Mark!*" She couldn't figure out at first why she was asleep on the couch alone, then her mind jolted her back to reality, and it started again. She wailed and cried and stomped up and down the stairs, just wanting to hear something other than her own voice. She turned on every light, got the revolver out of his drawer, and went to the treadmill in the parlor. She got up to running speed, barefoot and in her pajamas, but didn't notice till the soles of her feet grow sore and felt like they were on fire. The sky was lightening, and a thunderstorm was blowing through. She was glad for it, something other than this monotonous stretch of the same thing day after day, and went out into it. As bolts of electricity sparked and brightened, she ran into the front yard and knelt in the grass. Big raindrops were pelting her head and it felt like someone was tapping her with a stick. She was soaked through in seconds but didn't care and invited the danger of the lightning and hoped that God would strike her dead. But he didn't.

Back inside out of the rain, Sara dripped on her refinished hardwood floors. She slipped while running to the bathroom to find a towel and she laughed. She wasn't sure if was the drugs or the booze, but she was ready for more of them. *Music may soothe this savage beast*, she thought and went to Mark's stereo, his sacred stereo he hated to share with her. Yes, Frank would do, so she inserted Sinatra, yes, "Summer Wind." What a beautiful melancholy sound. She could almost smell the ocean, even though she was a million miles away. Ahhh…Frank's soothing voice, then the big brass punctuation. Yes, that was nice, that steady beat, da da…da da…da da… da da. Too slow, something else. Eject, search, rockabilly, no, soul music, Marvin, yes. He would do. In went the CD, volume loud, *who cares*. There were no neighbors to worry about. "Isn't that why we moved here?" she said to no one. Sara was panting; her heart was racing even though she's drunk enough to be knocked out. Dawn finally blasted over the ridge that Sara cursed for its big black presence, keeping the light from her. Sara twirled in time to the sad slow music and remembered when she and Mark were in Las Vegas, gambling and doing blow and getting drunk off their asses, renting a suite they couldn't afford and spending their inheritance and loving each other. She remembered intense love, sex, anger, madness, drugs, and violence. He hit her, right in the face. She had to wear sunglasses everywhere she went after that. Didn't matter, she forgave him. It was the drugs; he didn't mean to do it, she hit him first, after all. Sara ran to the mirror in the hall and checked her face. Was it still there, the mark he had left? She shifted her head from side to side, then shook it violently as if trying to shake loose out of this dream. She whispered, *"Where are you goddamn it!"* Then she lay down and passed out on the floor.

When you live in the mountains of southwestern Virginia, winter comes early; Sara knew this all too well. When she and Mark first moved to

Delbarton, they had a foot of snow by Christmas. The New Year wasn't any better as far as the weather was concerned. They put their new woodstove to good use that year, burning almost three cords of wood by February. She could see him, in the barn standing tall, like Paul Bunyan, grinning like a raccoon. You couldn't pry that ax out of Mark's hands, though, he loved chopping wood; he'd say, "A man who heats with wood gets warm twice." Sara started her first fire of the season with trepidation. It was hard for her to imagine doing it correctly without Mark's supervision. He always coached her with advice on just how many logs to use, "You always need three, hon," the right amount of air flow, "The top vent should be open and the bottom vent closed," and when to turn on the ceiling fan to help circulate the warm air around the room. But she managed just fine, even with her nerves still a jumbled mess as she noted it was going on week four, alone.

There had been numerous findings around the site where Mark had last been seen on Red Rock trail. There were a shoe and some bones found by cadaver dogs, but the tests proved them to belong to an animal and another hiker. Another hiker recovered Mark's cell phone too, just yesterday, but still no Mark. After that news, Sara finally stopped calling his number. The sheriff said there were a thousand calls from their home phone number starting the day after he went missing, she thought for sure there would have been more.

The cold snap that blew through brought snow. Sara was more than discouraged because bad weather meant any search effort would cease now. She felt trapped in her body and in that house, but still she couldn't leave. She would receive calls from friends, albeit less often. Her mother still called just about every day and emailed too. Sara had no siblings or other close relatives in the area. Mark's brother had died last year and his mom the year before. Her only visitor now was the mailman. She tried to read, tried to distract herself, but most nights she fell asleep with the aid of whiskey and pills and for that she was grateful. Mostly she lived in some other time when life was spinning in greased grooves. Picture albums were strewn all about the place, in every room. Sara would roam from spot to spot, stopping and forgetting if she'd already seen that one. Her mother's voice would show concern at times, noticing Sara's slurred speech. Sara's mother never mentioned the slurring, and she felt sorry for her daughter left helplessly waiting.

The next week, the fifth since Mark's disappearance, the phone rang with a force of reckoning. Sara prepared herself, clutching the receiver with a sweaty palm. It was in fact Sheriff Lightner. They had found a body and thought it might be Mark. Sara readied herself for the two-hour drive to the coroner's office where her mother would be waiting with moral support.

Sara identified Mark's body. It was estimated that Mark had probably died just days before, ironically enough. Mark had fallen of course, possibly out of confusion or dehydration or the combination, had hit his head and died of exposure, they thought. The autopsy would reveal more.

"Oh Mom, now what?" Sara said.

"Well dear, we might as well go right to the funeral home in Glenley."

"No!" Sara said. "I mean, not yet. Let's just wait."

"Wait for what, dear?"

Sara's mother suppressed her concern.

"Wait…until the results. But still, I'm so relieved I guess, I mean at least they found him, right?" Sara stared out of the car window so that her mother couldn't see her cry. "At least he's still not lying there…alone… and cold." Sara sobbed into a paper napkin she had pulled out of the glove box as her mother sat silently, cradling her daughter's shoulder as best she could over the bucket seat.

Neither mother nor daughter could even acknowledge the state of the body. Even though it had only been days since his death, hungry animals hadn't wasted any time. The two women hadn't wanted to think about why his legs were missing below the knees. Sara preferred to keep the memory of her husband intact.

"Mom, you need to go…home, I mean."

"But dear, I can't leave you now, not like this. You'll need me to help you make plans, for the burial."

"No, not yet. Please Mom, I'd prefer to just go home and sleep and give it a few days, OK?"

Sara's mother was perplexed at this decision, but felt Sara knew what was best for her and Mark, and although she felt helpless, left it at that.

"Call me dear, as soon as you're ready, I'll come right down."

"It's OK, Mom, I mean, I'll be all right. Don't worry. I appreciate you coming all this way for this...the identification, that is."

And the two women parted ways.

Sara drove towards home, but first made a detour into the Southside Plaza shopping center. She needed to restock her liquor supply. She bought a case of Jack Daniels and proceeded home. Not wanting to wait, she grabbed a bottle, opened it, and kept it near on the passenger's seat. Driving was a challenge, and it seemed like she was trapped in one of those Google maps where if you click ahead in the scene you're pulled and stretched to the next spot on the road. She'd catch herself staring into space and then the road would squeeze into a smeared blur and then coalesce into a solid again. That scared her, *shit what didn't at this point*. But the liquor was working and in a strange way, it was a comfort to know at least she could depend on something to be familiar. The two-hour drive was hard, but not as hard as what she'd just been through, seeing her dead husband frozen stiff on a gurney and she took solace in the silence and darkness and the cocoon of the truck cab.

His skin, Mark, her Mark, was so, blue. No, gray, as gray as a dirty sheet. She couldn't get over that fact and kept thinking that if only she had him home she could cover all that ugly with makeup. *What a stupid thought, makeup.* But then it wasn't. *Why not? I could do it. He'll be with me, not there on some cold stainless gurney. Poor thing, how he must have suffered. But I can't think about that. I just have to get home.*

The key fit, the lock clicked, and the house was dark as a grave. Sara entered with apprehension, but knew she had a chore and had better get to it. Funny, she wasn't hungry, even though it had been hours since she'd eaten. Sleep didn't interest her either; she was on a quest with newfound energy. She pulled the key ring off the little black hook that contained all the padlock keys and marched out into the dark to the blockhouse. The little cinderblock outbuilding contained gardening tools, painting supplies, tarps, and her Total Trolley, an impulse buy she had purchased on a late-night TV bender and one that would now become useful. The handcart could double as a stand-up type with wheels at the bottom and a handle on top, or lay flat, with four skateboard-type wheels that rolled as smooth as silk over her hardwood floors. A folded-up tarp fit nicely on top of the trolley.

Sara pulled her finds into the mudroom next to the kitchen door, out of the elements for safekeeping, closed the door, and went to bed. The next day, only half rested, she called the coroner and told him she wanted her husband's body sent to Glenley funeral home, immediately. The coroner said the autopsy wouldn't be performed till later that week. Sara argued and cried and threw a momentous fit until the coroner couldn't stand it any longer and finally gave in, figuring what the hell, he wasn't going to tell if she didn't. The guy hadn't been murdered the coroner knew for sure, so why not let the poor slob go in peace.

The funeral director at Glenley called Sara as soon as the body arrived; the clock was ticking, and keeping a body on ice isn't cheap. Sara didn't care; she had no sense of time or money, none of those things mattered. All she wanted was to get her husband home. She thought of her life with Mark, in the country and everywhere they had lived, and figured, it was always Mark's way. Everything had to be as he saw it. Well now, it was going to be Sara's way.

Sara dressed and, with determination, drove the eight miles to town, if you want to call Glenley a town. Nothing more than two convenience stores, one that sold gas, one that sold beer, neither sold both, and the funeral home. Mr. Moore, the funeral director, greeted her with the appropriate amount of reserve and concern in his voice and invited her into his modest office/sales room where there was a sample of the elite coffins offered, urns, and picture books of flower arrangements from the local florist. Mr. Moore was quite concerned when he heard Sara's request to take Mark with her. Why, how, would she deal with the remains? Was she planning a service at her house, and wouldn't she want his assistance in the preparation of the body? Sara kindly declined Mr. Moore's help and explained that she had a plan. She said she was prepared and would take care of it—him—herself and not to worry, Buddy Simmons was digging the hole.

Mr. Moore was taken aback, even though this was not his first encounter with someone requesting the body without embalming it first. He was skeptical that Sara had completely thought this through and was worried she was taking this too lightly. There was a lot more to it, burying someone, and in her delicate state he wasn't sure Sara was up to it. Sara was calm, confident in her explanation, and asked to be directed to where she should park her truck. Mr. Moore resigned himself to her demands and showed her the loading dock on the opposite side of the building. Sara backed the pickup into the bay in a professional manner and spread the blanket that was to be used as a shroud out and over the truck bed. She stood nearby clasping her arms around her waist, attempting to keep warm; it was exactly thirty-two degrees. Mr. Moore's assistant, Miss Burk, helped guide the big gurney towards the truck with Mark on it, covered by what appeared to be just a single white sheet. At first, Sara was surprised at how small Mark appeared, then remembered he was missing his feet.

Mark was loaded into the truck bed like a sack of feed. His stumps were wrapped tightly in gauze, and Sara thought it a nice touch, this careful attempt at preserving his dignity, and smiled. Sara covered him with the shroud and slipped a bungee cord up and around his waist to keep the cover from blowing off on the drive home. Mr. Moore and Miss Burk looked on in wide-eyed wonder as the truck pulled out of view.

The trip back home was uneventful, except Sara realized that since she skipped having Mark embalmed he would in fact rot, a mild oversight. She kept a close watch on the truck bed in her rearview mirror, not sure what she was expecting and plotted. She'd take Mark home, deposit him, and drive to Franklyn for dry ice, another detail she had overlooked in her excitement. It was a nice day, even though it was a cold one. The sun was bright and it reminded Sara of days long ago when she was little, squinting into the bright light from her father's old Chevrolet. She missed her father to this day and cried for him like a child. That was the last time Sara cried. Instead, she took her mind to another place, a made-up place where everything was as it was five weeks ago. It was still warm and just on the brink of changing seasons. Her legs were still tan and Mark too retained a summer glow. She was excited about the pumpkin harvest and couldn't wait for her two-hundred-pounder to harden over for the picking.

Mark was much heavier than he looked, but Sara believed that if there was a will, there was a way: "time and pressure," Mark would say. She had the trolley set under the edge of the gate of the pickup. Sara pulled the body by the blanket, and he plopped onto the rolling cart with no trouble at all. Sara neatened up the cover, tucked it under and around Mark, and pulled the load into the blockhouse for safekeeping until she returned with the ice. Sara made sure to lock up, always remembering Mark's forgetfulness, and jiggled the padlock to make sure it latched. If there's one thing Franklyn had plenty of, it was dry ice. There were so many hunters in this neck of the woods, dry ice was all but a necessity. The clerk did give her a funny look, though, when she requested a hundred pounds of the stuff, but she figured she had better be safe than sorry, not knowing just how much it would take to keep a body from decomposing.

Sara felt smug on the return trip. Once home, she quickly took to the task of pulling Mark back to the house, and made a bed of dry ice for him to sleep on. Sara had arranged the area where Mark was to remain—well, for a while. She hadn't thought too much into the future; as far as she was concerned, it really didn't exist. All that mattered was now, this day, this bright shiny sparkly day, with her husband home at last.

Sara felt so proud of her idea, her best in a long time. She rolled Mark's corpse over the bed of rock ice all foggy and spooky like something out of a horror movie. His gray skin looked better now that she had applied makeup and combed his hair. Sara was exhausted but figured it was her lack of food and fixed a PB&J sandwich. She sat with Mark in the parlor eating in silence and watched him sleep. He looked so peaceful, if not sedate. Oh how she wished she could relax like that and remembered her bottle of Valium. As if a spark ignited under her, Sara stopped eating and retrieved the pills. Captivated by Mark's solemn state, Sara absentmindedly poured the contents of the pill bottle out into her palm; there must have been thirty or so. Sara nibbled at the pills like a horse eating oats and chewed them bit by bit, as if eating Cracker Jacks. She washed all of them down with Jack and Coke and finished her sandwich—why, she wasn't sure.

Another day had come to a close, just about, and Sara was getting so sleepy she couldn't stand it. She pulled the big yellow pillow off the settee and shared Mark's blanket, remembering how he hated her stealing all the covers, and gently pulled it under his chin tight. Sara laid her head close to his, pushing any ice chunks away from her and created a barrier with the tarp. She ignored the fuuny way Mark smelled—not bad, just funny—and closed her eyes. Sara turned on her side and wrapped her left arm over his chest and sighed.

Madelyn Rosenberg

The Eye Doctor

As a journalist, MADELYN ROSENBERG wrote about colorful, real-life characters in southwest Virginia. Now she makes up characters of her own. She is the author of eight books for children, including *Canary in the Coal Mine*, *How to Behave at a Dog Show*, and the Nanny X series, which is set in a fictional town outside of Washington, D.C. She lives with her family in Arlington, Virginia.

The call comes on a Tuesday. Harold Crane is watching a crime show in bed and one of the witnesses looks like a girl he knew in college. She is a woman now, with extra skin around her neck, but she looks familiar and he wants to wait for the credits to see if they name her. Sandy is asleep, her hair fine and brittle against the pillowcase. Crane reaches over her to grab the phone.

"You the eye doctor?" the caller says.

"Yes," Crane says, clearing his throat. It's been an hour since he's spoken out loud. "Yes, that's me."

"Need you to do me some eyes," the man says, his own voice warm and deep. "Rush order."

"I can accommodate," Crane says. "Don't get many rush orders; my clients usually aren't going anywhere." He laughs. The man does not. Crane becomes businesslike. "What kind of eyes are you looking for?" he asks.

"Well," the man says. "Human."

"Human?" Crane repeats. "These would be for a mannequin then?"

"They're for my wife."

"I see," Crane says. His lips are dry. "Well, I, I'd have to get her measured before I can do anything. Unless you happen to know whether she needs a twenty-two millimeter or a twenty-six? Even so. Doesn't she need a real doctor?"

"Don't much matter," says the man.

"But it does," Crane says, warming to the idea that one of his eyes—he's been painting them for nearly a year now—might be worn by an actual person. He wonders if he'll recognize it, implanted in the face of a stranger he passes on Ninth Street or Markham Avenue. "The shape, especially. Mostly what I've got are the little globes, but for human eyes, you know, some of them have stems, and they're not all round either. They're more concave, to suction into the eye socket, you see? She really should be measured and fitted by a professional."

"Whatever you have in stock will do," the man says.

"I don't—" *I don't understand*, is what he wants to say. "I believe I've got some that might fit a human," he says instead. Deer eyes were close, "I can't guarantee how comfortable they'll be. I paint them, but I don't blow them. She could try some on, figure out what suits her best."

"Try them on?" the man says, a laugh rattling in his throat. "I should have said first thing. *She's dead.* We bury her Friday."

It takes another few minutes to go over the details and Crane misses the TV credits as they race by, chased by commercials. He will have to wait for the rerun to check on his classmate. The caller hangs up, and Crane reaches for his notebook and writes it down, all he can remember.

He has always saved scraps of conversation, scraps of life, with the thought of penning a novel. But Durham, N.C., with its flat landscapes and two Super-Targets, has never provided him with quite enough inspiration. Dostoevsky never mentioned a SuperTarget. Besides, Crane is an artist, not a novelist. He accepts—almost—that the most he will offer the literary world is a snippet of cocktail conversation. He saves scraps of those too for the departmental parties he attends under his new but already yellowed title of "emeritus."

"What was that?" Sandy asks, her voice thick with sleep. "Harold?"

"Just a customer," Crane says.

"Late for a call. I thought something had happened to Jon."

Jon, their son, has a one-year teaching position at Columbia, and Sandy, who hasn't spent time in New York since the city had become safe again, is certain he'll be mugged each time he leaves his apartment.

"Jon's fine," Crane says, kissing her forehead. Her eyes are already closed. "I got an order. Nothing to worry about."

When Crane first went into semi-retirement after thirty-plus years of teaching art history and appreciation, the idea of toiling in his studio to create the masterpiece he had never created in his youth seemed a depressing endeavor. It was fully what everyone expected of him. "Now," Sandy said at his retirement party. "Now you can really *paint*."

Obligingly, Crane carved out a corner of the garage to use as his studio. He sat there for two weeks and painted nothing. One morning, to escape, he went to walk along the Eno River—alone, because Sandy was tired. He stopped for a map at the ranger's station and found foxes, stiff and stuffed, and squirrels and beavers and other frozen wildlife. It occurred to him then that someone must have painted the eyes, and when he researched it, he found that someone had; it was a specialty. Crane liked the idea of a specialty, and this seemed a proper fit. He had always been good at eyes. In art, it is where others usually failed; they could capture hands or feet or the veiled threat of a winter sky, but never the eyes. Everything people say about the eyes and the soul? It's true, and Harold Crane gets that. He can capture spirit, wildness, melancholy. He has never been much good with hands or feet.

They first called him "the eye doctor" back in art school and it stuck, revived now on his business cards and his website. Crane has always liked being called the eye doctor. He likes reviving dead things, making them look alive—hunted, perhaps, but not defeated. Not that Crane has ever hunted anything. He doesn't know any Jews who hunt, and only a few who fish.

"It's sacrilegious," Sandy said, when he told her about his plan. "Killing animals for sport. You like stuffed fish? Try *gefilte*." Crane had wanted to point out that gefilte fish was chopped, not stuffed, but this would not help his cause.

Three weeks after that, his first batch of eyes arrived, pale moons in a compartmentalized plastic case. Sandy watched him sort through the contents on the coffee table.

"Bass. Beaver. Have you got anything in there for lox?"

"People don't mount smoked salmon," he told her.

"Harold," she tsked. "Don't tell me you've lost your sense of humor." She'd already been diagnosed then, but it was early on, and she was still fighting, still laughing.

It is a relief that Crane can now go to his studio with a purpose instead of to an empty canvas, that he can open up the bottles of paint and mineral spirits that smell somehow less of chemicals than the rest of the house, which is steeped in his wife's illness. It clings to her clothes, an antiseptic, metallic smell that mingles with the too-sweet aroma of raspberry Jell-O, forever cooling in the refrigerator.

Crane's webpage is garnering attention and he is painting steadily, giving each eye more time than he should. He paints a number for practice, opens encyclopedias and nature books to the section on bobcats. He tries to capture in their eyes the languid motion of their bodies. He knows, of course, that people don't want their mounts to appear languid. They want them to look hungry, demonic, possessed; they want the world to envision it: Man versus claws and teeth. They want the world to know it is by the grace of God and a 7mm Remington Magnum that this creature is mounted in the study above the plaid sofa, while human flesh remains unmarred, save the loss of pigment from too much exposure to the sun.

FIRST THING IN THE MORNING, Crane's new customer stops by the house with pictures to ensure accurate work. He is a black man—African American—of medium height, built solidly with muscles that show even through his long sleeves. They aren't gym muscles, carefully sculpted, but casual, as if he delivers refrigerators for Sears.

Crane stands outside, waiting for the man to get out of his car. It is the week before Christmas, but outside it is fifty-one degrees. Crane isn't wearing gloves, though he has thrust his fists, balled, into the pockets of the thin wool coat he has worn for fifteen years—no need to buy a new one, for all the use this one gets.

"My wife had your card in her wallet," the man says, by way of greeting. "Thought you'd be black."

"Yes, of course," Crane says. He has handed out at least one business card a day, on the street, at the mall and on the bus, which is mostly populated with black riders.

"You ain't," the man says.

"No," says Crane.

"You sounded white on the phone," the man says. He nods toward the house, a gray, two-story colonial. "Your house is white. Still wondered."

"If you're worried about my work," Crane says, "I can show you some samples. I can do black eyes." As soon as he says it, he knows it doesn't sound right.

"Don't much matter, I suppose. Just so we get something in there," the man says.

They shake hands, too late for handshaking, and the man says his name: Watson.

"Crane," says Crane, though of course his full name is on the business card. "Harold Crane," it says. "The Eye Doctor. Glass Eyes Hand Painted. Taxidermy to Teddy Bears."

The man follows Crane into the garage, which looks, for all the world, like a garage. On one side is the car, the weed eater, the lawnmower. On the other Crane has put up some shelves. His paints are stored neatly in tubes and glass bottles. In the corner is the easel his wife gave him a dozen birthdays ago, and another easel, a new one, that she gave him when he retired. The eyes are on shelves and on the worktable he made out of a long wooden door. He stores the eyes in cases meant for screws and fishing tackle.

Crane opens one of those cases, a yard-sale find, and takes out a pair of eyes he made as practice to fit a wild boar. He is particularly proud of these eyes; he feels he's captured the right wildness, the right pigginess, if you will. They look soft and hard at the same time. There are no real whites, just a tan outside the iris, then the brown, and then the dark night of the pupil.

"These aren't human," Crane says. "But you get the idea."

The man takes one of the eyes and presses it against his own, something Crane has done many times to feel the coolness of the glass. The man nods. "All right then," he says. He pulls out his colored snapshots and spreads them on the table. Crane reaches for his magnifying glass so he can examine them more closely.

The woman in the photograph isn't smiling. Her hair is cut short, but it is, of course, the eyes he wants to look at, and one of them is closed. Her right eyebrow is arched, as if she's daring the photographer to take the picture. Crane flips to the next photo. Here, the woman's lips are painted pink to match the cheerful handkerchief in her lapel, but there is nothing cheerful in her face. Her white teeth show in only one picture, in what pretends to be a smile. But her eyes are open in this one, large under his glass. Crane finds them hot and accusing. "Like a woman scorned," he will write later in his notebook.

"Mm hmm. That's her," the man says, nodding. "Bonita."

"Is this how you want me to paint her, then?" Crane asks.

"That's her, I said."

Crane tries again. "She isn't smiling," he explains. "Or rather, it hasn't reached her eyes. I thought you might want me to paint her looking a little…" He searches for the diplomatic word. "Warmer."

The man throws back his head. His laugh is sticky, coated with tar. "Man," he says. "You something else, you know that? Do I want you to paint her *warmer?*"

He leans over the table, so Crane can smell his breath. Crane expects whiskey, but there isn't a trace of it; instead he smells something sweet and familiar. Peanut butter. "This is as warm as that woman gets," Watson says.

Crane backs off, embarrassed. "I see. Well. These are very good eyes," he says, choosing a matched pair from his drawer. "They're from a German ocularist. That's a glass eye maker." He feels obligated to use the word, to put forth what knowledge he has gained about his new profession.

Sandy, of course, objected to his ordering the eyes from Germany. Like many Jews of a certain age, she believes there is evil in all things German, and so she refuses coffee makers by Krupps and cars by Volkswagen.

"They'll do," the man says. "What's the bottom line?"

Crane has not fine-turned his pricing structure. Many people use eyes that aren't custom made and are therefore cheaper. Crane has to go low to compete. After all, this man could have ordered vintage eyes off the Internet, as Crane once did, for the novelty of it. They'd arrived by mail, singles, not pairs, discolored from wear.

He considers the circumstances: the rush, the time of year, the man's possible refrigerator-delivery salary.

"They'll cost you seventy-five dollars an eye," he says finally. "Is that all right?" It's a steal, Crane thinks, but the man doesn't agree.

He lets out a soft whistle. "Eye for an eye," he says. "Can you have them by Thursday?"

"Two days," Crane says aloud. "They'll be ready."

They shake hands again and the man leaves, humming a tune Crane has never heard before.

Sandy opens the door from the kitchen and pokes her head into the garage. She is dressed, though she hasn't combed her hair.

"Can I dump out this coffee?" she asks. "The smell."

"Sure," Crane says. "Sorry."

She pauses. "You're taking the job then?"

"Man needs eyes," Crane says.

"For his wife," Sandy says. They had discussed it all at breakfast.

"Yep."

"Eyes," she says. "My Rembrandt." She sighs in the same, defeated way she's been sighing for the past three months and goes back into the house, leaving Crane with his four-by-six images of Bonita Watson. He studies the photos again, searching for signs of joy.

Slowly, he sets a pair of eyes, twenty-fours, into clamps, side by side, and spaces them the way they'd be spaced in life. He decides to paint blood vessels first, hair-thin red lines, and then tackle the rest, working edge to center, light to dark.

As he works, he imagines Bonita in his head, what she'd sound like if she were a character in the stories he begins writing but never finishes.

"He's a cheat," she tells him now.

"Watson? Your husband?" Crane asks, to be sure.

"Who else would I be talking about?" she says. "I don't even know you."

"I'm just the painter," Crane says.

"He's a cheat," Bonita says. "Leaves me at home with his dirty underwear while he runs around with some woman at work. You watch, he'll cheat you, too."

"Secretary?" Crane asks, politely.

"How should I know?" Bonita says. "You think he tells me? You think he tells me anything at all?"

"I'm sorry," Crane says.

"It is what it is," Bonita says. "Too late for sorry now."

"Is it?" Crane asks as he breaks the seal and opens a small jar of paint, sable brown.

"Of course it is. I'm dead."

Bonita is mean company. At times Crane thinks he should bottle her laugh and save it for the villains in the Disney films Sandy has started renting recently, reliving Jon's childhood more than her own. But she has a sharp wit that Crane likes, an irreverence only the dead can afford.

Reluctantly, he takes his leave, allowing the eyes to dry before putting on a new layer of paint. Sandy is in the living room, a newspaper folded but unread in her lap.

"Did he say why he needed those eyes?" she asks, and Crane is delighted that she is curious—about his work, about anything. But he doesn't have an answer.

"No," Crane says. "He didn't say. To bury her with. Maybe she was an organ donor." Though he had read an article recently that said far fewer African Americans donated their organs—some superstitious, some mistrustful, afraid the doctor would let them die so he could harvest a kidney to turn over to a white person.

Back in his garage, back in his head, he asks Bonita.

"What if I told you he'd poked out my eyes with an ice pick?" she says. "And I bled to death, how about that?"

"He doesn't seem like the ice pick type," says Crane, who is uncertain people even own ice picks anymore. "He seems too easygoing for ice picks."

"You never know about people," she says.

He asks about the business card, where she got it, but that answer isn't as easily conjured. "Woman of mystery," she says.

And Crane replies, "You are that."

He finishes the eyes in just over a day. He thinks about calling Watson and telling him to come early, but Crane has grown used to Bonita sizing him up from the clamps on his worktable. There is fire in her eyes—enough so that he dares to use a touch of orange paint, among all of that brown, to create a tiny blaze. He uses his finest brush so there is only a hint of flame, but enough, he thinks, to warm the ice in those photographs.

He tops the eyes with a clear glaze and the result is natural, real, so they appear to be gelatinous until you touch them and find glass.

He wonders if the undertaker will put them in with clay or wax like they do in taxidermy. Or if Watson will pop them in himself just before they bury her. Crane has never touched a dead person before, except for his mother, and that was an accident. He had peeked into her casket to make sure they had the right body, wrapped in sheets. There were mistakes sometimes.

WATSON ARRIVES THURSDAY MORNING, PROMPTLY at ten. He is dressed in a suit, dark and pinstriped.

"Her sister's coming in today," he says. "You got 'em?"

Crane leads him into the garage and hands him the eyes in a green velvet pouch. His cat's ashes had arrived in a pouch when she died after eighteen years and Sandy, adverse to burying yet another animal under the lilac bush, decided to have her cremated. Crane didn't have any pouches, but Sandy had a few from her good jewelry. She was willing to spare one.

"A touch of class," she'd said. "If that's possible."

Watson eases the pouch open and pours the eyes into a pinkish palm. They aren't friendly eyes and they sure aren't the eyes of a dead woman. Crane holds his breath and waits.

"Ha!" Watson laughs his sticky laugh. "That's her, dead on. I wasn't sure about you, but you know? You're all right."

Crane smiles and breathes. "I'm so glad," he says. He feels relaxed enough now to ask a question, so he'll have something to share with Sandy later. "Do you mind my asking? What happened to her old eyes? Her real ones?"

"Eye bank," Watson confirms. "One nice thing she did in her life. Her sister had a cornea transplant, see? So this was payback. Corneas went to a boy in Ohio, they said. The rest went to some medical school. She didn't want to be buried with empty holes, you know. Made me promise to get her some replacements."

"I see," Crane says. "Tending to her last wishes, then."

Watson closes his hands together and shakes the eyes as if they're dice. "I'm covering my ass, is what I'm doing," he says. "I don't, she might come back and haunt me."

"I'm sure she wouldn't do that," Crane says, matter-of-fact, as if he is telling the man he's sure his wife would never make tofu for dinner then lie and tell him it was meat.

"Bonita," the man says, "was a bitch." He opens his right hand and rolls the eyes in his palm so they clack together. Then he closes his fist around them, dry, as if coated in ash.

"I can't pay you everything today," Watson says.

"I'm sorry?"

"Can't pay you your one fifty," Watson says. "Tell the truth, I didn't think you'd come through for me, figured I'd be able to demand my money back. Funeral expenses, you know. And Christmas. They add up. I can give you half now." He pulls out seventy-five dollars, mostly in tens.

"And the rest later?" Crane finishes. "When you're back on your feet? Perhaps in February?"

"Sure," Watson says, with a grin that makes Crane believe he'll never see that money. "February. That's fine."

"You have my card," Crane says.

"Right here." The man pats his wallet. He turns to leave and Crane leans against his workbench where the pictures of Bonita are spread out in an orderly row.

"Wait," Crane yells, and Watson turns. "Your photographs."

"Keep 'em," Watson says. "Until I pay you."

"What'd I tell you?" Bonita says, after the man is gone. "You a sucker, just like me."

"He'll pay in time," Crane tells her, though he knows she knows better. He doesn't need the money, anyway.

"Must be nice," Bonita says, as Crane sweeps the pictures into a neat stack and puts them away. Slowly, he begins organizing his brushes, his spectrum of colors.

Again, Sandy opens the door from the kitchen, and peers in. "He come by?" she says. "I heard a car."

"Right on time."

"How much did you charge him?"

"A hundred and fifty," Crane says, which is the truth, as far as it goes.

"You don't charge enough," Sandy says. Her hair is neatly combed now. "I have an appointment with Dr. Lee at two o'clock."

"I'll be ready," Crane says, and sits down on a worn wooden stool.

There will be no more money then, nothing left but this story and Crane opens his notebook to write down words like "cool glass," "ashy skin," and "tiny moons"—cues to help him remember. He thinks of the way the eyeballs looked in Watson's hand, the way they sounded when they clacked together, as if they were only marbles.

"That's her all right," the man had said. "Dead on."

Crane thinks of his own wife's eyes, of how they'll look if he tells her the whole story, later. No anger, no snap like there used be. For three months, her eyes have been misted over, saying: "Look while you can; we'll be closing soon." Always, Crane is forced to look away.

But he remembers another time, from before. Jon was still living at home, blaring music from his upstairs bedroom, the thud, thud, thud coming through the ceiling. Crane had come home three hours late and hadn't called, a last-minute decision to have a drink with some coworkers, who usually didn't ask. Crane usually didn't drink. But on that night he had two and a half gin and tonics that were still on his breath when he walked in the door. Dinner had been made and sealed, cold and congealed, with plastic wrap. Sandy's eyes had shown relief when she first saw him and then: flames. Who did he think he was, a playboy? He was a teacher, a husband—with a family, with *responsibilities*. No, he didn't have to come home at five o'clock like some black-and-white TV husband. But yes, damn it—Crane nods with pleasure, remembering the hard shape of the words coming through his wife's lips—*damn it*, she'd said, he did have to call and let her know his whereabouts. Which, for all she knew, were mutilated on the side of the road out in Walltown or in a cheap hotel next to a cheaper blonde off of U.S. 70.

Crane hung his head to take the beating, but inside, he'd smiled, assured of her love. He smiles now. Taxidermists had a noble calling. They revived the dead.

From the open tray in front of him, the eyeballs regard him, white as milk. Crane listens for the sounds of his wife loading the dishwasher, brushing her teeth, but hears only the quiet that will soon encompass the whole of his life. He puts down his notebook and reaches instead for a brush with a long, fine tip. He reaches for the orange paint.

Melissa Scholes Young

Oxygen in Use

MELISSA SCHOLES YOUNG's work has appeared in the *Atlantic*, the *Washington Post*, *Narrative*, *Ploughshares*, *Poets & Writers*, *Poet Lore*, and other literary journals. She's a contributing editor for *Fiction Writers Review*. She teaches at American University in Washington, D.C., and is a Bread Loaf Bakeless Camargo Fellow.

*Y*ou hang up the phone and think about what the oncologist has just said about your mom. You actually heard him yawn just before he said, "I'm sorry, Mrs. Price. I know this is a lot to take." You're not surprised, but you weren't really expecting your mom's life to end like this. You thought there'd be a fight, some medical intervention, something to give false hope. He'd suggest radiation again just so you could protest "No, no. It almost killed her last time." Then she'd die like they do on television surrounded by machines beeping and gorgeous doctors shouting orders and earnest nurses with faces full of compassion. Instead, they were giving up. "There's not a lot more we can do for her. We'll try to keep her comfortable. I assume you'll want to take her home. To be more comfortable." And then you think "Did that bastard just yawn again?"

You sit in the car and stare at the phone. You flip it shut and remember how excited Vanessa was to give it to you for Christmas last year. "See, Mom," she said, "it has a camera and everything." You wanted to ask what for but you knew better. You'd assumed it was Vanessa calling earlier from California, not the doctor. This isn't exactly how you wanted to celebrate your fiftieth birthday. Flowers? Sure. A nice round of beers with a few coworkers? Maybe. Vanessa and her kids calling to sing "Happy Birthday" in an off-key round? Definitely. Driving your mom home to die? Not so much.

As you drive to the hospital to pick her up, to take her to your home for however long she'll last, you decide not to tell her. She probably wouldn't even understand. Like last week when you tried to tell her that her cat had died peacefully that morning, and she claimed she didn't have a cat. You'd driven the sick, meowing thing there yourself and told the vet to just do it. The vet assured you it was the humane thing to do, so you left before it was even over, just to get away from all that damn meowing.

You call work on the way to the hospital to let them know you won't be in again, that you'll need someone to cover the afternoon shift at the hotel front desk, and Betsy tells you again how sorry she is. And you end up consoling her as she whimpers and slobbers on the other end of the phone about how unfair life is. As if you didn't know. You decide to stop telling other people too, because you're tired of having to take care of their reactions. Somewhere in this you'd like to carve out a little space, a moment, maybe, to think about your mom dying. About how soon she'll let go and leave you alone. And about how relieved you'll feel when it's finally over and what a horrible person you must be for having thought that.

You need to stop for gas. The tank is only half full and who knows? You might hit rush hour on the way home and don't want to sit there on the freeway with your mom in the car dying, hoping to make it to the next exit on fumes. Not that it's actually that far from the hospital to your house, but what if you decide to take a drive? Your mom is in a drug-induced sleep most of the time anyway, the plastic tubes crisscrossing her face, hissing oxygen into her body. Why not lay her out like a child in the backseat and put a little blanket on her and drive to the coast? You'll crack the window and give her a tiny hint of fresh air—not enough to chill her or bring on a hacking fit—just enough to smell the saltwater, to hear the crash when the water hits the rocks and drowns all the noise, to feel the edge of Maine and know you can't go any farther. It would probably be fine to just leave her in the car while you walk a little. Just get your feet wet, maybe the hem of your pants, maybe even up to your knees. Just clear your head before you go home.

She probably wouldn't mind at all. You never minded all those nights alone as a kid, did you? The nights after your dad died and your mom started dating again, stumbling through the door, waking you on the couch, and reeking of wine and cigarettes. You remember her saying that she just wanted to dance, to feel wet sand at the beach, to float down the street. You remember thinking it wasn't the worst way people cope with death. She stayed. She took care of you and your brother. She did. When you leave your dying mom in the backseat of the car, you'll make sure her oxygen tank is full too before you go.

Once you gas up, you call the home hospice people again and ask for Sean, your assigned "home care assistant." You tell him that you're bringing your mom home for good. You tell him about the new *do not resuscitate* order she signed this time. You tell him you'll need another tank and the IV injections. He says he's sorry, and before you can stop yourself you say, "She's not dead yet." Sean is quiet, and then he says he'll send someone over in the morning with a supply list. You remind Sean that you have "the supplies" and you use air quotes even though you're on the phone and he can't see you. You remind Sean that you've been through this before. You don't need "someone" with the supply list. You need him.

By your count, this is her third attempt at dying. The other two times Sean and his hospice team called an ambulance and had her readmitted to the hospital. The first time she sat up and said, "I think I'll go take a walk now," pulled out all her tubes, and literally walked out the front door. The second time she shouted: "That toilet looks like it needs a good scrubbing. I'll do it myself!" She fended off the nurse by wielding a stinking toilet brush in the air, her robe flapping open to reveal her withered body. You laughed out loud at the scene, tears of relief, and your crazy brand was confirmed. Solemn faces staring at you. Accusatory glances. Of course you want your mom back in the hospital fighting not to die rather than home waiting to die, but how do you know which she'll choose? You've now been watching her die for years, maybe longer if you count how bitter she was even before the diagnosis.

It's a little hard to take her seriously these days. "Serving the body is never easy," Sean says in his soothing voice, "death affects us all." You wonder if he's reading some damn script or if his kindness is just part of the job like having enough pens ready at the hotel desk when you check in a large group. You can count on losing three or four pens for each twenty guests. By now you can even predict which old lady will steal your pen and tuck it into her purse and pretend she didn't.

Sean reminds you to take a moment for yourself. "Is there anything else I can do for you, Iris?" he asks in that voice again, and for just a moment you wonder... You wonder why people want to die in bed so much. You decide when you go you want to be in your car, listening to Harry Connick Jr's sexy voice, and driving to the coast. You'll hire a chauffeur so Vanessa won't have to drive.

When you pull up in front of the hospital, you park in a handicapped space because you know you can weasel out of a ticket with the whole dying mom thing. You decide to take the five flights of stairs just for the walk. Not to avoid her. You're wheezing by the third flight.

Finally, you get to her room, breathing so hard you're tempted to take a swig off her oxygen tank, and you don't recognize her. It's been three whole hours. For a second you wonder if you got off on the wrong floor and are looking at someone else's dying mom. She's curled up in her bed with the sheet up to her neck. She looks like a baby bird just hatched. All bones and wet feathers freshly fallen from the nest. You think she's not breathing and your heart goes all thumpy because this just may be the end. She may actually be dying. And you're not sure you're ready for the dying.

And then she takes a little breath, a puff of air, really, and you hear the rattle in her lungs. You listen to her coughing attack, the impossibility of clearing the lungs. You think about smoking, how much you hate, hate, hate it and how much you want, want, want a cigarette. You think it's her fault for dying, for smoking all those years and not controlling her urges, like you do, and limiting herself to one pack per week, like you do. But then you don't. You don't think it's her fault at all. Your grandpa smoked three packs a day until he was run over by a tractor on his farm days before his eighty-second birthday. You tell yourself that you'll never end up like her and that you'll never ask your own daughter to take you to her home so you can drag out your dying like this. And then you cry a little. Because no one's around to see it and your mom is not waking up anytime soon. Because when she first told you about the lung cancer, four years ago, the two of you were sitting on the back steps together, enjoying your after-dinner smoke.

"How long?" you asked.

"Months. Years. Who knows?" Cough. Cough. Cough.

"Can't they fight it? Chemotherapy and all that?"

"Oh, yeah. That they'll do. All of it. But I'll still die. Sorry, kid." Inhale. Exhale.

"But—"

"But what, Iris? People die." Cough. Gasp. Cough. Inhale. "Just don't let me go out like a goddamn vegetable. You hear me? Don't." She stubbed out her cigarette, picked up the butt, and put it in the pocket of her housecoat. "Pick up your butt. Don't litter, Iris."

When the nurses have given you the basket of drugs and oxygen tanks and pages of instructions and you get your mom in the backseat, a wave of panic slams into your chest. You think about calling your brother again, but you don't want to hear him tell you how busy he is and how he can only come by for a little while on Tuesday mornings. You don't want to hear him offer to use all his money to hire strangers to come into your house and take care of your mom so he doesn't have to. "We both have to deal with this, Michael," you'd say, and then you'd cover your mouth so he wouldn't hear you do that laughing/crying thing because you know what you just said isn't true at all.

She grunts from the backseat and you say, "What? Mom? Are you OK?" and she doesn't answer. You pull the car to the side of the road and shut off the engine and listen for her breathing. But all you hear is your heart doing that little thumpy thing again and cars zooming past and you think again about how much you'd like a cigarette just to calm down a little and you wonder if it's OK to smoke in your car with your mom in the backseat dying of lung cancer. Then you hear the pressure release from the oxygen tank. The image of the two of you engulfed in a ball of fire pops into your head. You think about how cruel the little warning is on the side of the oxygen tank with its skull and crossbones. You'll have to tack the little sign back up again on the front door: "Caution. Oxygen in Use. No Smoking." And for some reason that whole image just makes you lose it. You're laughing so hard your mother grunts again from her sleep and lets out a little fart and starts hacking and your giggles turn to tears. You start the car again and pull into traffic without yielding. Horns honk and cars swerve out of your way. You give them the bird.

At home you knock on Jimmy and Evelyn's door because they said if there was anything you need just ask. So you ask Jimmy to carry your mom's eighty-pound body up the stairs to the second-floor bedroom just so you don't have to touch her, to feel her bones and remember her flesh, to think about crying in your mom's soft bosom after your first fight with your ex-husband. You hate yourself a little for that, for not carrying your mom after she carried your body as a child and never refused, but it's done and you don't dwell on it.

You get the covers all nice and tucked in around your mom and then give her the eight o'clock pills which you have to sort of force down her throat and wipe her chin where the water spilled and ask her if she needs anything. She doesn't answer. You aren't sure she can. It'll be easier when Sean gets here with the IV medicine. She opens her eyes for just a second, so you grab her hand and say, "Mom. It's me. It's Iris. Can you hear me?" but she just grumbles again, hacks up some bloody phlegm, and passes out. You watch her eyelids flutter and then listen again to make sure she's still breathing. Gasping breathing.

It's almost dark so you decide to go in the backyard and cut some hydrangeas. They're blooming pink, and pink has always been her favorite color. You stay a little too long in the backyard, avoiding the house, and then reward yourself for all you've been through with your last cigarette of the day. It's the smart thing to do since you can't smoke in the house anymore. You huddle in the bushes like a thief, the red glow of your cigarette tip in the dark. You've never felt anything in your whole life so good.

You check on your mom again and since she seems to be sleeping, you call Vanessa on the other coast. When you ask about her day, she tells you about the twins' first tee-ball game and how Trent hit Brent with his bat and you think again that your daughter should have followed your advice and not named her children so carelessly. Poor kids, kindergarten will be hell. You don't say so, of course, because you are only listening these days and not telling Vanessa what to do anymore because you respect her as an adult and are no longer going to treat her as a child if you want to be a part of her life. You do want to be a part of her life and you wish that your daughter wasn't an entire coast away. You might not say no right now to a little hug, a little human touch. You wonder if Sean might offer a back rub in the morning. You won't say no.

When your daughter asks about her grandmother, you tell her she's fine, no better and no worse. "You'll come out for the funeral, won't you?" you say and then Vanessa is crying on the other end of the phone and you're sorry you said anything to hurt your baby. You didn't mean to at all. You were just looking forward a little to seeing her. That's all.

"Just tell me you're not smoking, Mom. Just say you're not," Vanessa says midcry and you think this is not what you need right now. You tell her you love her and hang up the phone.

You can't sleep, so finally you drag the little TV into your mom's room and watch the late-night shows with her. You look at her face to see if she has any reaction. She doesn't. You think about how she would pretend to stay up late and watch the shows when she was really just staying up to make sure you came in by curfew and see if you wanted to talk. She loved Johnny Carson. And then you really look at your mom's sunken, wrinkled face and you wonder if you'll look like her when you are dying one day. You hope not. You think about how much you love your mom and how much you don't actually want to be like her at all. You check the gauge on her oxygen tank, change out the IV bag, and put a crocheted hat on your mother's head to hide the yellowed strands of what's left of her hair. A midnight cigarette is just what you need to finally sleep.

YOU'RE AWOKEN THE NEXT MORNING by a soft knock on the front door. You must have fallen asleep in the rocking chair again. You run upstairs to check on your mother before you go to answer it, to make sure she's still alive. She's sitting up in bed, staring straight at you with drool sliding down her chin. "You," she says and closes her eyes again. You see the clock on the nightstand and try to remember if you gave her the midnight pain medicine. You must have or she wouldn't have slept and neither would you. It's 8:32 now so she's long overdue for her morning meds. "Mom, do you need anything?" you ask, but you don't listen for her answer. You go to the front door and see Sean's brown curls through the etched glass. He has bags in both hands, and there are two women with him. There's no way to get your morning smoke now.

Upstairs, Sean takes over. He talks softly to your mother as he changes the sheets and sends one of his helpers to the van for a new oxygen tank. "Why don't you go make some coffee? I'll get her comfortable and then we can talk," Sean suggests and you wonder if he knows you'll duck out back to smoke while it brews and the smell of French roast covers your trail. You see a little smile at the corner of your mom's withered mouth. Is she smiling because it's Sean or because she knows what you're about to do?

Sean joins you in the kitchen. You pour him coffee in the World's Greatest Mom mug and you want him to think it's yours, that your daughter bought it for you when she didn't, and then you hate yourself for caring.

"I don't think it will be much longer," Sean says and takes a chair at the Formica table. He pulls out a chair for you too and nods toward it. You sit across from him and grip your coffee cup with both hands. "She seems ready to go."

"Ready to go where?" you ask. Sean reaches for the cream, stirs his coffee with a spoon. You wonder if it's a clean spoon. He clears his throat and looks at you and you think he must be deciding how to answer. You two have a rapport, a playful banter that you both enjoy. Sean gets you, understands that sarcasm is a deflection of the facts, the fact that she is dying and you don't know what to do.

"Sorry," you whisper. "I don't know what to do."

"You help your mother die. That's what we do. We make her comfortable. She seems ready."

You bite your tongue to stop yourself from asking "Ready for what?"

"Stephanie's going to go over the paperwork with you," Sean says. "Your mother is resting. Why don't you rest, too? Take a nap or something. Have you eaten anything?" You know he's just trying to be kind, but you would really like him to lie down with you, just spoon up against your back for a moment, he can even leave his shoes on, just so you don't feel so alone. You wonder if there is a checklist somewhere: Be sure the caregiver is eating and resting too. Check.

When Stephanie comes downstairs, you tell her the coffee is all gone, which isn't true and if she looked she could still see some in the pot. She pats your arm and asks how you are holding up. You hate her instantly.

Stephanie and her blonde bob and adorable scrubs with balloons floating on them. You imagine popping the balloons one by one. Stephanie unpacks brochures and paperwork. When she asks if you would like to see a grief counselor, you say, "Grief? She's not dead yet. She didn't die when you were upstairs, did she, Stephanie?" Her eyes grow wide, and you feel a little sorry for her. "Sorry. I've been through this before. I know the paperwork."

"Oh," Stephanie says, leaving her cute little mouth in an "O" shape. "I didn't realize that. I'm sorry."

"Just show me where to sign, Stephanie. That's all we need to do here," you tell her. "You can leave the other stuff and I'll look through it later." You know that's not true, but that's not Stephanie's fault. The first time your mother tried to die, you spent hours reading online. You made a list of questions to ask your hospice care provider. You called the insurance company and filled out all their forms for billing. You read the brochures on Guiding the Living Body to Beyond. You even called a priest because your mother was raised Catholic and you thought it was the right thing to do. You've never seen the inside of a church in your life. But then she decided not to die after all. She decided to live and fight and exist. The doctors gave her a year. She took more.

"Can I make you some more coffee? Something to eat?" Stephanie asks.

You shake your head no and get out the screened door as fast as you can before she sees you break. The door slams behind you too loud and you sprint to your car. You sit behind the steering wheel not starting the engine. Not leaving. You take the keys out of the ignition and throw them out the window onto the grass. You crawl over the arm rest into the backseat where your mother was when you drove her home. One of her hospital socks and some tissues are wadded up on the floor. You put the sock on your hand and make a little puppet. You curl up into a ball and stroke the plush cushion for comfort. You close your eyes. You stay.

When you hear another car door slam, you hunch down trying to make yourself invisible. After a minute you peek over the seat and see your brother at the front door. He hasn't seen you. He's expecting you to be inside, to help him face this. You smile because now he has to do it alone, to see her so close. You scoot out of the backseat for a quick smoke. You've got time, your sock puppet says. What self-respecting son would only stay a few minutes? Michael catches you, of course, moments later. "What the hell's the sock for?" he asks first.

"Don't you know?" you say.

"I just saw Mom. She's not good."

"Oh, really. You think we should call the doctor? Maybe she's dying."

"I'm not trying to be a smart ass, Iris. I'm just saying. Do you need anything?"

You blow your smoke into the space between you. You climb back into the car and squeeze your eyes tight to stop thinking.

Sean finds you lying down in the backseat. He knocks on the window so you roll it down a crack. It's only been a few hours, right? "We need to make arrangements for the evening shift, Iris. Can you come out so we can talk?"

You shake your head no.

"Your daughter called," he says. "She said she tried to reach you by cell phone. It'd be good if you call her back."

You ignore him. He squints through the window. He doesn't ask why you're hiding in the backseat of your car. You'd tell him how comfortable it is back here if he asked. Your favorite hiding spot as a child. He can climb in if he wants to, cuddle a little in the backseat. You don't tell him about how you'd like to get your mom, unplug her from everything, and drive to the beach like Thelma and Louise. Except Louise would be comatose and all, not really raising her arms up to feel the wind as you drive. The sunglasses and the scarf would help.

"Your mother asked for you. She was awake for a little while this afternoon. Her fever is high. I gave her a stronger dose of morphine. You'll need to give another through her IV at 8 p.m." He waits by the window for your response. Finally he says, "Do you want me to wait inside? I can get someone to come sit with her through the night if you don't want to. I just need to know what you want to do." He leans up against the car and looks toward the house.

Last night when you brought her home feels like a lifetime ago. It's been twenty-four hours and you are already losing track of time. You wonder if dying time moves more slowly than living time. You see the blood on his sleeve and want to reach out and feel it, see if it's completely dry or still a little wet. You want to make sure it's your mother's blood, maybe from the coughing or the changing of the IV. It doesn't matter from where, you just want to know that it's hers. He wouldn't dare bring in some other dying mother's blood on his sleeve, would he?

Sean stands with one hand crossed over his arm. He keeps bringing his hand up to his face, then flopping it down again and you wonder if he's a smoker too. That would work, you think. Finally, he leans down and cocks his head to the side. "She's ready to go, Iris. It's soon." You want Sean to stop talking, to stop being so fucking melodramatic, so you climb out of the backseat and walk toward the house, leaving him in the front yard. You hope he doesn't see the cigarette butts.

In your mom's bed is an old woman. A bag of bones, really. A body invaded with tubes, machines beeping, synchronizing their attack. You ask Stephanie to leave you alone with it. Stephanie ducks her head—you imagine the training video on sympathetic looks and demure nods—and closes the door behind her. The sound of the door stirs the body. It scans the room through filmy eyes until she sees you. "It's me, Mom. It's Iris," you say. You think it would be nice if she came to, just for a moment, so she might think you'd been there all along and not hiding away like a child.

"Where have you been?" she asks. She is your mom. You've come in after curfew. You shuffle your feet, trying to think of an excuse. Then she starts hacking away and her body doubles over and you have to rub her bony back through the spell and you can feel each vertebra of her spine as it shudders through the thin cotton gown and you remember staying up all night with Vanessa once when she had pneumonia and rubbing her back the same way, the heat from the fever warming your hand. You had to force yourself to stay, to mother. You'd never leave, of course, but there are moments when you think…you just want it over. You want the coughing and the dying to just stop. You want to stop waiting and worrying and you want your mother to be healthy and angry and bitter and funny again. You want to sit on the back steps and have a smoke with her and laugh as she tells you the story of the time she called your second-grade teacher a bitch for giving you a B in cursive writing.

"I'm here, Mom," you say. "What can I do?" She looks at you through her fog.

"You who?" she says, like the chocolatey kids' drink. "You who?" again as if it's a knock knock joke. And you know you can't do anything. You feel a little earthquake in your insides. Who are you if your own mother doesn't know you?

So then you decide.

YOU WAIT UNTIL SEAN PULLS out of your driveway before you try to call Vanessa back. You're supposed to call Sean at his home if you change your mind and want some help. You don't think you will. You don't really know what you'll tell Vanessa. "Hey, kid. Your grandma's not going to make it through the night. She's in a coma now. She was screaming, 'I'm scared. I'm scared to die. Hold my hand.' So they gave her a big fat dose of morphine coupled with some Versed to take the edge off the whole fear of dying thing. Knocked her out like a baby. Except the baby foamed a little at the mouth. Gross." You just don't know what to say, so you hang up after the first ring and you turn off your cell phone.

When your brother stopped by earlier, said his goodbyes with all his drama, and asked if you needed anything, you said, "Do you mean like staying with her tonight? Helping me help her go?" He gave you that you-know-I-can't-do-that look. You think Sean is a good man, not like your brother. You're tired of everyone asking if you need anything. Yes, I do, you'd like to say. Actually, I do. My mother.

So then you decide to stop thinking.

YOU WAIT UNTIL THE MIDNIGHT dose.

You load three syringes.

You watch her face slack into calm.

You listen as her breathing slows and the gasping stops.

You turn off the beeping monitor and wait.

You might like to go with her, to wherever she's going, just so you don't have to be left alone.

You hold her hand.

You tell her that you're scared too.

She squeezes your hand just a bit.

AFTERWARDS, YOU WILL SEE YOUR mother everywhere. In her death, she becomes your constant companion, your denial that you are in fact now an orphan. A motherless something. You will speak out loud to her ghost and insist she stay by your side. You'll keep track of her. Death doesn't break this habit in your mind. You will see her in the garden when you go out to water the hydrangeas and you say, "Mom, I was just about to do that. Give me the hose."

"Water them at the base, Iris. Not from the top," she says. Next week you will water them too much. You will watch them die. You won't try to stop them.

She'll be in the kitchen making cinnamon toast as she always did when you were sick as a child and say, "Don't forget the corners. Butter and sprinkle the corners, too." She will roll her eyes at you.

"Fine," you will threaten. "I won't eat the crusts then."

You will almost wet your pants one morning when you see her in your mirror. "Jesus, Mom! You almost scared me to death! What are you doing?"

"Brushing my teeth. What's it look like I'm doing?" she'll say.

You will talk out loud to your mother as you grocery shop and drag the trash to the curb and check in guests at the hotel front desk. She is healthy and alive and not hacking and dying. She will agree that it's hard to mother, to mother your dying mother, to mother your grown daughter, to find any of yourself in the mess. To do any of it right.

You will sit at the kitchen table with her addressing thank you notes from the funeral home. You will write: *Thank you so much for your kindness. Your presence was a comfort.* You want to write: *Thank you so much for looking the other way when you saw me sucking on a cigarette behind the funeral home.* Your mother will tell you the gory secrets of all the people who attended, who pressed your hand with their wet tissues. Sorry, they said. Your mother was a good woman, they said. As if anyone ever says anything else. They didn't say: Smoked herself to death, didn't she? They judged silently, sure. But who doesn't? "They aren't so perfect themselves," your mother's ghost will mutter.

You wanted to ask them all if they'd yet lost their mothers. Maybe you could form a club. You just want to know that someone else feels like this too. You might even let your good-for-nothing brother join.

One morning your mother's ghost will find you crying in the shower. She'll hand you a tissue and say, "You did OK, kid. Stop it. Enough." So you will send her over to Michael's house. She will knock politely, find him drinking coffee on his porch, reading the morning paper. She will grab the paper out of his hand and say, "You fucked up, kid. Punish yourself. Start now." You will laugh and laugh and almost forgive him. Then you will book a flight to see Vanessa and the kids. Soon is good.

You will tell your mother about Sean, about the fantasies you still have of him. One day you'll mention the dream you had where you were the patient and he took care of you. "Oh, did he, now?" your mother will say all saucy. You'll tell her it wasn't like that at all. But it was.

When she goes to work with you, your mother will make comments about what the hotel guests are wearing or insinuate what they may be doing later in their rooms and you will have to shush her. "Be quiet, Mom. They'll hear you," you'll say but that will just make her mock them even more.

You will smile a little at the absurdity of it all and mold your mother into what you want and need her to be.

Melody Schreiber

Bellyful

MELODY SCHREIBER is a freelance journalist and a program manager at the International Reporting Project, based in Washington, D.C. She received a bachelor's degree in English and linguistics from Georgetown University and a master of arts in writing from the Johns Hopkins University. Her articles, essays, and reviews have been published by the *Washington Post*, the *Guardian*, the *Atlantic*, *USA Today*, *Vice*, *Slate*, *Delaware State News*, and elsewhere; and she has appeared on CNN and *Feature Story News*.

I suppose it started with the shrimp scampi, although really it started long before that. Ellis caught me staring at a box of frozen shrimp scampi, gazing, really, my nose nearly touching the glass. I'd gone a whole summer, carefully rationing my cravings. But starting a new semester was always stressful.

"If you want it," she said, "just fucking take it." It was a very Ellis thing to say. Even now, when I find myself thinking about her, this is what floats in my mind—not her face, not that later image in the mirror of the ribs and hip bones poking out, but that disembodied voice, the studied rebellion of it.

She yanked open the freezer, almost bashing me in the face with the fogged door. The box was in her fingers, her hand slipping into her enormous Jane Eyre tote bag, before I could even blink. And there you go. Problem solved. She got off on that kind of thing—creative solutions to intractable problems. Like looping the exposed pipes in our little basement apartment with all of our crazy-printed scarves, or painting windows and landscapes onto the bare cement walls, fuck the security deposit.

Next, she scooped up a box of frozen scallops wrapped in bacon, and two of those triangular single-serve chocolate mousse pies. For bulimics, we really knew nothing about cooking.

"What are we celebrating?" she asked, as we sailed out under the Tenleytown Whole Foods sign, purses bulging, nary a glance back.

I didn't have to think. "Each other," I said, and she smiled, one of those ear-to-ear, all-teeth smiles that I lived for.

⌃⌄

IF YOU CAN'T UNDERSTAND WHY we did it, then I don't think I can explain it to you.

Of course, she always had half a dozen excuses ready. Ellis had her reasons worked out for anything she did, her proofs meticulously sketched, explanations prepared for interrogations that usually never came. (It was a product of being cross-examined by her lawyer parents at every turn, she said.) She did it because she hated checkout lines, she'd say. She did it because she wanted to overthrow the system, be the Robin Hood of food—even though she and I were the only recipients of her largesse. "Half the time, grocery stores throw all this out anyway," she would say, and I would always nod. I didn't bother to point out that they didn't need to throw out frozen food, that usually they threw out fruit and milk and that sort of thing. I didn't say it because I needed her. I couldn't do this on my own.

Of course she had the money, more than enough money—or her parents did, even if they pored over her credit card statement every month and called her when food charges showed up too often. Like that was a bad thing, like having your parents act concerned about you once in a while was some sort of tragedy.

It's just... Paying for the food made it different, somehow. More real. Like we were back to our old ways, and really, we weren't, we couldn't be further from where we came, everything was absolutely different this time. But as long as the food just magically appeared in our purses and freezers—and then disappeared just as rapidly, in midnight gorges, in between-class snacks—well, it just happened, didn't it? It didn't mean anything. There was no paper trail; it was off the record.

The clothes, when we started taking them, were the same way. "Stores build in a certain percentage for loss," she said in that logical, reasonable, I-used-to-work-at-Topshop voice. That's what she called it—loss—like the clothes had merely lost their way and ended up tucked into our tote bags and strewn across our basement apartment.

When really, buying the clothes—standing in line at Anthropologie, Ralph Lauren, Lucky Jeans, Juicy Couture, and handing over the plastic—would have been some kind of admission. Size 2, then Size 0, then Size 00. We couldn't let ourselves think about how nothing fit anymore—not even, as fall semester went on, the clothes from rock bottom, when we met.

୧୬

"WHERE DID YOU MEET?" THE drunk man asked. His name was Chris, or Paul, or Ryan. He was watching us in that way peculiar to men in their forties and fifties who sit alone in bars. They always projected an air of waiting for something, for someone, for their real lives to start, and it wasn't until Ellis started going to bars with me that I realized they were waiting for us.

"Rehab," Ellis said, which wasn't quite true, but as lies go, it wasn't so bad.

Chris-or-Paul-or-Ryan grinned. For some reason, men in bars found this answer particularly enthralling. We seemed so easily corruptible, she and I, answering only the call of our own urges, weak to our addictions. We were waiting for a man just like him to follow us into the darkness, to find his twisted inner nature and force it on full display—but he wouldn't feel guilty because, he would think, we went wrong long before we met him. It was the kind of impression that we cultivated carefully and that came naturally to us, all at once.

Not that we ever took these men home. Not our style. The unveiling of our bodies was always an opportunity for more hurt—the tiny breasts, the uneven bump of bones under tight skin, the fat that we knew was hiding on our thighs. We instinctively avoided it. Occasionally, we would make out with them in the parking lot, but we preferred to keep some mystery to the whole operation. We were femmes fatales, we told ourselves, not whores. And the whole puking-in-the-bathroom-afterward thing might seem off-putting to some guys.

Chris-or-Paul-or-Ryan was in his late forties, with a hairline that didn't like him any more than Ellis did. But there was something about him that made me lean forward. Intrigued. Guys like him, with their endless stories about their kids and the awkward pauses around their wife's name—they were a puzzle to me, something to crack, like Ellis with her logic games.

Ellis leaned closer to me, notching her shoulder into mine, our little signal to move on, but I wasn't done yet. I was obsessed, suddenly and completely, with what made this man whose name I couldn't even remember tick. He had everything he could ever need at home; why would he seek out someone like me?

When I think about it now, the real object of my obsession was, as always, myself. What did guys—what did anyone—see in me? What did the world need from me? Where did I fit?

Ellis had had enough. She slid from her barstool and sidled between my legs, putting both arms around my neck and kissing me full on the mouth. Chris-or-Paul-or-Ryan, who was now gawking at us with a goofy, hopeful grin, was utterly forgotten. Kissing Ellis was always so sweet, so pure. Like kissing a better version of myself—one who knew what she wanted, and how to get it.

I think most people assumed we were together, you know, romantically. And we were together. My life had never locked so easily into someone else's. But it wasn't romantic; it was more than that. We were partners. Partners in crime.

We would sometimes sleep together, curled into one another. We could both count each other's ribs, and we would run our fingers over each other's jutting bones in pretend concern. Look at us. We're so bad.

We felt so light sometimes, like we would just drift away on one of the freezing drafts that blew through the cracks around the door. We were always cold, all the time. We held each other in place, mutual anchors; we kept each other warm.

The making-out stuff, though—that was really just for the guys. It was the surest way to get them to pick up our tab.

cs

EVEN MOVING IN TOGETHER HAD been one of her schemes. When she was busy thinking up plans like these, you could almost see her brain clicking and whirring away. And once she got started, she was unstoppable.

She had called up her dad and convinced him that living with me would keep her on the straight and narrow. I heard her on the phone: "Yes, Daddy, that nice girl from the in-patient program, you know, the one I bunked with." Like our month of treatment had been a stay at summer camp.

She told them we would remind each other to go to meetings and "hold each other accountable." She used all the language of the half-dozen programs we'd both been in over the last decade. She painted the picture of two healthy, happy girls partying it up at American University, and her parents ate it up like a pint of Ben & Jerry's Half Baked. Her dad's secretary faxed a signed lease and wired a whole year of rent to the landlady the next day.

Even Ellis and I believed it, this plan to help each other, at least for those first few months.

❧

WE DIDN'T JUST STEAL THINGS. We stole people, too. We would read about someone in one of our history textbooks, or meet someone in a coffee shop or bar, and we would steal their lives. We constructed whole selves, whole stories. We wanted to be anywhere but in our own skins.

"My name is Jezebel. My mother named me that because she knew I'd betray her."

"My name is Veronica. My father named me that because she loves comics."

"My name is Bold Heart. My mother named me that because she hoped I would be different. Better than her."

❧

THE THANKSGIVING PLAN HAD BEEN her stroke of genius. You'd think a holiday about gorging yourself would be right up our alley, but the stress of going home was insurmountable. We told our parents that we were each going to the other's house for the holiday. They were so pleased that both of us had finally found a friend, they didn't question it—not even her parents. My parents never really noticed when I was there, anyway.

So instead of going home, we stayed right in our little apartment, burrowing into our underground den. We ordered Papa John's and Chinese food and Thai food and drank liters of soda, and of course we paid for it all—Ellis hadn't yet devised a way to steal delivery.

The Thanksgiving heist, as we thought of it, buoyed us for a few weeks, but soon we were lower than ever. We couldn't use the same excuse for Christmas. Our parents needed to see us, they said. We knew what that meant—they wanted to check up on us. It was unavoidable, and even Ellis was scared.

By now, we were lifting something every day, sometimes more. We went to a different grocery store each time—Giant and Safeway and Whole Foods—so we wouldn't attract too much attention. Ellis had a code about not stealing from bodegas—"They're just trying to make a living!" she'd say—but any franchise was fair game. I had decided, in the logic of that time of my life, that purging only once a day meant I didn't have a problem—like, what, puking every day at six p.m. was what every healthy college girl did? I didn't know how often Ellis was purging, but I'm pretty sure it was twice and sometimes three times a day.

Yeah. Even my parents were gonna notice.

We needed to keep our minds off of our inevitable parental doom. And that's when Ellis came up with the Great Christmas Tree Heist.

She mapped it all out—she actually had a hand-drawn map and everything. We scoped out the best spot the day before. First, Ellis read all the Yelp reviews of local nurseries. Once she found the one with the worst reviews—boasting both the most expensive trees and the surliest employees in the business, one that deserved to have its goods liberated—we went there to study the lay of the land. We picked out the best tree for our little apartment—not too tall, but not puny, either. She marked it on her map so we could find it again.

The next night, we waited until midnight to don ski masks and creep into the lot. Ellis had even found a pair of headlamps at REI. We crept through the silent aisles of Douglas firs and Colorado blue spruce. The whole place smelled like a new car. Ellis pointed out the one we'd chosen the day before, and I nodded crisply, in a very *Mission Impossible* sort of way. We surrounded the tree like police officers, hoisting it from the base. We penguin-walked it to Ellis's car and crammed it in the backseat. Every time a car drove by, headlights bouncing drunkenly on the road ahead, we crouched beside the car and held our breath.

With some wriggling and a lot of swearing, we finally stepped back to admire our handiwork. The top of the tree, with its spare needles stretching like fingers, hung out one window, and its base stuck out the other. I was sweating from all the exertion, and even Ellis looked a bit jumpy.

"All right, let's head out," she said, dusting needles off her parka.

I was looking around the lot. "No," I said.

Her head jerked up. "No?" she asked.

"I want wreaths," I said. "And garlands."

She stared at me for a moment, and then—that smile. I'd do anything for that smile.

We raced around the lot picking up shrubbery like we were on some kind of TV shopping spree, loading more loot into the trunk. Finally, Ellis slid into the driver's seat, and I took shotgun. The whole car smelled like forest, all spicy pine and sweet sap.

As she pulled out of the parking lot, a floodlight shattered the darkness. We both jumped, and I let out a little scream, and Ellis just floored it. The wind rushed in through the open windows in the back, an icy whistling in our ears, and we waited until we pulled into our driveway to dissolve into laughter—loud heavy whoops that we muffled only when the neighbor's lights flicked on.

∾

THE NIGHT BEFORE WE FLEW home—her to sunny California and me to shitty Vermont—she blasted Bob Marley so loud, she woke me up. I sat up in my bed and looked across the room. She was facing away from me, but I saw her reflection in the mirror before her. She was undressed, just a bra and panties. Her skin was stretched taut over her skeleton. That's what she looked like—a skeleton, standing there, like a dinosaur on display, all ribs and hips poking forward. It made me sick in an unfamiliar way. I laid back down and pretended to sleep.

If she'd seen me seeing herself, she didn't mention it the next day.

❧

WINTER BREAK WAS INTERMINABLE. WHEN I got back, eager to share stories of how my parents alternated between threats to send me back to the inpatient program and then forgetting about me and my problems entirely, the apartment was cold and empty.

I texted Ellis: "Hey girl when you getting back?"

Nothing. She wouldn't pick up my calls, either. For days, I wondered what I'd done to piss her off. Believing that she was mad at me was easier than worrying about what might have happened to her. Had she been picked up for shoplifting? Worse?

Spring semester started, but I paid even less attention to classes than before. I was writing a paper on Chinese pottery one night when I heard a knock on the door. I opened it and a rush of snowflakes swirled in. Ellis's mother stood in the doorway, colder than anything around her.

"Ellis is finally out of the hospital and in a new program," she said. She looked so much more tired than the last time we'd met, over the summer. Her skin looked gray and loose.

"She's not coming back," her mother continued. "I'm here to pick up her things."

Numb, I stepped back and allowed her into our little apartment, our cozy nest, now aching with cold.

❧

I WISH I COULD SAY we had a happy ending. That we reunited a month later, that Ellis gave her parents a big "fuck you" and she moved back to her real life. I wish I could say that it was a wake-up call for both of us, that we helped each other get back on the course we'd always hoped for. But the truth is, I never saw Ellis again. We talked on the phone a few times here and there, but whatever we'd once had together was gone, purged from our systems.

All I had left were the memories of all we'd done, so incongruous now with my lonely life that it was like I'd dreamed them. Or stolen them.

Dahlia Shaewitz

Leather & Lingerie

DAHLIA SHAEWITZ is a poet and fiction writer who recently left the little city of Washington, D.C., for suburbia. She aspires to open a funky cool book store in Capitol Heights, Maryland. Her obsessions include the rights of people with disabilities, training a low-literate workforce, and the artist known forever as Prince. Follow her rare tweets on Twitter: @dshaewitz.

ou can touch them," he said.

Adrienne was with a few friends feeling boisterous from the rum. They were experienced enough to not twitter like the embarrassed twenty-somethings that had just exited the shop.

"That's OK," she responded, shaking her head no.

"Go ahead, try them," and he picked up the two silver balls, revolved them several times in his hand, then presented them to her while taking a bow, like a knight presenting roses to a maiden. Except she was no maiden. She was old enough to be his mother and celebrating her fiftieth birthday in Key West with a bunch of friends for the weekend.

Adrienne wore all black to feel thinner, but she was a solid square from her thick bust to her Naot sandals. The salesman looked a good bit under thirty with a slight frame, a beard, and too much confidence for a guy his age.

She took the balls and imitated his hand movements. "How exactly do these work?" She looked him straight in the eye, emboldened by the balls and the rum.

"You insert them into your vagina and hold them there as long as you can. It strengthens the Kegel muscles—some women wear them for hours." His explanation sounded like a challenge.

Her friend Debrae perked up. "Oh! I'll buy them for you! It's her birthday," she added, turning to address the salesman.

"Happy birthday," he said and moved them to the electronics section along the wall. "We have other items here," his arm swept the backlit glass boxes that covered the lower half of the wall. Dildos of various sizes and colors shared space with what looked like plastic spears.

"How the hell does someone use that?" Adrienne was gesturing to a two-foot-long purple phallus on the far wall, but the young man stayed close.

"We have lots of customers for those, but the doubles are most popular, especially the electric ones. You can set the speed to what you like."

He looked Adrienne in the eyes as he spoke and she met them, determined not to back down from an uncomfortable conversation. Even for her, a hotel salesperson for twenty-five years, this was more intimate than walking couples to be married through the honeymoon suite. Instead of feeling strong, though, she found herself wanting to gaze at…Evan, the name tag stated. His brown eyes and long lashes were soft, in contrast to his cheekbones, distinct despite the scraggly beard.

He's too thin for me, she thought, then realized what she'd been thinking. I can't be turned on by a child, he's just a few years older than Kevin. Her son had just entered sophomore year at UC-Davis near his father's home.

She sidled away, not too quickly in hopes Evan would follow, to join her friends at the lingerie boxes. Next to them stood a large rack of leather, pleather, and plastic dresses. The dummies along the aisle were large-sized women, big busted, hippy, lascivious.

"How nice that your models aren't anorexic or ridiculously out of proportion like the regular stores," said Carmen, another buddy of Adrienne's.

"We get everyone," Evan responded. "This is what women want and it's what most men who come in are shopping for." He stood respectfully to the side as the women pointed out double-D padding and penis-shaped covers for the less endowed of both sexes.

Adrienne noticed a handful of young girls walking in as the door chimes tinkled, and after them an older couple around her age. "You're getting busy," she noted and nodded to the entrance.

Evan turned to look. "Someone else will take care of them. I'm taking care of you."

He met the dark blue intensity of her eyes with his doelike brown ones, and she finally let herself believe it. She had been holding her breath without realizing it and suddenly exhaled, her jaw dropping, lips relaxed. An old boyfriend had told her that he could never resist her lips, they were so sensual and inviting.

She changed her stance as well, shifting toward him slightly and looking for another toy to latch onto, to continue the conversation.

A whip—"I need a whip," she said, this time directly to her tour guide, ignoring her friends' discussion of swings and pole dance classes. The whips ranged from short thick brushes that wenches of the Middle Ages might carry on their hips to Indiana Jones–style long leather braids with red tips. She grabbed a long one and whipped it against the floor, the tip crackling like pop rocks on a sidewalk. Her friends whooped—"Girl, you know what you're doing! Where'd you learn that?"

"I'm a natural," Adrienne responded, feeling confident for the first time since Evan had entered her line of vision.

"Nice," he added and gently took the whip from her hand, wrapped it into a large loop, and placed it around her arm and shoulder. "It looks good on you too."

Her friends reacted to the tension they'd finally picked up on. Carmen and a couple others gave her a devilish look and headed back to the costume section near the entrance, but Debrae wouldn't budge.

"*That's* your gift, Adrienne! Let's go buy it. I'm getting it for you." The woman was oblivious. She chatted up Evan as she grabbed the whip from Adrienne's arm and herded them both back to the checkout counter. "I know I should get something good, but I'm thinking just maybe the edible underwear." She inserted herself between the pair with attentive Evan on her left and a despondent Adrienne on her right.

If it's that easy to pull him away, then he must not be interested. I'm so stupid, what does a guy his age want from me. Why pick old and frumpy when he can have one of them? She looked over at the three attractive young women who had made their way to the stand of balls where Evan had first introduced himself.

She turned right to the backlit, mirrored boxes and this time looked past the products to herself. She looked at her ruddy face that never tans, now puffy from drinking all day. She had no makeup on—big mistake, she thought. Her eyes were indistinct without mascara and her hair was wiry, gray roots a thin line at the scalp, crossed over by her beaded headband.

She only had tonight and the morning left, then they were driving back to Miami along the causeway from Key West. There's no time for romance. Romance? She knew she was kidding herself. What was she going to do? Make out in the alley? Invite him back to the condo she shared with four other women in their fifties? Even if he was brave and willing, she would need a few more shots of rum to let herself go.

Everyone had converged on the checkout counter—her friends, the other customers, Evan, and another salesperson. She took advantage of the busyness and slid over to the door, then pushed the tinted glass out. She felt the heat, somewhat tempered since the sun had fallen while they were in the store. She forgot about the bells on the door—the tinkling surprised her and she ran down the block to the corner, out of sight from the store windows.

Coward, she whispered to herself.

Her friends took another ten long minutes before they finally exited. She waved them over, chattering about the next bar they should hit.

"What happened?" Carmen asked. "That kid was hot."

"What kid?" Debrae joined in, still clueless.

"Kid. That's the word—kid. I'm not a pervert! Anyway, he's just good at his job. He made a sale, didn't he?" Adrienne snatched the bag from Debrae with a quick thanks, turning toward the pier. "Let's hit the Small Bar, I need a shot."

"OK," said Carmen, quickening her pace to catch up, and pressed herself into Adrienne's side. "I thought you might like this…that sales guy gave it to me."

Adrienne looked down at Carmen's hand and took the small black card with the name of the shop in elegant lettering: Leather & Lingerie.

"Not too creative, are they?" Adrienne snorted.

"Turn it over," Carmen said.

And there, in handwritten blue block print, EVAN and a phone number. CALL, it said.

Atossa Shafaie

Professional Mourner

ATOSSA SHAFAIE received a BA in English literature from George Washington University and an MFA in creative writing from George Mason University. She is a senior assistant editor for *Bartleby Snopes*. Her work has been published by *Scribes Valley, Dream Quest One, Coffee House Fiction, Fish*, Savage Press, and Winning Writers. Her flash fiction earned honorable mention by *Glimmer Train*. She is currently working on her first novel.

Ferri Khanoum waddles through her narrow hallway. Over the years, her rounding body takes up more and more space in the tiny apartment. She no longer bothers to distinguish between the temporary pain of last night's storm in her joints and the constant ache of disjointed hips. Just yesterday the doctor told her to lose weight. She always gets the same lecture. You must relieve the pressure off your heart, your bones, your knees. Lose weight and take your medicines. Why aren't you taking your medicines? From birth, her life was in Allah's hands. No little pill can keep her from the day He decides will be her last.

Kitchen windows let first light in. The horizon bleeds orange and red streams, diluting night. It is too late for the Morning Prayer. She feels more tired than she ought. Ferri Khanoum takes a bottle of boiled water and pours it into the large kettle to boil again. Such a shame; there was a time Tehran's tap water tasted so fresh it might have come straight from Mount Damavand. But many years back, Sade Karaj, the dam holding all the city's water, fell prey to overpopulation and seeping human waste.

Loose tea leaves brushed with cardamom steep in the small teapot. Stone-baked bread, creamy butter, and sour cherry jam, the same breakfast she's had since she can remember, neatly decorate the kitchen table. Her Babak liked *panir* with his bread and jam. Made from sheep's milk, the cheese has a tangy flavor. Ferri Khanoum never warmed to the taste of sharp and sweet at once. She still sets two places at the table.

She ignores the strange tingling in her left arm. Heat creeps through the window's seals and tea hisses on the stove, filling the room with a tangy sweet smell. She puts three large lumps of roughly cut sugar cubes in her small tea glass. She eats in silence. The photograph of her grandchildren looks back at her from the refrigerator door. Her son sent it a few weeks ago. Their little round faces are white and rosy. And blonde hair! Who would have thought it? *Her* son a Chicago doctor, married to an Amrikan woman. Allah is truly great.

Even though the letters Reza sends always have money, she never spends it. She saves it for buying new clothes, pretty things, for when her son finally asks her to come to Amrika. She looks at the box sitting on the middle of the table; simple, no carvings or tile work, brass hinges and dark wood. She would be sad to go. For the children it was easy to leave. But this is her home, her country. With all its scars and bad behavior, she belongs here. She sighs. Time to get ready for work.

Ferri Khanoum wears a loose long-sleeved dress that falls to her ankles, no buttons or zippers. Socks and plastic slip-ons, no laces or heels. The pins are a bit harder to place than they used to be, but she pulls her hair back in a bun and secures any stray silver wisps as well as she is able. She puts her *maghnae* on; making sure it covers everything past her hairline. The chador will go over it. They are very strict at Beheshte Zahra, even the young women have to obey Muslim Hijab. None of those loose scarves barely covering a tower of hair. She wonders what they do under there to get it so high, and their jackets, tight and short. But they have a right, don't they? They have a right. She squints at her watch; Babak's old Seiko, too big for her wrist, is still not big enough for her eyes.

"Ferri Khanoum?"

Hassan Agha calls from the street. He is always on time. She wraps herself in the black chador. Making sure the stove is off, she tries to hurry down the stairs.

"*Salam*, Ferri Khanoum," Hassan Agha says.

She smiles. He looks older these days. His shoulders crouch closer to each other and the hair in his ears seems to bloom. They start walking, and she wonders how many years they have gone to the bus together.

"Shall we stop and get some apples?" he asks.

They turn the corner. The market is just opening.

"*Salam* Ferri Khanoum," the market owner says.

What is his name again? How could she forget? She never forgets anything. She nods, pulling her chador closer around her.

"No apples today," Ferri Khanoum tells Hassan Agha. "We are late as it is."

The bus waits for them as they climb the stairs slowly. Small seats strain beneath too many people, the air stale with sour sweat. When they get on, no one gets up. Ferri Khanoum shakes her head. In her time the young people would have let their elders sit. As if he reads her mind, Hassan Agha burrows his bushy brows and points a finger at a young pair of girls listening to music with headsets.

"Are you blind? Get up! Get up and let an old woman sit."

The girls laugh and roll their eyes, but they give up their seats. Ferri Khanoum nods a thank you and takes the window.

Hassan Agha has only one daughter, his wife dead a few years now from cancer. He rides the bus to his daughter's house every day to help her with her work, cleaning vegetables, preparing dinner, watching over his grandchildren. Ferri Khanoum went with him once or twice. She is happy for her old friend that his family loves him so. A seamless dance of respect and gratitude, busy tasks in preparation for the man of the house's return from work. He has a good job, the son-in-law, but not a doctor like her Reza.

What a world. If only her husband were here to see their grandchildren's round little faces, scrunched-up noses, bouncing curls. They look more like their mother. But they are beautiful. Her favorite photo is the one of them holding up a sign. "We Love You Grandma." She reminds herself to burn some dried rue when she gets home, lest she jinx her son and his family with her good thoughts.

"How are the children?" Hassan Agha asks.

"Good, good. Your daughter?"

"*Alhamdulillah*, all is well," he answers. "Why do you not go to them in Amrika?"

Ferri Khanoum shrugs, but her chest hurts a bit.

"This is my home. Who has time to learn new markets and streets? Anyway, Amrika is no place for the aging. I hear children put their old parents in prison there."

"Prison?"

Hassan Agha's eyes grow wide.

"That is what I hear."

"I just don't like the thought of you all by yourself in that apartment."

"Psht. I'm fine. Besides, if I go that daughter of mine will have no reason to leave her poetry studies and come home, to her senses. She has always been a wild spirit, nothing a good husband won't fix."

Hassan Agha laughs.

"I remember another wild spirit who didn't marry as her parents wanted. That seemed to work well enough."

He winks at her. She pushes against his shoulder and blushes.

"That was a different time. Do you remember how all of us would laugh and dance? The most important things were fashions and frills. What did Babak and I know of the world?"

What indeed. The face of everything changed practically overnight with the big revolution. Many had died. Babak not only survived, but adapted and did well for them. Both his children away and one of them, at least, successful. She smiles sadly. Her husband used to cry at night, sometimes in her arms, sometimes when he thought she couldn't hear. She tried to show him how happy she was in little ways, but she felt his constant what if's nudge their way between them. The bus lurches to a stop with a large billow of black smoke. Hassan Agha waits until all the hurried people get off.

"Well, have a good day, Ferri *joon*. See you tomorrow."

He smiles and waves before climbing down the stairs and off the bus. The cemetery is another hour-and-a-half ride.

In Tehran, death is a good business.

Beheshte Zahra, where all of Tehran's dead are laid to rest, is an enormous expanse of over thirteen hundred acres. Ferri Khanoum feels strange comfort looking out over the neat arrangement of white marble slabs laying flat, a sleeping army of dead. There is the occasional dark tombstone, and a few decadently adorned with statues. She dislikes the statues; they break the beautiful uniformity of it all.

Carefully placed evergreens tenaciously conquer dry dust. Mausoleums line the cemetery's borders. Earthen bricks form pointed arches, giving entrance to small rooms. Bright cobalt and turquoise tile work adorns geometric lines, a subtle blush of color in an otherwise bland landscape. Babak wanted such a room for them, but Ferri Khanoum knows that unvisited mausoleums fall prey to heroin addicts with no better place to go than where the dead keep secrets. She prefers to lay beside her husband in the open air.

Her work happens in the heart of the cemetery where bodies are prepared for the ground. She has no appointments booked today, but there will be plenty of mourning to be done. Black veils engulf her as she enters the main courtyard. The women's shosteshou is to the left. Professional Mourners usually do not enter this building, a concrete world of sanitation and logistics. Ferri Khanoum hates it in there. It reminds her of the zoo. On one side of glass walls, women wait for their loved ones to be carted into a gray concrete room on gurneys, naked, a puff of cotton resting between their legs to hide indecency. On the other side, women in plastic masks wearing plastic gloves and plastic gowns hoist them into cement tubs like slabs of carcass at the butcher. Corpses are hosed down and washed with lye as daughters and sisters, mothers and grandmothers press their wet faces against glass, wailing. At the end of the day, when everyone is gone, cheek marks, tear stains, and handprints are wiped clean. Even when the rooms are empty, pain reverberates, soaked into cracks and crevices.

So impersonal, this is not the Quran's call. When her own mother died, Ferri Khanoum washed the body gently, praying over her in the privacy of a room where respects could be paid the proper way. But the world has grown since then, and dying is now an assembly-line event.

Ferri Khanoum stands a few feet away from the small opening at the base of the southern shosteshou wall. A body is pushed through the hole, cocooned in beautiful white gauze like a caterpillar ready for the next journey. Onlookers wait patiently to check the tag, as one would do at the airport baggage claim. A small group finally takes the body. They drape an intricate tapestry of paisley and gold over the soft white mummy. Old and worn, it has not been bought in the cemetery shops. Ferri Khanoum wonders if this is a full life being mourned or one cut down too soon.

Most Professional Mourners exaggerate their actions, pounding their chests like animals. But people find such things distasteful, and so they never pay. She is not there to make a spectacle. She just wants to be sure that all the dead have someone to lament them. Perhaps that is why so many people seek her out, hire her specifically, when they desire extra weeping.

She doesn't need the money, and the money isn't even good. Tradition survives only if remembered. Professional Mourners date back to the Safavid period, but the nobility of the vocation waned with time, and they are mostly looked upon as pests now. Ferri Khanoum felt that way herself, until she lost her husband. One day he just looked at her and doubled over. She thought he was joking. He always loved to tease her. They said the stroke was massive. They told her, as they pried her fingers loose from his collar, that he didn't suffer. Why did life offer so little warning? But then, what difference would that make? Gone is gone.

It was a simple funeral. Standing over his body, she was grateful for the women who gathered with her, even though they were strangers. Their cries diluted the shame of not enough people, no children or cousins, brothers or friends. Later, with her days empty, Ferri Khanoum found herself spending all her time at Babak's grave or watching the Professional Mourners do their work. One day, one of them took her arm and showed her how.

Ferri Khanoum looks down at the white cloth delicately absorbing a red film of dust. She weeps real tears and rocks back and forth gently. It is a life, and the life is gone, and that is a sadness. Bowing her head, she asks Allah to take the soul. A little boy tugs at his mother's chador.

"Who is that lady?" he asks.

"Shh, she is no one," the mother answers. "Don't look at her."

She feels a sharp jab in her left jaw. The heat of summer rises through the ground beneath her robes, clinging to her skin, drawing out her sweat and soaking her clothes. She shuts her eyes and waits for the pain to go away. It always goes if she waits long enough.

Little fingers touch her hand. Opening one eye she sees the small boy. He puts a ten-thousand Rial in her hand and scurries away. She hears the mother arguing with her sister, it is a waste of money. The sister says it's the Muslim thing to do. Ten thousand Rial buys nothing.

The day moves on. Families shuffle like cattle through the kill pen, lifting white cocoons above their heads. After the men pray, the women get their turn. Then the dead go to their graves, where Ferri Khanoum's tears cannot follow, straight into the dirt. Once lowered, the face is uncovered momentarily. The mourners can look upon their loved one once more before a heap of red earth and cement blocks separate them forever, and everyone can be sure the right corpse is going into the right slot.

Ferri Khanoum mourns over twenty more bodies. There are still many more, but it comes time to head home or she will miss the evening prayer. On mourning days, she tells herself she is doing Allah's work so if she doesn't manage five prayers, well, Allah forgives. The sharp pain is back, only this time in her arm. Her mouth feels dry, and the smell of sweat and rosewater suddenly makes her nauseous. Someone asks her if she needs help. She thanks them. They bring cola for her, which feels nice and cold going down her parched throat. Feeling revived, she refuses any more help and gets going.

As she makes her way back to her bus, she sees a young woman sitting at the side of the road, two small children running around her, a baby in her arms. She recognizes that rocking, the desperate desolate movement of someone who keeps time to a beat no longer heard by the rest of the world. Ferri Khanoum walks over to her and gives her the ten thousand Rial, adding four or five bills to it. The woman takes the money without even a spark of recognition. Ferri Khanoum says a silent prayer to Allah, for only his hand can bring this mother back, and her children need her.

Now her head hurts, a deep hammering. Immediately, a young man locks eyes with her and suddenly gets up and lets her sit. She has never been so happy to get in a seat and lean herself against the window. For the first time in all the years she has ridden that bus, she falls asleep. The bus driver wakes her at her stop. She apologizes to everyone and shuffles off, barely hearing the hellos of shopkeepers and friends as she walks home. The heavy fist just beneath her rib cage fills her with dread.

She reaches her door. Just before she goes in, Ferri Khanoum stops to look around her. She smiles at a group of young people huddled together under the trees in the park across the street. They drink tea and argue over books. The girls toss their heads in laughter, lightly brushing boys' arms in flirtation. How many faces has her country worn in one lifetime? She is glad things swing back to the center, no matter how slowly. The young need to be free, or Iran dries up with bitterness. Shadows begin to creep over swells of flaming sunset. The Azam plays on the mosque's loud speaker, pouring sorrow and faith across the city in a steady voice. It is a recording now, crackled, the same every time. Ferri Khanoum tears herself away. She can't miss the evening prayer.

A prayer mat keeps vigil in the corner facing East. Her family Quran perches along the edge. Ferri Khanoum washes her hands and feet, catching a glimpse of herself in the mirror. A small wave of shock rises in her chest. Is she really this old? She always thought herself akin to the trees lining the city streets; impenetrable, green, even when smog spreads grease on leaves and suffocates bark. But today, her branches feel weak, threaten to break.

Pulling her baby blue chador around her head, she wraps herself in the large square of thin cotton and tries not to groan too much as she gets on her knees. The prayer stone Babak brought back from Mecca sits at the center of the mat's border. The deeply etched lines in the stones face worn down by the faithful brush of her forehead. She would have loved to see Mecca. But when the opportunity came, only one of them could go. She is glad it had been Babak. He was always a bit more pious.

She mumbles the prayers almost subconsciously now, rocking gently as she speaks to Allah, counting absolutions on her string of beads. As the Azam continues, she bends her forehead to the stone. Suddenly her chest feels concave, unable to catch air. Her head spins and she sits back up. She cannot finish the prayer, but Allah forgives. Unraveling herself, she drops her chador onto the floor and makes her way to her bedroom, slowly, as though she wades through heavy water. Her heart beats furiously.

She changes her clothes and climbs into her bed, letting her muscles ease. The framed pictures neatly arranged by her bedside are of her children, her grandchildren, and her wedding day. She looks at her watch, too late to call Reza. She should wait until tomorrow. Yes. Tomorrow morning she will call her son and tell him to get her a ticket. Just a short visit, but she will go. She should have gone long before now.

As her eyelids grow heavy, she focuses on the wedding picture, so bold, the white dress clinging to her curvy figure. Her hair mimicked Elizabeth Taylor's. She wore red lipstick and pearls. And her Babak is handsome as ever in his Navy uniform, white and decorated with heavy gold. Ferri Khanoum falls asleep humming her wedding song.

THE NEXT MORNING, WHEN HASSAN Agha calls for her, she does not answer. He comes up with his emergency key and finds Ferri Khanoum neatly tucked in bed. He takes her cold hand and puts it to his cheek, sobbing soundlessly. Later, he sits at the kitchen table, shoulders hunched, dumbfounded, wondering who to call. He sees a box with his name on it. Opening it with shaking hands, he finds three envelopes: money for her burial, letters to her children and grandchildren, and a little something for the Professional Mourners who will weep for an old woman they never knew.

Debra Lattanzi Shutika

Mirrors

Debra Lattanzi Shutika is a writer and folklorist. She is author
of *Beyond the Borderlands* (2011, University of California Press), winner of
the 2012 Chicago Folklore Prize. She is a professor of English at George
Mason University and lives in Northern Virginia. She escapes to her
native West Virginia as often as possible.

Kate stops outside the door, catching her reflection in the
windows, her gut growling nervously, excitedly.

Minutes later she's inside with him. He strokes her face.
"Your skin is really remarkable." His oversized brown eyes loom behind
horn-rimmed glasses. He is standing very close.

"Thank you," she says, looking away. "Good genes."

"Hmm. You have this little pouch here," he says, gently touching the
soft skin under her chin. "You don't want to change that."

"That wasn't my plan…"

"I find it charming, actually," and he pulls off a latex glove. "It's important that my patients not look too perfect."

When he pulls back her hair, she feels his breath on her neck. She shivers
as he runs his finger along her hairline in a final inspection. Suddenly his
touch is gone. She takes in his trim Italian sport coat, the impossibly tight
trousers. With the glasses and that mop of hair he reminds her of—who?

"You can put this on," he says, handing her a paper gown. "I'll wait outside."

She folds her clothes neatly on the chair, covers herself, and sits on the
exam table.

The space is warm and tasteful. There are dappled blues and greens,
which she assumes are intended to soothe the naked who wait here. She
wonders why he bothers with the paper covers. This is, after all, a pretense of modesty. She toys with the idea of tossing them in the bin next
to the table where she sits, then smiles at her reflection in the mirror as

she imagines the young doctor's reaction, the Elvis Costello look-alike beholding her aged body.

She raises her head to inspect that small pouch he mentioned. She does look good, damn good, for a woman her age. Since she got down to a size four she's been proud, probably more than she should be. Most of her thirties her weight moved up. She still recalls the first time she hit double digits. Size ten becomes a twelve, then fourteen. Back then she didn't think about her body or her weight. At most she considered losing a few pounds. This fact she still finds remarkable. In her mind she is always that slim-hipped girl from 1989 wearing riding boots and a long pencil skirt.

After a loud rap at the door, the doctor enters. He is impossibly young for someone of his reputation. A hipster nurse follows behind, all in black, same thick-framed glasses, camera in tow.

"This is Minerva," he says, nodding toward the nurse. "She's here to help out, take a few Polaroids for your chart." He flips open a portfolio and studies her with his enlarged eyes. "So you're here for an abdominoplasty consult?"

She nods, and thinks of Dave, her ex-husband, who gave her the digital scale that brought her here. It wasn't his only Christmas gift, but it unnerved her. There were other, more subtle references to her size, and after Christmas she bought tummy control pants, followed by shape wear. Then she went nuclear: the Spanx store. She remembered asking for their "super squeeze" collection, famed for creating shapely silhouettes from the average woman's ample midsection. She shoved herself into the super squeeze with gusto, stretching into a youthful second skin. Walking out to the large mirrored platform in the fitting room, she looked curvy, fantastic really. Transfixed with the woman in the mirror, she twirled and struck a pose, then felt a small trickle of sweat puddle between her breasts.

The flash was sudden and all consuming. Her skin flushed, heat radiated off her body, and every pore oozed forth, the skin under the spandex a soppy mess. She recalled reading of instances where bodies have spontaneously combusted, leaving behind a pile of bone fragment and ash, and in that moment she knew it was possible. She ran back to the fitting room and tore off her clothes just as the seams of the super squeeze surrendered to her bulk. Her second skin peeled away as flesh bulged forth. Within seconds the super squeeze lay on the floor in a tangled slick mess. She looked up, hoping to find the slim-hipped girl of her twenties, but a different woman gazed back from the mirror.

"Kate?"

She looks up. The doctor eyes her quizzically. "I'm going to ask you to stand up here so we can get a better look." Dr. Costello points to a small stool in the middle of the exam room and takes her hand to help her up. There are mirrors in front of her, and she watches as he circles her, occasionally touching her skin with latex hands. "Minerva, take a few shots while I mark." He looks up at her, "These are your 'before' shots. I'm going to mark a few areas with this," he says, showing her a blue felt-tip marker. Seeing the look on her face, he adds, "Don't worry, I'll give you something to wash it off."

The marker tip smells pungent, chemical. She feels the wet line of ink run along her skin. He looks toward Minerva. "Take this shot, and be sure to get the length of the apron," he says, pointing to the hanging belly flesh that sags and occasionally gets caught in her zipper. Minerva pulls out a small ruler. It pokes her skin. The sound of the camera flash, click of the shutter, then the photo releasing, all are sounds she associates with childhood, the anticipation of good things. Costello holds the recorder close to his mouth, but she can still hear him.

"Patient is a forty-five-year-old white female, exhibiting signs of recent weight loss: large pendulous breasts, copious skin folds in the abdominal area, sagging buttocks…"

She glances down at her breasts, their size, once an asset, had become a liability.

He clicks off the recorder, slips it in his shirt pocket. "We'll cut here," he notes, pointing to a long blue line, "then we'll pull this flap down."

"Are you talking to me?" she asks.

"Yes. We'll start here," he says, drawing a small circle around her belly button. "I'll cut out your umbilicus, then pull the skin down like a sheet to here." He points to a line drawn under her "apron," which he lifts gently. "This will be your scar line," he says, tapping on the blue line that stretches like a smile from hip to hip. "All of these scars," he circles the appendectomy and gall bladder scar, "won't be here after the surgery."

"Where will they go?"

"When I pull the skin down, I'll cut them away."

"Oh."

He smiles. "Why do you want to do this?"

"I lost a hundred pounds, well, probably more like three hundred if you include my ex-husband." He laughs at her little joke. "I want to be able to take my clothes off with confidence, and I have all this skin."

"Very common," he said, nodding. "What do you want to do about your thighs?"

"I was just thinking the belly—"

"That's fine," he says looking up at her like a sincere child, "but as you want to feel confident, and I'm already in there, I think it would be best to pull this skin up and do a tuck here." The marker is out, drawing a short line beneath her bottom. "The additional cost is minimal, but the overall effect will be significant."

"How much? I've been saving for months for this and I'm not sure—"

He strokes his chin. "Five to six thousand, if you include the breasts."

"My breasts?"

"They look fine in a bra, but when I'm done, they'll look out of place, top old, bottom young. Just a thought."

"I'll need to—"

"Think it over. That's fine. You can get dressed. Stop by the desk to schedule," he says, assuming any consideration will take place in this room. After he leaves, Kate stands alone on the stool and notices her strawberry birthmark, just above her left hip. She recalls her mother's story about the mark, the result of a fairy's kiss. That will go, along with the others, and she knows she'll miss it. Kate looks up, not for the slim-hipped girl, but at the woman who took her place. She dresses and trashes the paper gown. Then walks out, breezing by the receptionist's desk.

"Ma'am," the girl calls, and she stops. "Aren't you going to schedule your surgery?"

"Not today."

Outside she stops in front of the building catching her reflection in the glass. She's OK with what she sees.

Karen Sosnoski

Too Sweet

KAREN SONOSKI'S writing has appeared in the *LA Times*, *Poets and Writers*, *Grappling*, *Bitch*, *Radioactive Moat*, *decomP*, *Identity Theory*, *Chaffee Review*, *Yellow Mama*, and *Camroc Review* and on *This American Life* and *Boundoff*. Berkeley Media distributes her documentary film, *Wedding Advice: Speak Now or Forever Hold Your Peace*. "Too Sweet" is an excerpt from her novel "Rosemary's Models," which takes as its starting point the real-life wood engraver Rosemary Feit Covey's reputation as a healer/shaman.

heir texts blip in: *U late!* (Mia). *Upstairs!!! Drinking!!!* (Lail). Looking up from the coffee shop/wine bar parking lot, Ellen sees her sisters, framed by the window. Spotting her, they raise glasses, brunette and amber heads tilting together. Both grinning. Like witches. Ellen imagines the cackle as they clink. Their mom was supposed to be with them, her presence the whole point of Ellen's three-hour drive—but Ellen doesn't see her. What the hell?

Trudging upstairs, sloshing semidark with soy, she realizes she is wearing the backpack she brought with her in case she found time to transcribe notes from her morning interview. No chance of that at two hours late! As Ellen arrives at her sisters' table, puts her cup down, shoves her backpack beneath, they exchange glances. "Ow, my foot," Mia snorts. "Be careful!"

At least Mom is here after all, eyes glued to a spot outside the window. Crumbs fall from her lips as she giggles and chews. "Mom?" Ellen begins, but Lail's hug smothers her words. "Good to see you," Ellen says almost sincerely. Lail draws back, rubs Ellen's arm in little circles. "That the sweater we gave you years ago? Might be time for an overhaul."

Mia shakes her head in time to thoughts which can only be negative—*no, no, no* as she rises to air hug Ellen. Ellen smells incense, maybe pot, as Mia grasps her shoulder, uses it as a bracing wall to push herself away. "What's the holdup? I gotta leave for work in forty-five."

Ellen ignores Mia, whispers to her mother. "Mom?" Mom's green eyes rivet towards Ellen's and away again. Her mouth works for several beats. "S-s-sweet," she pronounces mournfully.

"What's with all the cookies?" Ellen asks her sisters. "She never ate like this!"

"Never peed her pants either," Mia says. "Welcome to our world."

Her sisters are not quite drunk despite the near-empty wine bottle, but they are amped up, flashing bleached teeth and flipping hair as they attempt to catch Ellen up. Tapping the table, Mia tells anecdotes about loser men (who resent her outspoken "opinions," her "personal power") and loser therapists (who can't fathom a woman's having "opinions" about men that don't result from "her" pathology). In between Mia's "fucking men" stories, Lail touts her latest six-figure commissions—no longer just an interior designer, but a "taste refiner" and a "lifestyle saver." "For me it's all about teaching people how to live with art on every level."

Ellen listens and doesn't. Mostly doesn't. Her lip curls as she remembers her own first encounter with art on every level, six months ago, with a Rosemary Covey wood engraving, *House of Cards*. The print showed two women slumped together, just barely holding each other up, each wearing a skirt of thorns, faces lax in stupor, pain, or passion, oblivious to everyone but themselves. *Enmeshment*. Ellen recognized right away a version of her sisters. Now in the coffee shop as before in the art center, she crosses her arms in judgment, then hugs herself to take the edge off of her envy. That day she'd left her phone at home to escape the increasingly frequent messages: Lail advising that they need to talk about Mom. Mia ranting, voice rising in dramatic horror over another episode: *Mom groped my breast, most action I've seen in a while, but still!* Both sisters: *Daddy just can't live like this much longer.*

Ellen suddenly realizes her sisters are watching as she daydreams. They crack up when Mia says, "Uhuh, so I guess the kids are fine." Mom's chortle joins the chorus. Ellen shrugs off the question she supposes she missed. She *could* tell them she's researching a book on an artist whose models claim that she's a shaman. But now Lail, urban glam in red body suit and bangles, is bragging about her "fav star status." Cotton-sweatpants-wearing Ellen's just no Lail. No Mia either, who, popping a pill from a yellow-labeled bottle, downs it with wine before proclaiming Lail "my hero." Lail tips last drops of wine into her glass. "Mia, any man who loses you by definition is a LOser." Her fingers form an L-shape at her forehead.

Men flash half smiles in her sisters' direction. Even Mom seems to have caught the sexy mood. Grinning wolfishly, she swipes at the hips of an older gentlemen walking past. "Heh, heh," she intones. "Go for it, Mom," Ellen's sisters tell her, flushing, giddy.

Ellen watches her mother suspiciously. Until recently, anyway, Mom still had words. "Palish p-ponyish pink, like those frugals you eat," she might describe the sky. She has always been lyrical. And what if she groped her daughter? Mia's larger-than-life breasts ballooning from her lean frame are fantastic; Mom probably thinks the gesture never really happened, just as the breasts themselves aren't really real. Different does not always mean demented.

Fact is, although they live closer than Ellen does, Lail and Mia barely know Mom. They've always disapproved of her, her choices. As girls they hated their portion of the attic room that Mom designed. Its slanted roof cramped them; spiders multiplying on the skylight made them sick. They were annoyed by the proximity to Ellen, whom they accused of eavesdropping, then reporting back to Mom. Now when they visit their parents, Lail pays for herself and Mia to share a suite in a hotel if they don't go home early. The two indulge in massages and expensive wine—Ellen overhears the unsubtle references—when the family visit has been "stressful."

When *she* visits her parents without Jack and the kids—as she will tonight, Ellen sleeps alone in her childhood single bed. Sometimes she wanders into Lail and Mia's old room, smells lingering scents of their Love's Baby Soft. If she were to look in their dressers, she could find their teenage diaries, written in unsustained secret languages, could decipher once and for all the encounters she'd heard about indistinctly through the walls, escapades that left the two girls shrieking over rug burns on their backs and stains on their jeans and that left shy Ellen cold with fear for someone—her sisters? herself? possibly even the boys—as she pretended not to hear. But as her mother's favorite, Ellen has always considered her parents' home hers for better and worse.

Transported by memory, Ellen finds herself once again at age thirteen, gawky and big-toothed in her childhood living room with her pretty middle-aged mother, the pair donning hats for a twilight walk. Watching them from their beanbags, fourteen-year-old Lail and twelve-year-old Mia roll their eyes; in the background the TV blares. Because Mom can be ethereal, Ellen makes sure her parent wears her boots and winter accessories; then, both be-mittened, with the door shut behind them, the two link arms, inhaling it all: woodsmoke, winter's metal, dogs barking at a still-hidden moon. Mom's stride lengthens; her shadow looms. Passing the first neighbor's house, Ellen nearly has to run to keep up to hear Mom who will have started the "windows" game.

"See there, behind that one? The woman of the family is setting the table now, has the silver out, and wine, although they seldom drink..." Mom pauses, lets the premise sink in.

"Today is no holiday, of course, but it *is* a special occasion for the woman; her husband just doesn't know it yet. Tonight she's going to sit through the whole meal before she tells him her news—yes, she'll watch him wolf down his beloved meat, potato, and cream-clotted supper, then slurp down every last bite of strudel, peach apple, his favorite—and it won't be easy, this waiting. He's the kind of guy who *masticates* his food." Always, Ellen's mom rolls out the details definitively, a small smirk on her face.

"Usually this woman will do anything—re-feed the dog, invent a phone call to miss the sound her eating husband makes. But tonight she sits, hands folded, looking better, frankly, than she's looked in forever, dewy even, stomach roiling like it would before a test—but you'd never know. She's got her eye on him. Finally, he's taking his last bite. Chew, chew, food mashed onto those yellow teeth." (Mom's face scrunches.) "Swallow, swallow. He's sitting back, hands stuffed in his belt, stomach bulging. Now, she pounces. 'I want a divorce.'"

Ellen draws close to her mother, breath steaming, thrilled by the intimacy, frightened by it.

"In *this* house the mother is also making a special meal, but for the kids," Ellen might say peering through the next lit window. "She has to make them hamburgers with American cheese and potato chips and butterscotch pudding so that they'll be really happy for a few minutes before she tells them: 'Kids, I'm sorry, I ran over your dog.'"

Even though Ellen's stories are rushed copies of her mother's, if Mom is in the right mood, she will draw Ellen close to murmur, "So sad, so absolutely perfect." Absorbed in pretend gossip, the two forget they don't know their neighbors' real stories. Mom doesn't do Girls Night Outs. Ellen doesn't bother to learn the names of the kids in her grade three houses down.

Rounding the driveway to their home, they must steel themselves for reentry: the outside's wood-smoke mystery, even its cold, are easier for women like them to bear than the warming tensions of indoor life. Nearly untenable for these two the rituals of a home, the effortful comfort, the casual criticisms—Dad, not bad but impatient, exclaiming over the boots tripping him as he walks through the door, the smoke rising from the oven, "Why is this like this?" Or Lail and Mia, "What else does she have to do but cook and she can't even do that right?"

(No doubt Ellen's sisters have their own stories. In their house, the dinner is burning.)

"So why were you late?" Lail is asking, dropping her voice as if expecting a confession.

"I don't know." Ellen reorients. "The kids? Traffic. I had an interview. It's a three-hour trip."

"Ho, ho, ho," Mom chuckles.

"Well, let's take that as a segue," Lail folds her hands, looks from sister to sister. "She's going downhill quickly. What do we do?"

Eyeing the wine bottle, Ellen sips her coffee before speaking. "But Mom's happy, isn't she? She's eating. She talks." Mom leans back in her seat, hands resting on her belly. Eyes slitted, she's the picture of benevolence—nothing like the slender, wide-eyed dreamer Ellen knew.

"Oh please, can you stop? We know you've always put Mom on a pedestal, but my God, Elle, time to quit." As if arming herself, Mia pushes an onyx bracelet up her wrist. "Look, I brought her to the bathroom while we were waiting for you. She couldn't remember how to pull down her pants. When I tried to help, she strong armed me! I mean Mom was angry! I had to fight to get her pants off and then practically push her onto the toilet.

Once she was there, it went fine, although frankly listening to my mother poop is not my idea of fun. When it was over, well, Lail had to come help me. Lucky two of us were here, or Mom would be eating her cookies with her pants around her ankles! That or she'd have pooped her pants. Most likely both."

"Maybe Mom doesn't *want* your help. Maybe she just can't use her words right now."

"OK, Ellen," Lail says in her "managing" voice."I do understand how upsetting this is and you're not here every day, so the decline must seem sudden or sound exaggerated. But she's our mother too. And even if we haven't always been able to be as close to Mom as you have, we care about her. In some ways, it could be that our emotional distance allows us to be…"

"Cold." Ellen interrupts, heart pounding.

Unable to look at her sisters, Ellen follows Mom's gaze to the parking lot. A young woman with bobbed hair, curvy in tight jeans, swings her arms as she walks past the outdoor tables. Around her neck hang two pink scarves. Her close-lipped smile snags Ellen's attention.

Next to her, Lail's voice sounds both soothing and angry. "There are practicalities to consider. Mia's right, Mom's incontinent. And she does fucked-up things—tearing leaves off house plants, trying to move the stove. Believe it or not, Ellen, Mia and I are doing the best we…"

The young woman outside reminds Ellen of others, one a character in a story Mom told her years ago. *Just this week there has been a development in her private life: above the gum line of her upper right canine…* The other a young Rosemary Covey subject she interviewed last month. In the prints of this woman, an older man yanks her head by the hair. She sneers, eyes sharp on the viewer. In their interview, the model—what was her name?—lacked such ferocity. She was lovely but reserved. Even dull. Ellen sips coffee, trying to focus on the woman in Mom's story.

Meanwhile Mia rages, "I mean, family life has never been easy for me and now to bear the brunt of…"

Her mother's voice floats back to Ellen. *This young woman has let her back teeth decay, a secret kept behind closed lips even from her aged husband. She's sick of being eye candy but doesn't know how really to change. She wants a dark side. That power to disturb!* How old was Ellen when Mom told her this? Not much older than her daughter, Archer, young enough to think the tale was Mom's warning: brush your teeth or else. Now her imagination extends the story of the woman—Kate will be her name, and the old man, her husband Robert who develops a crush on the artist Rosemary... Inspired by other prints she has done of old men and young women, he commissions her to do one or more of him and Kate. She seems uninspired at first. He feels he must beg her to work on them. As a kind of hook, he implies they are sadomasochists.

In truth the only role playing they've done prior to modeling involved a single afternoon of Kate's halfheartedly tying Robert to the bedpost with silk scarves, something she'd read about somewhere and had decided to try for something to do. They couldn't kiss anymore...not with her secret. But then Rob had gazed up at her, confused, childlike, despite his many years. —"Darling, I think the shrimp cocktail doesn't agree with me," she'd apologized, untying him hastily, stuffing the scarves in her nightstand drawer. She'd flipped onto her side to reread her book (Wuthering Heights) *as Robert pawed her backside. "Snuggle me."*

"Ellen, what the hell, did you just check out or what?" Mia is in her face, squinting her heavily made-up eyes.

When the artist arrives at their house to sketch them for what is to inspire her later, more serious, work, they are unsure of how to begin. Robert asks the artist to choose the music, his tone condescending, flirtatious, and confiding all at once. Suddenly annoyed, Kate tongues a painful shard at just the right angle so that something sharp—old filling? slice of enamel?—(she's been afraid to look)—presses into her gums. Oh my God!—the break! Furiously, Kate pokes, unearthing the sliver, the last respectable bit. She swallows, entombing the evidence. Age twenty-eight and entirely missing a tooth! A bright pain radiates. As stars dance, the young woman wonders if she is falling in love with Rosemary.

Now Ellen's sister looks very drunk. "You're totally out there, in your own world. Might want to watch that identification with Mom, you don't want to end up like..."

"It's a disease, but it's not contagious!!" Ellen raises her voice. Heads turn nervously.

"No," Mia says, "but it *is* genetic. And there may also be some choice involved…don't dismiss me like you always do, I don't mean Mom chose Alzheimer's, but she did check out a lot from regular life, didn't keep house, didn't work, didn't pay full attention to her children."

Ellen's eyes fill at the injustice. Her mother had a life, an inner life! Lail rests her hand lightly on her arm. "So, Ellen, you do recognize she has a disease. I have to say I'm relieved."

"Didn't cook," Mia continues to grumble.

After the modeling session, Robert is angry at the artist. "I expected more from her. Enthusiasm, even involvement. Did you see the way her eyes narrowed? Made her look so old!"

"I guess I saw it. But she's not, well, not so very young. I don't know what I expected."

Seated on the loveseat next to him, rubbing her husband's back in gentle circles, the young woman returns to the moment in their act when her eyes met Rosemary's. Rob had been yanking her hair, which caused a shrieking pain to fill her head, but Kate ignored it. She'd ignored too Rob's hot-breathed, urgent whisperings that she "fight back, show her real stuff." Slowly, deliberately, still gazing at the artist, Kate had smiled a horsey smile—revealing everything. In response, a knowing shadow darkened Rosemary's eyes. Replaying this, shame quickens Kate's pulse. Tensing suddenly, she shudders as she only pretended to do during their modeling. She glances at Robert, but he has his face in his hands. "I need to brush my teeth and get ready for bed," Kate says softly. Heading for the bathroom, she realizes she has always known exactly what she expects from Rosemary.

"I'll stop the world and melt with you." Mia has stopped complaining and is mouthing the song playing on the café speaker as she smiles at a man with a weak chin smiling at her over the top of his computer. Ellen forces herself to rally, to try to explain how it is.

"It's confusing this stuff of the mind, never black and white. Yes, I've read the info you sent me, Lail. But you know yourself a clinical diagnosis of Alzheimer's isn't one hundred percent conclusive." Ellen consciously addresses both sisters, "As Mia says, Mom has always been different, more creative I guess than practical…" Ellen's mother stares back at her, eyes twinkling, baring her graying teeth. "Think of the quilts she made, her stories…"

"Creative?" Mia stops her flirting to retort. "Is that code for 'depressed'?"

"Sometimes, I guess. But..."

Mia nods knowingly and launches into her point. "It did hurt when she shut us out, so maybe we saw things differently, another side to her that you..."

Lail sniffs. "Right, Mia. Ellen, to address your concerns: we understand what she must have been going through; it's not like we're trying to punish her..."

But Ellen is back in time, ten years ago, a springtime in her late twenties. The sun is barely up as she steps outside and smells the air, fresh with thawing snow; grief claws at her throat. She lights an unfiltered cigarette stolen from a housemate, hoping the nicotine will numb her enough so that she can dress without sobbing, but even when she's done smoking, the shame nearly doubles her over. Nothing excuses her inability to read, play, think, write, love. And now it's the afternoon, same spring, and she's in bed, made it through another day of her part-time editing job, solitary work for which she wears headphones, hides in a cubicle, the only kind of job she can stomach. Trees make shadows on the walls of the bedroom she shares with Jack in the group house they live in with five others. For two hours before the others get home, she doesn't have to pretend. Watching the shadows, she wonders how long this can go on.

But her mother? At least as far back as Ellen remembers, Mom had her stories so real they became memories; her imagination, her other lives sustained her. Was she depressed? Never all the way through, not in all her lives, Ellen believes.

Next to Ellen, the Saver of Lifestyles is at it. "If you think about it, we are all in this together. Our different perspectives or memories can be helpful. I—Mia and I just don't think Dad can or *should* take care of Mom forever. He's still young, healthy. Frankly, he needs a life."

"How is taking care of Mom not a life like any other? I can take care of her. Jack and I can," Ellen says. She wishes Mom would sit up straighter. She imagines herself prodding her mother and her three-year-old to brush their teeth together. Would she give Mom an electric Wonder Woman toothbrush to match Mark's Spider Man? Nights she dreams that her old mother is back, urging her outside for a walk, pointing at the oak trees, exclaiming at the moon. This dreamt mother still drives, sews, dreams, and tells her stories. It is this Mom Ellen has always imagined writing for. Now after six months of shadowing her Rosemary, she's yet to write a word.

Mia's voice is rising. "It doesn't matter to me if you want to lie in that martyr bed, but you can't expect us to give you kudos or bail you out if you change your mind. Or if Jack does."

Lail gives Mia a look. "*What*, Lail? I mean, she's got two kids, it's not a high-powered life but…"

"Like a waitress's," Ellen snaps.

"Like an actress's you mean if you're referring to me," Mia retorts, "but I was about to give you credit. It's not surgery but raising kids is something. Again, it would be cheaper for us, probably easier for Dad and it's your…" Mia's hoarse voice shows her buzz is wearing off.

After the modeling session, Kate would have to wait months for the artist to finish the print. Finally, one morning while Robert is still in bed, Kate takes the scarves out of the nightstand and ties one in a bow around her head, wraps the other around her neck, and after putting on a fur-trimmed jacket, steps out in the winter cold. She wishes she had a dog to walk, perhaps a mittened niece to hold her hand, someone to distract her from her dread, but she makes the best of it, swinging her hips as she ambles. She smiles carefully as she trips up the steps to the art center; a guy beating a drum whistles at her. Inside, the just-opened building is nearly empty. Kate hurries up to the second floor before her courage fails.

"Oh, you're here," says Rosemary, looking up from her table, blinking. "I was just going to call you, didn't know if it's too early." But Kate can't respond. The prints are done.

Several show Robert alone, gristly, tough. One, titled Groping for Youth, *shows his hand pinching Kate's lace-clad behind. In the large print,* Sweet, *the only one she cares about, Robert grips her hair in his fist, yanking it so that the skin on her forehead stretches taut. Her eyes beseech, like an animal's. Her lips pull back from her teeth, in a sneer, revealing…*

"Are you OK?" Rosemary interrupts her thoughts. "It can be a strange sensation…people tell me…because of course that isn't really you, it's a composite, whatever I was feeling that day, mixed into you. And Groping for Youth, *well*

my husband gave me that title. Maybe it sounds mean, but if it is, it cuts me too! I'm ten plus years older than he is!"

"I..." Kate's throat closes. She'd expected so very much.

"You know, I made you somewhat fleshier than you are, I see that now, but I wanted that look, fleshy as in young, sensual, fertile, not fat, just full of... Your husband said you..."

Kate finally dares to look at the artist who is looking at, who can only see, the art she's made of Kate. "Feel free to call Robert," she tells her. "I believe he still owes you your fee."

That afternoon Kate calls the dentist. In six months, she has a brand-new smile.

Lail is swooping in for the final wrap-up. "So Ellen, I propose that next visit you come with us to look at nursing homes. I'll vet them, the top two or three. If you do that I'll, we'll, also consider your offer to take in Mom. It has to be a group decision, though, and no decision—i.e., letting Mom stay with Dad indefinitely—by default—we need to face it, that's no option."

Robert dies. Kate remarries a man her own age. Her sister, who'd felt alienated by her prior lifestyle, comes to visit. The two come across Sweet *while searching for childhood memorabilia in the basement. "Passing taste," Kate laughs and puts it in the junk pile.*

Ellen feels her mother's eyes on her, gentle as a baby's. She recalls Rosemary's eyes in the interview this morning, gentle even when her words were not. "My friends say I'm good at walking with people in their pain. It's true, I'll go to great lengths to achieve intimacy with anyone for my art. But it's also true that when the art is done, more or less, I'm gone."

"I'll visit the nursing homes," Ellen tells her sisters, quietly.

A flurry of activity ensues. Kissing the air and muttering under her breath, Mia weaves away to her job at the restaurant. Lail teeters downstairs to get her and Ellen lattes for the road. Ellen puts her hand on her mother's wrist, feels her slow pulse.

"Fuh, fuh, fuh," says Mom and then something like "clouds." Ellen draws her chair close, leans in, inhales and sighs, recalling. Just the other night, while they were snuggling, her five-year-old had rested her head in the crook of Ellen's armpit.

"I will always be born first," Archer told her fiercely, angry that night at her baby brother for preempting her snuggle time. "I'm your baby cub. You're my mama. I can track you by your scent. If you ever try and leave me, I will follow you wherever you go." Ellen had hugged her firstborn close, then sat up to disentangle herself. "I'm not sure that will always be good for you, honey. And you know, my scent may change." Archer sat up too. "You don't know what will always be good for me." The girl wrapped her skinny arms around Ellen. Archer laid back down and so did Ellen. Her daughter remained quiet for a long time. Ellen was beginning to disentangle herself a second time, when Archer spoke up in a loud, clear voice. "I'll track you by your essence."

Now Ellen takes in her own mother's scent—mildew, baby powder, gingivitis, cookies, something oily. She would never be able to track this woman in a crowd. The loss makes Ellen dizzy. Next to her, her mother hums peacefully.

"You two still sitting here?" Lail's too-bright voice startles Ellen as she hands her their lattes, begins forcing Mom's arms into her winter coat. "There you go."

"Sweet. Huh, huh," Ellen's mom is nodding her head, laughing, inviting Ellen to laugh too. Once upon a time, Mom transformed their neighbors, women with dull hair and muffin tops, men with balding heads and boring jobs, into fiery hearts whose stories filled Ellen so entirely there was little room for anything else.

Now Mom shudders vigorously before spitting out: "Too s-s-s-sweet."

"You coming?" Lail asks Ellen, cupping their mother's elbow.

"No, I'll have to say my goodbyes here. I've got my computer, gonna work now while I can. Did I tell you, I'm writing a book? It's inspired by a shamanic artist—this artist and our mom."

Over cookies, Kate's sister leans back, looking at her.

"What is it?" Kate asks. "Stop!"

"Sorry, I'm just thinking. You know the girl's smile in that nasty print we found? With those white, those exceptionally white, those perfect teeth? That smile could be yours!"

Kate's stomach turns for a hope she once had. An image of the artist's meaningful glance, her gentle eyes, rises and drops away. Then Kate's body, unregistered, unrecorded, forgets its visceral memory. Her mind has already left it far behind.

With a flash of something not anger, Ellen wonders when she'll be done with Rosemary.

"Could be!" Kate shrugs, smiling her perfect smile. She pours her sister some honeyed tea.

M. Jane Taylor
Behave, Sissy!

M. JANE TAYLOR grew up in the Maryland suburbs of Washington, D.C. She has worked as a newspaper reporter, a science writer, and a freelance writer and editor, and she likes to explore fiction inspired by her Appalachian family roots. She earned a master of arts degree in writing from Johns Hopkins University in Baltimore, where she lives with her wife, Autumn, and their dog, Jackson.

For the third time this week, Sissy has spent the whole long hot summer night buzzing around the apartment project with Skinny Marie and Theresa With No Arms, smoking pot and cigarettes and singing along with WPGC on Skinny Marie's transistor radio. Look how the twilight sky is glowing softly orange—and now the birds are awake. Flocking together in the treetops, they squawk and plump up their breast feathers.

"Guess I'd best take my ass home," Sissy says, "'fore Mama or Jack gits up and sees I ain't been ta bed."

Standing outside her bedroom window with Skinny Marie and Theresa, Sissy smokes one more cigarette and wishes she could fly away, far away, and never come back here again. Then she thinks about her little brother and baby sister, and she feels sorry and tells God she didn't mean it.

"Ground control to Sissy," says Theresa. "You still tripping or what?"

"Naw." Sissy slides her left foot out of its flip-flop and scratches her dusty heel. "Just thinking 'bout what I'm gonna do if I don't git it soon."

The early sunlight is starting to give color to Jack's petunias, which spill wildly out of the brick garden box in bursts of purple, pink, and blue. While a lot of the other garden boxes are full of weeds and trash, Jack plants theirs with petunias every spring. He keeps them watered, fertilizes them every couple of weeks, and pinches off the dead flowers in the evenings after work.

"You remember my cousin Bibby that lives in Front Royal?" Skinny Marie says. "She got rid of hers by drinking turpentine."

"Yik!" Theresa makes a retching noise.

"Well *I* ain't trying ta poison *myself* ta death," Sissy says. "Y'all ready ta help me up?"

Sissy's family lives in a ground-floor unit, but her bedroom window is just high enough to make crawling in and out of it tricky. Her friends have it down, though. Skinny Marie interlocks her fingers, and Sissy—taking a last puff off her cigarette, then flicking the butt into the petunias—steps into the basket. She holds onto Theresa's shoulders to steady herself, then leans forward and heaves her body across the garden box, halfway in and halfway out of the open window.

"Aw shit," Sissy says. Dangling from the ledge, she tries to back out of the window, wriggling and kicking her legs, but Skinny Marie and Theresa are shoving her from behind as they try to hoist her the rest of the way through the window. "Stop, y'all!" Sissy yells. "Wait!"

But it's too late. Skinny Marie and Theresa give one more push, and Sissy crashes headfirst into the bedroom, where her mama, Tildy, is waiting on her with one of Jack's leather belts in her hand.

"Uh-huh," Tildy nods and slaps the belt against her palm.

Bubba Jack is sitting next to her on the double bed that he and Sissy share, sucking on a purple ice pop and looking smug. He's naked except for a pair of Redskins boxer shorts, and all around his mouth is stained purple. "Yer in trouble," he tells Sissy.

Sissy scrambles up off the floor. "I ain't been doing nuffing, I swear!"

"Done snuck out agin, didn't ya little girly?" Tildy stands up and moves toward Sissy.

"So it's *you*," Jack says from the doorway, "that's been mashing down my goddamned petunias!"

"I'll teach ya," says Tildy, "ta be climbing in and out of windas and running the streets with that skinny dope-pushing bull dyker."

"Me and Skinny Marie was hanging out at Theresa's house, just talking and stuff," Sissy says, "and then I got tired and fell ta sleep on Theresa's couch." Sissy backs away from Tildy, but she's penned against the wall with nowhere to go.

"And don't think I don't know ya been stealing money out my purse agin," Tildy says. "Prob'ly ta buy dope off that bull dyker. Am I right?"

God if You kin git me out of this, Sissy prays, *I swear I'll never tell another lie or take Yer name in vain again*. The belt lashes her chest and arms before she even sees it coming. "Goddammit!" Sissy says. Her body convulses from the sting.

Tildy raises the belt and lets it fly again. It slices the air and strikes Sissy with a swish-smack, swish-smack, swish-smack.

Sissy puts her hands up to protect herself. "You wouldn't git away wif beating me if Daddy was still alive," Sissy says. "He'd knock yer teef out fer it!" She grabs the belt and wrenches it away from Tildy, slings the belt out the open window, and makes a run for the door.

"Ya little bitch!" Tildy flies at Sissy, scratching and clawing her like a panther cat. She catches hold of her by the hair, wrestles her down onto the bed, and dives on top of her.

"Git her, honey!" Jack hollers. Tildy's been giving him hell for three days straight, on a rampage that started out over his ex-wife writing bad checks in Tildy's name, so likely he's glad to see her taking it out on somebody else now.

Tildy's as boney as Olive Oyl, but she turns into a rabid beast when she's mad. Sissy tries to fight her off, but her mama's straddling her now, slapping and hitting and cussing her up and down.

Hanging on the wall behind the headboard, there's a faded dime-store print of a barefooted girl and boy crossing a rickety wooden bridge over a churning river. The sky has grown dark, lightning sparks in the distance, and the children have no idea they're being watched over by a golden-haired angel in flowing robes.

"Ouch," Sissy cries. "Careful of my earrings!" Wanting pierced ears but being too chicken to let Skinny Marie do it with a sewing needle, for the past two weeks Sissy's been wearing a pair of self-piercing sleeper hoops, the kind that push through your earlobes slowly and painfully. Straightaway, she realizes she ought to have kept her mouth shut.

Grasping Sissy's left earlobe, Tildy squeezes as hard as she can, and Sissy screams as the sleeper punctures all the way through with a terrible pop-popping noise. Sissy writhes and tries to get away, but Tildy lays on top of her and goes to work on the other ear. Pop-pop goes the sleeper, and Sissy screams again.

Sissy sobs.

"There," Tildy says and rolls off of her. "Mama did ya a favor there, didn't she?"

FRIDAY NIGHT AT THE DINING room table, Bubba Jack is slurping down a bowl of cornflakes while baby Cricket sits in her high chair and feeds herself applesauce with a spoon. She drops the spoon onto the floor, and the dog licks it clean. Sissy picks up the spoon, wipes it off on her T-shirt, and gives it back to the baby.

Tildy is still carrying on about Jack's ex-wife. "Ain't enough we're still paying child support on one, two, three, four..." she counts on her fingers, "six kids!"

"Aw honey," Jack says. This is day five of Tildy's fit, and Jack's been drinking since breakfast. "Calm down now, why don't ya?" He rubs her back.

Tildy hits him away from her. She picks up a lamp and flings it against the wall.

Jack runs his hands through his hair.

The dog goes and hides behind the couch, so that only the mop of his tail can be seen.

Sissy carries the baby to her bedroom, and Bubba Jack follows. Sissy puts the baby down on the bed and gives her Bubba Jack's toy shotgun to hold. Bubba Jack sits on the floor with his race car track. The baby sucks on the barrel of the gun and watches her brother play with his cars. His favorite game is to make them crash, which the baby finds hilarious.

There's a scratching at the door. Sissy goes and opens it, and the dog runs in and jumps up on the bed next to the baby.

It has to be at least a hundred degrees. The box fan sputters in the window, and the green gauze curtains bellow out into the room, flapping above Bubba Jack's toy chest and out over top Sissy's dresser, where they lap at a bottle of nail polish, a hairbrush, a tube of white lipstick, and then the curtains cast again and again toward the closet door and Sissy's tacked-up poster of Jimi Hendrix.

Sissy turns on the radio and pulls out her tape recorder. WPGC is hosting a singing contest—the grand prize being an all-expenses-paid trip to Atlanta, to record backup vocals for the debut album of a band called Lynyrd Skynyrd—and Sissy plans to win it if she can get together a good demo tape. Out of all the entries sent in, the deejays will pick thirteen semifinalists to come to the station and sing live on the air for listeners to vote on. Mr. Seymour the high school music teacher says Sissy's got a damn good voice on her. Anybody that's ever heard her sing says so. What's more, she's got the right look too. Sissy imagines the club gigs, her name in lights.

Sweating through her orange jumpsuit, Sissy tapes herself singing along with each song that plays on the radio—"American Pie," "Puppy Love," "Seasons in the Sun." But it's no use, with Tildy and Jack's brawling, Bubba Jack's fatal car wrecks, and the dog and the baby cutting up on the bed. She can't get a clean recording.

Then the deejay announces the song Sissy's been waiting for.

"All right now, everybody shut up," she says. "Here goes my song!" She presses the play button and sings, "These boots are made for walking, and that's just what they'll do…"

Something clatters in the other room. "And yer too stupid ta see," Tildy shouts, "that woman's bent on ripping us apart!"

The baby starts to cry.

"Goddammit!" Sissy slams the recorder's off button.

"I'm gonna tell!" Bubba Jack says.

"Tell who?" says Sissy. "You want Mama ta come in here, whup yer ass along wif mine?" She picks up the baby, who throws her arms around Sissy's neck and buries her face in her hair.

Bubba Jack makes an ugly face and sticks out his tongue at Sissy.

Sissy stands in front of the dresser mirror with the baby on her hip. She turns this way and that way. Is her belly getting big? It's hard to say.

Earl pops his head in the window. "Hey Sissy." Squatting in Jack's petunias, he leans in and kisses her, and his long hair envelops them both. He gives Bubba Jack a high five. "Hey man. What y'all up to?"

"Nuffing," Sissy says. "Ya got a cigarette?"

"Yup." Earl grins and pats his shirt pocket. "Got something better too."

BUBBA JACK IS SNORING. SISSY gets up out of bed and stares into the mirror. In the darkness, her face looks like somebody else. A stranger she's never met.

Bubba Jack mumbles in his sleep, rolls over onto his back, and splays out his arms and legs to take up the whole bed.

Barefooted in her T-shirt and drawers, Sissy tiptoes down the hallway to the bathroom. She pees, checks the crotch of her drawers, and cusses.

She takes the can of turpentine from underneath the sink, unscrews the cap, and sniffs the opening. It smells like pine trees and tar and something like shoe polish. There's an awful fruitiness to it, but not any natural kind of fruit. It reminds her of Froot Loops cereal soaking in a bowl of kerosene. She covers her nose and turns her face away. Cussing again, she pinches her nostrils closed, tips the can up, and pours the dense, lukewarm liquid into her mouth. The taste of turpentine is not half as bad as the smell. At first, it's like taking a mouthful of oil. Then her lips and tongue begin to tingle. She swallows, telling herself *do not throw up do not throw up do not,* and then swigs down some more of it. Then she lays across the sink and lets the cold water run into her open mouth.

Sissy goes to the kitchen for a glass of milk to settle her stomach, and she is startled to see her father, Gravy, there. He's sitting on a stool, drinking a cup of coffee.

"Hey Daddy," is all she can think to say. She thinks it wouldn't be right to bring up the fact that he's been dead some three years. "I didn't know you was here."

"Well," says Gravy, "I ain't really." He lowers his chin to his chest and drops his head left and right to crack his neck bones. "Hell," he says. "Ain't none of us is."

Sissy stares at her father. The moonlight streaming in through the window plays out a silent tune on Gravy's sunbaked skin.

He laughs, and so does Sissy, but she doesn't know what for. A part of her wants to run into his arms, and another part of her wants to run away screaming.

He holds out his cup of coffee to offer her a drink, in the way that he used to give her sips from his bottle, and she catches a strong whiff of whiskey coming off it.

Sissy shakes her head no. She's trying hard not to puke.

"What, too bitter fer ya?" Gravy sets the cup down on the counter. "Then what'd ya wanna go and swaller turpentine fer?"

"What?" Sissy says. "You spying on people now?" She shifts her weight from foot to foot and tugs her T-shirt down lower on her thighs.

Gravy says nothing. He looks her in the eye.

"S'posed ta be good fer a toofache." Sissy brings her hand up to her jaw. "Oh Daddy," she cries, "my goddamned toof is killing me!"

"You best behave, Sissy," Gravy tells her. "Are ya being have?"

"Uh-huh," Sissy nods.

In Tildy and Jack's bedroom, the baby starts squalling.

"Cricket's done woke up," Sissy says. "I better go git her."

TILDY AND JACK KEEP UP their fighting on Saturday morning.

After breakfast, Sissy heads for the door with Cricket on her hip and Bubba Jack at her heels.

"Where y'all think yer going?" Tildy asks.

"Nowheres." Sissy keeps walking.

"Out to the stoop!" says Bubba Jack.

"And who else is gonna be out to the stoop?" Jack asks, looking straight at Sissy. "We been seeing that Earl sniffing round yer ass," he says, "like a dog on a bitch in heat."

But Sissy's already out the door. Bubba Jack lets it slam behind them.

Sissy sits on the stoop with Skinny Marie and Theresa. The three girls pass a joint around while Bubba Jack and his friend Billy play with Cricket in the yard.

Tildy and Jack's hollering carries outside through the open windows of the apartment.

"I can't stand it, Jack!"

"Well I cain't take no more of this shit neither!"

"They still at it?" says Skinny Marie.

"What a drag!" Theresa grips the joint between her toes. She was born with tiny stubs instead of arms, on account of her mother having been prescribed thalidomide for morning sickness.

Sissy chews her fingernails.

"Go on back if ya want her," Tildy screams. "See if I'll stand in yer way!"

"Come on now," Jack says. "Why don't ya go blow it out yer ass?"

There is the sound of glass shattering.

Skinny Marie skootches closer to Sissy and puts her arm around her.

"If I was Jack," says Theresa, "I'd haul off and backslap her."

Three Koreans come out of the building next door. It's the old grizzle-haired grandmother, followed by a stocky middle-aged woman and a pretty girl who looks to be about Sissy's age. The girl is obviously pregnant, and she has an infant tied around her in a sling. They squat down and begin digging in the dry grass with forks. The stocky one is giving hell to the younger one in Korean. The old woman calls to somebody in the foyer, and a little girl with a page-boy haircut comes dancing out into the yard on her tippy toes. She runs over to Cricket and takes her by the hands, but Cricket pulls back and hides her face behind her brother's leg.

"It's all right," Sissy tells her. "Go on and play wif Sun Young."

Sun Young reaches out and tickles Cricket's tummy, Cricket squeals with glee, and they both tumble to the ground in a mound of shrieks and giggles.

Bubba Jack and Billy go and break off branches from the big elm tree, which they use to play at sword fighting.

Skinny Marie kisses Sissy's neck.

"Cut it out." Sissy pushes her away.

"How many times me and Sissy gotta tell you?" Theresa says. "We ain't no bull dykers!"

"Don't knock what you ain't tried." Skinny Marie smiles. "Ya know, Sissy—I could go with ya ta Atlanta, be yer manager."

"Earl says he's coming wif me," Sissy tells her.

"Earl don't know his dick from his asshole!" Skinny Marie takes the joint from Sissy and hits it. "I heard tell his mama caught him trying ta stick it in her beagle."

Theresa snorts and hoots.

"That ain't true, and it ain't funny neither!" Sissy says, but she can't help but laugh too.

"Sissy?" Tildy pokes her head out the window. "Bubba Jack Stokes!"

Sissy drops the joint and steps on it.

"Hey Mrs. Jamison." Skinny Marie lights up a cigarette to cover up the smell of the pot.

"What y'all doing out there?" Tildy says. "Y'all being have?"

"Ain't nobody doing nuffing," Sissy says.

"Ya'll better not or so help me... If I gotta come out there, I'll whup me some asses inta tomorra. You too, Billy! Y'all boys throw down them sticks!"

"You ain't gonna whup my ass," Billy tells her, "or my mama'll come up here and beat yers."

"Hmph," says Tildy. "You tell yer mama come on up here. I'd like ta see her try."

Tildy goes away from the window, and the girls relight the joint. The sun hangs directly overhead, scorching everything.

"Damn it's burning up out here." Skinny Marie fans her crop top T-shirt.

In the yard, the Koreans are digging up some kind of roots and putting them into bags.

"What y'all digging?" Sissy asks.

The old woman holds up a clump of wild onions for Sissy to see. "Soup! Soup!" she says, smiling widely, showing off grayish-pink toothless gums. She points at her granddaughter's big belly, then at Sissy, and makes a gesture with two fingers. "Im shin!"

"What the hell is she saying?" Skinny Marie asks.

The old woman cackles impishly, and the stocky one cracks up too.

The granddaughter frowns, pulls out one of her swollen tits, and sticks it in the fussing infant's mouth.

SISSY TAKES CRICKET AND GOES and knocks on the door of their older sister Skeeter's apartment. Skeeter and her husband live up the block, in the same long stretch of three-story, red-brick buildings, each one sharing one or two of its outer walls with the others. You can, if you want to (and Sissy and her friends often do), travel from building to building by way of a concrete rat's maze of dimly lit basement corridors—past dank laundry rooms and crammed storage lockers framed out with two-by-fours and chicken wire—without ever having to go outside.

Skeeter answers the door in her bathrobe. "Don't mind my house." She steps aside and holds the door open for Sissy. "I been laid up with a headache would bring a horse ta tears."

The inside of Skeeter's place is dark, and it smells like patchouli incense and stale cigarette butts. Sissy turns Cricket loose and plunks down cross-legged on Skeeter's shag rug.

"Mama still fighting with Jack?" Skeeter asks.

"I can't hardly take no more if it," Sissy says. "You ain't got no pot, do ya?"

Skeeter fetches a plastic bag from inside the cuckoo clock and gives it to Sissy, then she takes a seat on her purple velvet sofa, tucks her bare feet up underneath her robe, and hugs her knees.

Sissy pinches some of the weed, crushes it between her fingertips, and sprinkles it down the middle of a rolling paper. She passes the joint to Skeeter for first toke.

Skeeter blows smoke and says, "Jack ought ta give Mama one good pop in the mouth."

In the dimness, Sissy can barely make out the black-light poster on the wall above the sofa. It shows the profile of an Indian chief in psychedelic headdress. A dusty lava lamp sits on the side table, beside a large green ceramic ashtray overflowing with butts and ashes.

"Listen," Sissy finally says. "Ya know how ta tell if yer gonna have a baby?"

"Awwwwwww!" Skeeter gasps and covers her mouth with her hand. "Who? Earl?" She jumps up from the sofa. "Mama and Jack is gonna skin ya 'live!"

"Don't say nuffing," Sissy tells her. "Swear ta God ya won't! I don't know fer sure, but I been taking turpentine—"

"Turpentine! Ewww! That ain't gonna do nothing but make it retarded! If ya wanna git rid of it," Skeeter says, "ya gotta beat it out."

JACK'S DAUGHTER LORETTA COMES OVER for dinner. Afterwards while Tildy clears the table, Jack lights up a cigarette, and then Loretta does too.

Sissy can't believe it. She waits for somebody to yell at Loretta, but nobody says anything.

Loretta leans back in her chair, puts her feet up on the table, and blows smoke rings at Sissy.

So Sissy pulls out her pack of cigarettes too.

But as soon as she goes to light up, Jack reaches over and mashes the cigarette into her face. "Now yer gonna eat it," he tells her.

Sissy spits out the cigarette. "It ain't fair," she says, "if Loretta's allowed ta smoke and I ain't, when she's ten and a half months younger than me!"

"Well we ain't raising *her*," Jack says. "We don't git ta say what she does and don't. Now let me see ya pick up that cigarette and git ta eating it."

"Go eff yerself!" Sissy tells him.

Jack jumps up and unbuckles his belt.

Sissy jumps up too. She snatches a steak knife off the table and points it at Jack.

Jack comes at her with the belt.

Sissy gets an idea. Instead of running away, she stands her ground and begins to tremble and moan like a woman she saw on a TV show about exorcisms. Her eyes roll back in her head.

"What the hell's the matter with you?" Jack says.

Sissy drops her head left and right to crack her neck bones. Then, in a deep, hollow voice, she says, "You gonna talk ta *my* daughter that way?"

"What's she talking 'bout?" Jack asks Loretta.

"I tell ya what," Sissy waves the knife at Jack, "you ain't never gonna hit my daughter agin!"

"Yer crazy!" Jack puts his belt back on. "She's nuts," he tells Tildy.

IT'S AFTER MIDNIGHT. THE MOONLIGHT is strong tonight, and Sissy can't sleep. Staring into the mirror, she looks more like herself now. "Ain't gonna be no baby," Sissy shakes her head. "Uh-uh."

Behind her on the closet door, Jimi Hendrix is rocking out with his electric guitar, encircled by a whirlpool of light, color, and pure vibrational sound. Jack has threatened a number of times to tear that "hippie nigger" down.

"Yer 'bout the only one round here who gits me, Jimi," Sissy whispers. "I win that contest, I'm leaving this effing place."

TILDY'S STILL TAKING HER FIT come Sunday. Jack is watching the ball game and drinking Schlitz, while Tildy slams around the house, hollering and cussing at him and everybody else. Jack hollers and cusses at the TV. It's the bottom of the third inning, and the Orioles are down 2-0.

Sissy irons her hair. She puts on her suede miniskirt and vest with the beaded fringes, then steps into her suede moccasin boots. White-lipsticked, blue eyes painted black, Sissy goes to the hall closet, where Tildy keeps the cleaning supplies, and takes down the bottle of Carbona.

Holed up in her bedroom, Sissy works on her demo tape while Bubba Jack—shirtless, in cutoff blue jeans, a cowboy hat, and boxing gloves—spars with his boxing dummy. The baby lies on a pillow on the bed, sucking a bottle filled with orange soda.

"I'll kill us all, Jack!" Tildy yells from the other room. "I fucking swear I'll do it!"

Sissy wads up one of Jack's work rags and soaks it with Carbona. She holds the rag to her nose and mouth and takes a deep breath.

Bubba Jack watches. "Lemme try," he says.

"Uh-uh, yer too little."

"I ain't."

"Are too."

Something large thumps against the wall in the hallway, causing the walls and the floor to tremor. "Git off me!" Tildy screams.

"Hit me," Sissy tells her brother. "In the belly."

"Fer real?" Bubba Jack hauls back with his right fist.

"Wait!" Sissy takes another huff of the Carbona.

"Lemme," Bubba Jack grabs for the work rag.

"Uh-uh." Sissy shoves him away. "Hit me now."

"Uh-uh," he says. "Not unless ya lemme have some."

"Here," Sissy pushes the rag at him. "Hurry up."

He closes his eyes and breathes in the fumes.

"That's enough," Sissy says, but Bubba Jack clutches the rag between his boxing gloves and buries his whole face in it.

Sissy pulls the rag away.

He leans, staggers sideways, then shakes his whole body like a wet dog trying to dry itself.

"Now hit me!" Sissy braces herself.

He gives her a one-two in the gut, and she cusses and doubles over.

Bubba Jack dances in a circle and punches the air.

Sissy forces herself to straighten up. "Hit me agin."

He slugs her harder this time.

"Agin!"

"What the fuck, man?" Earl sticks his head in the window.

"Hey," Sissy says. "We're just messing around."

SISSY PASSES THE BABY OUT the window to Earl, then she and Bubba Jack climb through too.

The dog whines after them. "All right, Poppy," Sissy says. She lifts him through the window and sets him down in the petunias.

Poppy wags his tail, jumps down from the garden box, and goes charging around the yard in circles.

The gang walks down the road that leads out of the project. They cut through the field behind Vinny's Crab Shack and crawl through a hole in the chainlink fence at the back of the country club. Carrying Cricket on his shoulders, Earl leads them into the wooded part of the golf course, and they encamp beneath a gangly sassafras tree. Earl leans back against the trunk and wraps his arms around Sissy while Bubba Jack makes pretend he's a monkey and chases Cricket around the tree.

Earl takes a square of violet-colored paper out of his pocket. "Purple haze," he tells Sissy. "Makes ya able ta fly." He rips off a corner of the paper and places it on her tongue like a priest giving the Holy Communion. He tears off a bigger piece for himself.

"I wanna eat purple hay and fly," Bubba Jack says.

"Yer too little," says Earl. Instead, he offers him the cigarette he's smoking. Bubba Jack takes the cigarette and puffs on it. "Kin I go play wif Billy?"

"Go head," Sissy says. "But behave yerself."

She lays her head down in Earl's lap. Here and there, the twinkling pink sky breaks through the emerald canopy. Tree, sky, cloud, sun. Centuries come and go, and everything is blazed with electricity. Sissy is growing lighter, less opaque. She is floating slowly upward toward the treetops.

"Be cool, baby," Earl says. "Git back down here."

Sissy laughs—the sassafras leaves are a thousand tiny green hands that pinch and tickle—and her voice echoes in her ears as if she's laughing inside a tin can.

"Marry me," Earl hollers up to her.

Sissy stops laughing. "I'm fifteen years old years old years old old old…" she says. "And you ain't got no job job job…"

"The shit I don't," says Earl. "Ain't I the best purse snatcher in Village Court?"

SISSY LEAVES EARL AT THE country club. She needs to clear her head. Even her thoughts are echoing. She takes Cricket to the playground and pushes her in the baby swing, singing "Delta Daaawn Daaawn Daawn, what's that flower you got on on on…"

Sissy pushes and sings, and the baby soars higher, higher, and higher. Sailing above the top bar, she claps her hands and squeals.

"Stop!" Bubba Jack shoves Sissy away from the swing. His nose is bleeding and his shirt is torn. "What's wrong wif you?"

"What?" Sissy says.

"I'm telling!" he yells, picking up his baby sister.

"Hold up," says Sissy. "We ain't done swinging."

"I'm telling!" he shouts again as he runs home with the baby in his arms.

Sissy tries to follow after them, but her legs will only go in slow motion. She feels like she's running on the moon.

Someone taps her on the shoulder. The old Korean woman is smiling and stirring a large steaming pot with a long-handled wooden spoon. "Soup!" she says, and offers Sissy a taste.

It smells rich and spicy. Sissy sips from the spoon. The flavor is peculiar, but not altogether unfamiliar. More like a stew than a soup, with chunks of tender meat. Sissy eats several hearty spoonfuls.

"Tastes good," Sissy wipes her chin on her sleeve. "What's in it?"

The old woman smiles, stirs the pot some more, and motions for Sissy to have a look.

"Poppy!" Sissy screams and clamps her hand over her mouth. Bobbing among the carrots and the onions, the head of her family dog looks up at her with glazed and sunken eyes. Sissy gags and retches.

Wailing, she tries to back away and stumbles—but instead of falling down, she goes airborne again. She rockets up out of the playground feet first and on her back. Then, twisting and kicking to right herself, she spreads her arms like the Flying Nun and circles high above the grid of rooftops and parking lots.

"Oh wow," Sissy says. What was she crying for? She can't remember. The buildings, trees, cars, people—everything looks so small.

She flies to the country club to find Earl, but he's no longer under the sassafras tree. A group of golfers stare and point as Sissy zooms overhead. One of them hits a golf ball toward her. She catches it and chucks it into the sand trap. The golfer hollers and shakes his fist. Sissy hovers above the putting green long enough to pull down her jeans and take a piss.

She does cartwheels and somersaults in the air above the project, showing off and waving to the people down below. Mid-somersault, she spots Bubba Jack's friend Billy and his mama, Mean Pauline, a big-tittied biker moll with a headful of curly, copper-colored hair. They're tramping in the direction of Sissy's house. Mean Pauline has her fists clenched, and Billy is trailing several paces behind her.

"Shit's 'bout ta go down," Sissy says. She sighs, turns one last cartwheel, and spins toward home.

CRASH LANDING IN JACK'S PETUNIAS, Sissy crawls in through her bedroom window and is relieved to see the dog stretched out across the bed. She runs into the living room just as Mean Pauline begins pounding on the door.

Jack is in his chair with a can of Schlitz. There's a cowboy movie playing on TV.

Bubba Jack is on the couch with Cricket. He's still wearing the ripped, bloody T-shirt, and he's holding a bag of frozen corn to his nose.

"What happened ta yer face?" Sissy asks.

"Nuffing," he says. "Billy said we was white trash, then me and him had a fight."

Tildy comes marching out of the kitchen. "Who the hell's banging at my door?" She goes and opens it, and Mean Pauline starts mouthing off, saying how Bubba Jack picked a fight with her boy and blackened his eye.

"Looky here," Pauline shoves Billy forward. "Now if y'all ain't gonna do nothing 'bout it," she says, "send that little brat out here and I'll take care of it myself."

"Hold on a minute," Tildy says and shuts the door in her face.

Tildy braids her straight black hair into one long plait down her back. Then she rolls up her left fist, jerks the door open, and socks Mean Pauline square in the face.

It's on.

Tildy and Mean Pauline roll out into the yard, and Jack and the kids chase after them. Some of the neighbors come out to watch, and the crowd forms a circle around the two women. Skinny Marie, Theresa, and Earl are there too.

"Cat fight," somebody shouts. "*Meow!*"

Tildy's a good head shorter and at least fifty pounds lighter than Mean Pauline, but she's faster and wilier, and she's been itching for a scuffle. "Come on, bitch," she says. "I'm gonna fuck you up good."

Mean Pauline wears a set of heavy brass rings on her right hand. She hauls off and busts Tildy in the mouth, and Tildy goes reeling backwards and hits the dirt. She crawls up onto her hands and knees and spits a bloody tooth into the grass.

"Ha!" says Mean Pauline. "Saved ya a dentist bill, didn't I?"

Tildy charges Mean Pauline, and Pauline catches her and wraps her in a bear hug. They struggle, both women go down, and the back of Tildy's head bangs against the ground.

Jack runs over and drags Mean Pauline off Tildy, and Earl picks Tildy up and carries her toward the apartment.

"Put my goddamned wife down!" Jack tells him.

Earl drops Tildy, and her head bangs the ground again.

Mean Pauline breaks away from Jack. She bounds on Tildy and starts to choke her.

Gasping, Tildy tears out handfuls of Pauline's hair.

"Git her, honey!" Jack yells.

Sissy and Bubba Jack try to pry Mean Pauline's fingers off their mama's throat, and even the baby jumps onto Pauline's back and begins kicking her.

Skinny Marie, Theresa, and Earl root them on—

"Go y'all!"

"Take that bitch down!"

Bubba Jack gets Mean Pauline in a headlock.

Mean Pauline grunts and cusses, but she won't let go of Tildy's throat. She calls for Billy to help her, but he just stands off to the side and bawls.

Tildy is wheezing and turning blue.

She's killing her, Sissy thinks. She bares her teeth and sinks them into the pink flesh of Mean Pauline's tattooed right arm. Taking the cue from his sister, Bubba Jack bites down on Mean Pauline's left shoulder.

Mean Pauline howls and lets go of Tildy.

Tildy rolls over, wheezing for air.

Mean Pauline lurches forward and shakes off Tildy's children.

Tildy scrambles up. Screeching like some kind of wild animal, she rushes at Mean Pauline and claws her eyes.

"Ya picked the wrong day ta come knocking on my door," Tildy says.

When it's over, Mean Pauline goes stumbling back home, ripped and bleeding, and tufts of red hair, the color of new pennies, are strewn all over the grass.

Earl helps Jack carry Tildy inside and lay her down on the couch.

Skinny Marie claps Sissy on the back. "Y'all whupped that biker bitch's ass."

"Guess she won't eff wif us no more," Sissy says, smiling.

"Um, Sissy," Theresa says. "You might wanna go check yourself…"

Sissy looks down to where Theresa is pointing and sees a sticky redness staining her thighs. "Woo-hoo!" she shouts and throws her arms up. Then she grabs Theresa by the waist and dances around the yard with her.

LATER, AFTER THE SUN HAS gone down, Sissy sits out on the stoop with Skinny Marie and Theresa while Bubba Jack and Cricket chase after fireflies.

Honky-tonk music pours out from the apartment, along with the sounds of Tildy and Jack talking and laughing together.

Skinny Marie passes the joint to Sissy. "Ya know Mrs. Weber that lives on the top floor of my building?" Skinny Marie says. "She swears she seen ya go sailing past her kitchen window this afternoon."

"It was that purple haze Earl give me," says Sissy. "Like ta thought I'd lost my effing mind!"

Sissy snares a firefly one handed and uses it to draw a shimmering S on the sidewalk.

"That's mean!" Bubba Jack says.

"Nuh-uh," Sissy tells him. "Bugs can't feel nuffing."

She catches more fireflies and writes out her name in luminous capital letters.

The baby points at the sidewalk and squeals, squats down, and touches her finger to the phosphorescent green Y. "Hot!" she says, pulling her finger away and pressing it to her lips.

"Ya finish yer tape fer that radio contest?" Skinny Marie asks.

"Naw," says Sissy. "Not yet."

Virgie Townsend

A Friend Loves at All Times

VIRGIE TOWNSEND is a journalist, fiction writer, and essayist. Her short fiction has been featured in such publications as Tin House's *Flash Fridays*, *Gargoyle Magazine*, and *SmokeLong Quarterly*. She has contributed nonfiction to the *Washington Post*, *Jezebel*, and the *Huffington Post*. Find her online at www.virgietownsend.com or www.twitter.com/virgietownsend.

I am hunting you, Elisabeth. I pack a small bag and leave home before the sun's up. I go down to the lake where we swam as children and perch nibbled our toes, mistaking them for stout worms. I go back to the field where we found you, take off my gloves, and trace your imprint in the snow.

In my pocket, I carry the talismans of our friendship: a God's eye you made as a child from purple and green yarn, the dime-sized splinter that I extracted like a prize from the heel of your right foot the summer we were twelve, and the card you wrote for my seventeenth birthday, scrawled with the proverb, "A friend loves at all times, and a brother is born for adversity."

I go to your grave outside of town, but nothing touches the site except the gray granite marker and a veneer of ice. No roses or flags to remember a girl who could catch and name any insect. I think about leaving the birthday card, but instead I say a prayer and make my way to the road.

The sun is rising over Victorsville. To reach the closest town before nightfall, I will walk away from Victorsville toward the west.

On my heels are the elders, wearing dark suits with pearl cufflinks at their wrists, and carrying the word of God. They wanted to put you in the ground and forget you, Elisabeth. They went around Victorsville with a white cloth sack and asked for any objects that could remind us of you and your sin. They say that memories are like heavy stones in my pocket weighing me down, pulling me closer to the earth and away from heaven. They say that you're not in heaven, but your unborn son is.

The road is unplowed, so to avoid the elders' detection, I walk where the snow is thinnest. In my bag, I have my father's hunting knife, a bottle of water, three currant jelly sandwiches wrapped in wrinkled tin foil, a change of clothes and shoes, and a photo of you. When I see a trail of footprints gathering behind me, I take out the knife, cut down branches from the pines lining the road, and try to dust them away.

The sun shines through the trees, but it's cold and the road is empty. Snow creeps into my boots and melts up from the hem of my dress. Numbness starts in my pinky fingers before moving toward my thumbs. It reminds me of playing piano scales at home, where it's warm and they must now be searching for me.

Yesterday the elders burned that white cloth sack filled with memories of you. They placed it on the church altar, lit a long match, and held it against the bag, where the flame nibbled a corner before consuming it. The auditorium filled with smoke and the scent of charred paper—report cards, your sketch notebooks containing drawings of star-shaped cornflowers and black-throated sparrows with dashes of gold and brown along their wings, a fourth-grade Sunday school craft project with cotton-ball sheep staring up vacantly at their stoic, bearded shepherd, photos of you wedged between your eight siblings, and photos of us, holding up bunny ears behind each other's head.

When only a small pile of ashes was left, the elders scooped them up with bare hands and offered the dust to our God, who takes away the sins of the world.

Your family and I watched from the back of the church, hands folded on our laps. We know the teachings. To cry for those who bring shame on themselves is to partake in their shame. To look back is to look away from future glory.

Now all that remains of you, I hold in my pocket.

I left in a hurry. I don't have much of a plan, except that in the next town, I'll show your picture around and ask if anyone saw you there. I'll look for a small home with asphalt roofs and white vinyl siding made to last 'til kingdom come, or a convenience store with its name written in chipped paint on the front window. When I find that kindly place, I'll peek through the windows and see if there's a woman inside alone. A woman who's on her own will help me, I think. I can show her the God's eye and proverb. Then I think she'll understand the things we'll do for a friend who feels like a sister.

You would be proud of me, Elisabeth. We've now both left Victorsville. Isn't this the adventure you always wanted? Is this the adventure you thought you were having before you realized you were pregnant, before you walked into the field and lay down in the snow?

The miles go on. Shadows grow longer. I move forward and lose track of how long I've been walking. I stare ahead until my vision becomes blurry, but I don't lower my gaze. With my eyes still fixed on the road, I rummage through my bag with my right hand, feeling for the water and half of a sandwich. I raise them to my lips, but taste little.

When I see the first street lamp ahead of me, casting its pale orange eye over the snow, I know I must be close. As a reward, I stop beneath it and lean against the cold, curved stem, shifting my weight between my feet.

The town is less than a half mile before me in a valley. There's a church with a cross steeple at the intersection, and the road I'm on now turns into a street—a real street like I've never seen in Victorsville. It leads up a hill and has lines of cars rolling up and down it, a stream of headlights, as people return to their homes.

The sun is low in the sky. I close my eyes and see you. I see you the way you can see a light on in a room, but your eyes are shut tight. My heart is pierced like a kite in the branches.

I keep walking. I put my hand in my pocket and turn the mementos over in my dulled fingers: a God's eye, a splinter, a proverb.

Jourdan Woo

Curl Up and Dye

JOURDAN WOO enjoys traveling, reading, writing, and daydreaming.
She currently resides in Washington, D.C., with her family.

On Valentine's Day, the zombies always showed up for a makeover. I
didn't really know where they went during the rest of the year—they
were like birds in migration—but on Valentine's Day they came
staggering in here, hoping for love, just like everyone else.

I arrived at exactly nine, like I did each morning, and used that extra
hour before the beauty salon opened to tighten up the lines between the
hair care products and adjust the chairs so they all faced precisely the same
way. I loved selecting the music for the day—nine-hour-long playlists of
'80s hits that reminded me of more carefree times.

I was walking through the glass door when I was greeted by the shrill
sound of the phone. I rushed in, reached over the counter, and picked up
the cordless business line. "Curl Up and Dye," I said.

"Oh. Hi, Dotty." My spine straightened the way it did whenever something wasn't right. There could only be one reason why Dotty was phoning
the salon so early.

She hammed it up with a nasally voice and a big loud cough.

"Cut the bull, girl. You're calling out because of the zombies, aren't you?"

She paused long enough to tell me that I'd guessed the truth, and she
finally confessed that they made her uncomfortable.

"I can't say it makes me happy to hear. In fact, your attitude disappoints
me."

She gave me some crap about how she found them disgusting, and how
zombie vanity was unnatural.

My anger rose. "A customer's a customer. That's all there is to it."

I hung up before I could say something I'd regret. I felt a mixture of irritation and disbelief that one of my employees would act this way. I debated calling her back and telling her not to bother showing up for work. Period.

I went behind the counter and pulled up the day's schedule. It was one large block of fuchsia with hardly a break in between. There were the zombies to consider as well. They were notorious for not making appointments, and they were dangerously impatient. Keeping a zombie waiting too long was like playing Russian roulette. No telling when they'd suddenly get hungry. But hell, we're all a little cranky when we haven't eaten, right?

No matter how I tried to shift things around, there was no way I could avoid the pileup that was going to be caused by Dotty's absence. I'd recently hired a new girl, Crystal, who wasn't scheduled to start until the following week. Right then, I calculated that a pair of nontrained hands was still better than none.

Twenty minutes later, Crystal knocked on the front door. Judging by her lack of makeup and simple ponytail, she must have left her house right after I called. I liked that she wasn't a dawdler.

I unlocked the door and pushed it open. "Hey, hon, thanks for coming in on such short notice."

Crystal stepped inside and shook off the February cold. "I'm thrilled to be here," she said with the perk of a Mary Kay beauty consultant.

"Got a lot of energy, I see. That's good. You'll need it."

"Am I the first one?" Crystal asked as she looked around the empty salon.

"It's just you and me until we open. I wanted to get you in as early as possible so we can go over some things, help you get situated."

She took off her coat, and I noticed her clothes.

"Lord, girl," I breathed. "This is a salon, not a club."

She wore one of those flouncy, *mini*, miniskirts and her top was so low that between the two she was going to have cleavage peek-a-booing from some part of her all day long.

"I was in a rush," she explained, "but I wanted to look nice." She ran her hands over her skirt, smoothing down the fabric. It looked even shorter wrapped against her curves.

"Guess it won't hurt your tips," I said. After all, I was a glass half-full kind of gal.

"Sorry, just a little excited. Today's a special day, kind of a dream come true, really."

I wondered what young girls dreamed about these days. "You got a boyfriend?"

She laughed. "Oh no, nothing like that. It's just…" She hesitated. "Is it true that today the zombies come in?"

I cocked an eye at her. "You squeamish?"

She shook her head.

"You ever work with zombies before?"

"No."

Oh dear. "A zombie virgin." I sighed. "I'd like to tell you that you don't have to work with them, with it being your first day and all, but it's going to get busy, and you'll probably have to roll up your sleeves."

I thought back to those early days when I first started working with the undead. I remembered how flustered I got, trying not to be too obvious about wearing rubber gloves—or staring. I never discussed it with the other girls, but sometimes when I got a customer with one of those gashing head wounds, I would close my eyes while doing their shampoo so that I could really feel the mushy bits between my fingers. I recalled the wet and sticky texture, the sweet, pungent odor of old blood.

I didn't quite catch what she said, but when I looked up, I felt a heat stain my cheeks. I cleared my throat and shoved my hands into my smock. "It can be a little weird at first. You got to get used to the loose skin and sometimes when you're washing their hair, parts of it will just fall out. When that happens, there's nothing to be done about it. Most important thing is not to panic or else they panic, and that's never pretty." I hoped she wouldn't get it in her head that they were gross, but she seemed fine, more than fine in fact. She seemed eager and earnest, and as an employer, I liked those traits best.

"Let me show you around."

I marched across the salon, Crystal just a few steps behind. "Obviously those are the chairs where the girls do their magic, and back here is where you'll wash hair." We stopped in front of one of the oversized basins, and I pointed to a shelf behind the sink. "Here's where we keep all the towels and shampoos."

"Seems pretty standard," she said.

"Except for the zombies," I added.

She grinned. "Except for them."

I squared my shoulders, ready to lay down the law. "Just a few things. If you have to go to the bathroom, make sure you tell someone. Same for cigarette breaks. We get busy, can't have people disappearing.

"I know it can be tough, but don't let me catch you gawking. We treat our zombies just like all our other customers.

"Also, try not to let the smell get to you. After a while, you get used to it, and it's no different than all the other chemicals we use." I thought for a moment. "If you feel like you want to vomit, just go out back and have a cigarette or sniff some ammonia. It'll clean the stench right out of your nostrils.

"You can use gloves if you must, but use the clear latex brand in that drawer to your left. We don't like making a fuss." I turned my attention to a shelf behind the sink. "Shampoo in the orange bottles are for humans, black bottles for the undead. Got it?"

"Separate shampoos?"

"Zombie hair is more delicate." A pretty obvious fact, but of course she had never worked with them before. "With all that rot, you got to be careful not to dry the scalp out anymore than it already is. We've tried all sorts of things, but dog shampoo seems to work the best.

"We put it in these pump bottles so no one thinks we're calling them something they're not." I gave Crystal a pointed look.

"If I tell you that we're getting low, take the black bottles and fill them up with the extra shampoo in the storage room. If you have any trouble, just come and get me. Don't go whispering if there are any zombies in the salon. They're so sensitive to that kind of stuff. They always think you're talking about them.

"If you need extra smocks, towels, craft materials, you'll find it all in the back."

I led Crystal to the front of the store. "Any questions?"

"When do the zombies come in?"

"Hon, don't worry. They're real nice. You'll see." I gave her arm a motherly pat.

"I can't wait. I've always wanted to see a real zombie. It's like seeing a vampire."

I squinted down my nose at her nonsense. "Honey, you know they don't exist."

She paused. "Or like an eclipse. It's rare and special. That's what I mean, dream come true. I think it's cool that you let them in your salon."

I stood a little taller. "You know, we were one of the first beauty salons that started accepting them as customers. Don't get me wrong. In the beginning I was worried it'd be bad for business, afraid that the other customers would get freaked out. But it seemed like the right thing to do. After all, it wasn't their fault that the Twinkie factory dumped all those preservatives near their graves, but that's another story.

"Ever since the zombies started coming around for Valentine's Day, business has been better than ever. People get curious and want to know. Even those who are too afraid to come in today, they come in on other days, and they always ask what it's like, doing up a zombie.

"Just shows you why it's important to be open-minded," I added, knowing a story is more powerful when there's a lesson to be learned.

"You know what's been more rewarding than the money is the way they're always so grateful, like we're real miracle workers, and not to seem all high and mighty, but sometimes it feels that way too.

"Last year, a guy came in here, poor thing. We had to Krazy Glue part of his face back on. And when you're able to do something like that—really piece someone back together, I imagine that's what a doctor feels like when he's stitching a person up." I was suddenly eager to share. "Do you want to see some before and after photos?"

"Really?" she asked, like I had just offered to give her a ride on my 1964 panhead duo-glide Harley.

"Actually, it's more like after pictures. You'd be surprised how self-conscious they get about the way they look." I frowned. "It's sad, really.

Everyone should be comfortable in their own skin."

I pulled out a large blue album. The binder was worn and cracked. "I'll skip the first part. Those are just humans."

I flipped halfway through the book before holding up the page with pride. "This was my very first zombie. See that right part of his head? It's papier-mâché and a wig. Brilliant, isn't it?" I ran my hand lovingly across the photo. "He was great." I remembered how jumpy he was, but as I started his transformation, his dull eyes seemed to clear with trust. I lingered a moment longer before turning the page.

"Here's another one. She was a darling." I met Crystal's saucer-wide eyes. "It's not true what they say—that they only eat human brains. When she came in, I thought she'd been rolling in the mud. Turns out it was chocolate cake. Imagine! Chocolate cake!" I chuckled. "Everyone knows they're not so tidy."

Crystal giggled.

I sighed with nostalgia and flicked through a few more pages. Every one of those makeovers meant something to me. Sure, they could be pretty disgusting. The smell of rotten flesh, the mangled limbs, the exposed guts… the bad skin. Still, the truth was, since they'd started coming in, I'd grown a soft spot for them just like I had for ugly babies.

The bell jangled, and we both turned to see Leigh-Ann walk through the door. "Shoot. Lost track of time." I reluctantly closed the book.

BY MIDAFTERNOON, THE SALON HUMMED with voices and hair dryers. *Love Is a Social Disease* blared from the speakers. Occasionally, I glanced over to Crystal's station, making sure she was OK.

True to her word, she wasn't at all squeamish with the zombies. She seemed to have a special way with each one. The way she squeezed a shoulder or when her hands lingered on an arm, and how she handled each head of hair with loving care. I felt a swell of satisfaction about my decision to have her come to work today. There was something about Crystal, a quiet determination and sense of purpose that reminded me, well, of myself. My only concern was that in her desire to be attentive, she wasn't moving through the customers as quickly as she could.

I got a zombie with an eyeball hanging out of her socket. I mean, it was really drawing some attention, and I had to snip it off. The hardest part was trying to convince her that it probably wasn't working anymore. I wanted to get a glass eye but couldn't find one on such short notice when one of the girls suggested using a marble. Genius really. I told the zombie how the marble swirl really made her eye pop. She left, another happy customer.

I had already skipped lunch due to three additional zombie walk-ins about the same time. Two of them were in and out—just a little stapling here and there and some silly putty to cover the marks, but the third required completely new hair, extensive lip work, and a false set of teeth. Though that meant I'd run over into my next appointment, when a zombie pleaded with his cloudy eyes, I just couldn't say no.

My back ached, my feet were sore, and I desperately craved a cigarette. Even though the salon was in full swing, I walked to the front counter and told Sheila that I was going to run out.

WHEN I RETURNED FROM MY break, I felt refreshed, bobbing to the music. God, I loved Poison. Why'd they have to break up?

Suzanne, a regular, was already waiting for me in my chair.

"What'll it be, hon?" We eyed each other through the mirror.

She wanted Shirley Temple curls. Lots and lots of Shirley Temple curls. Though it was going to make her pumpkin face look even rounder, I believe the customer is always right.

I finished putting two-thirds of Suzanne's hair in curlers when I realized that Crystal wasn't at her sink. I glanced around the salon. Zombies stumbled around like overgrown toddlers, magazines littered the floor, and there weren't enough seats for everyone waiting. A human customer looked at her watch in annoyance.

I turned to Leigh-Ann whose station was next to mine. "Where's Crystal?"

She looked around. "Bathroom?"

I clucked my tongue. "She knows better," I mumbled under my breath. I turned my attention back to Suzanne, but the empty space at Crystal's sink beckoned like a bright-red warning.

"Leigh-Ann," I said again. "You know if she had any zombie backlog?"

She paused for a minute, comb in hand. "Come to think of it, she had three waiting at one point. Took so long washing out the blood with the first one that the other two started to hover over her sink."

My jaw dropped in disbelief. "And you didn't think to tell me? You know it's her first time."

"They're always hovering." She saw my expression, and her eyes darted around before she lowered her voice. "Didn't I tell you that one day there'd be trouble?"

"Hold your horses. Nothing's happened."

Yet.

I snapped the last curler onto Suzanne's head, and gave her my you're-going-to-look-fab-fab-fabulous smile before leading her to a seat under a hair dryer. I turned the dial, set the timer, and told her I'd be back to check on her in twenty.

I walked with purpose to the two separate bathrooms. The first door was locked, and I gave a quick, stabbing knock. "Crystal? You in there?"

"It's busy," said a man's voice.

I turned to the second door, but it was also locked. "Crystal, is that you?"

"Uh…hang on."

Between the music screaming from the speakers and the door smothering the girl's voice, I couldn't tell if she was Crystal or not. After some hesitation, I decided to wait. Curl Up and Dye did not harass its customers in their more intimate moments.

When the door finally opened, it wasn't Crystal after all. I rushed to the back entrance, into the little alley where all the girls took their cigarette breaks.

No one was there.

Crystal seemed too conscientious not to heed my advice and leave the floor without telling anyone. With long, steady strides I went to the last place Crystal could be. The moment I walked into the supply room, the familiar stillness of the space greeted me. I normally welcomed the way the music fell away to a distant muffled sound, and how the neat, orderly arrangements of supplies contrasted the bustling chaos on the other side of the door. But this time, I didn't feel that sense of tranquility that I loved so much. This time, the silence and stillness felt dangerous.

A puddle of towels lay on the floor, and the bottles, though still on the shelf, no longer stood like rows of graduating cadets.

I reached down to pick up the mess when I heard a noise. It sounded like a soft whimper. Before I could react, a low growl—a very distinctive zombie growl, caused my stomach to drop faster than you could say "Conquistadora."

I thought about all the hard work I had put into the beauty salon, making it the best in town, and how a death by zombie would be bad for business. Still, it was difficult for me to move. I tried to speak, to call out, but my voice was lost in some hidden pocket in my throat.

When I heard another groan, my heart sank. The noises came from the far side of the room, and two aisles of shelving blocked my view.

I found myself hoping that the zombie would eat all of Crystal with nothing left to discover. Everyone would think she had unexpectedly quit. I turned it over in my head a few times before shaking the thought away. I knew that wasn't right…or Christian, but then, wasn't there a saying in the Bible about looking the other way or something? Before I could convince myself, I remembered that zombies weren't so tidy. There was no getting out of this cleanly.

My legs felt like they did after I finished a step class wearing my ten-pound ankle weights, but I concentrated and willed them to move like I willed myself to do all my life: one step at a time. I hoped I was being quiet, but it was hard to tell beyond the rush of blood in my ears. As I moved closer to the sounds, I looked around for a weapon, anything I could use to pierce through the brains.

I made it down the second aisle. A faint shadow cast by the overhead lights told me that they were right around the corner. I sensed the movements more than saw them, and they felt low to the ground. I pictured Crystal sprawled on the tiles, a zombie hovering over her, gnawing on ladyfingers. Can't wash hair without fingers, and I prayed I wasn't too late.

A bottle of dog shampoo lay on its side near my feet, and the cap was open. A ripple of annoyance cut through me because liquid had leaked out and the edges were starting to dry. That was going to take ages to mop up later. I stooped slowly and reached until my fingertips brushed the plastic container. It rolled quietly toward me. I clutched it to my thumping chest, prayed that the industrial size would make a dent when crushed against the side of a head.

After a long, slow breath, I pivoted around the corner. Arm raised, shampoo bottle ready to be launched, my eyes settled on the scene. Fear turned to confusion, then shock, before finally settling on some strange combination of fascination, disgust, and excitement.

Crystal's skirt was hitched around her waist, and she straddled a zombie who lay on the ground. She was lifting herself up and down. Up and down.

She massaged the decomposing flesh on his chest before a hand trailed down to a wound below the rib. She plunged two fingers into the gooey opening. "Oh yes. More," she breathed before picking up her rhythm.

The words snapped me out of my trance, and my first sensible thought was that maybe Crystal shouldn't be riding him so hard. Zombies have been known to have things break off. I shook my head, dismissing the thought. It was none of my business really, how hard or how fast Crystal was moving. A girl her age should know how these things worked.

I started to see red, and not because of the blood that began to seep out of the hole in his gut. There was a part of me that had a mind to shove Crystal right off him. He was a zombie for God's sake. It didn't seem right…or natural. Plus, where did she get off thinking she could sneak in a screw at my salon! With one of my customers!

This girl had a lot of nerve. It wasn't even her break time. The more I thought about the muck she made, and her blatant disregard for my salon, the more steaming mad I became.

I was ready to rip her a new hole to match her zombie boyfriend's, but I couldn't take my eyes off her fingers moving in and out, her body moving up and down. My hands clenched with the memories of washing hair all those years ago, and I tilted my nose, hoping to catch a whiff of that one-of-a-kind smell.

I felt something besides anger, and it gave me pause. The zombie wriggled underneath her. His head lolled around, seeming relaxed. The two of them together no longer looked so strange.

I backed away quietly, keeping my eyes on the feast of love. Despite the activity in the salon, I really needed a smoke.

In the alley, my hands shook as I lit the stick. I didn't know what I felt, because things felt all mixed up.

I sucked slow and hard, the tobacco becoming a long line of ash. It was Valentine's Day, after all. I flicked away my cigarette, and a smile spread across my face.

Morowa Yejídé

Heathens

MOROWA YEJÍDÉ's novel *Time of the Locust* was a 2012 finalist for the PEN/Bellwether Prize, longlisted for the 2015 PEN/Bingham Award, and a 2015 NAACP Image Award nominee for Outstanding Literary Work. Her short stories have appeared in the *Adirondack Review*, the *Istanbul Review*, and others. She is currently a PEN/Faulkner Writers in Schools author and lives in the Washington, D.C., area with her husband and three sons.

It took three cups of coffee at the kitchen table for Mia Taylor to get the strength to go out to the mailbox. Even before the government shutdown, she and Harris had stopped checking the mail until the box was nearly bursting. And as she sat at the kitchen table in the stupor she had been in since four o'clock that morning, the possibility of having to stop and speak to her neighbors as she checked the mail sickened her. From the stoops of their rowhouses where their mortgages were being paid and their bills covered, they would want to know how her husband, Harris, was coming along in his contract job out in McLean, how her three boys were doing and if she'd signed them up for science camp (early-bird registration was only five hundred dollars per child). "We didn't see you and Harris at the neighborhood association social the other night," they would say. Mia would have to respond with bullshit: how Harris was doing well and didn't mind the long commute, how their boys were getting to be as tall as the Washington Monument, how she'd been so busy working on her novel. And she'd say it all with a smile. She'd say it with a clear understanding that they didn't really care and that they were just comparing notes. They didn't know what it was like to try to live and battle the minions of circumstance without a firm grasp, without the superhuman strength that the nation's capital required.

Mia rose from the table and ambled slowly down the hallway. She kicked the Hot Wheels cars and Nerf balls littering the floor out of her way, her stomach souring with every step to the front door and outside. And by the time she lifted the little aluminum door of the mailbox nailed to the brick and pulled out a heavy envelope wedged between past due credit card statements and cutoff notices, her hands were trembling. The envelope—it had arrived at last—was battle scarred with red ink, smudged fingerprints, and scratches. A list of names on the return address label glared up at Mia from its worn front. Long, serious names, all in accusatory uppercase letters, printed in angry ink. "NOTICE OF DEFAULT" bled through the patterned underside meant to keep these kinds of things private. She looked up and down the empty street (thank God nobody she knew was there) and back at the envelope.

Mia stared at the names that read, "Sherman, Horowitz, Brennan and Rubin." She imagined the four of them lounging together on plush lawns in Fairfax or Potomac after tiresome days at the firm, holding martinis and cigarettes, shaking their heads about the heathens. In the late evenings, over Angus steaks and asparagus tips, Sherman, Horowitz, Brennan, and Rubin would continue discussing the masses that had no savings, had not participated in pretax expense accounts, had not contributed more than three percent to their 401k plans or paid their credit card balances within thirty days. The ice in their Waterford glasses would clink as they prophesied the fate of the fiscally weak and the doom of the national budget. They would lament the constant threat of a city peopled by the unworthy, a town filled with fools marching to destinies no different than those draining social services in Ward 7 and Ward 8.

The mortgage was two months in arrears. Mia had learned that "arrears" was a special word for being dangerously behind on important expenses. They bought the house at a bargain, considering that many of their neighbors—refugees from other cities and other lives—bought at nearly double the price. Then the company where Harris worked before contracting downsized and he was laid off. "We've not met the projections the shareholders expected," Harris said the CEO announced, calling the employees together like delinquents at a school assembly. In the eternity it took for him to find work while his severance pay dwindled, they'd maxed out the home equity to pay for Harris's technology consulting start-up, which tanked in the recession bloodbath.

The weight of the envelope pressed into Mia's hand. *This is how it happens*, she thought, staring at the thick envelope. Not the why or when. Just the how.

Mia remembered that day at the dinner table after the children had wandered off to play and the dishes had been cleared. She and Harris sat together in the crushing quiet at the table, floating on a barge of dread.

"Maybe I should go back to work," she finally said.

Harris stared down at where the plate had been.

"I checked into some daycare and after-school programs, Harris."

Harris looked at Mia, his eyes red and empty. "We've been through this and you know it's too expensive. You'd be working just to pay someone to look after the boys while you're at work. It wouldn't make sense." He stood up. "I told you I'll handle it," he'd said as he headed for the door.

Mia remembered how the sound of the front door closing echoed through the house long after Harris was gone. In later months when he left on the slightest whim, she speculated that he was out doing what men do when the need or opportunity presents itself, when the urge to make a female smile overtakes them, when noble designs are destroyed by disappointment: see other women. She considered this when she found a phone number in his jacket pocket. And Mia supposed that every time Harris gazed at her—sideways when he believed she was not looking—he was reminded of how their life together was shipwrecked on the beach, how he hadn't been able to steer them clear. He was no longer able to bear—Mia reasoned—the worried, ruined landscape her face had become. It troubled Mia that this did not bother her terribly; not because she didn't care about her marriage, but because it had somehow landed on the list of things she felt she could no longer do anything about.

On move-in day, after they took the FOR SALE sign down and put the new curtains up, Harris was triumphant. It was a long way from their cramped apartment in Columbia Heights. He confessed his joy at giving her something that would make her happy; that he would have worked ten jobs for the way she beamed ultraviolet when she saw the master bath and the granite countertop and the kitchen island. The way Harris held his head high and his shoulders back on their first trip through the aisles of Home Depot told Mia that all of this was so. The shine was gone now, replaced by dark circles and disquieting murmurs. They hadn't looked each other in the eyes since February and instead focused on pieces that together were no longer whole: forehead, lips, an earlobe, an eyebrow.

When Mia arrived back in the kitchen, she dropped the thick envelope in the wicker basket on the floor next to the refrigerator, atop a landfill of unopened mail. Many of the envelopes were speckled with lime Popsicle juice and strawberry milk the kids had dripped on them in the course of going in and out of the refrigerator. She picked up a bottle of ibuprofen left on the counter the night before and swallowed three. A boom shook the ceiling and Mia heard screams of delight from upstairs. The five-year-old twins were jumping off the top of the bunk bed again. *Dive the Cliffs*, Mia thought, their favorite game. She was too tired to reprimand them about not using the ladder, and a crushing guilt stopped her from interrupting any of their escapades in the wake of disappearing trips to Chuck E. Cheese and treats from the toy section at Target. She opened the pantry door and stared at the shelves, trying to remember what it was she was going to make for breakfast. Oatmeal?

When Mia turned around, Sean, her youngest boy, was waiting. He smiled at her, holding the edge of the blanket he'd pulled from his bed. "Can we have soda with our pancakes?" he asked. In his three-year-old mind soda with every meal was reasonable.

Mia looked at his bright little face, eyes full of the wonder of bugs crawling on sidewalks and the marvelous composition of dirt. "Yes," she said. In recent weeks she had begun to fixate on the small things she felt she could offer her children: overindulgences of sugar, staying up past bedtime, and Saturdays in the middle of the week.

She thought she heard the doorbell and froze, her reflexes honed from months of responding to certified mail deliveries and shutoff courtesy visits from utility servicemen. Was there someone at the door or was it her imagination again?

"Did you hear the doorbell, Sean?" she asked.

The toddler shook his head. "No, Mommy. We can have pancakes too, right, Mommy?" he asked.

The phone rang and Mia thought about the calls from collection agents and decided not to answer it. She had gotten into an argument earlier that week with a guy who called at eight o'clock in the morning. "If you paid your bills we wouldn't be calling you," he'd sneered before Mia hung up on him. A few weeks back, when Mia had launched into an exasperated litany of explanations with another bill collector, the boys bickering and crying in the background, the representative commiserated with her. The agent (no longer concerned that the call was being recorded) confided that the job was a strain on her conscience, since many of the issues she was obliged to call and badger people about were things she herself faced on a monthly basis. "It's been hard for us all," she said.

But most of the bill collectors enjoyed playing judge, reminding Mia that her life wasn't anymore difficult than anyone else's. Now she cursed herself for forgetting to unplug the phone last night when she had gone down to her basement office to skim through another unfinished manuscript, to start and stop another repayment plan. She ended up swimming the Internet instead, awash in a sea of wealth-enrichment seminars and infomercial clips. She consumed the ads like opiates, addicted to the solitude and secrecy of being underground, of dulling reality with fantasies of prosperity in less than thirty days. She read a financial article titled "Take Charge of Your Life," which instructed readers to slash budgets, sell what was of value, and borrow from family and friends to pay off debt.

That last one about borrowing from family stuck with Mia a bit, and she spent a full nine days contemplating whether or not to ask her father for a loan. She had always felt that asking him would have been an admission of failure. At the height of her regression to the insecurities she held as a child, she obsessed over how he would insist that she had been wasting her life with unrealistic aspirations, that she had not married well, and that starting a family before going to graduate school had only sealed her fate. "We didn't do things like this in our day," he would say. She wondered what her mother would think, had she lived. "You can reach me with your mind," she'd told her from a Washington Hospital Center bed at the fourth stage of breast cancer, Saint Jude dangling from a locket around her neck. She'd saved the locket for reasons she could not explain, other than that it bore witness to the putrid way of things.

Mia heard shrieking and laughter from the twins upstairs and then something crashing to the floor and breaking.

"The phone, Mommy," said Sean.

Mia's head was pounding and her body throbbed and she walked past Sean, saying, "I know baby," and headed to the bathroom.

"Don't take too long, Mommy," he said.

In the bathroom, Mia sat on the edge of the tub trying to clear her mind. She could hear Sean playing on the phone; she'd told him not to do that a thousand times. "Hi. Hi. Mommy's busy. Hi, I'm three…" She went to the sink and filled it with cold water and submerged her face. She could hear the faint clanking of the copper plumbing the real estate agent said would last forever. In the quiet of the cold liquid, she imagined the foreclosure sign stabbed into the earth in front of the house like a grave marker, their hopes and dreams buried beneath it. She thought of her boys and the security of their future bleeding out with every passing day. And when she thought of the runaway train ride that her marriage—their lives—had become, how she and Harris had let each other's hands go, both of them bracing for the impact alone, she wanted to cry.

Then Mia remembered something else that traveled through time and dimension and water to find her. *You can't lose what was always yours*, she heard her mother say. She remembered how she'd been holding her hand and listening to her talk those final days, her voice dry and hoarse from the chemotherapy. And even in those last hours when her mother was trapped in a bog of nausea and pain and outrage, still wanting her life more than the relief that death would bring, she'd been defiant; a heathen to the gods of despair. "Remember this: We have what we had in the beginning," she'd said.

And Mia remembered when she and Harris talked and laughed over Lo Mein and grape soda on the tattered floor of their first apartment, how they stood watching in awe as their newborn boys slept in a crib, how sunlight filled her when she rendered thought to paper.

Richard Peabody is the founder and current editor of *Gargoyle Magazine* and editor (or coeditor) of twenty-two anthologies including *Mondo Barbie*, *Conversations with Gore Vidal*, and *A Different Beat: Writings by Women of the Beat Generation*. He won the Beyond the Margins "Above & Beyond Award" for 2013. His latest book is *The Richard Peabody Reader* (Alan Squires Publishing, 2015).

After graduating with a BFA from SUNY at Buffalo, Lisa Montag Brotman moved to Washington, D.C., attended the Corcoran School of Art, and received an MFA from George Washington University. Brotman received two individual artist awards in the visual arts from the Maryland State Arts Council. Her work has been exhibited in the United States and Europe, and in the Washington, D.C., area, including the Corcoran Gallery of Art, St. Mary's College, George Washington University, Washington Project for the Arts, five solo shows at Gallery K, and retrospective exhibitions at both Maryland Arts Place and the American University Museum at the Katzen Arts Center. www.lisabrotman.com.

Through the cold liquid and the blackness of her mind, Mia heard Sean pounding at the door, his little voice cracked with panic. "Mommy, are you there?"

"I'm coming," she said, rising from the water.